AN ACCOMPLISHED WOMAN

AN ACCOMPLISHED WOMAN

NANCY PRICE

Coward, McCann & Geoghegan, Inc.
New York

The author gratefully acknowledges the following for permission to quote from copyrighted materials:

Holt, Rinehart and Winston for the excerpt from "The Silken Tent" from *The Poetry of Robert Frost* edited by Edward Connery Lathem. The copyright 1942 by Robert Frost. Copyright © 1969 by Holt, Rinehart and Winston. Copyright © 1970 by Lesley Frost Ballantine. Reprinted by permission of Holt, Rinehart and Winston, Publishers.

W. W. Norton and Company for an excerpt reprinted from "Archaic Torso of Apollo" from *Translations From the Poetry of Rainer Maria Rilke* by M. D. Herter Norton, with permission of W. W. Norton and Company, Inc. Copyright 1938 by W. W. Norton and Company, Inc. Copyright renewed 1966 by M. D. Herter Norton.

Harvard University Press for excerpt from "A Loss of Something Ever Felt I": reprinted by permission of the publisher and the Trustees of Amherst College from *The Poems of Emily Dickinson,* edited by Thomas H. Johnson. Cambridge, Mass.; The Belknap Press of Harvard University Press. ©1951, 1955 by the President and Fellows of Harvard College.

Library of Congress Cataloging in Publication Data
Price, Nancy, 1925-
  An accomplished woman.

  I. Title.
PZ4.P9465Ac   1979   [PS3566.R49]   813'.5'4   78-12456
ISBN 0-698-10964-3

Printed in the United States of America

Gratitude is due
Howard, John, David and Catherine
Michael James Carroll,
and Connie and Koert Voorhees.
This book was advanced by a residency
at the Michael Karolyi Memorial Foundation
and completed with a grant
from the National Endowment for the Arts.

"*Abject as this picture appears,
it is the portrait of an accomplished
woman.*"
—Mary Wollstonecraft

1

The open car came over the hill too fast, fenders and running board a streak of sun. Hot summer light was brilliant on the man, woman and baby in the front seat. Halfway into the valley, sheep clogged a narrow English road—the car roared down on them, skidded to a crash on the stone bridge beyond, and burned. Catherine, flung from her mother's arms, fell on the broad backs of the sheep, but Janet and Rob, crushed in metal, were black wicks in flame and smoke.

When the impact echoed away in corners of cottage yards and oaks on the hill, brook water ran on, as tranquil a sound as the steady crackle of fire, or the low baas of the sheep.

Catherine slid over dirty wool to the ground, face up, sun and clouds in her wide eyes; she gathered the summer air in and screamed it out, a baby's wail as fire mounted and water bubbled, and bees, hovering, settled again in the weeds.

Voices came, after a while. They found Catherine in bracken that was hot and green and smelled of sulfur. Broad Derbyshire voices mouthed English like cud.

"The car came over the hill a fat sight faster'n it ought—smashed into Dabney's sheep, smacked into the bridge, burnin', burnin' both of 'em instant—Christ!"

"Don't look on it, Sally!"

9

"The childt's all right. They've fetched the doctor, and Rector Trapp's come."

The odor of sulfur was carried on the hot wind along with a smell like burned fat.

A new voice boomed. "I believe they must be the young Buckingham couple." There was unction in the voice: full pews on Sunday morning. It moved off, and other voices moved in, dropping and turning sour.

"They're all rich Americans visitin' Marleyshall." A dry female voice: lace curtains, boiled ham on the dresser. "The lady and the childt always was with the tall chap. Got a butterfly net."

"That tall chap's half brother to the burnt one there, says the rector."

"Nothin' the doctor can do as'll mend those two in the motorcar—he's lookin' the baby over."

"Kettle's on the boil and it'll be noon—shall you come eat?"

A sheep coughed. There was a far chain of whistles, a rattle and clink. Then came the shrill authority of colliery hooters over the sound of winding engines and shunting trucks, pit screens, locomotives.

2

The car had smashed and burned, the lawyer said. Mr. and Mrs. Buckingham were—fortunately—killed at once.

It was appalling, Lord Marley said; his face showed as much shock, leather for leather, as the rows of books behind him.

The lawyer had always admired Marleyshall's views: from these library windows you could see for miles over farms and collieries. His face suitably grave, the lawyer surveyed Nottinghamshire.

Bill Buckingham would have to be told that his only son was gone, Lord Marley said—but where was Bill Buckingham? In some sanatorium near Boston, probably. His old friend in steel. He'd been going to pass the business on to his son, and now he had to be told he had no sons left. No grandsons.

The baby hadn't been hurt at all—thrown clear right out of her mother's arms, the lawyer said. They were keeping her in hospital until further notice.

Ah yes, Lord Marley said, roused from his memories of Bill

Buckingham's foundries. The baby. What was her name? Some old-fashioned name, Elizabeth or . . .

"Catherine," the lawyer said. Did she have relatives left besides her grandfather in the sanatorium? Any guardian?

Nobody, said Lord Marley. Her nanny was in the nursery upstairs—she could be sent to Nottingham at once. No, Rob had been an only child, and Janet had been an orphan . . .

Hold on, Lord Marley said—the baby's half uncle . . . stepuncle . . . he didn't know what. He'd almost forgotten the fellow was there at Marleyshall. Lord Marley stared out at fields and pits. Right there at Marleyshall he was: young chap named something Wade. Bill Buckingham had married Wade's mother—one of those late-in-life marriages to your nurse. Tall fellow. Fond of butterflies. Better tell him first, then tell the rest of the crowd. It was appalling. He rang the bell.

The butler told the footman that Lord Marley wanted Mr. Wade.

"Whatever for?" whispered Daphne Hacket. The butler's voice came clearly from the landing to the hall below.

"Wants a game of mah-jongg," Alice Gresham whispered back, and then laughed at Mary Ross and Daphne. They walked through French doors to the lawn, their strapped slipper heels sinking in the turf. Tea was being served under the oaks.

"Janet's gone motoring with Rob and Catherine to Nottingham, because Rob said *he* was going to take her and the baby to the doctor this time," Daphne said.

"Otherwise . . ." Mary Ross said, her eyebrows almost disappearing under her bangs and headband, "it wouldn't be hard to find Thorn Wade."

"About three feet away from Janet," Alice said. "With the baby between them, of course."

"Of course," Mary said. "Did you see her new motoring hat?"

"Jack Laird would also be three feet away," Alice said, sitting down at a tea table in the shade. "Handsome thing."

"But if looks could kill," Mary said, and laughed, and whispered that they all knew where Janet's *husband* would be, didn't they? But there was the butler with the bread and butter, and the rest returning from the stables, and then Ethel Daniels came running across to the tea table with the news, the horrible news her maid had got from the butler, and they all just sat there.

"She was here only this morning!" Mary cried. "She was a dream in the blue outfit she sent to Paris for, and that hat . . ."

"Who's going to tell Jack Laird?" Daphne said. "Here he comes—who's going to tell him, for God's sake?"

Horses stamped in the stable stalls; harness jingled. "Lord Marley wants the tall chap," said the footman to the groom. "Motors in the old lizzie round and about the fields."

"He went by here an hour past, walkin' through the park," said the stable boy. "Happen he catches specimens."

"There's Wade comin' now just by the church corner," the groom said, and the three men stared from the stable door at the young man walking the pink gravel path through the deer park.

"Poor relation," said the groom. "Hasn't even got ridin' boots."

"Always drivin' the Buckingham lady round, and the childt."

The young man came closer. His thick brown hair was on end; the pockets of his suit coat bulged with heavy objects. He looked into the oaks above him as if he saw them, as if he found them interesting.

"Poor relation," said the groom firmly.

The footman stepped into the sun, but then he turned around, stiff with importance. "The Buckinghams smashed up," he said. "Killed—all but the childt. Mr. Wade's next of kin, so he's got to be told."

"In the phaeton?" cried the groom.

"Tourin' car," the footman said, off down the pink path toward the young man.

"Christ!" said the stable boy. "Car like that! If 'twas me got the handlin' of it . . ."

3

Lord Marley told Jack Laird it was appalling. Laird, after all, was in steel, and was American, and had got some capital from Bill Buckingham somewhere along the line. And he was such a good friend of Janet and Rob's. He could understand how appalled Marley was, having to tell Bill Buckingham that his only son was dead, and his daughter-in-law.

It took time, because matters were arranged with the lawyers in Boston—Bill Buckingham was in that sanatorium for alcoholics:

he couldn't do much. Thorn Wade turned out to be the baby's guardian. He'd have a tidy bit of money from Janet's estate, and he was going back to America with the baby. Didn't need a nanny, he said. Had a man meeting him in London.

Everybody went to London to see Thorn and Catherine off; it was the least they could do.

"Jack Laird's obviously prostrated by it all," Daphne said on the train platform, looking past the gate to where Jack talked with Thorn Wade. "Jack was desperate for Janet, and he's so good looking, too. With money."

"All those clothes Janet had," Mary Ross said. "And with those looks."

Steam and smoke rose to the station's far glass roof to meet the smoke of London looking in. Isolated in the flow of passengers and porters, Jack Laird, Thorn Wade and Catherine formed, for a moment, an island. A woman on the platform smiled at Thorn: his suit was speckled with lint, and his arms were full of baby, baby bottle and trailing pink blanket.

Alice and Mary turned away from the gate to find a taxi; they skirted pigeons, a young man in a wheelchair (wounded in the war, no doubt) and a grandmother in a black bonnet. It wasn't absolutely necessary to wait and see the train leave, Mary said.

Daphne lagged behind, staring through the gate. "She should have married Jack!" she said under her breath. Then she ran off after the others, giving a last look at the two men and the baby who were like an island in the crowd.

"I'll have Catherine, and my work," Thorn said. Catherine was asleep, her fuzzy head on his shoulder.

Jack glanced at a passing pair of silk-clad legs. "A bachelor with a baby? Why don't you go back to France?"

"I can work in the States. Janet wanted Catherine raised there. Rob didn't care."

"Janet's ideas!" Jack ground his cigarette stub into the platform with his heel. "She was spoiled."

"I've bought a house that belonged to a friend of mine," Thorn said.

"So you're going to write books about bugs, and change diapers. Lord. You'll have to find a woman."

"Tubbit's all right." Thorn glanced at the little man with an immense brown mustache, standing guard by their luggage nearby.

"He's from where I was born in South Dakota, and he cooks . . ." His voice trailed off in the hesitant way he had. "No. No women. And no children. Janet said—"

"What?"

"Well . . ." Thorn hesitated. "We don't kill the young like tomcats do, you know. If Catherine has sense enough—"

"Her mother was smart, for a woman! She didn't get that way stuck off—wherever you're going. Where are you going?"

Thorn didn't answer. Jack lit another cigarette. "Raise a baby with nothing but two men, no women, no teachers but a self-appointed—"

"I was with Janet almost a year before." The locomotive at Thorn's back hissed. "She made me Catherine's guardian. There really wasn't anybody else." Thorn gave Jack a faint, apologetic smile. "You said she was smart. For a woman."

"Too damned smart! Too smart to be fooled by a poor kid talking about bugs and following her all over with a butterfly net! She used to laugh at you, by God! She never laughed at me! Or Buckingham."

"No." The grin was gone from Thorn's face. "Neither of you were funny."

"I was serious as hell. It wasn't her money. Buckingham wanted that. I wanted her." Jack looked at Catherine asleep on Thorn's shoulder, her fist curled at his neck. "I played it wrong," Jack said.

The man with the brown mustache took Thorn's luggage up the train steps; Thorn turned to follow him. "Thanks, then . . . thanks for seeing us off," he said, gathering the baby blanket around Catherine. For a moment he stood at the top of the steps staring down at Jack, his eyes widening and very blue. "She was hard to catch," Thorn said.

Jack blew smoke through his nose for an answer, and stared back. The train jerked, slid forward.

"Without a net," Thorn said.

4

"Without a net," Thorn said to no one but the ocean breaking against the ship's side. Women in floppy hats and fluttering frocks giggled, passing the young man at the rail who talked to the sea.

"What did he say?" whispered Irene.

Gladys looked over her shoulder. "Who?"

"Dad's driving my new coupe to New York to meet us—come to Newport with me!" said Mabel.

"I think he said, 'Without regret.'" Irene glanced back. "He's so tall and so—shy looking. Those blue, blue eyes and nice brown lashes all around. Really not bad. Knobby. Kind of rumpled up, makes you want to cuddle him, tell him Mommy's here."

"You're a card, Irene! Besides, he's got a baby. Listen, when we get to New York—"

"Baby!"

"A little baby. Some Russian left over from the revolution carries it around for him. At least that's how it looks. I saw him in the first class yesterday when I was sneaking a smoke. Come on, Irene . . ."

5

Hot in New York. Hot on the long trains west. Finally Thorn bought a used Model T and a baby carriage, and wedged the carriage between front and back seats so that Catherine could sleep in it.

She looked at him with Janet's eyes, except that hers were bluer. He had a thick wad of cash in his breast pocket.

Karl Tubbit drove the car in the silence he seemed to inhabit. He followed directions and found his world acceptably solid, to judge from the forty-year-old face with its observant eyes, the mustache threaded with gray. If he caught any glint of shock in Thorn's long-lashed eyes, he kept it to himself. If Thorn's face looked bleak sometimes, Karl Tubbit watched it with the same interest he gave to the heat lightning that was flickering on the horizon as they drove into Michigan.

Thorn bought a foot accelerator, and then muffs. After he'd raised the seat a dozen times to dip the gas stick, and put grease in the wheel cups, and knew every knot in the floorboards, the car seemed to be his. He had the crackle of money in his hand, and the thought of more money waiting in banks, and a man to pay for and carry with him. He had to give the man directions: have Catherine's bottle filled and warmed, pay the hotel bill, carry the bags.

"Without a net," Thorn said against the down on Catherine's small, hard skull. Under the baby's fuzzy hair, that bowl of bone—like his mother's skull, smiling from beached seaweed and shells, her familiar teeth the only familiar thing, except for William Buckingham's ring among her scattered finger bones to tell who she was. Thorn pressed his mouth against Catherine's sweaty skull and tasted salt. Full of milk, she jerked her arms and legs, and blew bubbles. William Buckingham's grandchild.

"Better stop for gas," Thorn said.

The old farmer who brought the gas looked in at Thorn and Catherine. "Where's your mama?" he asked the baby, his weather-creased face deepening its wrinkles in a smile.

"I'm her mother," Thorn said. "Her father's dead."

"Now that's a shame!" said the farmer. "What a pity!" He watched the young fellow riding off down the road with his father and the baby. Lost his wife. Now that was a shame. "Good luck!" he yelled after them.

It was still hot when they got into Detroit; the lake air hadn't started to cool the city toward dark. Thorn's back stuck to his shirt and his shirt stuck to the car seat, and Catherine dribbled on his shoulder. He put a clean diaper under her glistening chin and pushed the windshield open farther.

The city he knew seemed to waver above the hot pavements like walls beyond a fire. "Turn left on Woodward," he told Tubbit.

Miles of city blocks. Then Detroit thinned out, little by little, to a few houses in the sand of an old lake bed. After a while Thorn said, "Turn right."

A worn gravel road wound through open country. A few elms were vertical strokes on flatness, with scrub oak and sumac here and there. Tall grass baked in silence. If Karl Tubbit wondered what they were doing there, his face showed nothing. He'd seen a lot of cities by that time, growing at the edges after the war. Godawful land, this was. Worse than South Dakota.

Now the road was striped with cottonwood shadow. A break in the trees showed the country house of some Victorian—a house twice as big as Thorn remembered. Afternoon sun repeated the wooden scrollwork in black on white clapboards.

Tubbit stopped the Ford in weeds by a sundial. The front yard was mowed, and wide porches looked out on a cottonwood grove, and sumac.

"Your cottage is behind the house," Thorn said. "It's got three rooms, I think, and everything ought to be clean and ready . . . better get some milk warmed up for her as soon as you can." Trailing baby blanket, he swung his long legs out and over the running board, Catherine in his arms, and felt for Tubbit's keys in his pocket. Tubbit took them without a word, and then Thorn found his own.

The house loomed before him: his house, heavy as the rest of it and thick with stillness. He unlocked the front door, and when he swung it open, its round, beveled window streaked rainbows in and out of a hall and parlor, like scared things flying. Then the presences of old Professor Zeidart and his wife came forward with the scent of what had been their house before they died, and the feeling of rooms full of empty air.

Catherine was asleep on his shoulder. He walked into the parlor and looked out a window. The house and its cottonwoods rose from a sea of coarse, waist-high grass. The grass lay deep and still in the heat, except where the first currents of lake air parted it, a furrow like the wake of someone walking into water, deeper and deeper, walking away.

Catherine stirred in her sleep, turning her head to suckle his bare neck. When he squinted he could see the great clumps of milkweed in the meadows.

There were stamps from old letters in a candy dish. Souvenir plates gathered dust on the mantel. The mantel mirror continued its slow loss of silver, darkening the air it held to a perpetual afternoon. Antimacassared chairs spread their arms by a blackened hearth with ghosts of evenings spent in this room: Thorn and Professor Zeidart intent on the veination of an insect's wing . . .

Windows filled with leaves made the dining room shadowy. The kitchen breathed out the scent of old juices, like its knife-scarred chopping block. Boards in the back hall creaked with voices as acrid as the smell of coal climbing the cellar stairs, or the red of the barn behind the house, fired by the late sun.

Thorn walked outside. He found nothing in the barn but straw on the floor and a shaft of dusty light. Holding Catherine close, his cheek against her small, damp face, he looked out at the sea of grass around this island, and heard what might have been the sound of rain. It was only wind rising in the cottonwoods.

Tubbit's cottage was across from the barn in the abandoned, ratty sprawl of a garden. Thorn picked his way through the yard

and climbed to the porch. "You'll be all right here?" he asked
Tubbit at the door. Tubbit nodded, holding the door open.

The small parlor seemed to lie under a snow of starched doilies. Thorn sat down between chair arms stiff with crochet, and
fed Catherine her bottle of milk while Tubbit went back and forth
from kitchen to bedroom, unpacking.

"Breakfast at six, I'd say. Catherine wakes about then. Lunch
at twelve or so, and dinner at six?" Thorn said to Tubbit as he
passed and repassed. "You can do as you like about the cleaning
. . . doing the laundry . . . I'll have a study upstairs near
Catherine." Tubbit glanced once at the young man, nodded,
then disappeared to rattle grates in the kitchen or drop loads of
kindling in a box. Catherine made her rhythmic cooing sound as
the milk descended in her bottle.

Thorn's house was only a big shape against the dusk sky when
he walked back. A bulb under a frill of gray glass yellowed the
back hall; another spilled light down the front stairs. Catherine
woke as they climbed. Her fuzzy head bobbed against his jaw; her
eyes blinked at gardens of wallpaper roses up the stairs and down
the hall.

Catherine's room was still light enough to show the white
enameled palisade of a new crib. Kicking her arms and legs, she
lay there, fallen from her mother's arms, idle afternoons, her reflection in a silver teapot, the sound of metal smashed on
stone . . .

Then he heard the plane, far overhead. Its whine increased,
until he cried, finally, "Hear it?" and then "Hear her?"

Full of milk, Catherine made a contented, gurgling sound and
smiled; she was all compact and bound somewhere, pumping her
arms and legs like an engine, and she crowed.

Her mother would grow fainter and fainter now, like the sound
of the plane flying west. Janet Buckingham would shed details
with every day and night, becoming smaller and fading . . .

I

How do you tell an arrowhead
from a stone?

By the way rock
takes on meaning. Not much.
Enough to bind a shaft to.

Arrowheads are stone, mostly,
but a glint of light, an edge
always runs to a point along the grain

until you feel as much as see
a wedge of flint
rough-cut to go straight.

"Thorn Wade?" she said to his cowboy face and fringed blue eyes. "Oh—Rob's half brother! Stepbrother?" Janet Buckingham laughed against her parlor's sunny, blowing curtains and the screaming of gulls from Boston harbor. "Well, anyway, you're here for a while?"

"He's about my age," she told her husband before dinner. Rob ducked to see himself in her table mirror and slicked his hair to black leather, squinting through cigarette smoke. "You could have told me. He looks like somebody's poor kid brother—how's he going to fit into our set?"

"I wrote him to come on, work at Harvard or whatever. Dad put him through college and now he's graduated in bugs from Michigan and his mother's dead." Rob put down his brush and glanced at the maid waiting by the bedroom door. She said dinner was served.

"He can see the Cape," Rob said, going out. "Follow us around England if he wants to, carry the suitcases. He's just a kid. Wasn't even in the war."

Didn't he think these Beacon Hill houses were amusing? Janet asked Thorn. She had light gray eyes, so light that the pupils seemed black as bullet holes. Her accent was New York, not Boston. He'd lived in France—didn't he see these high, narrow Boston places as rather Old World—brick sidewalks up and down hill, and everybody up in arms just now because there were electric signs spoiling the view across the Basin?

Thorn ate steadily and answered politely when Janet kept asking questions in the bold, fashionable way, laughing.

Yes, he'd been born in South Dakota and his father had been a minister, and his widowed mother had gone back to France as a nurse . . . she had a family there—miners—in a town not too far from Paris . . .

Yes, he knew Paris, knew a lot of—she'd met Rob's father when she was his special nurse, and after she'd married him she had cancer . . .

No, she was drowned, and they finally found her. Thorn watched Janet's fluttering eyelashes and Rob's fingers tapping the tablecloth.

No, he couldn't go on for graduate work—had to get a job— had a project started on the Monarch butterfly.

The house was a present from Rob's father, Janet said, and did he know his stepfather was in a sanatorium again?

They went to the library for coffee. Prohibition was too late for some people, Rob said.

Thorn's eyes were nice, Janet thought, but he certainly wasn't their style—so quiet. What was he thinking? He didn't have any French accent, but maybe this country still seemed strange to him. He watched them beneath his dark lashes as if he lived in those eyes of his, reflecting upon her, then Rob, then the house.

He stopped at the portrait of William Buckingham in the drawing room's gauntlet of painted faces. "You look like your father," he said to Rob.

When they got to the library, he ambled back and forth, so tall and skinny and shabby, actually reading the titles of the books: rows and rows of them like leathery, paunchy old men.

So he was really nobody, and she wouldn't have to find him girls, or not much, or entertain him. When he was settled by the fire with coffee, Janet lay back in Mr. Buckingham's horsey-smelling leather chair, knowing how the firelight gleamed on her bare arms flung above her head, and thought he was a nice kid, and must feel how he was a poor relation.

Rob talked about how he was managing the family business now that his father was in the sanatorium again. Thorn listened.

Business talk. Janet's mind wandered, but not for long: something kept bringing her back to Thorn Wade. Rob's voice went on, but was Thorn giving him all his attention, or was he interested in something else, too? She was sure after a little while: Thorn was including her as he listened. He was interested in her silence. He was aware of the space she occupied in the room, quiet in the leather chair, watching them.

2

At ten the next morning there were klaxon blasts outside: two Overlands full of friends. They came in for a noisy breakfast. "We're going to the Cape," Janet told Thorn when he came down. "You're not unpacked, are you? There's room for you in Ray's car."

So Thorn rode in Ray Gardener's car with Ray, Alice Gresham, Mary Ross, baggage and bottles, and watched glimpses of the Atlantic get bluer and closer between ocean bungalows.

Then they had a flat. It was late when they nosed in last among expensive cars that stood up to their running boards in grass at the back of the Buckingham beach house.

Sand and sea were bright as the Mediterranean. "Take these, will you?" said Ray to Thorn, tossing gladstones into the sand. "What was that last name again?"

"Wade."

"All they say is 'No swimming suits on the street . . . no swimming suits on the sidewalk'!" Alice Gresham's high voice preceded them through the grass and around the house. "That's all you hear on Nantucket."

Mary Ross shaded her sharp black eyes to look at a beach already alive with the Buckinghams' red umbrellas and a gramophone shrieking away among the gulls. "Nantucket's so Victorian," she said. Tennis rackets were stuck in sand near the porch steps; somebody's Mussolini straw hat speckled the bannister with shade. They climbed past striped suits dripping on the stairs, and halted on the porch.

"A flat?" cried Janet, jumping up from creaking rattan. "Poor things—you must be melted!" The living room had windows full of light from the sea, and smelled of spilled whiskey, and scarlet geraniums planted in brass buckets.

A blonde speared lobster from a bowl. Three young men were

lounging among Sunday papers on the floor. A girl with short black hair stared at Thorn's suit. "Here's everybody you know," Janet told them, "except Thorn Wade, who's Rob's stepbrother from Michigan. Thorn Wade . . . Daphne Hacket, Ethel Daniels . . . " She gestured with the half-empty glass in her hand. "Stan Burke, Bill Bailey, and Walt Lavalle."

Chatter, the clinking of glasses, and the nasal jazz voice outside, howling to beach and sky. The floorboards of the house were worn and wide; they set off the red lobster on its bitter blue tray, and a chocolate cake beside it, half gone, shedding crumbs into somebody's crystal set. "Choose a bed upstairs, and then take a dip and cool off," Janet commanded above the talk. A yacht swam past a window like a fish through an aquarium.

Thorn was wearing that same suit—Janet smiled at him as he went upstairs; they were all looking him over. When he glanced back, his eyes were quiet and blue; they traveled over the faces and the room in one grave sweep. Then all she could see was his long, wool-clad legs going up between two gladstones.

It was so hot. They swam, or sailed, or talked to the tinkle of ice—or a ukulele Daphne could play best, she said, after exactly three gins. Ethel and Stan decided they were in love and locked themselves in the biggest bedroom which, unluckily, was the route to the bathroom. They couldn't, they said, possibly switch beds with anyone because it would be bad luck, so when they finally opened the door, everybody carried the bed to another room and locked them in, until Stan ripped sheets up and climbed down to say the honeymoon was over. So they all went to New York, and Thorn was the only one who was sober enough to drive back. He didn't, he said, drink much. When Alice asked him why not in that piercing voice of hers, he said he was really enjoying himself.

"He's nothing but a kid," Rob said to a midnight ceiling and Janet, who had just told him she was pregnant. "A poor kid. Goes around looking at things. What's he thinking?"

"You're changing his whole view of life," Janet said in a flat voice. "Just imagine that." She took off her earrings and bracelets and threw them into the bedroom's dark that echoed the surf's thud and hissing.

The last of summer's crowd danced cheek to cheek across gritty floors, got sick one more time on three-mile hootch, and decided to go back to Boston. Thorn carried suitcases out through a litter of newspapers, a Kodak somebody had smashed, plates of eggs left over from breakfast . . . "See you all at the Patterson party!" yelled Daphne as the last car pulled out of the yellowing grass. Thorn looked back. A maid was folding beach umbrellas. The gramophone listened to the sea from a sand dune, its black trumpet stuck in its ear. No one was wading into the Atlantic's blue gaze of light.

3

September was hot, but it rained for the Patterson dance. The Pattersons always threw the first big party of the season, Janet told Thorn. She said it would be big, and expensive, and—by midnight—drunk, and it was.

Janet was only half drunk by twelve o'clock. She sat near the dance floor and watched its polish shimmer with the colors of panting and shrieking dancers and the repose of the long buffet. Behind it all flowed the Charles, carrying its bridges and lights beyond windows, balconies, and rain.

Janet wasn't listening to Russ Schmidt, whose mouth was only a few inches from her ear. He was one of Rob's buddies from Harvard Law days, and four drinks ahead of everybody. He whispered that he adored Janet, always had adored Janet, always would adore Janet, while Ethel and Stan argued about strike breakers, and Walt Lavalle dragged Daphne through high kickers on the floor, trying to teach her a new step.

Thorn was sitting alone. Janet's bored glance swept over him and then returned to him. He was by himself, wedged in a little bamboo chair against frocks and tuxedos that jigged past to the "Japanese Sandman."

He had such an adolescent, roosting look—couldn't Rob's father at least give the kid money for a decent tux? Janet leaned through a cloud of cigarette smoke, narrowing her eyes. Thorn was embarrassed, she supposed, sitting there all alone, his thick hair mussed, as usual, his black socks showing above his big shoes. "Shush my kind of girl," Russ crooned in her ear, exhaling bourbon.

Janet leaned away from the bourbon, not listening: she was curious. She wanted to see the expression on Thorn's face. All she could see now was what looked like loneliness: a kid all by himself, watching a dance. He always looked a little grim; it had something to do with the long lines of his cheeks and the straight line of his mouth, and then those peculiar, really beautiful eyes. She ought to go over to him. She ought to ask him why he watched women the way he did; she was drunk enough. Then he turned, and she saw that he wasn't embarrassed, or even lonely.

"Come on," Rob said, and swung Janet up and away from Russ. He pressed her against his tux and the hot, brown plane of his cheek. She let him push and pull and turn her, her bare arms and pink silk legs pumping, her white beaded frock twinkling. She didn't notice she was dancing; she kept trying to see Thorn. Mary Ross's black-eyed face bobbed past, and Alice yelled something over the saxophone's bleat, her mouth a red-rimmed hole.

Thorn had gone over to the buffet: she caught a glimpse of him taking a swallow of punch, his Adam's apple bobbing. Then dancers intervened with the seesawing hands and shoulders of a tribal rite, babbling and shrieking. There Thorn was—she saw him again—mussing his hair with one big hand. The buffet table floated its serenity of glass and porcelain like water lilies. Above his thin cheeks Thorn's eyes moved over sweating Harvard men, band instruments wailing like cats, and girls as bold and narrow as young boys.

4

Soberly, in the fall daylight on Boylston Street or the candlelight of the London Club, Janet sometimes watched Thorn Wade, thinking how compact, how finished Rob looked beside him. Even the youngest man in their crowd seemed more in command of his clothes than Thorn. Thorn's clothes seemed to wear him: he stuck out of them, the nape of his neck vulnerable as a baby's, his feet bigger than anyone else's. His eyes never darted lightly about, smiling or polite or simply bored like other people's. Back from his days in the Harvard collections, he regarded Janet's new Martial et Armand frocks with the same profound attention he gave the pumpkin pie or Rob's description of a remodeled De Haviland plane.

It provoked Janet a little. In the midst of desultory conversations of he-said, she-said, or let's-go, she put on the modern act that was only beginning to be the style—the Tame-me-if-you-can Tomboy who twisted and jerked as no lady had ever done. The Tomboy skipped into a room and perched on a chair arm. She shot into a car or up a gangplank by herself, disdainful of masculine support, or said "tough" things. "I'm having a baby, and it's kicking!" Janet told mixed company in their opera box between acts. "Isn't that exciting?"

When Jack Laird came from Chicago, he had the new styles of flirting down pat. The man talked tough right back, squinting his eyes a little, taking up a dare that was so different from the old shy-rosebud technique, though Janet supposed it all ended up the same. But there was this new sexy edge to it, and though Jack Laird wasn't the dangerous game he would be in twenty years, he was dangerous enough with his glossy black gaze and his beautifully tailored suits and the way he still felt about her. He decided to go to England with them, and all the way over on the boat she kept up this new fire-with-fire business with him—no more than a stab of your eyes (when you should be looking down) or a toss of your head. Jack was fascinated, and that was all Janet wanted.

The crossing was perfect: warm and sunny. Thorn lay on the first-class deck watching his tanning kneecaps, or the immense hairbow of a passing child, or gulls that hung overhead on the wind.

Janet stood at the rail with Rob, her eyes on Thorn. "He looks better."

"I wrote Dad's banker." Rob lit a cigarette in his cupped hands, watching the water creaming away from the bow. "He sent Thorn some cash for clothes and the trip."

"Thorn's mother nursed your father—"

"Thorn is family—that's what it is. The old man finances poor relatives all over the place—it's the old Boston Tradition. Someday I'll have to pass the bucks around."

"Not my bucks."

"No . . . your bucks," Rob said. "Your baby."

Janet walked away to Thorn. "You're getting browner," she said, and smiled.

Thorn glanced up in time to see that amused look in her eye: there was an entomology text open and fluttering on his hairy legs. Illustrations of the dorsal and ventral views of termites marched from one margin to the other.

Janet sat down in the next chair, throwing off her robe. The ruffles of her swimming suit slid up almost to her knees, and she yanked at the ruffles, then lay back. The sun glowed through her eyelids, but she thought she could feel something else beside that heat: Thorn's attention trained on her, like a gun muzzle, a lens, a question.

Rob walked by with a nod just as she opened her eyes. Thorn watched Rob stroll off down the deck, then turned that dark-rimmed, sad awareness on her, level and quiet.

"He doesn't want the baby," Janet said.

She couldn't believe she had told him something like that, even while her words were still vibrating in the air between them, making his eyes wince in reflected sunlight from his open book.

She couldn't look into that gaze of his—she watched cloud shadow flying across the water. He'd say something trite and comforting, she supposed. How it was her baby, anyway, and she'd love it.

He said nothing. When she looked at him, finally, she met that wincing, squinted look of his. That was all there was. Cloud shadow blotted the rail, the deck, the lifeboats, the deck chairs, the deck and rail again, and ran off across the sea.

Rob strolled back down the deck to stop by lifeboats still covered with khaki canvas. He lit a fresh cigarette. What were Janet and Thorn talking about? The sun between clouds hit them like a spotlight, and Janet sat in a queer privacy of sun and looked at Thorn, her knees sticking out of one of those new bloomer outfits.

When he came up, they didn't notice. Janet saw how Thorn's peculiar eyes were glinting, blue-green threads in their blue, and a shimmer of color she knew was herself, reflected in their sadness.

5

The present Lord Marley was fond of progress, Rob said, and so was his son. Alice Gresham watched the coal towns go by the limousine windows and said she'd heard it was "black money" that built Marleyshall. That's what friends told her. First black from the Liverpool slave trade, she said, scowling at the grime on her new kid gloves, and then from coal in Sheffield. Their limousine climbed the last Midlands hill and there was the brick and stucco pile of Marleyshall on the forest's edge. At least that was romantic, Daphne said, and the place looked big enough for an army.

Lord Marley met them in one of the huge drawing rooms to ask about Rob's father—how was his old friend in steel? Then nobody ever saw much more of him than a broad smile from a doorway or a chauffeur waiting for him by his car. He thought it was an honor to have the first Buckingham grandchild born at Nottingham, and where were there better doctors? His furnaces reddened low-lying clouds at night; the pits steamed by day. Above steam and smoke, massed winter trees hid deer parks, gardens, stables, and tennis courts. If blackened men from underground looked up as they trailed home at dusk, they could see only Marleyshall's chimneys, or the steeple of the old church halfway down to town.

Autumn and early winter had been fine in Scotland, but this February weather was rotten; everybody said so. They motored to Devon or weekended in London or lolled at Marleyshall. Jack Laird was part of the Buckingham crowd now, and somebody said (in Torquay or shopping on Piccadilly or somewhere) that Janet would have done better to marry him. It was clear that he'd been (and still was) in love with her, and equally clear that Janet couldn't stand the sight of her husband, and clearer yet that Rob Buckingham had found prettier things to look at than a wife in her eighth month.

Janet was quieter; it was her condition, everyone said. She smiled her quieter smile at Jack, and would not drive with her husband in the fast car he drove too fast. Jack stood ready with his phaeton and lap robes, but Janet rode with Thorn in his rented Ford. She was learning about insects and flowers, she said, and Jack was a dear, but he didn't know a mandible from a mandrake, a fact he couldn't deny. Well, said Jack in his curious Chicago accent, bastards might kill themselves in fast cars, but she deserved comfort. "I'm perfectly comfortable," Janet told him, smiling her new gentle smile, and rode off with Thorn.

What did those two do, up to the axles in country mud at all hours, or walking slowly through the park, down farm lanes, rummaging in old sheds for wasps or whatever? Janet left the stucco facade of Marleyshall to raise its eyebrows of brownstone over its windows all day if it chose; she was studying the world, she told her friends. She had never seen it properly before. It was ravishing, she said.

"She's keeping a journal," Alice said. "She goes off on walks early every morning." Alice was watching Janet and Jack Laird against the tennis court hedges. "All by herself."

"Jack looks like a movie star, I think," Daphne said. "Like what's his name . . . Fairbanks."

"He's got money."

"If she wanted to make Rob jealous . . . "

Alice laughed. "They talk about bugs! And flowers!"

Snow fell, melting into brown farmlands.

Janet's small head, helmeted against the wind, turned to Thorn's touseled and sun-streaked one as they rode high in his rented Model T down cowpaths and winter fields. She watched his profile from the cocoon of her fur-lined collar, her lips pink with rouge, her eyelids shiny with grease, and listened to Thorn explain what he knew she didn't need to know.

What use would it ever be to her to know about insects and flowers? She asked herself that, and sometimes she asked Thorn, her voice going up in exasperation. He didn't know. He was going anyway, he said, and she was welcome to come along.

She flirted with him sometimes when they were off for the afternoon (straightened his tie . . . patted his cheek). It was the least she could do when he was driving her all over the countryside. He acted as if it were the least he could do to show he didn't mind it—he never blushed, or tried to kiss her, or fidgeted. He just waited quietly, as if flirting were something she had to do.

And all the time he patiently explained what he knew she didn't need to know, but she learned it—got her teeth into it, as if hard facts were some exotic food her pregnancy made her wild to have. She listened to the usual daylong chitchat at Marleyshall, but what she craved was the truth about carpels and corms, or the pupae a farmer's plow turned up to the sun.

This bumblebee was a *Bombus lucorum;* that was a *Bombus pratorum.* She gritted her teeth sometimes—dug her fingers into

damp Midlands dirt that always smelled, just a little, of sulfur
from the pits.

She brought facts back to Marleyshall like stones, lumps of lichen, or galls, and put them down near a timbo hat or Paisley bag
whose intricacies she had no name for—and yet intricacies had
names, just as the dark, reddish-purple flowers of Hedge-Wound-
wort were *Stachys silvatica.* Facts underlay them—solid, like biting into an apple, like rooting down. Like the blade of a saw. An
ax helve.

6

Janet, half awake on a March morning, wondered where she
was—London? Devon? No, she was waiting for the baby at Marleyshall. Fields were greening out there in the dark. There were
windflowers at the forest's edge.

Dawn came earlier now. The clock in the church tower below
struck quarter and half hours, while dressers and tables began to
stand out from the bedroom walls, dark gray against light gray.
Rob's watch and chain, dropped with his studs on a gilt chair,
picked up small gleams like eyes. They watched Janet as she
climbed clumsily from bed and came and went across thick carpets.

Marleyshall's broad stairs were carpeted, runners locked with
brass rods like spears at each riser. No one heard Janet go down.
The butler was shaving. The half-dressed maids yawned and
complained far up under the roof. The cook was putting water to
boil with a clang of pots, talking to her cat in the damp cellar
kitchen. Janet stepped through the conservatory's French doors
and left Marleyshall's deer park for the farm lanes, a notebook
under her arm.

No one missed Rob and Janet at breakfast; they hardly ever
came down, but had coffee sent to their room. It was ten o'clock
before Rob asked a group at the stable if they'd seen Janet. He
shrugged, looked up at the gray sky, then sprang to his saddle and
was soon nothing but a spot of color among horses and horsemen
in a spring field.

Thorn watched Rob ride off; he stroked his mare's nose absentmindedly, his blue eyes moving across stone walls to fields only beginning to flush green at the root. Then he handed his reins to the groom and struck off on foot down the deer park's gravel. The groom shrugged, watching the lanky fellow go. Didn't have a proper riding suit. Not much polish. A poor relation. When he led the mare off, he looked back, and Thorn was letting himself through the woods gate. He disappeared past the lichen-scabbed church wall.

Beyond the church a road, bordered in yellow grass, had thawed to mud. Just as Thorn passed the bare brown whips of a hazel wood and skirted a farm cart, he saw the print of a small, high-heeled shoe in the ooze.

Thunder came closer and closer, and the wind smelled of rain now. Janet was probably back at Marleyshall by this time; she never walked far. "How can I walk in shoes like these?" she would ask.

He passed a cottage whose vine-covered wall was turning faintly green like the fields, suffusing with leaves almost too small to see. The forest came to the road with the noise of wind in a larch grove, and then the lavender and black of oaks. "Maybe it's a question of what we're for," she had gone on to say, walking ahead of him through the din of the larches. "You can walk. You can think—when you sit watching and looking peaceful, that's what you're doing. Asking the right questions. That's what you're for."

Her small head in its bell of felt had turned away from him; her hair frayed and blew at its edges. Thorn had watched her wrap her full coat closer and pick her way down the ruts beside these oaks. Her legs looked naked. One of her arms, flung out for balance, clinked with metal rings.

Thorn glanced up. Rain was coming now, moving over farmlands and collieries like a phalanx with shimmering spears, blotting out miles of open country ahead, field by field. Only a great gray-black barn and a copper beech were not fading yet: they still showed their textures of stone, timber, and leaf against the curtain of rain: a colored poster pasted on smoke. He began to run.

Big drops splatted around him and on him; thunder cracked. He vaulted a fence and made for the barn's open door. Lightning flare spotlit the barn as he ducked inside. It bleached a straw-scattered dirt floor and straw heaps against the far wall.

It lit Janet's white face across dim and dusty air. She knelt there in a pile of straw, hands on a stall beam as if she were trying to rip it from the wall. Thorn stared at the red splash her silk dress made against the dirt and straw, recognizing guttural groans he had heard more than once in a peasant hut; they came from the half dark as if an animal crouched there.

She gasped when she saw Thorn, then had to go back to the wood; she pitted herself against it until his belly knotted in rhythm with her cries.

"Should I go get help?" he said, kneeling beside her.

"No!" she cried and groaned, and groaned again. "The head! I can feel the top of the head already!"

When she could rest, she lay along the beam, panting, eyes shut, brown hair plastered to her cheeks, rouge smeared across her mouth. Thorn wet his handkerchief in the downpour sheeting across the doorway and wiped her face and neck when she pushed her dress down and off her arms. It was too tight and only in the way; he helped her get it over her head, and she knelt in her pink chemise, glistening with sweat.

Her panting breath was the only sound in the barn except the steady rain on the roof. The pain convulsed her again; she dug her fingernails in the wood and moaned.

When she could lie along the beam, he wrapped his coat around her, but she threw it off when the pain came: she was beyond caring whether she was covered, and he, kneeling in the straw by her as she alternately pulled and clung, worked with the body under his hands that was half naked and suffering in a few layers of silk that were only in their way.

Sometimes he held her, sweating and slippery and shivering, against his chest, murmuring into her soaked hair. Sometimes she bent over the beam, moaning that her back hurt her so, and he rubbed her hips and the lumpy strung bones of her spine.

The rain lessened to a quiet, pattering fall, leaking through the roof to stir straws in rivulets down the dirt floor beside them. When the lightning died away, they had less light to see by.

Janet wouldn't lie down; she knelt there grunting and moaning, clinging to the beam or Thorn. She cried in short gasps, her face streaming with tears. Then, with a last scream of hers, the small, live body of a child dropped red and slick and hot into Thorn's hands, a child who was yelling already, her eyes wide open.

Thorn and Janet babbled words they never heard or remembered: two half-naked, sweating, blood-smeared creatures bent over a third, who lay on Thorn's shirt in the straw and yelled back at them. There was the human face, and the perfect human body. "Oh!" Janet kept crying, "Oh!" her gray eyes blinking in her white face, her hands hovering, afraid to touch. It was Thorn who wrapped the shirt around Catherine as Janet lay back in clean straw, sobbing.

"Lie still," he murmured, groping for his coat flung on the stanchion; he tucked it around Janet and laid her own coat over her legs. Catherine's screams became whimpers and then stopped as she grew warm in the hay. When he could, he tied off the cord with his shoelace, and cut it, and waited for the afterbirth, remembering a midwife's talk in lantern light, and the sound of splashing water in a basin, and the horrified eyes of a young father not as old as he was now. Janet lay exhausted until he brought her Catherine, warm in the bundled shirt, and scooped clean straw to heap over Janet's feet against the damp air.

"I'll go now—run all the way. They'll come, and send for the ambulance." His long, lean face was as sober as hers, but then they both smiled the same kind of smile, and he pushed her wet hair back from her face as if it were his own. There was a smear of blood on his eyebrow; she brought one hand from beneath the coat to wipe it away. Naked to the waist, he was shivering, but he laughed. "She's trying to nurse already." Heads close together, they watched the small red face creep along the wet silk of Janet's chemise hunting something it had never tasted, whimpering.

Thorn glanced over Janet's body just as she did, trying to think how baby and breast could be brought together. Janet's chemise couldn't be slipped down enough; Janet half sat to see if she could pull it up, but Thorn said, "Wait," and stood up to get a hand in his trouser pocket. One of his bare arms and a shoulder flushed gold suddenly: returning sunlight threw the shape of a ladder against the barn wall and glittered on the knife opening in his hands.

He came down to squat again, and slid a hand between layers of silk while he cut two slashes in the cloth. He worked carefully to the bare skin, his full lower lip bent with the thinner one above in the grim look he often wore. Then his dark lashes lifted and he smiled; they both smiled, gray eyes into blue. She heard his knife click among coins in his pocket, saw his thick hair shine against dark beams overhead, and he was gone, running through weeds, vaulting the half-fallen wall, dodging puddles up the farm lanes.

The baby's mouth touched skin through one of the slits, homed to a nipple as a compass points to north, and fastened on it—Janet's exclamation echoed in the dark barn, a lonely sound. She shut her eyes to bring Thorn's hands back, and his bare chest, and his arms around her, and the low, flattened voice that still seemed as close as the rustle of the straw, or the echo of screams.

When she opened her eyes they were full of tears, although she had come through, and floated in an absence of pain like clouds or mist, and the child moved in her arms, sucking, making little sounds. Rob's child. Sky was clearing beyond the barn door; copper beech leaves, new and red, flickered against patches of blue.

She had come here before. A ladder leaning before one of the windows brought her the memory of Thorn kneeling near it. One great bumblebee queen, all polished leather, plush and lacquered gauze, had clung there. Thorn would not take her as a specimen; he wouldn't even tamper or touch, but knelt to observe. That was all. *Bombus terrestris,* he said.

The last of the rain gathered and fell everywhere from eaves and leaves, and Thorn's absence was as real as the spaces between the slow drops, between ladder rungs, between far off cries of rooks. Janet stared past door and beech leaves, tears running into her ears and down her neck. When the cars came, and the ambulance, she was still crying, and the women crooned over her, and Thorn wasn't there.

7

Everyone said Janet was a wonder, recovering so quickly from such an ordeal—all alone in a barn having your first baby in a thunderstorm! How lucky Thorn found them afterward. Imagine doing everything by yourself! She shouldn't have gone out walking alone like that, but who thought the baby would be that early?

"He's always there," Daphne told Mary and Alice. "Sitting by her bed in that same old suit with his messy hair, and they talk and talk."

Mary Ross tapped her cigarette into one of Lord Marley's Chinese vases. "What about?"

"I drove down there yesterday and waited in the hall, naturally—I didn't want to interrupt—and they were talking about how he went roaming over his part of France when he was a boy . . . stayed in awful peasant huts and haystacks and whatever, looking for moths, because he didn't have money . . . "

"Well, anyway, she's got her figure back," Alice said.

Janet had her figure back. She sat in a hospital room filled with roses and boxes of candy and cards with storks and booties on them. She remembered blood. There were slivers still working out of her hands. Her body had pushed Catherine out, and now the baby extracted milk from her, efficient as a plant root, solid as an apple, and true to laws, like a stone or a gall.

When Thorn came the first day, there Janet was among the roses and candy and booties. She had on the silk negligee that was the only thing she'd bought to be ready for the baby—for the blood and the screaming.

She couldn't just lie there and smile at Thorn the way she smiled at anybody, could she?

She said "Thorn!" and held out her hands.

He had to come and take them, splinters and all. But when she pulled his hands a bit, softening her eyes and her mouth, he only bent a little closer and asked how she was, and she said she was fine, and he sat down.

Look at him! Too big for his suit, with one finger absentmindedly running around his collar as he talked. He didn't look at her; he looked at the cards propped beside him that said, "A Parents' Joy" and "Baby Makes Three" and "A Little Sweet Someone Has Come!" He said he'd been out in the fields; he was going to the barn every day—did she remember the *Bombus terrestris*—

"You really don't understand," Janet said in a peculiar voice, watching him with her half-shut, pale gray eyes.

He didn't look at her. He said he knew he didn't. He couldn't . . . did he know, she asked, that her mother and father had both wanted a boy? They tried and tried to have one after she was born. Her mother had died trying. So think of it—she'd killed her mother just by being a girl. Thorn sat there, thinking of it, she supposed, while she went on about the private schools, and the father she'd seen as little as possible. She'd told him all of this once. He listened, knowing she was telling him again because, as she said, he didn't understand. You couldn't expect too much, she said, and now there were tears in her eyes. You just couldn't expect . . . and now she had Catherine. He didn't understand. Thorn sat there and looked as if it were his fault she had to tell him again and again, and of course it was.

He didn't say he was sorry. He didn't try to change the subject. He just sat there, mussing his hair in that absentminded way he had, and his expression looked as lonely as she felt. He didn't understand either, he said. He didn't have an answer in the world. So they looked at each other.

Then those deep blue eyes of his stopped darting around the room. He opened them very wide and took a deep breath.

His mother had waded into the ocean off Florida, he said—a tall woman. Her face was round until she smiled, and then it seemed three-cornered and French. What you remembered was the eyes, and the piled hair that must have been black when she was twenty-one and had her passage money, and could go be a nurse in America.

No older than he was now, and nothing to her name but a steamship ticket and the address of some distant relative. But she was sure there must be dirty floors she could scrub in New York. Leaning over the rail with no money in her pockets, watching the same Atlantic. She'd crept on her knees with a pail and rag along the corridors of some buildings they passed when they sailed from New York, probably.

"But she got through nursing school," Thorn said. "She got a job in Sioux Falls, South Dakota, and she went all those miles by train through a foreign country." He sat thinking about that for a while, and then said she'd met his father in the hospital. She'd met both her husbands in hospitals.

He thought he could remember sitting with his mother in the front pew of a church. A skinny black-gowned man who must have been his father waved his hands at the ceiling. And he remembered his mother cooking chickens all the time. The farmers left chickens on the back porch to pay the minister for a wedding or a funeral or a christening.

Dust blew through every crack in their old house—he could remember that. He remembered his mother drawing pictures for him in that dust, while his father lay in bed, coughing. He was sure he could remember that coughing.

Then it stopped. The man in bed had coughed his way into a box in the church. Thorn hadn't understood any of it. All he knew was that they were going to somewhere his mother called "France."

"She was going back home because she had to: my uncle had been killed in the mine, and they had two little girls, and my grandfather was old." There had been black dust in his grandfather's house, and the roofs of row houses crowded the sky away. He lived at the bottom of them as if he'd been dropped in a well. Cousins slept in his bed; he ate at a table with strange faces and strange food and not a word he could recognize. Everything seemed black except his mother. She came home at night like a clean sheet of paper or a white flower, white as milk in her nurse's dress, with the money.

Thorn wasn't looking at Janet: he was looking out at Nottingham's chimney pots.

But then he made her laugh, grinning and turning his hat around in his big hands. His cousins were girls: sharp elbows and knees in bed. Sharp voices. They taught him the word for the funny thing he had in front before he knew any other French at all. His Aunt Marie was a great, bosomy creature (he demonstrated with his hat), who washed floors and sheets and children with the same swooping, hard-handed zest, while his grandfather sat, toothless and dozing, in a dry spot. Women and girls knew everything in that house, and Annette Wade came home every night with the money, in her clean whiteness.

Thorn looked at Janet, aware that he was repeating . . .

"Hello!" said Bill Bailey at the open door. "How's the new mother today?"

Rob was with him, and they were carrying bunches of flowers. The nurse came to put the bouquets in water. The two men stood by Janet's bed and talked in cheerful tones and looked uncomfortable, as if they would rather be somewhere else.

Janet watched them closely, and she wisecracked and talked back, as if having a baby were something you did to be even more attractive. A hospital was a place where real women went, mysterious women, and they lay in silk negligees among roses and laughed, knowing delicious secrets.

After Rob and Bill were gone, she felt the pads and belt under her negligee, and the splinters in her hands. Thorn was still sitting there with his straw hat, not looking at her. A baby was crying in a room down the hall.

8

Janet couldn't sleep much. She'd never slept alone before, or had so much time to think. In the dim hospital nights she had nothing to do but smell her roses, or wait until it was time to feed Catherine, and so she lay and thought about what Thorn was trying to tell her, trying to explain, as if he were a curious bit of rock she had come across: she turned the thought of him over in her mind and barely sensed the way he was shaped and made plain.

His aunt and his mother and his cousins all stopped short, Thorn told her. That was the first, he thought, that he noticed. If he tried to make a picture of the feeling, it was like an invisible wall that he wouldn't have known or felt was there, except that he saw how it stopped his cousins and mother and aunt. Halting, they had a look in their eyes, and so he knew he was special. They stopped short. For a while he thought there was something he didn't know about himself, and of course there was. ·

"Marthe and Claire and I got dirty, and fought, and ran away," he said, "but they got a whipping, and my aunt just scolded me, and told my mother. It wasn't fair."

Could Janet imagine how it was . . . his cousins lying beside him at night, both of them still hot and wet with crying? It was such a small house that when his mother and aunt talked in the kitchen, their voices were clear through the thin lath and plaster. He'd torn his clothes, his aunt said. He'd fought. And then the two women laughed softly under the lamp. When sobs shook his bed, they measured the distance between his cousins and him, like an echo between them, the first of all the things he couldn't understand.

Marthe and Claire must remember the whippings, and the tight braids that pulled their eyebrows back. He remembered the magical house door that stood open to the waiting street, with boys running just beyond the doorstep, and when the first of the boys came in, his aunt and his mother and his cousins stopped short, halting before the boy. So he knew by their eyes that his friend was special, too, and so was the next boy, and all the others. The voices and hands and eyes stopped short of even the smallest boy, leaving him to the other side of the transparent wall where the door was, and the street and river and fields.

He fought. He didn't know why—because the boys were waiting for him in the street, perhaps. He had to explore because the mine was there, crouched in the fields over its black hole. He had to go to the woods because the gypsies camped there. He had to go to the farms because the cider was done, or because Maurice dared him to swing from the fodder hook in his uncle's barn. But he knew (did he?) that the mine and woods and farms were there for everyone, weren't they?

No, of course—they weren't. Every day was a hard fight to get through. He didn't know what went on in a mine, so he was laughed at, and they jeered because his father wasn't down there, or anywhere. He came home choking on his rage, or too tired to eat, or wild eyed with some daredevil trick. There were Marthe and Claire in dark dresses and pinafores, setting the table, and the house was warm and safe. It wasn't fair. Tomorrow the Hebert boys would be waiting to chase him again.

Everything had to be known and done and suffered through, and no help, and no place to hide. He looked at Janet with his half-shut, vulnerable eyes.

And yet there was the door of the house, open on the street always. Nobody thought it strange if he stood at the edge of a fight, yelling with the rest, or listened to what the blacksmith told his cronies between hammer blows. He jumped in the creek, ran shouting through the woods, and came to the meadows at last to lie watching the insects, their world within his world.

He didn't ask if Janet had ever felt that way; he sat turning his hat around in his hands, and in the silence between his words the nurse brought in ice water or a glass of milk.

"Couldn't you stay home?" Janet asked. "Why did you have to go out?"

"They saved the nicest things for me," Thorn said, startled, his hat frozen in his hands. "A piece of bread and jam," he said. "Pudding."

"Will you step out and wait?" said the nurse to Thorn. "It's time for the baby's feeding."

Thorn sat in a chair at the end of the hall, his hat on his knees. When Catherine was carried away, he came back to Janet's bedside, his eyes very wide and very blue. "Bread and jam," he said. "Pudding."

Sometimes, in the hospital nights, Janet tried to remember the door of her house in New York open to the city street. The maid had always pinched her ankles when she fastened her high shoes with the buttonhook—she could remember that. Her long underwear was folded over her ankle, and then her stockings had to be pulled up over it and fastened to a scratchy belt around her waist.

She had had a muff. There was a white dresser in her nursery that had bluebirds painted on it. She couldn't remember ever being hurt or mad or even tired when she came home from the park with the nursemaid, and nobody had ever saved anything for her. She took her bath and then she had her supper in the nursery and then she went in to see Papa unless he were going out. And then she went to bed. She couldn't remember ever being alone, not even when she was asleep. Later she was always with the girls at her school. You weren't allowed to go out alone.

Nottingham lay dark outside her window under a few streetlamps. She didn't know that town, or any other town; there were no maps in her head of creeks and quarry pools and rotten logs where ants tunneled.

Sometimes she fell asleep and then, in the depths of the night, there would be a brilliance flooding through her door. A rustling white blur came to her bed, and a baby wailed. Efficient hands unbuttoned her gown. A woman's crisp voice above her was as wide awake as if it were noon.

Trying to raise herself on one elbow, trying to focus her eyes, Janet felt she had been sleeping while adults attended to the world. Catherine nursed and Janet watched the bright hospital hall where equipment was wheeled by and women sat writing at a high desk. Nurses laughed at three o'clock in the morning.

She could only remember her house in New York from the front, she told Thorn. She had never been allowed to go out the back way. But once she had gone to play with a child who lived next door—she remembered going upstairs behind a maid's starched apron bow. Then she had looked through curtains on a landing and seen suddenly—like a child in a dream—her own house as the neighbors saw it. Raised as if in air, she saw all that was so familiar turn a blank stranger's face to a child in a window.

It had been necessary to smell good from the very beginning, and you were not to chatter. Her father liked to see her embroider, so she was very good at it—she had embroidered a woodland view for his fire screen. No one asked what you were thinking while you embroidered. Her father told her that she was pretty, and she cried because she was so happy.

It wasn't Thorn's fault, Janet said, while he started fumbling for a handkerchief and she was wiping her eyes and nose on the sheet. She could start somewhere. She could find out how Rob managed her money. It came from cotton mills. She wondered if cotton mills ran all night. She blew her nose.

"You know how beautiful you are," Thorn said. "None of the others have Jack Laird following them around, or Bill, or Marley. 'You common people of the skies,'" he quoted awkwardly, turning his straw hat around in his hands (it was really too early for a straw hat), "'What are you when the moon shall rise?'" But he wasn't complimenting her. He was comforting her, with that embarrassed or guilty look in his bleak eyes.

And then the doctors said that she could go home.

What a lot of attention she got. Everyone came from Marleyshall to drive her and Catherine and Catherine's nanny home in triumph. It was really very nice.

And what a pretty figure she had now—they all said so.

They went to London when she felt strong enough. There was a holiday in her honor at Windermere. Catherine, swathed in cunning baby things, traveled along with the nanny, who was reliable and adored her.

Janet talked to Thorn sometimes. Sometimes he watched her with Jack Laird, or Bill Bailey, or Lord Marley's son, down from Oxford.

Janet was charming, and Rob saw it, all right. He took her away from the men's admiring glances with his Boston manners that could be just as smooth as the English gentry's.

He wanted her to get some really good clothes, he said, when they went to Paris in July.

9

But Janet had screamed there in the straw. Thorn had rubbed her back, and held her, trying to keep her warm. She'd been wet with sweat and blood and tears, the way an engine turns in its grease. Her body had done all that. Now she put charming new clothes on it. She fed it from Lord Marley's porcelain plates and crystal. It danced. It sat around in chairs.

She didn't see Thorn very much. He couldn't make conversation about fashionable things, of course. His clothes weren't right. He actually said once that he didn't know how to play mahjongg. When she was circled by masculine admiration, he drifted off. She hadn't been quite herself in the hospital. It was fun to have her figure back, and be able to flirt again when she felt like it.

And yet Thorn was so seldom where she was. She looked for him (never seeming to), just as she never seemed to remember, surrounded by men, that their admiration could be seen as a comfort.

Sometimes Thorn was there, and she felt how he was once removed from Daphne's chatter, Rob's loud laugh, the flutter of Alice's hands . . . aware and alive behind those wincing, shadowed eyes.

She wasn't stupid. She began to notice that when she had Catherine in her arms, the women came to coo over the baby, but the men kept their distance most of the time. They glanced at the little girl, an object they didn't need to know about. They waited for the nanny to come and take her away . . . all the men but Thorn.

After that it was harder to find Janet. It was such fun, she said, to play with Catherine. She wanted to see her when she smiled the first time.

When Jack Laird went by the library on his way to the tennis courts, Thorn was holding Catherine and reading to Janet. It was a fascinating book about the home, Janet said when Alice asked her. Did Alice realize that we've taken industries and education out of the home, and organized almost every important thing— except housekeeping? Except raising babies? So we're Neanderthals there, because housekeeping and babies weren't as important as weaving better cloth, Janet said. Or learning Latin.

Good Lord, Ethel said, they were telling each other the history of their lives. She'd heard bits and pieces. One or the other would hold Catherine while they talked, talked, talked—all about how his mother had fought to get him educated, or whether if you had a defect of character you should be taught that it wasn't one— such serious faces, good Lord. Whatever they talked about made them stare at the rest like strangers sometimes—it gave you chills. Sometimes Janet looked as if she'd been crying, and other times the two of them went off into giggles if you said the simplest thing. Honestly. Nothing but babies, babies, babies.

What could Bill Bailey and Jack Laird and Marley do—Alice Gresham asked in her high voice—learn to change the baby's "nappies"? Jack Laird was the cleverest, Daphne said: he had a niece in Iowa, and could talk about babies, too.

Daphne and Ethel and Alice sat in the sunshine watching Janet. Luncheon was served on the lawn every fine day now. The crowd lounged about in tennis dresses or riding jackets, and spread maps and timetables among the dishes.

Thorn was bent over Catherine as she lay on his knees, arms and legs jerking in the sunlight, laughter bubbling from her in little chirps. She grabbed a lock of his hair and hung on with a monkey child's grip; Janet had to lean close and pry Catherine's fingers loose. Thorn was laughing, but Janet freed his hair and then, in a small, quick gesture, smoothed it back. Jack watched from one of the tables.

"Marthe was the oldest of your cousins?" Janet asked.

"She wouldn't let me help in the kitchen," Thorn said. "She told me I should be studying. But if I wouldn't go away, she'd play number games with me, and she was quick. She always won." Smiling, Thorn saw Marthe, her hands in dirty water, her hair piled up anyhow over her bright eyes. She beat him and laughed, and he said she ought to be a banker.

Thorn stared up at the facade of Marleyshall, remembering how the grandfather called then, waking to wail for his dead wife, piping like a child's whistle that he wanted his pipe, his tobacco, his bowl for spit. Marthe had to wipe her hands and go to him.

"What was it you felt?" Janet said in her low tone, watching Thorn's face.

"I don't know . . . she had to go take care of grandfather then. I waited for her a little while, there in the kitchen. Then I stood at the door, and there were the Jaubert boys, wanting me to go off with them in their market wagon."

Janet sat in the shade, holding Catherine, while Thorn tried to describe the kitchen that had no windows, where the lamp glazed pails of water beside him, and he heard his grandfather's old voice, thin as willow peel. He had stepped out in the street and felt the sun. When he rode off in the wagon, he looked back and thought he saw—for a moment—Marthe's white apron in their open door among others down the street.

Thorn shut his eyes for a moment. "I always think of that," he said. "I never can forget it."

"Mary's mad about Venice," Alice was saying.

"Let's go over the Brenner before it gets too hot." Mary Ross yawned.

"Then Mother married, and I left that house. I walked out in a fancy suit nobody in that town could afford." Thorn wasn't looking at anyone; he pushed his shoe against a daisy in the grass and watched it tip. "Aunt Marie and Marthe and Claire stood in a row and looked after us, like people do in dreams, when you can fly and they can't." He tipped the daisy over again, and said he'd help out Marthe and Claire—the minute he had any money he'd help them out. He'd talked to his mother about it, and she understood. It wasn't fair, she said. But they'd send them money, and help. And they had.

"It's just that you can buy such gorgeous gloves in Venice," Mary said.

Shade turned the linen cloths turquoise. Leaf shapes kept up a constant movement, reflected in silver, china, glass. Lighting a cigarette, Rob Buckingham watched the smoke thin away on the warm air. "Three o'clock at the stable," he said under the talk of hotels and opening dates.

"At least they haven't got the Volstead . . . drink your way across the whole damn Continent without a flask."

"I can't come till four," said a blond girl in a riding skirt, while Bill Bailey cried, "The Orient Express!"

"I despise trains," Walt said.

"St. Louis to Chicago and nothing but soda pop!"

Janet and Thorn, alone at their table, looked at each other over Catherine's fuzzy head, and then Janet began to laugh, her head tipped back.

"Claire could pantomime anybody," Thorn said. "She could 'do' the tripe dealer's daughter . . . holding up her breasts, you know, one in each hand, waiting for customers."

"Oh!" wailed Janet softly.

"And the laundress in town took in both washing and . . . " Thorn glanced over his shoulder, "men. Claire did her: she showed her scolding the butcher's wife—telling her that she ought to keep her husband cleaner. We'd yell, 'Do it again, Claire!' but of course nobody ever knew how clever she was."

Catherine dropped her toy, and Thorn bent to pick it up, trying to explain how he'd thought Claire was teasing him one day— he thought she was only impersonating an unbelievable Claire: his cousin Claire whom one of the Jaubert boys was going to marry.

She couldn't be serious—not Claire! He had laughed at the way she looked with her eyes down and her face as empty as an empty stage, counting threads in a camisole for her trousseau! He was sure she'd look up, and laugh her naughty laugh, and mimic the tobacconist . . . there the man went, toddling by the door, drunk at noon and blowing his nose with a sound only one description could possibly fit!

"But she just sat there, putting cloth together. Talking about the sheets she'd need, and the tablecloths." Thorn was watching the grass at his feet, his elbows on his knees, as he tried to explain how he felt about women and cloth. It oppressed him to watch them drag it over muddy streets or up stairs. They tended cloth. They were always aware of it. They had to learn to fit it to their bodies, and they fingered it when they met.

"Aunt Marie said Claire was lucky to get married at all," Thorn said.

Janet watched Rob blow cigarette smoke across the facade of Marleyshall; it thinned and rose above his broad shoulders that were square like the square facade. He sat with one riding boot up and across his knee, and squinted at the valley.

Thorn said he might have some tea, if Janet didn't mind? Did she want some? Janet thanked him and said no, and watched him go across the grass. Holding Catherine, she looked down at her white slippers, side by side among a few daisies. If she squared her shoulders, stiffened her neck, and squinted? She tried it.

Nothing like presence or command—more like a woman smelling something bad. She went and sat down beside Alice.

"Skirts are six inches in Paris . . . they never did get up to eight, Dolly says." Alice made room for Janet and Catherine.

"Just lying on the Lido in the sun . . ." Mary said sleepily.

"They send up a rocket and a fiesta starts, and everybody dances—all day!" Daphne said. "All night!"

"And eats garlic. Ugh!" Ethel screwed up her face.

Janet raised her eyes to Marleyshall's brown stone and stucco. It loomed over her, solid with the presence and command of generations of Lord Marleys. "Why garlic?" she asked.

"I haven't an idea!" Ethel said. "Wear it in strings around their necks!"

Catherine was dressed in yellow, and Janet in green. Janet was being careful not to crush her bertha against the chair: she felt that carefulness. Her hip sash was out of the way, and every pleat of her skirt fell gracefully, and she knew she was thinking of that, too, not listening. Her brown hair had always been curly; now it flipped prettily over her ears—she knew it did. She was as slim as ever. The silk chemise and step-ins slithered against her flat stomach.

Her hands had been full of splinters. She had seen Catherine's blood-smeared face between Thorn's head and her bare thigh. Thorn sat with a teacup to his lips, his thick hair catching glints and streaks from the sun. His big ears were pink in the light; he perched all arms and legs among the men talking about horses.

The air was soft and warm on her bare arms . . . she could almost taste it. She could almost feel the shape of Thorn holding that cup in his knobby hand, a lock of hair blowing over one eyebrow, his quiet eyes moving from Walt to Rob to Stan. Then he got up, put down his cup, and walked away among the trees.

"There's a black stage, she says, and the girls will come out like visions, and then the lights go out and all the lace they have on will glow. Cost thirty thousand."

"What did?" Janet asked, handing wet Catherine to the nursemaid.

"It's radium paint," Mary said.

"The lace number at the Follies."

Janet put down the cup and saucer she had reached for; in the

bulbous silver world of a teapot she saw Thorn striding off
through the deer park. "I've got a headache," she told Alice and
Mary. "I'm going for a walk."

Janet strolled downhill through the park. Crystal beads on her
bertha and sash shot sharp, small rays of light in the sunshine.

The path through the oaks was dry, but their trunks were still
striped black with the night's rain. Sun through a ceiling of new
leaves hardly speckled the grass. When Janet was out of sight of
the lawn tables, she ran around the scabby lichened church wall,
but Thorn was already out of sight past the bend in the lane.

Catkins hung everywhere in the hazel wood now—was it those
she smelled, or dog's mercury? Her white slippers were already
muddy; she picked her way around puddles. Air brought scent after scent to her: rank green of trash in a farm cart . . . then apple blossom. Beyond a privet hedge the flowering trees hung over
an open cottage door. There was a red brick pavement inside,
and a Dutch oven before the fire, and a young woman was black-
leading a stove in the pearly, shadowy interior. It passed before
Janet's eyes: a scene delicate as a Vermeer; yet what she felt was
not delicate—that thirst to know again—she would go in and
watch. She would learn to blacklead a stove . . .

But the very presence of spring and sun was funneling down-
lane on the wind from where Thorn must be walking out in the
open fields . . . out where the barn was. With the sound of the
larch grove she was passing, Janet felt that wind cool her bare
arms and flatten her voile dress against her like a hand. Thorn
had known what to do. What had she looked like? Her face felt
hot. Her stockings had been hooked to the garter brassiere. They
had wrapped her in blankets and carried her on a stretcher
through the low barn door. Her chemise and brassiere were torn
and spoiled; she had never seen them again, or the red dress.

She stopped before the hedgerows stopped and looked up and
down the road. She'd just fed Catherine; milk wouldn't come
through her dress. She bent to pull her stockings up.

Then she left the hedgerow behind with its briskly twittering
sparrows, and there was the barn. It loomed in the weed-grown
field, huge and gray-black in the blazing light of meadows. The
copper beech was green now; the barn door was like an open
mouth. Every weathered board of it seemed to her to have been

waiting ever since the thunder and rain to see her standing here at the end of the hedgerows.

How hot the light was. Sounds seemed piercing: there was a sharp procession of whistles from a colliery across the meadows. As she stepped over the fallen stone wall, she felt nothing but the picture she made: all green in green weeds, her white shoes and stockings twinkling over the wall, slim and sheer and warm and cool, a heartbeat fast in her ears and neck. Looming closer and closer, the barn breathed its dampness from its broad door. Even before she stepped in, she was trembling with memory.

Odors of earth and straw and fodder—they were enough: the air seemed to vibrate now with her remembered panting and screams. A few strokes of sunlight, thick with dust, spotlit a shaggy beam, cobwebs, a straw tuft. Beyond in the dimness, brooding upon her, was the stanchion whose splinters had driven into her hands, and the piles of straw.

And Thorn. Just as she felt herself crouching there in his arms, she saw him kneeling in the light from a window, his startled look on her. With no warning, even to herself, she ran to him as he came to his feet, her eyes already shut before her lips were on his cheek, his mouth. The barn's silence closed around them: the dark, secret air, the straw piles that would be soft to lie on, rustling . . .

Janet came to herself with the window frame pressing against her back. Thorn held her hands; his eyes were so close that the barn seemed blue. Then he walked away to look out the door, his face turned away from her.

"What do you think about yourself?" Thorn said at last. "What are you planning to do?"

The present returned a little. There was the smell of the barn again, and a rustle of wings somewhere above them, and a faint buzzing.

"And why do you want me?" Thorn kept his eyes on the fields beyond the doorway. "To revenge yourself on Rob? To explore? Or do you want power—the kind you have over Jack—adoration?" Thorn's words seemed to be forced out of him. "What's Jack supposed to adore? What am I?"

The buzzing seemed very close to her. She felt like a child in her ruffles and sash and beads and white stockings, staring at him. His hands had been on her in this barn; he'd rubbed her back while she screamed. Why didn't he do something with that hair of his, always too thick and not parted? Far away a farm cart creaked through the fields and was gone.

"You mustn't care about me," Thorn said. "You know what I want—something that doesn't even exist." He smiled a little. "I'm your kid stepbrother-in-law who doesn't fit in, wanting a woman . . ." He stopped, kicked his toe into the dirt floor. "I've got funny ideas. I ask funny questions. You've got all kinds of men to choose from . . ."

He stopped then, watching her face. Some animal ran over the barn roof. She heard the wind in the leaves of the beech.

"Why don't you want respect?" he asked.

After a while he walked past her and crouched again in the window's hot sun. His pencil and paper lay there on the straw pile, and he picked them up, his face grim with the mouth's downturned line, the jut of his chin.

But he had to look up after a minute or two. Her eyes filmed and filled; she let tears drop down her face, not knowing they were there. When he stood up, she sobbed in his arms, the barn echoing and seconding a misery the whole world stood witness to with its leaves and sunlight and moving air.

Then she pulled herself fiercely away from him and shook her head until a tear spattered his chin, and grabbed his coat to unbutton it, and pulled off his tie. She stripped off his shirt, and his tight collar, never once looking in his eyes. When she laid his clothes on the straw pile, she hung over them for a second, and he saw teardrops fall from her face like sparks in the sun.

She stood before him again, rubbing her wet eyes and sobbing the way Catherine laughed—short, breathless sounds—and then pulled her dress up and off and kicked it away, and kicked her chemise after it. As she pushed off her step-ins and stockings, tears ran shining down her breasts, so that her naked wetness against his bare chest was something he already knew, and so was the wideness of the fields beyond the barn, and the almost dark stanchions and beams, and the smell of the straw.

10

Every window was open. Curtains billowed like sails. The summer wind was both smoky and fragrant; unbroken by more than an oak or two in its fifty-mile sweep, it struck the facade of Marleyshall.

A figure just beyond the blown curtains looked into a pier glass. Cloth hung flat to its hips, then dropped unevenly almost to the floor, dangling between pointed shoes. The sleeves were too long with their flopping cuffs, and an immense collar dwarfed the head.

The figure took a Castle stance, one buckled shoe flat on its pinched heel, the other on its tip a step behind. The unsmiling mouth puckered a little and the face tilted, looking under a helmetlike hat that was almost as low and close as a blindfold. Then the body twitched sidewise, shoulders slung back, hips slung forward, hands cocked at the hip-riding belt. The face gave the pier glass a last unsmiling look, then rode the heap of clothes out the door, through the hall, and down the brass-strapped stairs.

A maid was hurrying across the hall below. "Were you ringing for me, Mrs. Buckingham?" she said to that descending face.

"Tell Mr. Buckingham I'll be back for tea, please," Janet said.

Thorn's wrists stuck out, as always, from his white cuffs and dark sleeves, and his boots were already dusty from the road. He helped Janet into the Model T on the Marleyshall drive. When she looked out from the driver's high seat, Janet saw Jack and Rob coming up on horseback behind the tennis court hedge.

The spark and throttle levers were set; Janet checked them. Rob and Jack cantered up and sat their restless horses; they watched Thorn crank, hanging on the choke wire, his coat pulled up and hair falling over his cowboy face. Jack said something to Rob, and laughed.

Then the engine caught—Janet pulled the spark lever down. The engine died just as Thorn stepped on the running board to climb in. "Get a self starter, buddy!" Rob said, grinning.

Janet set the spark and throttle levers back to ten minutes to three. Thorn cranked again. Rob was watching Janet now, and so was Jack.

The motor roared, Janet moved the spark and throttle to

twenty-five to two again, and it killed. The horses pranced side-wise. Thorn stood up to rest a minute. Rob pressed his boots against the flanks of his mare and reined her in. Jack cantered up to the driver's window, his black eyes opaque with the look Janet expected. She looked away. She looked at Thorn.

Thorn's eyes were faintly dreamy with that smile of his. Janet laughed. His blue eyes spangled with laughter then, and she put her head back, laughing, and set the levers again, laughing, and waited until the motor began, still laughing, and when the car was roaring they rode, laughing, down the long drive, shrieks and whoops sprinkling back to Rob and Jack.

"He's funny, all right," Jack said. Hot summer sun bleached the landscape's greens and blues. The old car stood against those misty pastels: a black hole shot through a candy box.

Jack's eyes were still on the disappearing car, but he heard Rob swing his mare around with a spatter of gravel, and saw that Rob was scowling.

"I'm driving Janet and the baby to Nottingham tomorrow," Rob said.

II

Aerialists inch out, clowns
staring down, teetering,
bicycling backward across the air
until we laugh. Until they strip,
and their grace bows
to our stunned applause, and there's no net
below.
There never was.

1

It's none of Karl Tubbit's business. If a kid just out of college wants to raise a baby somebody left him, that's the kid's business. If he wants to write books about butterflies and can pay good money to somebody to keep house for him, Karl Tubbit will do it. He's no fool.

Karl Tubbit's no fool. He is what he is, and he knows what he knows . . . he was raised along the Custer Battlefield Highway. Folks in South Dakota said she was a battle all the way, and everybody cussed 'er.

That highway sank to bare stone bones every spring when the frost went out, until driving it in a wooden-wheeled Ford loosened your back teeth. Then Tubbit's old man was paid to take out a team and drag timbers loaded with rocks over it, until it got smoothed over some and ran through one more year of drought.

That road was what Tubbit watched, even when dust storms hid the curve it made before it straightened out for town. He knew where to look for that road at every break in the windbreak and every crack in the chicken house. By the time he'd been married, and lost a daughter, and a wife, and was forty, Karl Tubbit was watching for a way to take that road out for good, and any way was fine with him.

His aunt heard of somebody named Thorn Wade advertising

55

for a "man of all work," which was what he was, all right. So he took the Custer Battlefield Highway into town, where a lawyer asked him if he' d mind going to England and back, and then set- tling in Detroit, whatever kinds of places those places might be.

That was the last he saw of the Custer Battlefield Highway— some gravel running by a lawyer's window. He sold his farm. Now he keeps two houses and cooks good food for Thorn Wade and the baby, and is what he is, and knows what he knows, and will stay that way. Yes. Hard-rutted as a gravel road.

2

It's none of Karl Tubbit's business, but he ought to know some- thing about kids: his little Irma was ten when she died, and she al- ways was her daddy's girl. He ought to know a little more about children than Thorn Wade.

Thorn Wade was from Ferrisburg; he found that out. His aunt asked around, and it turned out that Wade's father was one of those lame-duck ministers they get for little towns. All the Pro- testants get together, minus the Lutherans, and try to keep a church going. About every seven years there's some kind of crop, and then they buy some hymnbooks, or maybe pipe water into the parsonage. Thorn Wade's mother was French, and she took him back there to raise when the minister died. Wade could talk French all right. He got letters from there.

It wasn't any of Tubbit's business, but Thorn Wade's nothing but a kid himself, so how's he going to know how to raise a little girl?

Living outside Detroit was fine, even if they didn't have a neighbor closer than a mile—Tubbit was used to that. He got those two houses cleaned up, and Wade spent money on them, too. By the second summer the garden was in pretty good shape—he hadn't been a farmer for nothing.

It's none of his business. He keeps two houses, and cooks, and washes, and irons, and has a nice garden started—there's really nothing wrong. Even when he thinks about it, he can't say there's anything really wrong.

But Wade's just a kid himself, and he doesn't know you can't let a little baby loose the minute she can crawl. Before long, Catherine's eating whenever she feels like it, and she even sleeps whenever she wants to, and wherever she wants to—just drops anywhere, and Thorn covers her up.

Beats all. Wade follows her around, and she's pushing doors open when she can't even walk yet, crawling around where there's germs and poisons and stings and grass stains. My God. You can tell Wade doesn't have to get her duds clean, and she wears holes in everything. She'll lie out in the long grass all morning, tasting grasshoppers, flies, ants, happy as sin.

And when she learns to walk, off she goes with Wade behind her—you can see him for a mile in that grass, tall as he is, and a little track in the field ahead where she's toddling along, wet, probably, talking to herself and getting filthy—Wade doesn't know beans about kids.

So she never hears the word *no*, of course, unless she's about to get killed, and Wade spends an awful lot of time with her, so she's spoiled. Karl Tubbit could have told him.

She's such a cute little thing, but has she got a mind of her own.

At first he tried to make suggestions—said he'd be glad to build her a play yard all fenced in. Wade said thanks, but she was all right. If you ran out and picked her up when she was crying because she'd skinned her knee or something, Wade didn't like it. Cute little thing bawling, and he'd say, "Put her down." Wanted to have all the say-so.

But everything was really all right. Catherine was growing up nice and healthy, even if she didn't have a kid to play with. She got funny ideas, though, playing by herself all the time. When she wasn't even three, she learned to take the telephone off the hook, and there Central was, saying, "Can I help you?" So Catherine gets the idea that Central runs the telephone company, just because she answers every time the kid takes the receiver off the hook. Could you tell her she was all wrong? Hell, no. So independent. Thinks she knows everything, when she's all wrong. She'll sit on your lap, and then the next time she won't let you hold her. Independent.

The thing was, Wade never bothered to set her straight. She was positive that there were women flying every damn plane that went over, and women driving all the trucks on Seven Mile. He told her to go watch the trucks, and she did, but she was still sure about the planes.

And then Wade began to take Catherine down and let her run all around Detroit before she was even ready for kindergarten, and you should hear her talk about things she didn't even understand. Followed folks around, and Wade followed her, talking to everybody. Somebody called Irish Mac was blind and played a violin, and he said the Black Hand was a police squad out after another Black Hand from Italy. Fellows in a garage told her about planetary transmissions.

She said you had to figure things out. If you didn't know what people were doing or what they meant, you asked them. Sometimes they answered you, she said. Sometimes they told you that you were cute, and a little lady. Sometimes they said not to bother them, and where was your mother?

3

"I don't know what good it does," Catherine says. "And it makes me feel so crawly."

A Monarch caterpillar has reached the edge of Thorn's bedroom desk. He puts it back on the potted milkweed plant it came from.

"The kids are all right," Catherine says.

The caterpillar, exploring the air above it, waves about on its leaf.

"No. They're not." Catherine fidgets. She picks up Thorn's magnifying glass and looks at the whorls on the ends of her fingers. "But the room first. It's got little chairs and little tables—that's the first thing that makes you feel crawly. We know we're little, and it's worse when we're way down there, having to look way up all the time. Big chairs make you feel bigger, and everything is real then."

The caterpillar begins its long descent to the desk once more. It passes the milkweed leaves it has stripped to fretwork balconies with its colossal appetite, not mistaking a single leaf for the way down.

"The teacher's so friendly . . ." Catherine's voice dwindles away. She twists a short lock of hair behind her ear into a corkscrew, as if she could wind thoughts out of her skull that way. "There isn't any reason for her to be that friendly. As if she doesn't want us to notice that she really doesn't enjoy being there. Because why would she want to be there with so many little kids and nobody her size?"

Thinking and twisting the lock of hair, Catherine puts both legs over the arm of the oval-backed chair. Its framed plush roses watch Thorn with an occasional yellow eye, and its bent legs seem to buckle slightly under the weight of Catherine's hard thought.

"Friendly all the time." Catherine scowls, then shoves her rear under one arm of the chair until she can get her head under the other. Now she lies looking at an upside down Thorn watching a milkweed plant that grows downward from pot, desk and floor. "And the kids are crawly, too."

Thorn lifts the caterpillar back to the plant again. Catherine comes to stand beside him, her head on his shoulder and his arm around her. "Why do that?" she asks after a while.

"I'm seeing how many times that caterpillar will be able to climb down and hunt for something to suspend itself on—it can't wait forever. It's changing to a pupa under its skin. This was its last instar, remember?"

"If you keep bothering it, it won't have time to hang itself up," Catherine says. "Then what?"

"It won't be able to hang. It will just lie down and change into a pupa, I think."

"Write out 'metathorax,' will you?" She takes the piece of paper, puts it in a pocket, and watches the caterpillar reach the desk surface again. It's traveling faster now.

"Remember that kid on the streetcar I told you about, that was watching to see if people were watching her all the time? That's the way some of the girls at school act, wanting the teacher to notice them all the time. They get silly little voices and lift their shoulders up and hang their heads on one side . . . ugh! And some of the kids are scared; they just sit and watch, or they cry. So why do they come to school if they don't like it?"

Now the zebra caterpillar finds itself once more on a leaf. "The girls have little silly voices and wiggle themselves around, but then when they get to the toilet room or out on the playground, they aren't like that. I like the boys best."

Now the larva's agitation is eloquent: the body pleats and unpleats past pot rim and down to the desk. Its dark brown, cream, and yellow bands trundle in a straight line; dark feelers stream behind its foraging head. "It's not going to give up yet," Catherine says. "Did that other one make another silk button?"

"No," Thorn says. "It finally gave up and couldn't climb."

"It'll get all out of shape lying flat. So will this one. The butterflies won't come out right."

"It had already suspended itself and started to change its color, and it couldn't go back and do it all over again."

Catherine watches the caterpillar lifted from desk to plant to begin its descent once more. "The boys stand around and watch the girls smiling at the teacher and jerking and twisting, and then they start making a lot of noise or picking on each other, and that makes the teacher notice them—they want the teacher to look at them all the time. That's what I can't figure out."

Catherine isn't watching the caterpillar; her blue eyes are remembering, staring out a window. Suddenly her hands press hard on the edge of Thorn's desk and push her away. "I don't want to go to school," she says, walking out. In a few minutes Thorn looks up to see her going across the garden to the gate in Tubbit's fence. Tubbit put it up to keep the rabbits out, and the sand. Catherine shuts it behind her.

4

Detroit was sure growing; Tubbit could see that. The road to their two houses was half gravel and half sand, and it was worse when the gangs of men started to come and lay streets and sidewalks for blocks and blocks: a new subdivision. They even put up street signs: Northlawn, Roselawn, Cherrylawn . . . you could see that new cement grid squaring off the blocks of high grass and sand.

There was a dead dog rotting in a ring of yellow grass by Seven Mile, Catherine said, and she thought the worms had lived in him all the time, and just came out when he died. You could see her squatting down by the thing for hours, watching, for God's sake. Then she said that the flies laid eggs, and the eggs turned into worms. She liked to write down the fancy names for everything, and her "notebooks" had the flies' names in them, and pictures she drew, and whatever she'd heard from Irish Mac about the Oakland Sugar House Gang or the Little Jewish Navy Gang. A Jew in a junkyard drew her a picture of how to build a still from old boilers and pipes, and she got Wade to help her try to build one. It worked, too.

Sure was quiet and lonely around there for her, but she said she liked it. She got so dirty lying on her back watching the sky, or crawling around pressing flowers and leaves or sticking bugs on pins. But then the steam shovels came when they started building houses a mile away. She said the shovels had names like "Tiny" and "Sambo" scribbled in the dust on their cabs, as if they were elephants in the zoo. She loved to go to the zoo. The men in the shovels answered her questions for a while, and then they only told her to go make some sand pies and put lots of raisins in. Every time she wanted to know something, they laughed, and the carpenters must have made her mad, too. But she climbed around in those houses as they went up, and made all kinds of little pictures about how houses were built.

Running around a big city. Well, at least she finally found out that the nurses didn't run the hospitals. She had crazy ideas when she was little. Thought the teachers ran the schools and the secretaries ran the offices, just because there were so many of them. Tubbit could tell her, but she thought he just stayed home and washed and ironed and cleaned and cooked and didn't know.

If anybody had asked him, Tubbit would say Catherine was happy, and he supposed there really wasn't anything wrong about a little kid learning about a city, but she was such a little kid.

Poking all around. The Poles lived in Hamtramck, she said, and they fought and yelled about Jews, and listened to Father Coughlin on the radio. Coughlin talked about the Red Fog of Communism, she said, and what "indecent women" did, and Catherine asked a lot of questions about that, all right.

She wanted to know everything. Every cop in Hamtramck was a bootlegger, she said, and that was why the Black Hand couldn't touch Hamtramck. The Sanders stores sold chocolate hearts for Valentine's Day; Catherine wondered how they got the little red hearts inside. She liked to lick the cinnamon off, and then he found them in her coat pockets later in a ball of fuzz.

Wade took Catherine when he voted at some school. She talked with people waiting in line about the Good Citizens League, and they got mad and yelled. She said the school smelled like chalk and wet shoes.

But it wasn't any of his business. He shut up as much as he could, and kept out of Wade's house except when he was working, which was what Wade seemed to want. He was paying good money, after all.

And everything was really all right, but Catherine was sure a funny little kid, and people didn't know what to think. It was really Wade's fault. Even little girls only two years old have sense enough to sit by their mamas on the streetcar, dressed up pretty in bonnets and all—they don't go stand by the motorman and watch him and bother him with questions—when Catherine doesn't even have her hair curled, and wears whatever she feels like, which is usually pants. She'd be so cute if she wore nice dresses and had her hair curled.

<h2 style="text-align:center">5</h2>

She wasn't even ten years old, Joe Perry told the cook. Came in the hotel and had to reach up and tap on the coat check desk so the girl knew she was there and wanted to leave her coat and hat. Not even ten, and she just came in the hotel like that. For dinner, she said.

"No kiddin'," the cook said.

Just came to the dining room door. Joe couldn't get over that. Just came to the dining room door and waited to be shown to a table. He thought she was a kid staying there and kind of held her off, thinking somebody was going to come and take care of her, of course he did. Didn't even listen to what she was saying. Kids were a pain in the neck in a hotel.

God, the feet in this business. Joe untied his shoes. The great big hurting feet.

"You're telling me?" the cook said.

But finally he started listening to what she was saying, and she was saying very politely that she would like dinner, please, and was there a table? And no, nobody was with her. So all he could do was take her to a table, and when they got to one of the new ones the management made them put on the dance floor—God knows why, when he had too many tables already—she sat down and began to read the menu.

"Doesn't take them long to learn how to spend your money," the cook said. "Did I tell you my wife wants a 'dinette'? I cook all day, and she wants a 'dinette' in the kitchen."

Well, sure, he asked the kid right away if she had some money, and she said why did he want to know that? Did he ask the people at the other tables whether they had any money? Kind of made him mad, being talked to like that by a little kid.

"Kids are sure gettin' smart these days. Razor strop is what they need. In the right place." The cook was picking dried flour paste off the side of his pants.

So he took her order and there she sat all by herself at a table. It did look funny, a little kid like that, but she didn't look like it was funny to her. Acted like she did it every day. Just sat there and ate, and when she was through she asked for the check, and gave him a good tip. Other people thought it was funny—they watched her pay the bill and then go out through the lobby, a little kid like that, hardly half as big as everybody else—and damned if she didn't buy a newspaper before she paid the check girl and got her hat and coat.

"Maybe she was a midget," the cook said.

Heck, no, she wasn't a midget, just a little kid, awfully cute and dressed nice in a dress and Mary Janes, and she put on her hat and coat and just went out. Right out through the door, and it was getting dark. Just walked in and ate, and walked right out by herself, like she owned the place. People shouldn't let kids run around like that. Not even ten years old.

"A 'dinette,'" the cook said. "I cook all day, and now we got to have a 'dinette.'"

6

"A single bed," Catherine says.

"And do you think he gave me anything for my birthday?" Adele Pinney says to Grace Duffy.

"What do you want, honey?" Grace says to the little girl standing before them.

"He did not," Adele says, one eye out for the floor manager. "Not even a nickel card with a penny stamp on it. Nothing. That's what I got."

"I'd like to look at single beds," Catherine says.

"You ought to ditch him," Grace says. "What's the matter, honey? Where's your mama?"

"Maybe she's lost," Adele says.

"I'd like to look at single beds," Catherine says. "You advertised some single beds in the paper last night."

"You'd what?" Grace asks.

"There's a woman over there by the chifforobes, kind of looking around," Adele says.

"Is that your mama, honey?" Grace says. "That lady over by the chifforobes with the blue—"

"I'm all by myself," Catherine says.

"If she's lost, we ought to tell old Pinchbottom, if he isn't back in baby cribs with you-know-who doing 'inventory,' which is a new word for it if ever I heard one," Adele says.

"Honestly, Adele, you're a scream!" Grace says. "Are you lost, honey? Why don't we go see if we can find the floor manager, and he can find your mama?"

7

"I think maybe if I wear a dress," Catherine says.

Thorn closes his book, and Catherine crawls into his lap and sighs. He reaches into the pocket of his sweater for her favorite candy: the hard raspberries you suck and then crunch.

"I stayed on the streetcars like we said, and I only got lost once." Catherine rattles the candy against her teeth, watching the fire, and Thorn can hear the rattle through his jawbone against her skull.

"People don't ask each other where their mothers or their fathers are, or why they're not somewhere else, instead of on a streetcar. But they asked me that all the time."

The smell of red raspberries. Tubbit is making more noise than usual in the kitchen.

"Lots of people don't like children. Especially when they're not dressed up. I'm not going to wear my slacks any more—I'm going to wear a dress all the time, and this hairbow, and smile a lot. If I can remember."

She's sucked the raspberry candy down to the crunch. "Why don't *you* have to smile?"

Thorn bares his teeth against her fluttering hairbow as she turns, pushes against his chest, and gives him a disgusted look. "Silly! I mean smile when you talk to people. When you ask them things."

"She can come and eat now, if she's not too tired." Tubbit stands in the doorway.

"Give her a big piece of pie, too—she's hungry," Thorn tells him.

Tubbit hasn't lighted the candles. Thorn pushes Catherine's chair in for her and finds some matches. Tubbit is talking to himself in the butler's pantry. The darkness outside makes this supper seem different to Catherine, eating alone while Thorn leans back in his chair, his eyes sharply bright with the candles.

"There's a long line of people waiting to get soup and bread downtown," Catherine says when her plate is nearly empty. "I heard a lady say she was going to the welfare, so I followed her to another streetcar. She kept crying. The little kid with her said her mother was crying because her kids were hungry." Tubbit brings the pie in.

"I asked a Negro lady, and she said her husband doesn't even make thirteen cents in a whole hour at Ford's in the 'nigger department,' and I asked her what that was, and she didn't know," Catherine says.

"We can go to the Ford plant and ask to see it," Thorn says. "If you want to."

"That won't be very nice," Catherine says. "They won't like it when we ask. But I could wear a dress and my hairbow." She watches the candles flicker in the breeze as Tubbit goes out. "That lady just kept crying, so I gave the kid all my money but enough to get home, and jumped off the car real fast and got on another one, and I saw a man sleeping in a parked car nobody had gas for, he said. He said sometimes people have to rip holes in the seats and stick their feet in to keep warm."

Tubbit makes a small sound, coming back from the pantry with

Thorn's coffee. Catherine looks him over thoughtfully. "You went sneaking up on that fellow with the still, remember?" she asks Tubbit. "And that horse you rode when you weren't supposed to? And the time you hitched a ride on the boxcars when you weren't even nine? Even if you didn't ride streetcars."

Tubbit says nothing.

"I'm sorry I was late for supper, and all your good stuff got cold," Catherine says. She's dead tired, Thorn can see that, but she rides a wave of excitement yet, and looks at them both with alert yet preoccupied eyes, as if her real concerns are elsewhere.

"Streetcar motormen have swollen legs all the time," she says when Tubbit has gone out. "The cars are sure dirty."

She yawns as if her jaws will crack, and huddles in her chair, watching the candles. "I got one of those city maps, and I only got lost once."

The telephone rings in the front hall. They hear Tubbit go to answer it. "Hello?" he says.

He comes to the dining room door. "For you," he says to Thorn. "Somebody named Jack Laird."

8

The De Soto passes mile after mile of Detroit's bungalows through winter cold and monoxide, and turns outward past the mile roads. Jack Laird grins at the car ahead, not at Dorothy beside him. "You will," he says.

"You're awfully sure of yourself," Dorothy says. She runs a hand up her silk stocking from ankle to knee, and catches Jack's eyebrow going up in that boss-of-my-company look (the profile a bit like Ronald Colman's?).

Five Mile Road. The door of Joe's Meat Market slaps shut where the De Soto's reflection slides across store windows. Curbs are black with coal smoke on snow; streetcars jangle and spit sparks at the curve ahead. A paper Garbo plastered on a streetcar's flank goes smiling into the dimness of a viaduct.

"What a story," Dorothy says. "A bachelor with a baby? That's a scream."

"He wasn't even her real uncle." Jack scowls through the windshield. "Answered the phone and it was the same old Thorn. Never thought he'd hear from me again."

Dorothy yawns and opens the *Ladies' Home Journal* in her lap. Women smile up at her, wearing aprons or diamonds. "I'm a Bride of 6 months—but I've already learned this lesson. It doesn't pay to use a cheap, unreliable baking powder. Getting married on $20 a week takes courage nowadays . . ." "In Paris, they're tinting teeth to give them sparkling brilliance." "Meet the GIRL MEN want to KISS." "I've seen girls *lose out* time and again because their skin lacks that velvet-soft alluring quality men respond to." Dorothy shuts the magazine and explores with her tongue to see if there is lipstick on her front teeth.

"He writes books about butterflies. Has quite a reputation in butterfly circles," Jack says.

The De Soto turns west past Six Mile Road and begins to speed through a strange-looking country. White streets and sidewalks lie empty for miles, though street signs are in, labeling deserted fields. "Good lord, look at this," Jack says. "There's the Depression for you. Whole subdivision laid out, and that's the way it stayed. Wilderness."

Dorothy turns in her seat to look out the back window. The car has left paired tire marks, two lonely lines, block after block. Some trees and bushes stand in house lots full of snow, but there is nothing more to see but a few tumbleweeds blowing across untracked miles.

Thorn is watching the car come, his level, bleak gaze finding it, following it when the De Soto is only a small black spot. But Catherine doesn't see it through a window stuffed with rags. The dark, gutted little house Catherine visits is warm. Violet's fire snaps under fringed newspapers spread on the mantel: ladies' corset ads and pictures of patent-leather slippers. Headlines plaster the wall Catherine leans against; the overpowering smell of vanilla and cocoa rises with the steam from her cup and Augusta's cup, mixed with odors of naphtha, starch, and her snowpants' wet wool. Dogs prowl outside, keeping hungry men away.

Violet has stopped shushing Gertrude because Catherine and 'Gusta are listening; whiskey has got her staring into the fire. Now Mary will begin one of her slow stories, Gertrude will join in, and both will talk in the clear, precise voices liquor gives them in the beginning, while it makes them forget Catherine, who sips her cocoa and waits beside bloomers and long underwear and sheets that belong to rich people and are dripping into papers on the floor. Six-year-old Augusta is almost asleep beside Catherine and baskets of clean, ironed laundry.

"He had a pleasure for the ladies, and it was a pleasure—and then you had the babies," Mary begins, looking around vaguely for the eleven-year-old who comes to play with 'Gusta. She forgets what she looks for, the whiskey burning her throat. "We get the best of it."

"Leroy makes some babies," Esther says to the bottle in her hand.

"Hard to have as hell. 'Gusta took a day. Put the ax under the bed like the niggers say—she popped out just like a cork."

"And Leroy tryin' to get in the house."

"Didn't make it. Jewel got every one of her teeth into him."

"Some bitch."

"She hated a fuss. First time you laid out a howl, that dog turned her back. 'Gusta givin' me all that trouble, Jewel had a look on her askin' as plain as a nine-months belly why in hell was I makin' that racket."

"You ought to have sang." Mary shovels some stolen coal on the fire. "My mother'd sing and grunt like she was rowin'. 'I Walked in the Garden Alone' was what she'd sing. All the kids was born to it, and that's what we heard first, and that's the way."

"Pass the whiskey," says Mary.

The fire flickers around the black coal like the voices flicker around death; Catherine listens, doubled up against headlines of foreclosures, kidnapping, suicide, and breadlines. Chocolate as dark as blood cools in her cup, and danger and daring hang in the air among Dr. Denton sleepers and wet sheets.

The voices are slow and deliberate and dignified, and the bottle passes from hand to hand. Whiskey is the stuff women drink to bloodshed and pleasure, to keeping fed and warm while dogs prowl. And the children are the prizes, milk-smelling and warm. They lie in clothes baskets along the wall; the reeds creak softly when the babies move. Toddlers watch the fire from their mothers' laps under the traveling bottle.

Darkness spreads; the snow gleams blue. "She plays alone out there?" Jack asks, looking from the living room window. Snow blankets miles of empty streets and lots turning gray-pink with dusk. "Is that all she does—wander around, or keep up with lesson sheets?"

"Aren't there any children out here?" Dorothy smiles at Thorn. He's so tall, and that buttery-brown hair. Wonderful eyes with a fringe of brown lashes all around. Strange when he looks at you. Kind. In a Victorian horror of a house—lumpy davenport, French doors, pink marble fireplace, tiled front hall. Now a maid with a doily on her head will come in with tea. No . . . here's a man with a mustache like a peasant's. With drinks.

Dorothy runs her tongue over her lipstick and smiles: she can see herself in a long mirror between chairs—slim, a cigarette in one red-tipped hand. She poses in the depths of the glass like a movie star, set off by yesterday's plush and sepia, then takes the glass offered by a stone face behind a mustache. Imagine Thorn and the Mustache raising a little girl . . .

"She can go to school or not, now that she's almost twelve. She'll have to decide that. We have a group of . . . families living near here," Thorn says. "About half a mile away. They come to the fields around here to pick berries in summer: this area used to be a berry farm. Catherine's at one of their houses now, I think. I don't ask where she's going, of course; it's no business of mine."

Catherine runs home across pearl gray snow. The heat of Tubbit's kitchen makes her cold face and hands sting and her nose run; she wipes it on a mitten rough with snow crystals and shuts the door hard, sitting on the floor to get her boots off.

Tubbit grunts. "There's company for supper." Catherine yanks until her shoes and galoshes come off, buckle straps wagging. When she throws her socks on the radiator's leprous ribs, her socks smell like feet. "Ugh!" she says. "Rust," says Tubbit. Sighing, Catherine takes the smelly things with her up the back stairs.

"No business of yours?" Jack's feathery eyebrows rise; he sloshes his drink in his glass, watching Thorn.

"I tutor her, of course. We go all kinds of places together, or she goes by herself. We have friends in. She takes tests to satisfy the Board of Education. That's a reason I settled here: one of the Directors of Personnel for the schools is a friend of mine, so we're left alone. Just lately she's been writing. Poems. She won a prize book in the Young Writers' Page in the *Detroit News*." What a changeable face the man has, Dorothy thinks. Sad sometimes, and his whole look apologetic and shy. But he has other looks, when his eyes aren't shy at all.

"Poems?" Jack says in a preoccupied voice. "But why not let her go to school?" There's a long silence.

"How interesting," Dorothy says at last, raising her voice a trifle because she hears light footsteps on the stairs. The little girl must be coming. "We can't wait to see her." She catches the startled shine of Jack's eyes, and turns. The little girl standing in the doorway is pretty: short brown hair, a clean blouse, and long pants that are damp around the cuffs.

"This is Catherine Buckingham," Thorn says, hearing how that name must affect Jack. "Miss Short. Mr. Laird."

"How do you do?" Another pair of strange eyes, Dorothy thinks. Such a light blue, with whites like pearl. Her face looks good, especially those cheekbones. A nice thin body.

Catherine sits on the edge of a chair, her brown oxfords resting side by side on the carpet as if she intends a polite stay within range of the conversation, like the large vase on the floor nearby, not ill at ease, simply listening. Dorothy hands her a long box.

"You look . . . so much like your mother," Jack says.

"Thank you," Catherine says, checking his face with a quick glance because his voice sounds strange. She opens the box.

A miniature child lies asleep under the lid. Catherine lifts her out, and the eyes open, sad and quiet above the poised hands and the rosebud mouth. They fix their agate melancholy upon some point as distant as the moon.

"Do you like her?" Jack asks, a peculiar smile still on his face.

"It's nice of you to bring me a present." Catherine spills a doll brush, comb, hand mirror, and a wardrobe of dresses out of the box. They have the look of possessions of the dead as they lie beside the doll's deep gaze.

"Her name's Patsy, and she stands up," Dorothy volunteers in the silence. "And she shuts her eyes. You can put her nightie on and tuck her in bed, and dress her, and feed her . . ."

Catherine's mouth, changeable as reflections in water, puckers with thought. "Thank you very much." Her short brown hair, like the painted hair of the doll, falls forward, half covering her ears.

Catherine sits looking at the doll for several minutes. The only sound in the room is the crackle of the fire and a muffled clatter from the kitchen.

"Dolls are like pictures in books," Catherine says at last. "They aren't supposed to be the same size as real things." Her eyes shine, and then she laughs so triumphantly, with such delight, that everyone smiles, Dorothy and Jack a little uncertainly. "But it gets a little hard about here," she adds.

After a perplexed pause Dorothy says, "Hard?" There's a line between her plucked brows. "A doll?" She forces warmth into her voice. "Dolls are for fun!"

There's a silence in the room again. Dorothy, rattled, hears a clock ticking out in the hall. Are they supposed to sit here and let a child think? Think about what? Something the child has said or done has antagonized Dorothy, yet the little girl's so pretty, and so polite, and Dorothy loves children; she often says how much she loves children.

"I know they're supposed to be for fun," Catherine says at last, politely. "I've seen them in the toy departments." Her face grows a little pink, as if she is aware that she offends.

"Dinner is served," Tubbit says from the doorway.

9

After breakfast the next morning Tubbit ushers Jack Laird into his small, overfurnished living room with a triumphant air of having been—finally—consulted upon important matters. As he sits down across from Jack, Tubbit's dark eyes gleam; he is stiff with his attempt to mask his satisfaction.

"I came because of Catherine's grandfather, you know. He hasn't been able to keep up with her progress at all—he's been sick," Jack says. "Mr. Wade's stepfather. But now he's better, and he wants to know how she's getting along." He sits back, takes out a cigarette, and waits.

"Yes," Tubbit says. "Yes. Well . . ." He lifts a crocheted doily on the arm of his chair, looks under it, presses it flat again under his palm. "It's none of my business, of course. I'm just a man-of-all-work . . ."

"You're loyal to Mr. Wade, I know."

"He's been good to me, here in the Depression. Sure couldn't find another job as good."

"But you're fond of Catherine?"

"Why, she's just like my own little girl I lost! Known her ever since she was a baby—"

"Mr. Wade is too strict with her, do you think?"

"Strict? Him? Never says no to her! Never has! Treats her like . . . I don't k̄ ow . . . like somebody grown up who can go around—why a man went after her when she was downtown last fall, and she talked it over with Mr. Wade, and said it was just one of the 'risks' of going to see things!"

"Goes alone, does she? In the city?"

"Off all day lately! If I don't like it when she's not here for meals, she comes and tells me she's sorry she was late. He takes her most places, except when she rides all over on the streetcars alone. Watches her, I guess, while she wanders around—police brought her home once! Fellows with revolvers tracking up the hall, mouths hanging open when they heard she was 'only' exploring the university or pawnshops or the General Motors Building or the Statler Hotel—I don't know where she'd been."

"And she doesn't go to school?"

"He says she can go if she wants to, so of course she doesn't want to. And there are kids about a mile away, and the whole school's full of them, but their mothers sure don't let them play with her! She wants to take them off to the docks, or maybe sit with the colored people on those stoops on Brush Street with the geraniums in tin cans. As long as the kids learn what they're supposed to, she thinks they ought to be able to stay home from school—"

"Mr. Wade just lets her do as she pleases, then?" Jack stares at Tubbit through cigarette smoke.

"It ain't right!" Tubbit bursts out; his gray mustache seems to bristle. "That's what I say. He has friends in and she's right there, talking away just like she's grown up—staying up late. Always has! And isn't she kind of . . . well, don't you see what I mean? Kind of . . ." Angry, Tubbit fiddles with the pins holding a doily down. "They don't like it."

"Independent?" Jack raises his dark eyebrows.

"She wanted to know how to keep house, so I taught her all

kinds of things, you know—washing and ironing and cooking and so on, because she's real smart—she learns fast. But then she didn't come to work any more with me, she said, because she thought she knew how to do it! Only eleven, she was, and she said she knew how to do it!"

"She seems happy," Jack says.

"Oh, she's happy! Happy as a lark! Taking an old radio apart by the hour—finding out how toilets work—water all over the place! I don't know what the two of them got to see in the furnace stoker, or clouds going over. Reciting poetry. Raising caterpillars all summer long. Of course, those books Mr. Wade writes are something to see, and they cost plenty, when half the country's going to bed hungry every night!"

"It sounds good: that she's happy. You don't think she should be taken away from here?"

"Away?" Tubbit's eyes lose all their fire in seconds; his mustache quivers. "Away where? Catherine? Oh no, she's really all right. I wouldn't stand for it if she wasn't. She's happy here." He grips both arms of his chair with his big red hands.

"Well, thanks for telling me. I'm going to talk to Mr. Wade, but I wanted to see you first," Jack says, getting up.

Tubbit, going with him to the door, watches him cut across the snow and stubble of the garden. Then he shuts his cottage door and follows, to finish getting breakfast in the big kitchen, his eyes fixed and his thoughts elsewhere. The table is set in the dining room; he carries in the butter and cream.

Sun on snow lights the dining room, a milky light that almost combines Catherine, Dorothy, white tablecloth, china, and yellow butter balls into a domestic scene. Dorothy is quite aware of this effect; she smiles happily at the little girl as Thorn and Jack come in, and even bends toward her.

Catherine's eyes, level and cool, have nothing to do with such an effect. As he picks up his napkin, Jack feels that self-possessed look, but his voice assumes it isn't there. "Well, honey," he says to the childish pink mouth and the tips of the ears pushing through bobbed hair, "did that doll of yours behave herself last night?"

"It's a very nice present," Catherine says slowly. "I'll always think of you—"

"Honestly, Thorn!" Dorothy breaks in. "Raising a little girl without a doll!" She tips her head as she leans toward Catherine, smiling. "She's your pretend baby, honey, and you can be her pretend mother!"

Catherine doesn't smile back. Dorothy's head wagging is something she watches, and she examines Jack's face, too, and says nothing.

10

"I promised your stepfather I'd drop in—he told me where you were." Jack looks around Thorn's cluttered study; books are spread open on desk and floor. "He's been a help to me. Loaned me some capital." He scowls. "But it's none of my business."

"No," Thorn says.

"But I did love Janet."

"Yes."

"My God!" Jack glares at Thorn's study walls, ranked with butterflies in cases. "I tried to get something out of that Tubbit of yours at his house this morning. I distinctly felt that he doesn't think everything is just right here—especially her staying up so late and talking with your friends, and roaming the city, and not going to school . . ."

"I'll talk it over with her," Thorn says.

"You don't have anything to say about what she does?"

"Not if I can help it. How can she—"

"She's just a little girl!"

"What were you doing your twelfth year?" Thorn says, and knows, and smiles.

Jack blows a cloud of smoke at cased-in butterflies. "That's different." Thorn doesn't answer. "What would Janet say?"

"We talked all that spring about how she was going to raise Catherine. Wherever we went that year, we talked about it. Not so much about how as how not, and the how is the hardest part." The look in Thorn's eye infuriates Jack. Seeing it, Thorn looks down.

"Running all over the East, and then England, with her crowd—"

"I didn't have any money, you know," Thorn says. "You don't pass up chances when you don't have any money."

"You and Janet! Always—" Jack stops, hearing Tubbit's knock.

"The luggage is in the car," Tubbit says.

Following Thorn and Tubbit down the front stairs, Jack smells the old-house smell: years of dinners and furniture polish, summer damp, coal fires.

The mantel mirror is dim; it shows the passage of the three of them among its propped-up plates, then reflects an empty hall that echoes a car's roar, and its slow dying away.

When the black car grows smaller and smaller across empty house lots and then disappears, Catherine turns from the frost-starred front door window. "What'll I do with this?" she asks Thorn, looking down at the Patsy doll. He shrugs.

"What did you do with dolls when you were little?" she asks.

"I remember sleeping with a teddy bear that was old and dirty and hard and smelled like sawdust."

"Then you didn't practice feeding and dressing and undressing and putting to bed and all that stuff?" Catherine laughs, a free sound, as if a presence had been lifted and withdrawn.

"You think you should?" Thorn asks, going into the living room to poke the fire. "Herb Jensen's bringing someone called Bill Downing here this afternoon." He drops a new log in place.

"I know. How would you ever practice? And why does everybody think dolls are fun? Is it supposed to be fun to put a real little girl to bed, and dress her and undress her and feed her and all that?"

"They call dolls 'toys,'" Thorn says.

"I *know*," Catherine says. "But what's fun about dolls? And what can you learn?" She plumps down beside him on the couch and puts her head on his shoulder. "I could stick books in front of that doll, or bandage her all day long, and I wouldn't *learn* anything, would I?"

The room is still, except for the fire. Catherine's blue eyes sparkle; she tucks her chin in, staring at the doll on the rug. "They gave me something they wouldn't use—they wouldn't practice with a doll! They weren't really interested in it at all!"

She twists a lock of hair, deep in thought. Thorn leans back and looks into the fire. *But I did love Janet.*

"I'm supposed to like something that's all cold and dead and little that they're not interested in?"

Thorn watches the fire.

"They didn't really see me, or really listen to me—it's the same old thing that happens, but this time . . ." She stops, her face flushed, then jumps up to stand near the big vase, the doll between them. "You didn't either."

Thorn doesn't move or speak. His deep blue eyes are fixed on her.

"And you looked like you hadn't done anything wrong, but they'd think you had."

The small, little-girl face, the hair over pink ears, the starched dress and skinny legs. Thorn gets up; his face is hidden as he runs his fingers through his thick, taffy-and-tobacco-colored hair.

"Tubbit thinks so, too." They stare at each other, and the words lie between them, like the doll. "He doesn't like you, either."

The front doorbell jangles through the house.

Catherine's voice drops. "Not even your friends do—not Jim or Freddy or any of your girlfriends—Sally or Edna or Mary-alice . . . or Mr. O'Brien. When he comes to talk about what you're teaching me, he doesn't really like you, either. He gives me those tests and hopes I won't know everything I'm supposed to, because then . . . but why?"

Tubbit's footsteps go down the hall outside the shut living room door. Catherine whispers, "Why doesn't anybody—"

Tubbit opens the living room door. His eyes run over Catherine and the doll she picks up; he doesn't look at Thorn.

"Hello!" Herb Jensen says, stepping into the cozy family scene, beaming, shaking Thorn's hand. "I've brought Bill Downing here—meet Thorn Wade!"

"I'm glad you could come," Thorn says, shaking hands with Downing. "This is my niece, Catherine Buckingham."

Bill Downing is a middle-aged businessman like Jensen, and proud of success in a depression. He's never met an author like Thorn Wade; he doesn't know quite how to talk to such a man. But he can talk to a little lady who sits down as quietly as a lady, holding a doll across her knee like a stick of wood. "That's a pretty doll you've got there," he says. "What's her name?" But he has already shifted his attention away from her, alert to the other two men.

"Patsy," Catherine says, her face still pink. She slides the doll under her chair. "You were with the Union Guardian Trust?"

"That's right." Downing hardly hears her; he's tense with his respect for Wade. "I haven't had much time to work with Monarchs, but I heard about you from Jensen here, and I wanted to meet you—I've got your book. I was breeding Monarchs until I changed jobs. I've collected data on egg laying and larvae."

Jensen talks about Batesian mimicry. Thorn explains his method of tagging. Tubbit puts more wood on the fire.

Downing feels fairly sure that the Monarch hibernates; Jensen thinks it might fly south. Catherine sits in silence. Are Monarchs really distasteful to birds? Downing wants to know. Jensen describes a new kind of breeding cage he saw in Ohio. Their eyes glow as they flicker over the room and Catherine; they share knowledge as if it is some secret vice. What does Thorn think about larval cannibalism? Jensen sips his coffee by the fire and says that pine trees are so often a roosting site—why?

Catherine listens, her hands in the folds of her starched dress. Her light blue eyes move from one speaker to the other. The doll lies under her chair.

The clock in the hall strikes four. Downing looks at his watch and says he's amazed. It can't be so late, can it?

"Catherine?" Thorn says.

Jensen and Downing look at the child. Her short hair swings forward on her flushed cheeks, and her look is so peculiar that both men stare. Then she shrugs her shoulders.

"Well!" Downing cries. "Young lady! We've been jawing on and on about butterflies, now it's your turn. Tell us about your school! Tell us about—"

"Yes, do you like school?" Jensen, like Downing, feels uneasy; they should have paid more attention to her. Both, in the same instant, are rather annoyed: why didn't Wade send her off to play, not make her sit here? "My daughter Sally is about your age, and she says she likes school—sometimes!"

There's a pause. Catherine looks down at her shoes. "I don't go to school." She looks at Downing, and he wonders if the child is handicapped in some way; that would explain—

"Have you looked at the cremaster magnified? That might answer your question," she says to Downing.

"My question?" Downing has a beaming and fatherly look on his face, just as Jensen has.

"You wondered why the pupa gyrates so long. You thought it was trying to embed the cremaster in its silk pad."

"Um, well, yes!" Downing's smile fades. "Yes . . . I'm sure

the 'cremaster,'" (he puts the word into quotation marks with his voice), "has to be embedded . . ."

"Yes, it does," Catherine says. "That's why you'll see spines on it, sticking out like a brush."

Downing scowls a little. "On the cremaster?"

"Yes. You can see it if you look." Jensen and Downing exchange identical glances. "That's why your idea's wrong," Catherine goes on. "The spines have little hooks on them—look and see—and they lock tight in the silk before the pupa—"

"Well!" Downing says, looking at Thorn, not Catherine. "You've made observations?"

Catherine's face is pinker now; her voice trembles. "So the pupa doesn't gyrate to embed the cremaster in the silk."

Thorn says nothing. Neither does Downing or Jensen. "Watch it and you'll see," Catherine goes on, gripping her hands tight in her lap. "It's trying to dislodge the larval skin. That answers your question."

"Ah . . . well . . . that's fine!" Downing says in a second or two, his voice a little high. "That's a great help, young lady!"

"You were with the Union Guardian Trust, you said?" Catherine asks the same question she asked hours ago; Downing is suddenly aware of it. "The Department of Justice hasn't found anything wrong yet—maybe our banks could have gone on; they didn't have to close. What do you think?"

"Are you studying banks?" Downing asks, his eyes on Thorn, his eyebrows raised.

"No," Catherine says. "When I heard you were coming—"

Downing laughs. "I don't know, honey—it's late, and I'm afraid we'll have to be going. Tell you what: you and I will have to get together and talk about it someday." He looks around for his matches, a cigarette dangling from his lips.

Jensen knocks his pipe out on the hearth. "Couzens will support Roosevelt yet, they say."

"Good thing, too," Downing says, lighting his cigarette and getting up to go. "They belong together."

11

The two children come out of the silence behind Tubbit's fence: fields of dead grass, and scrub oak brown with dry leaves.

Tubbit's garden is embedded in lake-bed sand, and wet enough to look lavender in a February thaw. He trucked in dirt that was dirt cheap—dirt he'd never seen the like of in the Dakotas. Catherine rode on top of hundreds of wheelbarrow loads of sand he rolled out of that garden, and dirt he rolled in. His spade sheared sand down neat as the walls of a grave, and he filled those yellow holes with black and gold mixed.

The garden's curves came from the garden hose: Tubbit put it down and took it up until he liked what he saw, and then sliced the grass away to a deep ditch, so the dirt rose in domed beds. Spring, summer, and fall the flowers massed themselves there, beautiful and hardly ever picked, until their dead blooms and withered leaves disappeared as silently as the dust disappeared from Catherine's dresser top, or clean clothes appeared in her closet, smelling of starch.

"Hey, go on—pick a nice bunch!" he'd call to Catherine, and sometimes she'd take one or two flowers, making such a pretty picture in the sunshine. When she was little she said she loved Tubbit, and kissed his bald spot, or sat in his lap, sometimes. She watched him garden hour by hour in the patterns he followed patiently, while the patient flowers bloomed in orderly progression.

Even now, when nothing is growing yet, Tubbit's garden is raked and neat, but the sand-drifted silences behind the fence are different. Sand sifts into the garden, grain by grain, and dead weeds look through the chain-link fence, just as the children do.

Catherine doesn't see or hear them; she's squatting outside Tubbit's fence where drifts of sand are as smoothly curved as Tubbit's flower beds, but unstable and shifting. The snow has melted away from the furry gray lump of a rotting field mouse at Catherine's feet.

The small boy, followed by his sister, trots around to squat beside Catherine. "He's sure dead," he says.

The mouse doesn't smell but the boy does, and so does his sister. They've come from somewhere out of sight across wet fields: their old shoes are soggy and full of sand.

"That your house?" asks the boy. He shivers. The thaw has come and gone again with the last night's rain, and his hands are red with cold.

His sister says nothing, but she's shivering, too. The clothes they wear aren't thick enough, and too big. Their upper lips shine like snail trails; their eyes are half shut against wind or, perhaps, against everything. Maybe it's only the wind and the sunlight striking under the boy's cap and the girl's mat of hair. "Come in and get warm," Catherine says, standing up.

"We ain't cold," the girl says quickly.

"Well," Catherine says, not looking at either of them, "I'd like to have you come and see my house, if you'd like to."

They follow her, passing Tubbit's cottage and entering the bigger house's kitchen in silent single file, their scent joining that of Tubbit's pot of oatmeal on the stove. Their eyes are slits; they look at everything without seeming to look at all.

"Won't you sit down?" Catherine asks. Once barely seated on the edges of chairs at a table, they might be watching her. "I haven't had breakfast yet," she says hesitantly, while they perch and wait. "I'd like it if you'd keep me company and have some, too."

They stay where they are, never looking at each other, until Catherine fills three bowls, pours on cream and sugar, and brings spoons. With one quick glance to see her pick up her spoon, they dip their own into oatmeal glistening with mounds of sugar.

She could give them hot chocolate. There's toast made, and there's strawberry jam. But she waits, gathering clues, and offers nothing more. When the bowls are empty, she asks, "Would you like to see the house?"

They take up their single file behind her, walking through the pantry to the dining room, through the living room to the hall. Catherine hesitates again at the stairs. "My bedroom's up there."

They nod, not seeming to look up at all. "We'd better be going to school now," the girl says. "Much obliged." The boy follows his sister through the garden and past the gate, latching it carefully behind him. They disappear through the cottonwoods toward the school more than a mile away: a tall smokestack, a long roof.

"Just look at that," Tubbit says, seeing them go. He hasn't wanted to stay upstairs with Thorn, watching them through a stair window. "Got nits, I bet."

12

"Without a net," Jack says to his empty office and the telephone receiver in his hand.

"Hello?" says Thorn. That hesitant voice. Jack can see him in
that messy house of his, knee deep in caterpillar droppings, bent
over the telephone like a maid over her mop. Apologizing for being alive.

"Jack."

"Well. How are you?"

"Worried. I've been talking to your stepfather—you know he's
been discharged?"

"No."

"Well, he has, and he makes sense—wrung out, I guess."

"That's good. I don't hear from him much."

"So I figured." Drawn up before the office mirror, Jack smiles
at the reflected executive: sleek black hair, sleek black eyes. "He
doesn't like what you're doing with Catherine."

"What am I doing?"

Jack blows his breath out, exasperated. "Don't pretend. I've
been there. What kind of life is that for an eleven-year-old girl?"

Thorn allows a long pause to lengthen from Detroit to Chicago. Then he says reluctantly, "She went off to school today."

"She did?"

"She said she wanted to try it. Visit, you know."

"Visit?" Jack's heavy, sharp emphasis crackles in Thorn's ear.

"She hasn't visited for a few years, so she thought she'd like to
go take a look."

"I hope you dressed her right."

"I believe the ticket from her outfit said she was dressed like
Shirley Temple."

"Well, that's good, that's—you should encourage her."

"Encourage her to what?"

"Get out in the world! Spread her wings! Learn from other children." There's silence on the line. "I'll tell Dorothy. My company's going ahead on that branch in Paris, and we're off this week.
I'll send our address when we're settled."

"Congratulations on your marriage."

"Thanks. Give Catherine a kiss for me. When we're in the
States again, we'll drop in."

Thorn puts the receiver back and pushes the phone away.
Through the front door's round window he can see the smoke
from the stack of the John J. Bagley School across miles of white
fields, streets and sidewalks.

13

The John J. Bagley School is new red brick and white stone. Trampled snow is a path of slush past a playground fence. The double doors clamp shut after Catherine.

Sunlight floods down a stairwell upon more children than Catherine has ever seen in one place: a bedlam of yells and slammed locker doors and chatter of boys in shirts and ties and knickers, boots laced or buckled to their knees, and girls in cotton dresses like hers.

As Catherine watches, a loud bell thrums through the building, and halls grow still as they empty. Doors shut. She is left with dark rows of steel lockers and the sound of adult voices and a typewriter. She feels the orderliness: students have begun their work.

"I'd like to visit school today, please," Catherine tells a woman she finds sitting before the typewriter in the school office.

"Visit?" The woman's chair squeaks as she straightens her back and looks at Catherine. The little girl is pretty and nicely dressed; she sees that at once. It's the child's businesslike tone that—

"I'm here with my uncle. From England."

That, of course, explains whatever has made the secretary hesitate, her back rigid. She smiles now. "Did he come with you?"

"No."

"I see. Just a moment." The woman goes to an inner office and whispers there. Returning, she asks, "How old are you—about ten? And what's your name? You can leave your wraps here."

"Almost twelve. Catherine Buckingham."

"How do you spell that?" The woman writes it on a card. "You must be in sixth grade or so?"

"I don't know."

"Come here then, and I'll show you. See that door with the picture of the snowman on it? That's the sixth grade room, and your teacher's name is Miss Crane. Give her this card and she'll know what you're there for." She smiles at the little girl who thanks her politely. "I hope you like our school."

As Catherine walks down the dark hall, bright worlds of strangers glow through the windows of the classroom doors. The students at their desks are hard at work, like secretaries in offices or clerks in stores, businesslike and grown up. A little nervous, she steps into an empty room for a moment. There's nothing in it but blackboards, an upright piano, and some violins laid on chairs.

She picks up a violin carefully, the way Irish Mac taught her. When she plucks a string, there's the sour twang of off-key catgut. The piano is no help; it's out of key, too. Tuning the violin by ear, she knows what's so strange about it: it isn't full size. None of them are, and neither are the bows bristling with broken horsehair.

She draws a bow across the strings. It would make Irish Mac shudder. Mac's blind, and sleeps under the stairs of an old warehouse off Riopelle Street where rumrunners unload, he says. He can smell Canada a half-mile away across the river, and he can hear the bootleggers' speedboats come in from Riverside. He sleeps in newspapers; he says they keep you warm in winter . . .

"What are you doing out of your room?" A plump woman stands in the doorway.

Catherine lays the violin down gently and takes the card out of her pocket. "I'm visiting today."

"Well," the woman says, looking at it, "you belong in Room 112." She hands the card back.

"Yes," Catherine says. "Do the children have violin lessons?"

"We have orchestra after school three days a week." The woman's voice is irritable; she keeps her eyes on the hall. Suddenly she yells, "George Mead! You march right down to the office!" She leaves Catherine to the violins and the piano.

Catherine finds Room 112. Perfectly round and white, the picture of a snowman on the door has lumps of coal for a smile.

Catherine takes a deep breath and opens the door to meet a roomful of lifted faces. The orderly rows of desks and the books on each desk breathe of habit and order she breaks into; all the eyes are full of that easy habit, too, and something else she can't identify.

Before she gets to the teacher's desk, every pair of eyes is down and reading intently. The teacher whispers that Catherine should take the fourth desk in the second row, and read chapter two in this book about the settling of Detroit, and the teacher is glad she came to visit, and she hopes Catherine will enjoy herself, and when it's recess, she'll introduce Catherine to the children.

Catherine tiptoes to her desk, surrounded by the quiet readers. How still they are. Maybe they'll ask her questions about what's in the book . . . maybe it will be too hard. But everybody looks about her own age, and it seems so queer. How can they teach each other very much? You almost always learn from older people.

She opens her book, remembering that once she'd imagined there would be all ages of children in each room, and that the children would agree on what they were going to learn each day.

How businesslike it is. She's ashamed to think of all the time she wastes.

Catherine glances around her. All the children seem to have the same book, open to the same chapter. She can see the same picture everywhere.

Beginning to read, Catherine keeps trying to think why the book seems so different from any books she can remember. It's so easy to read; that's part of it—she's never seen a book with nothing but easy words, and sentences that seem to say only one thing at a time. And the pictures fill up so much of the space. One picture shows Cadillac and his boatloads of Frenchmen and Indians. Their faces have no more expression than the sides of their canoes, and the river they row upon is as smooth as the sentences. There are a few facts. She memorizes them, feeling surrounded by all the others who must be memorizing, too.

When she's sure of all the facts, she looks at her desk. It seems quite new, like the rest, with its metal legs bolted to the floor. The students sit in rows like people in buses. They can look at each other's backs, or the teacher at her big desk in the front. If they look sidewise, they can see charts titled in large, clear letters: Reading, Spelling, School Service Club. Books stand along a table by the chalk rail, propped open at an equal distance from each other. The pictures on the bulletin boards are spaced neatly, too.

She'll make some charts when she gets home, with names of all the books she's read, and the words she always has trouble spelling. Her room ought to look neat, like this one; Tubbit always says she ought to straighten it up.

She darts a glance at a girl with barrettes in her hair, and boys with fancy ties and big hands. One has a leather pocket on the outside of his high boot. The teacher sits watching them all. How quiet they are.

The room is so neat. The clock's hand jumps from second to second above the teacher's head.

Catherine looks at her desk again. It has an inkwell with a hinged lid, and a groove for pencils and pens. It must have been new not very long ago, and smooth to write on. Now it's covered with a cobweb of letters and numbers and pictures scratched or cut into the wood.

Catherine looks at her desk for quite a while. There are deep cuts in the center—why would anyone put marks there? If you tried to write on top of them, your pen would skip and spatter.

Every desk looks like hers. Catherine sits without moving, her eyes on Cadillac's smooth face.

She's listening to the changing quietness of the room. The silence she walked through is overlaid with a hundred small noises now. The boys' thick-soled boots have always scraped and clicked; there are the usual coughs, a riffle of book pages, the creak of a desk. But she hears whispers now. A smothered giggle.

The girl across from her seems to be reading. Catherine watches from the corner of her eye. The girl has propped a book just like Catherine's on top of another. Her eyes seem to be on Cadillac's canoes, but her right hand, moving only its fingers, is scribbling. Carefully, never moving anything but its fingers, the hand behind the book folds a scrap of paper it has scribbled on. Then the hand creeps under Cadillac and over an inkwell and pokes the back of the girl in the seat ahead.

Catherine waits for the girl to turn around and take the paper, but she never makes a sign that she felt the poke at all. Then her right hand creeps up behind her back slowly, grabs the note, creeps back, and unfolds the note below her desk top. Catherine sees the girl slowly drop her head to read it; in a minute the girl repeats the maneuver exactly, passing the note to the boy ahead.

Catherine looks around her again. Books lie open on every desk; twenty-five Cadillacs look up at students who aren't reading any more. A couple of children have their eyes on Catherine, but they shield their faces with one hand. Some are staring at nothing. A blond boy rustles papers inside his desk, his eyes on the teacher. Near the front of the room another boy traces and retraces some part of the marks on his desk, the movement of his hand hidden under his book.

What are they waiting for? Why don't they work, or talk to each other?

Catherine blinks, and looks again. Everything being done in the room now is furtive; it is happening in small hideaways, wherever a student's back, or a book, or the bulk of a desk provides shelter.

Shelter from what?

Then Catherine meets the teacher's eyes. They are moving from desk to desk, from one child's blank face to another.

III

Who named them Dock, Dodder,
Corpse–plant, Clammyweed
Toadflax, Fat–bellies, Horned Bladder–
wort, Spotted Cowbane, Tickseed,
Greasewood, Hairy Vetch, Stonecrop?
Lovers, found flowering innocently, are given such
names with a vengeance, but who envied Soursop
that much?

1

It was none of Karl Tubbit's business, but he'd helped raise her, hadn't he? Out there in the middle of sand and streets where nobody lived but them. From '30 on nobody was building houses; the Depression was something to see in a city like that. Catherine's grandfather had lawyers, and they saved some of his money, anyway, so when he died Catherine got it, and Wade had enough to keep going, and nobody could say Karl Tubbit hadn't helped his relatives, or kept a nice little nest egg hidden away.

So everything was really all right. They were snug as a bug in a rug when half the country went to bed hungry every night, and breadlines stretched for blocks, and the few houses built a mile away stood empty, their windows knocked out. And Catherine was healthy, and Wade got his books printed right along.

You couldn't say anything was really wrong—not when Catherine was growing up to be such a pretty girl, and was smart, too, and happy, most of the time. She was always happy when she was working by herself at home, and it was nice to see her with her school books and lessons, getting ready for tests like a kid should. She didn't want to go to school, she said. Not ever, until college.

"The kids don't go to school to learn things," Catherine said one time. She liked to watch him when he made cookies, and she'd eat the raw batter, too. "They just do what the teacher tells

them. They want her to like them. They throw their school papers in the trashcan after school!"

She'd looked so cute when she was dressed up to go to school.
"Miss Crane told the class how well they'd worked, but she still
acted like she was smarter than they were, and so they had to be
watched every minute. Kids know when somebody doesn't really
like them."

"Teachers are real nice ladies." That was all he could think of
to say.

"Would *you* like to spend five days every week with people who
think you're little and dumb and have to be watched every minute?"

Well, he didn't know. It wasn't any of his business—but was
that any way to raise her? Letting her decide that school was
"crawly"?

If she tried to go play with some of the kids after school, she
said the mothers didn't like her and the houses were "crawly"—
he heard her talking to Wade. She told Wade the mothers stayed
home all day and "did what Tubbit does." Kind of made him
mad, except that she was lonely; you could see that.

A couple of times Catherine brought some child home and
showed all the things she was doing. The place was always a mess:
insect collections and plant presses and two old cars spread all
over the barn and her paints and all. The kids trailed after her,
and sometimes they came back once or twice, but it never came
to much. Catherine got so excited about her "projects"; she
couldn't see that most kids wanted to just play, or maybe listen to
"Tom Mix" or the "Lone Ranger" or "Jack Armstrong the All-
American Boy" on the radio after they'd been at school all day.
But he always had cocoa and cookies for them.

It was like she kind of wilted a little, and all Wade did was listen
to her while she told him how people were nicer to her if she wore
nice clothes, or smiled a lot, or acted shy. She should have
learned something from that, but Wade never said boo—he
should have told her that she mustn't look people right in the eye
like she did, and expect to be treated like she wasn't just a little
girl. Sometimes Catherine looked so sad—she should have been
out having fun with kids her own age, or having company. It
wasn't as if he couldn't cook real well. Everybody always said the
food was good, and Wade couldn't say Karl Tubbit ever objected

to having company. Set a real pretty table—had the flowers and candles and everything.

He wondered if Catherine would have spent a lot more time at his house if Wade hadn't told her not to come—he was sure it was Wade kept her away. As if he'd do the wrong thing, or tell her any lies, like Wade had. Well, maybe Wade didn't really lie, but he didn't tell her what was what. Let her make all kinds of mistakes.

But at least she didn't wear all that makeup, and shoulders padded out like shelves, and naked legs above dirty white shoes and socks. He didn't know . . . he'd grown up on a farm in South Dakota, and there were girls and women all around—he had lots of relatives on the Tubbit side. He always knew girls were girls— no matter how much they didn't like washing dishes or sewing, and were always hanging around the barn or acting wild or even fighting. They got started in school and they settled down. His own sisters were tomboys growing up, but there they were now, married and good housekeepers and mothers just like his own mother, even in this depression that still wasn't over, no matter what Roosevelt said.

And Catherine didn't drive around with boys in cars. Young squirts hanging around drugstores waiting for a war to come. They'd probably get a bellyful of war before they were through.

Every now and then he got a letter from Jack Laird from some-place in the world—Laird said he'd been a good friend of Catherine's parents and wanted to keep track of her. Even when all the trouble started with the war in Spain, and Hitler, and Mussolini, he got a letter from Laird every now and then.

He always wrote Laird back. He told him how Catherine got some of her stories published in a high school magazine, and how she was going to college pretty soon because she'd passed all the tests. Just about the time Catherine got to be seventeen, he wrote Laird that Wade was taking the news from Europe hard, especially when the American ambassador came home for good from Berlin, and then Barcelona fell, and Germany went into Czecho-slovakia. Wade had sisters in France—not really sisters, but Wade felt like they were. He worried a lot about them, because he hadn't heard from them in a long time, and didn't even know where one of them was. He started talking about going over there, and Catherine could start college. Maybe he'd go over the end of the summer.

Laird wrote right back. He was divorced now, and he was coming to Detroit with his secretary, he said. He wrote Wade, too, asking if they could come visit. Nobody knew that Laird had all the news straight from Karl Tubbit. Why should they? Laird was interested in how Catherine was getting along. That was all.

2

The Chrysler takes Woodward Avenue out of the heart of Detroit, traveling through the shadows of new leaves. Mile after mile of the city passes in hot sunlight.

"Now that I'm divorced?" Jack Laird says, squinting through the Chrysler's windshield.

"I'm a private secretary." Shirley's voice is cool.

"Paper, mister?" A boy on a curb pokes a newspaper through the car window, the headlines crowded with Czechoslovakia, but the light turns green and the car leaves him behind.

"She must be seventeen now," Jack says after a while.

"Why go if he won't be glad to see you?"

Jack's eyes look deeper and less sharp under their heavy brows. "She hasn't anybody except Thorn. Her grandfather's dead now. And I haven't seen Catherine for a long time—six years. Look at this."

"What?"

"The way they're building out here!" Jack laughs. "He thought he had a regular wilderness to himself, and now the city's come and got him!"

Shirley looks at the new brick houses. Young trees are growing in every yard. Shrieking children play among wagons and tricycles on the sidewalks. The streets are named for fruits and flowers: Roselawn. Cherrylawn.

"Same old dump," Jack says. Beyond the last row of new houses is sand, and then a grove of cottonwoods; a gravel road disappears behind their fluttering screen. When the Chrysler turns a bend in the gravel, a Victorian house shows itself beyond a garden and sundial.

Shirley wonders if her seams are straight. Awareness of the backs of her legs has run through her consciousness since she was twelve: paired lines. Stepping out of the car, she executes a pretty maneuver, looking over her shoulder and down, one leg lagging behind, then the other.

Jack watches, running his eye over her without seeing her, thinking of Thorn. Shirley turns to see a man coming through the garden. "Hello!" she says.

While the pleasantries go on, Shirley thinks he's very nice. Tall, with thick hair that's half brown and half gold, and a still young face, and such eyes.

The Victorian house is dark after the bright sun. A young girl in slacks stands among old, tacky chairs in the gloom. Shirley listens to Jack's voice beside her, heavy, hesitating. "And this is Catherine? My secretary, Shirley Chase."

"How do you do?" A pale face and pale mouth turn Shirley's way, not smiling, yet not hostile. "Would you like a drink?"

"Fine," Shirley says, taking a chair.

"You've got a Custom Imperial," Catherine says.

"We've been reading about the fluid drive," Thorn says.

"Would you like to take a look?" Jack's voice sounds so strange to Shirley. The room is growing lighter. "We won't hold dinner up?" Jack says politely.

"Not a bit." Thorn continues to sit where he is, looking up at Jack, not intending to go anywhere, it seems, and content to see them go.

"We'll be just a few minutes then," Jack says after the smallest pause.

"Take your time," says Thorn.

When they've gone out the front door, Shirley crosses her legs and smiles at Thorn, whose face is clear now. He wears a polite expression, inquiring about Chicago, her job, the trip.

The hot sun yellows the porch steps and sidewalk as Jack follows Catherine. "Do you drive?" Jack asks the back of Catherine's head, staring at her long, straight brown hair that's like a squaw's, hanging down her back.

"Yes, I do."

"Jump in, then—here's the key." Catherine takes it without a word or look, walks around the car once, then climbs behind the wheel. Seated beside her, Jack opens his mouth, but before he can speak, Catherine has turned the key in the ignition and the car smoothly circles the drive, takes the gravel road out and back, and noses into place again among long cottonwood shadows.

Jack laughs a little. "You've been practicing with an Imperial?" That profile of hers! Janet . . .

"I've read about the fluid drive. Mind if I take a look at the engine, Mr. Laird?" Catherine climbs out; Jack follows.

"Won't you get—here, let me—" Jack stares at the serious young face, the brown hands already raising the hood, twirling this, running over that. "Interested in how things work, are you?" he says, grinning at her.

"I'm interested in engines." Catherine's light eyes with their clear whites are on Jack, and the look on Jack's face. "The pair of turbine fans—"

"Oh well," Jack shrugs, "don't know how it works myself." He leans against the car and lights a cigarette. "Your mother and I used to go driving."

"She drove everywhere, and that was when the roads were bad!" Catherine says. "She knew how everything worked."

"I can't say I remember her driving . . ." Jack stops, frowning. "Prettiest girl I ever saw," he goes on. "Looked just like you. Thorn can tell you. Men crazy about her." He watches Catherine's profile, but sees nothing more than the steady reflection of metal in one of her calm eyes. "And you're seventeen." Jack moves a little closer, hearing the warmth of his voice echo slightly from the raised hood. Janet's eyes. The voice he had never forgotten at all.

"Could I take a look under sometime?"

Jack draws back as she slides the hood down. "Lots of curiosity?" He laughs. "Poke around in it any time . . . ask me questions. Just don't take it apart so it can't be put together again." His hand on Catherine's arm steers her toward the house.

Shirley stands at the window now. "Such a pretty girl," she tells Thorn, and watches Jack and Catherine.

Thorn seems to be looking at Shirley: his dark blue eyes are politely attentive. A bit too attentive to be so. "She looks like her mother," he says, and drops his dark-lashed gaze to his glass.

"You were all Americans abroad once, Jack says." Shirley imagines flappers and bathtub gin. Thorn's not as old as Jack. One of these father-daughter things where you flirt around with the fascinating Older Man. She bets Catherine does.

"Her parents died in a smash-up." Every movement Thorn makes, however slight, is in the direction of the hall and the door;

even the drink in his hand seems to quiver in anticipation of voices approaching. "I was drunk, I think, when I promised to be Catherine's guardian." He smiles, listening. "But there wasn't anybody else." Shirley hears Jack's voice.

Now Thorn's tone is different: "So there I was at twenty-one— baby in one arm, 'nappies' in the other." He's already at the door.

Shirley can see the girl clearly now: she stands between the two men, but closer to Thorn, and she isn't smiling. She doesn't look pleasant without a smile, and she doesn't seem to care. Is she normal, or is there something . . .

Incredible! That long hair of hers hanging beside her face and down her back! Nobody lets their hair grow like that. It's not the slacks, it's that hair, and that washed-out face without any make-up. But most of all it's the way she stands there with her hands in her pockets, closer to Thorn, as if they both know that she'd be pretty if she had a permanent, and some eyebrow pencil, and mascara, and they don't care. Shirley narrows her eyes. And lipstick, for God's sake. She's got to have lipstick.

Jack's eyes are on Shirley now; she gets up, smiling, prepared to join Catherine in chitchat against the men as foil, as audience. Poor kid, Shirley thinks . . . probably feels awkward and shy . . .

But Catherine stays where she is, unsmiling, as if she belongs where she is, and Shirley is something she watches with a certain curiosity. There is nothing else in her look at all.

So Shirley stands with the smile still on her face, wondering what's going on.

3

Catherine straddles a low elm branch in early morning light; she picks caterpillars from stripped leaf veins and drops them in a cheesecloth bag. "Always wriggling and smiling," she says.

Thorn glances up to where Catherine sits. Staring down at him, she has the preoccupied look she wears to judge the world. "Always rubbing against things," she goes on.

Thorn says, "She's young, maybe twenty-one. Good looking."

"She thinks I ought to wear lipstick, and she told me I'd look pretty with my hair curled."

Thorn doesn't answer. Catherine picks a leaf, looks at it, lets it flutter down to Thorn. Light through the trees tints her oval face with a slight green underwater glow. She grips the branch with her knees. Blue shadow falls over him in the grass. The elm leaf she dropped is riddled, its spring green oozing.

"What if Jack came wriggling and grinning in, painted and curled up, and you'd know how hard he'd worked just to look that way—and what if he sat down and posed, just rubbing up against things and looking sleepy—just begging . . . smiling, smiling, smiling!"

Thorn is close to Catherine's slender, dangling leg. Her hands that hold the cheesecloth sleeve pull her shirt tight over one breast; the other is hidden by brown hair that drops between leaves and her thoughtful profile.

"You don't have to," Thorn says, but turns away. She stares at his back, as if aware of a flaw in the clarity between them.

"And he didn't know my mother at all! He doesn't talk about anything but how pretty she was, and how she had men around her all the time."

A steam shovel near the school begins work with a distant grunting sound; Catherine looks over Thorn's head to where the shovel drops with a clang. "Acted as if I were a puppy sniffing his Great Big Machine. He said he didn't know how it worked, but I don't think he'd tell *you* that. 'Just don't take it apart so it can't be put together again'—that's what he said!"

Catherine swings her slim leg up and over the branch and drops into the grass with the cheesecloth in her hand. For a minute they stand together in the blue early morning shadows.

"Not your idea of 'first love'?" Thorn says. Sun strikes small points of light in his thick hair. He drops his long-lashed eyes then; the corners of his mouth, pulled down slightly, give his long face its sad, descending shape.

The pantry window frames Catherine and Thorn, facing each other under the elms. Watching them through the kitchen curtains, Tubbit holds his breath.

They cross the weedy field without looking at each other, almost like sleepwalkers in the blowing grass.

4

"Up early?" Shirley stops at Catherine's bedroom door and smiles. Her lips are dark red, her robe a plain and chaste white silk, and she has just taken fifteen wire curlers out of her hair and brushed it into small ringlets, sausages, and waves. She bats her mascara-thick eyelashes at the bottles and card files and Catherine's blanket-covered bed. Catherine is hanging cheesecloth sleeves on a rod to dry.

"A relative of yours?" Hands on her hips, Shirley stands before a watercolor on Catherine's wall. The middle-aged woman in the picture looks back at Shirley, calm and self-possessed.

That long hair, just hanging down . . . Shirley glances at Catherine and gives her a pitying, big-sister look. Poor kid, stuck out here alone. Shirley can't help but pose for Catherine; she knows how fashionable she looks, head to foot. Poor kid. Shirley fluffs her hair with one hand and says, "I thought it was a colored photograph at first. It's so . . . true to life."

Spring light slides along Catherine's smooth cheek and glistens in her long eyelashes and eyes that hold no little-sister admiration or shyness at all. She pushes her hair back, throws it back with an abrupt toss. "She's me—about fifty-five or sixty, I suppose," she says, pulling a dresser drawer open. "My room's so crowded because I have to keep my ant colonies here."

"It's you?" Shirley asks, and feels angry. It's something about the way Catherine stands, or her voice . . .

"I've tried it in the basement, but it's too damp," Catherine says. "Look—she's pulled off her wings." She holds a covered jelly glass out. "That means she'll lay now."

Shirley takes the glass. A huge ant climbs the side; below her on the dirt lie two narrow, wedge-shaped wings. "But who painted that?" Shirley asks.

"I don't know. I found it in a secondhand store downtown." Catherine is watching the ant, not Shirley. Then she glances at Shirley's hair and makeup and white silk with alert, preoccupied eyes, as if her real concerns are elsewhere. "She'll make a hole, and live on the energy from her wing muscles. She doesn't need her wings now. In a month she'll have her callows to feed her, and then hundreds of worker ants."

"That's interesting," Shirley says, staring at Catherine. The middle-aged woman in the picture watches her, as calm and self-possessed as Catherine. The woman's eyes are creased deeply at the corners; jowls are forming at her oval chin. Wrinkled neck and gray-brown hair are painted without compromise; age spots are scattered over the hands in her lap. "I'd better go get ready for breakfast." Shirley hands the jar to Catherine and rustles down the hall.

Catherine looks past cottonwood branches at her window, and sees Thorn and Jack facing each other on the drive beside Jack's Chrysler. Nothing of what they're saying reaches her open window; she turns away.

"What would Janet think?" Jack squints against the light and Thorn, and picks a bit of tobacco from his lip. He scowls at the moth-eaten army blanket spread between the Chrysler's wheels. Catherine's wrench and pliers hold the blanket down against a wind that smells of rain.

"I've tried to do what Janet—"

"For God's sake—she looks like the Okies from the Dust Bowl! Get her some decent clothes, can't you? She's got some money left, hasn't she?"

"Not much," Thorn says. "The crash pretty well wiped out the Buckingham money, and Janet's, too. I saved enough to live on and send her to college."

"She could be a knockout, like Janet was. But where's she going to get if she looks like that? Seventeen, and she doesn't even know how to put on lipstick—and what does she do out here all by herself, month after month?"

"Write. Study. Help me with my books."

"Her whole life? She could be seeing the world, having fun with kids her own age!"

"It's what Janet wanted," Thorn says. "We don't know. It's like a game of tennis without a net, without any . . ."

Wind strikes the sumac and the cottonwoods. Their thin branches whip. Rain pocks the dry sand. The shape of the wrench at Jack's feet makes his hand twitch; for a moment he feels it, heavy and cold, between him and Thorn's single glittering eye in a face half turned from him.

But the wrench is under the car yet when Jack looks. Only

Thorn's face has changed; something sharper than regret clouds his eyes before he drops them to the car sparkling with rain.

Following Thorn into the house, Jack carries himself stiffly. His heels click on the back hall boards. When they join the others at breakfast, he doesn't say much. He sits watching Catherine, and Shirley, who's almost the same age as Catherine, after all—a couple of years' difference. Shirley's a beautiful kid; even old Thorn gives her the once-over now and then. But Catherine just sits and listens to Shirley chatter away about Thorn's cousins in France, and the book that Thorn and Catherine have to finish before he can go overseas. Shirley was a deb, and now she's the fashionable "career girl" just out of college: she's got the new style down pat. She's all business in the office, but she lets you know that she's really very feminine and as much in favor of marriage as the girl next door.

"Then you're planning to go to France?" Jack asks. Tubbit is passing rolls, his face without expression.

"As soon as I can," Thorn says.

"I'll probably start at Gilman College this fall," Catherine says. She's been watching Shirley with an unsmiling face, as though she's trying to understand some complicated process, like a fluid drive. "Thorn really does need to go to France."

"Won't you find college a little . . . hard to get used to?" Jack says. He looks at Thorn. "She hasn't had many young people around, but at college she'll be living in crowds of them." Janet had those eyes of Catherine's, and when Janet dropped them and then raised them suddenly, or looked sidewise . . .

Thorn doesn't answer. Neither does Catherine. Watching them, Jack thinks he picks up something in the air between them. They don't look at each other. Neither wants to answer him. Has anything happened? No way of telling. "You know I've got a niece just about Catherine's age and a nephew a little younger," he says. "In Iowa. So I know a little bit about high school kids."

"I don't know where I'll be going in France," Thorn says after a pause. "I'll start at the town we lived in and try to trace my cousins."

"If we aren't in the war by September—or Hitler isn't marching through London," Jack says.

"You'll have to see the World's Fair when you go to New

York." Shirley tosses her silky hair and smiles, and when she gets up from the table she moves inside her clothes somehow; that's quite a trick, Jack thinks, surprised. He watches her get into the car when he opens the door for her, fluid as a snake with a grace Catherine doesn't have at all. Catherine says goodbye, pushing at that sloppy hair. She doesn't smile.

Alone in the car, Shirley and Jack carry a faint uneasiness away with them; it gives an edge to their voices. "So Thorn's really going to France," Jack says after a while. "You didn't get very far, talking to her."

Shirley's voice is high with amazement. "She really doesn't care how she looks! She really doesn't think it's important. Can you imagine? It's just not natural, is it? Any girl—"

"She hasn't had a chance!" Jack says, tapping his fingers on the wheel, waiting for the light on Six Mile Road to turn green.

"Did you say anything about her visiting your sister's family in Iowa?"

"I talked to Thorn and Catherine about it, and then I mentioned it to Tubbit. Maybe she'll do it." The light changes. "I'll ask my sister to come with me. She's got two high school kids— she'll know what to do about the way Catherine looks. She's a smart woman. She'll know what to do."

5

The old bathtub, made for some midget, is hardly four feet long. Catherine sits doubled up in high water, looking at the islands of her knees.

Water pipes are clanking as they always do. Between clanks the house is still, emptied of Shirley's chatter and Jack's deep voice. They've gone.

Water runs from the tub without a sound, descending, a warmth falling from around her. He's going to France.

He ought to go. Catherine gets out and grabs a towel. Try to find Marthe, and Claire, whose husband has simply disappeared. Catherine looks at the bathroom wallpaper's swans and fountains without seeing them, and starts pulling on shirt and slacks. France seems far away, but not as far away as Thorn under the elms this morning.

The hallway with its patches of light from open doors looks strange, and her old room looks like somebody else's. Thorn's door is ajar; she hears him shut a dresser drawer.

Thorn turns, hearing Catherine in the hall. His eyes are wiped clean of any expression for a moment, seeing hers. "Ready to go?" he asks. "I've got the sleeves."

She crawled into that bed when she had nightmares, or when she was sick. The carved leaves on the headboard have shreds of nightmare clinging to them: once she lay there damp and feverish, holding on to him while the world wheeled around them. His dresser has brass drawer pulls with three circles on them. His mirror creaks when he tilts it. She would know the faint scent of this room anywhere.

"Right here in the daylight," Catherine says. Her mouth feels dry. "You look . . . bright. Loud. As if all of you is talking." The oval-backed chair watches her with its roses. The highboy's dark bulk crouches on its lion's feet.

"Arnold is coming to photograph the *Danaus* plate at three, so we'll have to be back by then." Thorn goes by her and down the hall to the stairs.

The late spring days are warm, and the first butterflies crawl from chrysalides, wet and pulsing. Hands as familiar as Catherine's own hands palm the butterfly bodies . . . they catch the undersides of the wings gently between thumb and fingers, and she cannot watch.

Thorn books passage on a ship sailing from New York in August. Tubbit will stay and take care of both houses. Tubbit fusses over Catherine. She looks so tired, he says. She ought to rest more. Let Thorn work on the book—go out and lie in the hammock for a while this afternoon, and he'll make some lemonade. It's as hot as summertime, and not even June.

The hammock swings in the coin-shaped shadows of new leaves. Space between Catherine and Thorn rings with far-off hammer blows.

"What's the matter?" Catherine says to Tubbit's tulips, not Thorn. The neat flowers watch them both. She hears the ice shift in his glass.

"It's been happening all the time lately." Her voice quivers and then goes on. "It started under the elms that morning Jack was here. That's why I stared at you, remember? I couldn't talk."

"I couldn't talk either."

"You felt the same thing?" Catherine's voice has relief in it, then sharpens: "Well, what started it?"

"Outside that morning?" Thorn doesn't go on for a while. The hammer blows cascade through distances.

"I said wasn't Jack your idea of first love?" Thorn says at last. "I said he ought to know how to make love after about twenty-five years of it—supposing he started at fifteen."

Thorn's head, bent like that, with glints of sun on it—"Yes!" Catherine cries. "And I thought that you must know how as well as he does—you're about his age—you've had all those girl-friends, and Sally, and Dot . . ." Catherine stares at the tulips. "How did you know that was when? I saw you, and then I imagined . . ." She stops.

Thorn walks away. His long legs take him through the twinkling shade and sun fast. He goes up stairs two at a time and stands at his study window, eyes shut, a glass of lemonade untasted in his hand.

After a while he opens his blue eyes that are as bleak and inward with distances as a sailor's or a plainsman's. Below his window Catherine is on her hands and knees in the grass, Tubbit's tulips a bright background. She jumps up as he watches, her bare arms and legs still light with the long winter. He hears her running upstairs, and then the clash of glasses jammed together.

"There's an ant flight!" she calls to Tubbit, who is bringing a plate of cookies through the garden. On her knees again in the grass, she balances on one slender arm and hand.

The ant princesses are like splinters of glass in the air, on the bark of the cottonwoods, in the grass. At every movement their long wings glisten. They pour out of the ant hole like a trickle of cellophane.

Tubbit walks through a cloud of them, waving his hand to keep them off the cookies. A princess drops to the plate, dragging one of the small males attached to her. Catherine crawls on her knees looking for the queens who have already torn off their wings.

The book on Monarchs is nearly finished. Thorn works on the map of migration paths from breeding to overwintering grounds. That night, at work again, he can hear Benny Goodman on Catherine's radio, slithering through "Don't Be That Way." Goodman's clarinet is shut away with her as she closes her door.

At breakfast it's the same as always: light comes through vines over the windows, and the old china with the Greek key pattern is on the table. He hears Tubbit go out the back door, heading for his cottage.

"How did you know when it began out by the elms?" Catherine takes a deep breath to steady her voice. "The morning Jack was here."

Thorn's dark-lashed eyes meet hers for a second, darting away again. Long lines are beginning to form on his cheeks; they accent his grim mouth. "I don't know. I think . . . it's the eyes." He won't look at her. "And it wasn't the first time with me."

"I know that," Catherine says.

"No." His eyes are dropped to his fist on the tablecloth. "I mean with you."

Neither one of them says anything more; they get up after a while without a word. Catherine begins her hour of piano practice. An F on the piano is flat again, and scatters a Czerny exercise with small sour twangs. Tubbit comes back to gather up the breakfast dishes. Thorn has gone up to shave.

She can sure play that piece fast now. Tubbit stands in the dining room, listening. Rips right through it, then tackles it again. Sounds real pretty.

Laird thought he'd get Catherine to visit in Iowa with his sister and her family after Thorn goes. He wrote that he'd bring his sister with him—it would look better, he said—older man with a young girl, you know. Seemed queer to think of Catherine that old. Laird said his sister could buy Catherine some new clothes and have her hair fixed. And then Laird wrote: "Watch Thorn for me, will you? Write me if anything funny happens."

Now why did he say that? Why watch Wade? Ought to have written, "Watch Catherine." She's so jumpy. Sad, sometimes, too—wanders around. Doesn't want to leave home, probably, and go to college. It'll be good for her, but he'll sure miss her. Sure will.

But she'll come back to visit. When Wade's in France, she'll be back. Listen to her play that piece. Makes a pretty picture at the piano in that flowered bathrobe. Makes her seem so grown up.

But look at that: neither of them touched the nice warm muffins. She'll miss the home cooking—she'll come home and see him, that's what she'll do.

Catherine stops right in the middle of her piece—just quits. He looks through the dining room door to the parlor. She isn't doing anything. She's just sitting there.

6

Sunlight follows its slow morning and afternoon course along Thorn's desk, into his wastebasket, across the corner of his bed. He tries to concentrate on the patterns of migration and overwintering he pulls from his note cards. But there are no orderly progressions for some things. Luna moths flutter, pumping up their wings, or float across his room.

Looking up in late afternoon light, he sees a moth swoop between him and Catherine's flushed face. She stands in his doorway.

"We could marry each other," she says. "You're younger than Jack. People like us get married all the time. We could wait until I'm twenty."

She stops a luna as it drifts near; it balances on her palm. "But you don't get married just because of this," she says after a little while. Her bare feet step into a patch of sunlight on his rug. "How long does it last?" The luna flies from her outstretched hand.

"I have to go to France."

"Do you want to start, and then leave when it's not over?"

"I don't know," he says.

The lunas crisscross the sun between them, wings green as the undersides of spring leaves where a white down pales the color. One clings to Thorn's rolled-up sleeve. Along the tops of its wings a purple-red branch shape with one bud is drawn. It wears shoulder capes of pale yellow fur; the white abdomen pulses. Antennae more branched and fragile than a snowflake plume from its dark-eyed head.

"Then I've got to think about it," Catherine says. "Not go flying off like I've been doing."

Thorn tries to smile a little, tries to meet her eyes. "That's the idea, I suppose. Feeling better?" His eyes are almost blue-black.

"No." Catherine shrinks against the doorway, her eyes wide, the pupils shrinking with the light over his shoulder. "You're still talking to me with your hands . . . even your clothes! Why?" Her voice goes up, exasperated.

"Maybe that's what Jack and Shirley were after, leaning and rubbing and smiling. Wanting us to feel like that."

Catherine sorts out memories. "But what would they do with us if they got us? They're not the kind of people we—"

"Maybe they don't think that far ahead. What would Shirley do with me?" Thorn starts to laugh, but his white shirt sleeve rolled on his brown arm seems to hang before Catherine's eyes, and his long fingers press white silk—

"Sorry!" Thorn cries.

She's already out of sight down the hall. "I didn't think!" he calls after her, but the only answer is the sound of her bare feet on the stairs.

He slams his study door behind him and goes into Catherine's room. The house echoes, empty. He picks up Catherine's pillow.

The pillow smells like her hair.

Janet's head against the sun, between him and the sun. "To be pinned down!"

Did Janet's hair smell like this? Thorn shuts his eyes. The books have sold well. Go to England and study the damsel fly. Go to France . . . track Marthe and Claire . . . make them let him help them. Go now.

When he opens his eyes, a woman watches him from her picture frame, her eyes twinkling slightly, her mouth barely smiling. The pillow smells of shampoo and fresh air and naphtha.

There are neat rows of empty jelly glasses on a bookcase, and the backs of volumes of Forel and Wheeler bulge like fat breakfronts, full of facts. A skinny Frost. A Dickinson leaning against a *New Poetry*. Shakespeare, art books, chemistry, and a battered *Alice in Wonderland*. All the doors have been open, and when she came home . . .

The wild flower book. He picks it up and a dried fern falls out. "Why do some beautiful flowers have such ugly names?" she'd asked him once. "Vetch, for instance. It sounds like the nasty-sounding names for women or intercourse—the ones people scribble on walls downtown."

Thorn puts the fern in the book and the book on the shelf and sighs, turning away.

The very pattern of the curtains conjures up Catherine.

Beyond the open closet door her clothes keep the shape of her arms in their quiet sleeves. Her plants on the windowsill are confident planes of green, waiting for her to come back. The woman is confident in her frame, waiting for her to grow old.

The upstairs hall smells of beaverboard, always has. The bathroom smells of soap; wallpaper swans swim in layers among improbable fountains. Crouched on its paws, the bathtub waits for a midget. The toilet's water tank seems to harbor a frog; it croaks with a pull of the chain.

Afternoon groans to an end with a steam shovel digging another cellar among the houses they can see from their windows now—new houses in sand and hot cement. Beyond the barn and the garden and Tubbit's cottage there are still meadows of grass, and an elm; Catherine lies on her back in the shade of it.

Above her the clouds slide on air, whipped cream over glass, and the scent of that air surrounds her. March after March her kites rode a kite string into that sky. They rose until they were too high to see, while all around her were the smooth, empty streets littered with bud sheaths—streets that are swallowed up now, lined with parked cars.

Catherine squints against the bright blue above. She tied the kite to a tree and strapped on her roller skates. She could feel the clamps biting through her shoes, and locked the key in its six-sided slot to tighten them. Her fingers smelled of metal.

And then the pull. She held on to the kite string, waiting. And the slow, cold pull of the wind came down from somewhere near the sun where the kite was, but the kite was too high to see, so the pull seemed to come from the whole force of the sky—the slow, cold, steady pull that she pulled back against. Lonely and cold, the pull began near the sun and pulled tight from the kite, down-light and down-wind and down-March.

Until, leaning back, she felt a roller skate wheel, the first one, turn. And then another. And she—tethered to that sky—picked up speed, crack by crack, over bud sheaths and dead twigs and her own shadow, until her skates began to whine on the smooth, unused cement, hitting one crack—clack—and the next—clack—and then clack, clack, clack, what a hum through the wheels to her feet . . .

Fast as flying, then—flying and hanging on. Until the wind turned. Until it shifted and pulled her cross-lots across sand and stopped her somewhere among fighting sparrows in the bushes. The earth smelled of thaw. Her feet were numb yet with the hum of flying.

But now the elm above her moves against that sky, and is heavy with leaves. The very weighted swing of its branches plays on her. Lying here, remembering the pull of that air, she is tight like a kite string or a mouth, and spring air cannot so much as breathe across her without making her quiver.

Catherine sighs, a kind of sob. The blue of her eyes sparkles with the sky through elm leaves, and her sun-streaked hair flows over sand.

Thorn looks through cottonwood leaves to the pink sky. He'll have to find her—where would she go? He feels every sense shock him with the last heat of the day pressed against him. But Catherine turns on her stomach and puts her cheek in the warm sand. The immensity of clouds and sky and memory are out of sight; all she can see is a pebble, a few blades of grass.

She props herself on her elbows. The sand is so warm in the wash of elm shade; it meets her body at every surface pressed upon it. She can shove her fingers in it, and the mark stays. She can toss it into the air and it blows away.

Thorn walks through the garden and climbs a ladder in the darkening barn. No one in the loft above the car. The old tomcat, mouser, father of dozens, shines two yellow lenses from a barn beam and yowls. But Catherine begins to smile, lying flat in the sand with its quiet warmth against her cheek.

The barn keeps the scent of long-gone horses and old wood, dust and mouse-riddled hay, and spring's evening wine is mixed with it—Thorn breathes it in: barn and spring night. He climbs down. The tomcat's four paws hit dirt behind him: the cat is alerted by footsteps. Thorn says, "Catherine?"

There's a slender shadow in the doorway, hands spread to the splintered wood.

"I've been thinking all afternoon," Catherine says to the dark, dusty air of the barn. All she can see is the blur of Thorn's white shirt. "I want to go on. In case we can get through to the other side." He says nothing. "In case we want to marry when it's all over and we can tell. We could, you know."

"Yes."

"How long does this last?"

She can see him a little better now; he raises two big hands, palms up, in a gesture that seems French, and says, "You'll go off anyway, you decided. To college."

"It's hard to leave when it's not over, I suppose."

"Pretty hard."

"I've thought of waiting until you come back, and I'm out of college. But I'm old enough, and you'd be . . ." Her voice trembles, and she stops, then goes on. "If it doesn't change everything. It will. I think it will. But why should I be scared of that? Unless, after it's all over, we decide we shouldn't marry. But that wouldn't stop us from being—friends, like we are."

"No." He waits, letting her think in this dim place, saying as little as he can. "You'll have to hide what you're doing."

"I know. And I'll have to go to college, and you'll have to go to France."

"We agreed that would be the best thing."

"There's something . . ." Catherine's voice is softer as she turns away; it strengthens as she turns back ". . . in the air. Can you feel it? All the time we've been talking, ever since this morning, colors are different, and everything feels like it's touching me . . . it almost seems to hurt."

"It gets worse," Thorn says from the depths of the barn. "Take it slowly. Don't start at all unless you're sure it's what you want."

He takes a step toward the twilight. Night wind off the lake bends sumac outside the barn door, then releases it in a rustle of leaves.

"I want to begin," Catherine says. She is quiet then, thinking, and might be alone in the barn; there's no sound but the night wind in the leaves.

He feels her hands on his shoulders. "I'm not afraid," she says.

"No," he says in the second before all that will scare them both explodes when she kisses him.

It's worse than he thought it would be—the dark, the spring dark, this voice, this mouth.

Whatever they're saying makes no sense, but he won't grab, or take. He thinks of nothing at all, and will not touch her, fighting not to be there, Janet's face between him and the English sun. Her hair smells of soap and fresh air, like her pillow. And then she breaks away from him, and runs toward the house in the darkness.

7

All night long the house carries on its secret conversations between one board in the stairway and another in the back hall . . . between the downstairs clock and the busy click of Catherine's alarm. All night long there's no footstep on the stairs. He won't come in, not when she ran away.

He's not there at breakfast the next morning, either. She has to go and find him.

"Come and eat," she says through lips that seem to have turned to cement. He's her uncle, and Thorn Wade, and the hundreds of things he has always been. Yet he seems to be ticking like a time bomb, screaming like a siren . . . Thorn puts his book down and turns to her in a barn that is full of nothing but the blue of his eyes.

He won't make one move. He won't even look at her much, but keeps back, increasing space and silence, and cancels even the waiting out of his eyes and voice.

"You want me to do everything," Catherine says when Tubbit has left the house. They haven't eaten much breakfast. Breaking the silence in the dining room is like breaking one of the windows—smashing into ivy leaves and sunlight.

"It's not that way in movies and books," Catherine goes on. The silence presses upon her with the weight of all that Thorn is now, sitting there.

"You said the women always sit and wait," Thorn says at last. "And dress themselves up to get attention."

All she can feel is Thorn. He seems ten times as big as he has ever been. There seems to be nothing in the dining room but Thorn. "It's awfully hard," she says.

There's a shout from the garden: Tubbit is after one of the cats. They've been digging in his asparagus patch again. Catherine goes to the window. "Female animals don't just sit and wait and look pretty—they take care of themselves."

She stares through ivy leaves where colors from the garden flowers are like stained glass. "If I go to college and get to know men my own age . . ." She stops. "It's awfully hard for them, too."

Catherine hears the chink of Thorn's coffee cup on the saucer. "So why should I have to do it all, if it's easier just to wait for somebody else?" Her words seem close to her own ears, echoed from the window glass.

She begins to laugh as she hears them. Or is she crying? She doesn't know or care. She swings around, her long hair flying, and runs to Thorn. "I want to kiss you—all morning!" she cries.

Catherine stands before Thorn as he rises, rubbing her wet eyes and laughing. A teardrop falls from her face like a spark in the window's sunlight.

8

Thorn bends over the proofs of the new book: a man in his thirties with thick, gold-brown hair. His lower lip clamps firmly shut and turns down, as if it knows something the fringed eyes won't tell: they dart so quickly up and away, withdrawn and blue. The old house hasn't changed one of its sounds or shadows; long grass and sumac and scrub oak ring it in.

New brick houses are rising nearer and nearer now; the hammer strokes beat on the morning air. And when Thorn looks up, who is he? The careful calm of his face brings all of him to mind—the complete shape you might think the moon is, until it grows, night after night, from the dark, and at last glows there, round and still, and is itself completely, and always was, but you didn't know.

So what has changed is you, not the moon. When you've seen all of it once, it can go back to its thin rim, but you feel the roundness, the absence of what's there.

Is she as complete and bright to him, too?

All day they're alone, working on the book. They hear Tubbit, punctual and plodding, getting their meals and cleaning and leaving the house to them again, and there Thorn is, working over the long strips of proofs.

She has kissed him and hugged him ever since she can remember anything . . . what doesn't she know about those long eyelashes or the downturned line of his mouth? She has seen him bundled against the cold, or nearly naked in summer heat—no pose his body can take is strange to her, or any play of muscle, or angle of elbow or knee or narrow hands.

And yet if she bends to fit her mouth on his, her long hair covering the proofs, until he straightens up and his arms close around her, who is he? Who looks from his eyes when she opens her own? When his long eyelashes lift, someone new is living in those eyes, and the house is as strange around them both as if she has never seen this place before.

"Have a good night's sleep?" Tubbit asks every morning. Catherine opens her mouth to say yes, and there, between Tubbit's ordinary smile and the dining room window, are two eyes, bare and blue. Their look changes the room. Tubbit's face is as unfamiliar as a peasant's in a Brueghel village dance.

"Yes," she says, "thanks. How was yours?" The ritual words bring reality back: the room, Tubbit's face, Thorn's eyes looking out the window now, not at her.

But when meals are over and Tubbit leaves the house, the silence begins. It hums without any noise behind what words they say.

Catherine types an editor's name and then stops, because nothing but Thorn is in her head. The shape he makes in the room behind her has a final quality, as if he were the answer to every question, or all questions combined to make one man.

Thorn sits in the breeze from the window. It ruffles his thick hair and makes the paper tremble in his hand. He stops dictating, seeing her eyes.

The kissing isn't enough. At night Catherine curls in a tense ball in her bed, thinking how to begin, or if she should, or if she can. The condoms he'll have to wear. The act that can't be—dignified. Can that be what it's all about? Not there. Not with that. How could anybody?

Night wind, dense with rain, rushes through the cottonwoods.

Climbing from bed, Catherine finds Thorn's room alive with the sound of waterdrops on glass: a dark, sheltered place where he lies sheltered again in sleep, until she touches him.

Nothing but a change in his breathing tells her he feels her head on his shoulder, and her body settling against him. She elbows her way up to sit and pull off her nightgown, and wriggles down again, and falls asleep instantly, as if she has broken through this decision into rest.

Thorn lies awake, watching daylight come slowly through win-

dows like wet diamonds, watching the girl in his arms emerge
from the dark in her long hair, her breath a feather stirring
against his chest.

9

Now Thorn's bed is the center, the heart of what has always
seemed to be there: two houses in the cottonwoods, the bowl of
the sky over roads leading in all directions. Each morning the
birds wake them; each morning wind blows through Thorn's bedroom curtains and smells of spring.

"I don't want to try it just yet," Catherine says, listening to the
birds.

"You don't have to try it at all," Thorn says.

"I have to." Catherine twists a lock of her hair in an old childhood gesture. "I'm getting used to no clothes."

"Exploring," Thorn says.

"Exploring." Catherine has twisted the lock of hair tight; she
lets it go. "I have to try it . . ." she sits up, one breast pink with
its long pressure against him ". . . because it's one of the last
things I can learn with you for a while. If I can figure it out."

Sun reflected from the bedroom wall edges her tanned arms
and white breasts in luminous light, and furs the edge of her hair
with bright tendrils, but her light blue eyes are sad and very still,
looking at him. "Then we have to leave," she says.

Catherine runs a hand down Thorn's long cheek and furry
chest to follow the swell of hipbone under the skin—so different
from hers, like the shape of armor through flesh. Then she comes
down to hide her face in the warmth between his neck and shoulder. "But this isn't enough," she says, her lips moving against his
throat.

Spring breeze carries voices from one of the new backyards.
She feels him trying to swallow around a lump in his throat. "I
mean—it won't be. Not even when I've got it figured out, and we
make love—it won't be . . . enough."

A dog barks. Someone races a car engine, drowning the yowl of
the barn cats waiting at Tubbit's cottage steps, and the slam of his
screen door.

"All *right*," Tubbit says in a cross voice to cats wreathing his ankles in fur. "All *right*. Let me get it in the dishes at least—get out of the way."

The cats eat, then disappear in the barn again, sleeping away the growing heat of the morning and the noon sun. The old house seems stuffy to Catherine when she wanders around it after lunch. The beveled window in the front door makes rainbows of the afternoon sun, just as it always has.

Catherine chinks money in her hand, going through the yard past the sundial. The bus routes make a map in her head, and she can go anywhere. The salesgirls in the stores will stand behind counters, their eyes roving over expensive things as if they are in charge. Secretaries in the General Motors Building type in long rows; the place seems to house nothing more important than that constant sound.

When Catherine turns and looks back, the barn watches her go. It's full of her unfinished "projects" that aren't enough, either.

If she goes to a library, she can sit and read among bookshelves like the treasuries of Ali Baba, floor to ceiling, where women sit at their librarians' desks and seem, in the still rain of sunshine through dust . . .

Tubbit's in the garden pulling onions: his white apron gleams in the green. They're having chicken tonight, he's told her. And chocolate pie.

"Northlawn," says the first street sign.

A woman hangs wash in one of the backyards at the end of a new white walk. Her apron is ruffled and pink, and a cat follows her, keeping in her shadow. Catherine can smell meat cooking. "Bett-eee!" somebody calls close by. "You come in now, Bett-ee!"

It's hot, but she's worn slacks anyway; she changes buses along Livernois and remembers where to get off to go to Jemmie's tenement rooms on Brush Street.

"Where you been at?" Jemmie says, pulling her black bulk away from the door to let Catherine come in. "We ain't seen you for the longest time!" Her beautiful chocolate eyes go over Catherine carefully while her white teeth smile. "You been poorly? Set down and I'll make us some coffee."

"No—I'm all right." Catherine pushes her hair behind her ears and sits down at the table. "How's Audrey? And Bassett?"

"Grown like spring beans, just like you. Bet you won't know

either one." Jemmie puts a cup on the table before Catherine. "Wish we had ice."

Catherine sips the hot stuff. Jemmie looks at her again, hesitates, then drinks her coffee in companionable silence.

"You growin' up," Jemmie says at last. Long friendship makes her relax, leaning back; her eyes run over Catherine again. "Gonna fix yourself up, girl? Some nice young man come along, you wants to be ready."

Big feet take the stairs three at a time, and Bassett slips through the door. Catherine says she wouldn't have known him and shakes his hand; Jemmie grins. "Just a sight for sore eyes, ain't he?" she asks Catherine. Bassett hitches up his very fashionable trousers, slicks his slick hair slicker, and prowls the room for a while. Then he sidles up to Jemmie and smiles.

"What you want?" Jemmie asks. She looks up at him and then chuckles. "Oh, go on, help yourself."

"Just takin' in a movie with Sally," he mumbles, ducking to find Jemmie's purse behind the breadbox. "Be home 'bout ten, Mama."

Jemmie winks at Catherine as Bassett clatters downstairs. "Just a cock rooster spreadin' his feathers, that's all. Told you he was growin' like spring beans. Did I tell you what happen to Annie's George Nathan?"

Catherine must hear all the news now, the stories told and embellished on hot nights on Brush Street stoops while the children play under the streetlights and the young folk go off to good times for nickels and dimes. The hot sun slides down the wall; traffic-rush pours through the open windows with the smell of tar and frying fat.

"Here come Audrey," Jemmie says. "She got a good job at the Crown Hotel cleanin' rooms. Got a real good job."

The door opens only a crack . . . opens a little more. A thin young woman stands there, and behind her a young man. "Audrey?" Jemmie says, a peculiar sound in her voice. Audrey draws back quickly and turns, but the young man is already going downstairs with a fast click of heels before Jemmie can get to her feet. "Audrey!"

Audrey comes in and closes the door behind her. "Catherine!" she says. "How you doin'?"

Audrey was plump and pigtailed once, and she fought the boys up and down her block. Now she's tall and thin and very tired, and old enough to match glances with her mother and not look away.

Jemmie stares at her. "You lettin' that Everett Polk walk you home again?"

"I got a good job now," Audrey says, sloshing the coffeepot sideways, then pouring a cup. "Mama tell you? At the Crown Hotel, and I get the room tips all to myself."

"That Everett Polk—"

"I need a little fun, don't I?" Audrey says to no one in particular. "Work all day, I need a little fun?"

"You *get* a little fun, you don't watch," Jemmie says. "How you gonna find a nice young man—"

"Like you, Mama?" Audrey sips her coffee. "Like you done?"

"Prettiest man!" Jemmie cries, glaring at her daughter. "Prettiest man ever made a shadow, he was!"

"Well, that Everett he ain't exactly ugly," Audrey says proudly. "You see him in his fingertip, and them pegged drapes, and you watch him jitterbug, Mama!"

Jemmie grins. Then she laughs: white teeth, liquid brown eyes. "Just like her mama!" she tells Catherine. "Got the eye for the pretty man, just like her mama!"

"Well, sure!" Audrey is grinning too. She shrugs. "I got my paycheck, I can have some fun. I don't give him no more than he can dance down or drink up, do I?"

"Soft hearted for the men." Jemmie's continuing chuckle simmers with pride. "You gonna do all right, girl, you keep the good job."

"Sure, Mama." Audrey's eyes are dark slits above her smile. She leans her elbows on the table and spreads her knees, her dress hitting the corners of her boniness. "Get me a place of my own," she says to the contented black face across the table.

"Sure," Jemmie says.

Buses snort and roar in the hot street. "Mama!" a child cries, and a window slams up. High above the rush of traffic two women yell at each other, and their children. Listening, Catherine remembers snow, a cup of chocolate, babies in wash baskets along a wall.

"You gonna get prettied up one of these days, girl?" Jemmie asks. Catherine turns to see both of them watching her. Jemmie smooths her apron and glances at Audrey.

"Yeh," Audrey says. "Maybe get your hair cut, and curl it. Ought to be pretty."

"You gotta look nice, honey. Some rich boy come along, and you get married, have a nice place . . ."

"Maybe some lipstick." Audrey squints at Catherine over her bony fingers.

"Do *you* like to fiddle with that stuff?" Catherine asks.

Two pairs of eyes meet hers, startled, and then Jemmie laughs, her fat shaking. Audrey's laugh is as sharp as her bones.

"Honey," Audrey says kindly as Catherine gets up to go, "Sure I do, but *you* fix yourself up and some man gonna just *beg*! You gonna look real good." She pats Catherine's arm at the open door.

"Thanks for the coffee." Catherine hears their goodbyes ricochet ahead of her down the narrow stairs. Their door shuts on laughter.

10

Hot. Tubbit mops his forehead over the ironing board and watches Catherine in the garden. Not doing anything, just wandering around and looking. Sure is getting tanned, and it's not even July. Just roams around all day. Thinking about going to college, probably, and Wade going off to France. But she ought to eat more.

Just roaming around. Now where's she going? He watches her off down the dusty gravel road. Movies, probably. About time for the matinee. If he peels apples for the pie now, maybe the ironing will dry out. Think of living all alone here, keeping up these two houses. Lots worse jobs.

Off to the movies. When she doesn't even enjoy it, seems like. Comes home and talks to Wade and gets mad, and then they start to laugh, sometimes. They laugh at a lot of things you couldn't see anything funny about. Or Wade tells her how he grew up with two little girls in a mining town in France, and talks about invisible walls and them saving nice things for him, and his mother making money as a nurse—you get bits of the story, running in and out with the plates.

But movies are something you're supposed to have fun at.

Shadows of clouds race the bus across green fields. Catherine has to get off where the bus stops, right in front of the drugstore where boys lounge against the outside wall. She's got slacks on and she shakes her long hair over her face, but the whistles begin anyway, and follow her to the ticket office. She takes her change and goes in to the smell of dusty seats and popcorn.

The audience is mostly Saturday afternoon couples, scattered like islands in the ripples of empty seat backs. Their faces darken and lighten with the screen. The girl behind Catherine keeps saying, "Don't! Now you stop that!" while the look-alike chorus girls are pointing their legs and arms together to make pinwheels.

It's a double feature, so most of the day's heat is gone when Catherine comes out, blinking in the bright light. "What do you want?" she says to a long-legged boy sprawled on a drugstore step.

"Oh, hey, Sugar, what do I—"

Catherine breaks in. "Did you whistle?"

"Yeh, Arnie," another boy says, "what you want, Arnie? Tell the lady!"

"G'wan!" the boys chorus. "Tell her, Arnie!"

"I don't know you," Catherine says.

The boys are watching. Arnie leans back and runs his eyes over Catherine. "Sure, you know Arnie Carney, beautiful—how about a date?"

The boys shout approval.

"Why did you whistle?" Catherine asks.

Arnie looks at the others. He pops his eyes out and "mugs" for them. "'Cause you got such gorgeous top drawers, baby!"

The laughter seems to hit Catherine, as if they are throwing it through the hot air. "Ever done any French kissin'?" somebody says, and snickers.

"She ain't so bad from the back, either!"

Two girls from the theater go by, their arms around each other, hurrying, chins in the air, braving the whistles and shouts. Catherine backs away and runs down the street where the bus is waiting in front of the dime store.

There are men on the bus who look like men in the movies, but the girls and women don't. Most of the women have hats and gloves on, hot as it is, and the girls are wrinkled and look tired, or bored.

It's so hot that Catherine gets up and stands behind the motorman where the rush of air from an open window blows on her hot face. A movie smile grins at her from an ad: Mrs. Eugene du Pont, III. ("My pores seems so much finer, my skin clearer and brighter" is printed under her face.) Two women in another ad are not smiling. ("Mary is a very careful mother," says one balloon above their heads. "Not always, her bathroom paper is terrible," says the other.)

When Catherine gets off at Seven Mile and the sound of the bus dies away, she can hear a meadowlark in the fields of wild grass that still ripple, long and green, between the new houses and the road through the cottonwoods. Tubbit isn't in the kitchen but Thorn is in his study. When she puts her arms around him, he gets up, glancing once at her face, and holds her, and waits, the way he always does. Watching her as she turns away from him, her face hard with whatever she has brought back with her, Thorn says, "How were the movies?" and gets an indecent kind of sound for an answer.

"You have fun at the movies?" Tubbit asks at supper. Catherine hasn't eaten very much; neither has Wade. Hot weather, probably. He brings in the apple pie.

"Oh—" Catherine's eyes are bright, and she laughs. "Same old thing. The women race cars and smash through roadblocks, and they've got all kinds of troubles with City Hall, or a Rival Mob. Or maybe it's a Principle—they've got to stick to some Principle. And the men change clothes and put on makeup and wait around, or visit jail."

"Sounds like a gangster movie," Tubbit says.

"And the second feature was full of men trying to get in a stage show—of course, some of them only want to get married. One of them finally gets the part . . . when the girls finally notice the men and kiss them, that's the end."

"Either one of you want ice cream on your pie?" Tubbit asks.

"I'd like some," Catherine says in a funny, tight voice.

"You want some ice cream?" Tubbit asks Thorn.

"I guess so," Thorn says. "I need to cool off, too."

Catherine is laughing when Tubbit goes out. When he comes

back with the ice cream, they're both gone. They're laughing somewhere upstairs. He goes to the bottom of the back steps and yells, "Hey, you better come enjoy it before it melts!"

So they do, but it doesn't cool them off much. When the sun goes down, lights of the new houses begin to show only a few blocks away. Cottonwood leaves move over the lights, making an intermittent sparkle where once there was nothing but the darkness of fields.

Catherine walks for a while after supper, trying to remember where the little houses were. Dogs had guarded them. Women hung washings to drip on newspapered floors, and passed whiskey bottles over the babies cradled in their laps. Now new houses line the streets; men in shirtsleeves water their lawns.

Two small girls are playing jacks on the sidewalk under a street-light. Women's voices come from a porch nearby: a desultory conversation cut into neat measures by the creak of a porch glider. There had once been long grass here, insects ticking, the lazy zing-zing-zing of cicadas in the elms, and dark that spread on all sides as far as she could feel it. She had run miles in the dark sometimes to race the moon, or stayed out all night to watch dawn come.

The girls have spread their skirts in a circle, their bare legs angled to make a diamond-shaped space for the jacks. A smaller child watches, and tries to stuff a toy bottle in the rubber *O* of a doll's mouth.

The same stars are overhead, and Catherine still knows the names of the gods and animals wheeling up there: cobweb shapes drawn between lights, dead men's lines chalked on a blackboard, a net to keep you from falling through into blackness.

The chink of jacks on cement pauses for a moment as Catherine comes into the light. "Hello," she says.

"Hello," one little girl says listlessly, shoving sausage-shaped curls off her forehead.

There had been a grove of sumacs here where the last new houses are, where the street sign says, "Northlawn." Catherine once piled snow in a heap among the sumacs, working until she sweated in the cold, heaping snow higher than she was. Then she lugged water from the house to pour over the snow pile until it was a glass mountain. She dug a doorway, burrowed in and up, heaved armfuls of snow out, panted white breath. At last she had a cave where she sat in the dark, listening to the cold, feeling how it crept closer and closer, until Tubbit came yelling for her, and Thorn told him she was all right, see, she built herself an igloo like an Eskimo.

Houses of ice. Summer tents. A hole roofed with boards and sod until even Thorn couldn't find her. She stayed hidden for days, leaving notes on the kitchen table when she could sneak in to say she was still alive, and where did Tubbit think his cherry pie had gone? She built her houses farther and farther from the sight of the roofs in the cottonwoods, until she slept, alone and afraid, where she couldn't see home at all.

The streetlight's circle shades away into dark. Looking back, Catherine sees the little girls watching her go, their hair ribbons as alert as ears, and more alert than their eyes. A radio is playing from an open window in the lot where her hideout hole was. A pilot aims his high plane for the light dying in the west. "Jeanie!" a woman calls from the sumac grove, from the miles of blowing grass that lead anywhere . . . "Time for bed now—come on!"

"Northlawn." The last street sign. Tubbit and Thorn brought her here in the old Model T when the houses were on an island of shade in a sea of grass.

The gravel road crackles under her sandals; sumac fronds reach from the dark. They'd parked in a patch of weeds by the sundial, Tubbit told her once, when the front yard was nothing but a field that had been mowed.

Cottonwood leaves shiver against the dim house wall. An island, and inside the island the house. Inside the house, Thorn. Stopping at the sundial, Catherine turns to watch, through the clear, hot air, the spreading lights lapping closer, north and south, a crescent of sparkle from which voices come, and the sound of cars, barking dogs, hammer strokes.

Catherine shuts her eyes, then turns to run toward another sound: the heavy rustle of water in air: Tubbit's sprinkler on the dark garden grass. Catherine kicks off her sandals and runs through the cold and hissing ring that is delicious, shocking.

"Come on out!" she cries, hurrying to the back door and calling up the stairs. "Thorn!"

The house is still hot from the day. Thorn comes to the top of the back stairs, a pair of pants sagging at his waist and rolled up to his knees. "Come out under the sprinkler!" Catherine says, darting up and past him, pulling off her shirt as she goes, kicking off her slacks, rummaging in her closet for a swimsuit. Light from the hall flickers over the planes of her body as she squirms into the tight tube, ties the halter, and is out in the hall again to pull him past the wallpaper roses and down the stairs.

Holding hands, they leap through the dense, hissing wheel and cling together in the center where the double nozzle spins. Mouths open, eyes shut, they gasp and shudder.

What's going on? Tubbit slides one of his kitchen curtains aside. Out in the sprinkler. Well, it's hot enough for that to feel good, but they better move it now and then—it's hard on the grass, jumping on it that way. "Move the sprinkler once in a while!" he calls, but he doesn't know whether they can hear him, shouting the way they are. Like a couple of kids, not just one.

The hissing wall of water blots everything out: stars, houses, garden, as they hang on to each other's warm slickness. Grass underfoot, half mud, sucks at their feet; silvery adders of water swarm down their skins between water bursts. As they shiver and gasp, the swinging swords of the water jets, inches from bare skin, build a wall between them and summer and spill into their laughing mouths.

Cold. Frozen to the bone. To step into the hot garden at last is to wrap themselves in warm wool that smells of roses and tobacco plant and damp earth; they crave warmth and dryness, as if winter rain has soaked in, or they have fallen through ice. Teeth chattering, they find towels in the dark bathroom upstairs and shed their dripping clothes in the tub. When they rub each other down, they scatter bits of grass from the newly cut lawn.

She has to choose. Nothing is enough. Cold kisses aren't enough, or cold skin against skin, turning warm under her hands.

She has to choose. Thorn's room is dark, but she knows what to do. Scared, she has to go on choosing, asking, "Is that it?" when it hurts, "Is that the way?"

And then she knows it is, just as you recognize the moon. And why shouldn't they both be crying?

But then it's funny, so they laugh.

11

Thorn wakes at dawn. Catherine sleeps in his arms under a tangle of long hair like Janet's brown silk, but Marthe and Claire have been whispering in his dream: "Come on! Before Mama wakes up—hurry!"

He was so little, and his legs were too short; Marthe and Claire had to carry him over cobblestones in the autumn air before dawn.

When they came to the beech wood it smelled bitter and wet with the first frosts. Down on all fours in the dark, the three of them stuffed beechnuts in sacks and pockets while the man who owned the trees slept in his dark house. Its facade beyond the grove grew pale with dawn, like a face turned their way.

"Wash your feet in the horse trough before anyone sees!" Then he climbed into bed like a piece of ice to thaw between two others who smelled of air and forest floor. Beechnuts, buried near their back gate, had the rich, oily crunch of larceny itself, and danger, and daring.

Go to France. But nothing can bring back pigtailed adventurers in the mushroom hollows and flower fields, cramming elderberries into purple mouths. Until there were polished shoes and petticoats to keep clean. The sharp eyes of boys after church. Blackened lamp chimneys to be scoured. They watched him leave that house for good, their voices soft, their eyes avoiding his.

Birds are beginning to sing. Thorn smooths Catherine's hair back, but damp strands stick to her cheek. He looks at his big hand, and the skin beginning to wrinkle in the loose web at the base of his thumb. Catherine's small hand touches his breast on the sheet. If the smallest women had been chosen as brides for centuries—what had been left on the spinster heap?

There had been the wideness of her childhood, and the thirst. Now would her days narrow, like a funnel? The smell of sun on dust. The calling of rooks. "If Catherine can't win, at least she can *know*"; Janet's voice, and the rustling of straw in the barn. He had been young, with no wrinkles on his hands, and he hadn't wanted a cripple.

He eases his shoulder and arm away from Catherine's weight and sits on the bed edge. Cool air plays over his bare skin.

Catherine's small breasts are pressed together under her arm; first light follows her jaw line, coils in her ear, picks out the down on an arm, the gleam of stretched skin on a kneecap. But she is guarded even in sleep: her self plays over her, armed, like Pallas Athena, even against him. And she has approached him, step by step . . . she has bled and been hurt by her own choice, exploring him, and will know what it is, and what it is not, and he can be that for her. A robin warbles on a branch at the windowsill; the morning air is damp.

Now Catherine half wakes, sighs, gropes for the sheet and, with the ease of a solitary sleeper, appropriates the whole bed. Her bare arms, flung above her head, are fixed in their curve like wings; her hair ripples away from her sleeping face. If her face were hidden, her body would still express the reticence, the self-respect, like Rilke's poem about the sculptured torso, "breaking out of all its contours like a star: for there is no place that does not see you. You must change your life."

There's a blade of grass on his pillow, and another on the sheet. Thorn holds them in his hand, watching them melt and swim under his wet eyes. Not to be thirsty to know and to explore. To be smart and defiant and determined not to fail. Hobbling, smiling, dragging fashionable clothes along. Clinging. Soft. Sweet. Sly.

"Don't!" Catherine says at his back. She pulls him around and kneels, hugging him. "Don't worry about it—I'm not as worried about the future as I sound—I'm happy—look!" She leaps out of bed in the first shaft of sunshine, pulling him with her past the oval-backed chair where a child, for a second, is curled up, twisting a lock of hair, thoughtful.

Two serious faces in his creaking dresser mirror. Two bare bodies as expressive as faces, half green with the light through June leaves. "We're the same people," Catherine says. "It doesn't change anything, the way all the songs and movies say it does. But it's nice, and I like it, even if you do get used to it." She faces him, holding him against her with a tight grip. "I had to know, didn't I? You were only sixteen when you started!" She pulls his head down to kiss him, and murmurs over and over how she loves him.

"And it's only love," Catherine says, letting him go. She leans toward her mirrored self, bare and lovely as a statue. And what if

Pygmalion, able to shape his Galatea, had dared to stand back and let her shed her own marble chips like eggshell?

"See how green I am?" Catherine asks. The sun through leaves makes her look like a woman under water, washed by that green light. "Wait until you come back home." She scowls as she bends to her reflection; her breasts, firm and green, lengthen a little, and her hair slides over them. "Caterpillar!" she says to herself in the mirror.

12

July comes, and the days pass, heavy with leaves and rain and the force that locks the two of them together in dark or light, at the top of the stairs, in the barn's dusk, in deep grass. Has she tried everything there is to try? Catherine asks, dragging a sheet downstairs to the cool parlor. They lie in the dark beside the tall china vase, listening to night noises through open windows. The Chinaman on the vase is watching them from his round window, Catherine supposes, his teapot and his cup before him.

"And what if people don't know each other the way we do?" Catherine asks.

Insects fill the darkness beyond the parlor windows with the scraping of chitin on chitin, rasping of plates, wing covers, leg segments, until the sound of cars on Seven Mile Road is veiled in whatever the insect chorus is saying over and over. "I'm so happy, and so are you," Catherine murmurs in Thorn's ear. "And I'm safe here. That's the trouble." The moan of a truck thrusts through the insect curtain to underscore her words; Thorn reaches out to touch, for a moment, whatever his hand finds: a smooth thigh, a breast.

Catherine laughs, and tickles him, but when he grabs for her, she's gone past the vase and the mottled glimmer of a fireplace mirror. Her bare feet whisper on the hall floor. He catches her in the kitchen, snatching her up, tickling and kissing her, muttering nonsense from shared books and jokes, silly spells when they had rocked and snorted and wept with laughter, man and child together.

"Oh, don't!" Catherine begs at last. "My stomach's sore from laughing, and I'm so thirsty!" She's giggling yet, held high in his arms, his face against her breasts that vibrate with her laughter. He has only to bend her backward, looping her hair up with one hand, and turn on the kitchen faucet with the other. The water is cold and delicious; Catherine pulls his head down, too, and they share, biting into the rush of it from the old brass faucet, until their mouths are cold when they kiss.

The brass faucet glitters with sun at seven o'clock the next morning: Catherine watches Tubbit turn it on to fill the teakettle. "Summer's going to be a hot one," he says, clapping on the kettle lid. He can hear Wade coming downstairs. "Here's the toast," he says, handing Catherine the plate.

When Catherine puts the toast on the table by Thorn, he doesn't look up. Tubbit is in the kitchen. "It's like learning to drink coffee," Catherine says softly, sitting down and taking a sip of her own. "You depend on it. You get used to it." She smiles at Thorn. He doesn't smile.

"Already seventy-five in the shade," Tubbit says, coming in with the eggs. "And it's not even eight o'clock."

Thorn tries to swallow a bite of toast. He doesn't want to talk, or look at anybody. Christ. But the memory of dawn comes back . . . only a few hours ago . . . even if he doesn't want to think of it: the birds singing, and he was dreaming, and he'd reached for Catherine. He gets the toast swallowed with a drink of coffee. No, not for Catherine. She'd been smaller than he was—was that it?—and was *his*, for that second before he'd stopped, wide awake at last. Christ.

"Seventy-five. I just checked," Tubbit says.

The girl he'd reached for hadn't been Catherine. Catherine sits before him buttering her toast; her long hair shines in the morning light. The girl he'd grabbed had been smaller than he was, and had wanted to be conquered—made herself his quarry. Until he woke, and she was Catherine.

Catherine puts marmalade on her toast, her calm eyes on Tubbit. "You eating marmalade with your toast, or toast with your marmalade?" Tubbit asks, grinning.

"Toast with my marmalade—if it's *your* marmalade!" Catherine says, and Tubbit laughs.

The girls on postcards presented their bloomered bottoms like a dare—he'd seen the postcards before he was ten. Not like any girls or women he knew. The boys giggled and pointed. The cards were dog-eared, and it was all right if men saw you looking at them.

"Seventy-five in the shade," Tubbit says, going out.

Catherine had known, even half awake, that there was something wrong. The arrogance. The domination. "Don't," she had murmured in her drowsiness.

Thorn watches Catherine crack her boiled egg and knife it neatly out of its white cups, until his throat eases enough for him to swallow another bite.

"Don't," she had said.

Catherine's calm glance follows Tubbit out the swinging door, then meets Thorn's eyes before he can look away.

13

August, and the last day. Hot wind stirs the leaves over Tubbit's cottage where he naps after lunch; the sun drops to meet black clouds at the horizon.

Kneeling on Thorn's bed, Catherine runs her fingers through his thick hair. "I feel small . . ." she says. "No . . . it's not really being small." When she lies beside him, her eyes are so close to his that he can see the multicolors of their blue. "Just . . . unimportant."

The cool sweep of the crooning electric fan brushes over their bare bodies, over and back, over and back. "Except when they talk about love, and then you're important, kind of." Catherine's voice is muffled now against his shoulder. "Or if you have babies. But not really. Babies don't really count."

Thorn says nothing; Catherine lies still. The breeze has stopped; leaves hang limp in the hot air. "I never noticed there was nobody like me in the garage, learning about transmissions," Catherine says at last. "Nobody like me was ever asking questions at the Ford Hospital."

The first thunder rolls like a barrel over the roof; the sun goes under. "You feel as if you've lost something, or . . ." Catherine sits up. "As if it's been taken away and you didn't even know it. You keep on thinking you can do things—" Thunder peals again; lightning flashes. "And nobody ever says you can't. They don't need to."

Now the space they occupy is dim, like an old photograph, and has the quality of pictured air. "That's why I don't think we should write each other," Catherine says. "You'll have enough trouble over there, and I have to do it alone. Besides . . . you'll be back before long." She bends to kiss him; leaves through the window turn livid green, fluttering beyond the monotone dusk of the room. "I don't really believe I can't," Catherine whispers against Thorn's mouth. She sits up again. "I don't."

"No." Thorn's face is turned away from what light there is; she can see only a shadow. "You don't."

"Did my mother ever believe it?"

Thorn lies without moving. "She said she never really had a choice. She got married. It was so easy."

The green darkens; the silent garden is as intense and deep as a jungle, waiting. Catherine watches it, both hands pushing back her long hair. "So where can I go?" she asks.

Storm wind thrusts suddenly into the room's close air, smelling of rain and distances. The fan hums back and forth like a toy. Then the rain's tattoo strikes a hundred leaves at once.

Thorn swings his feet to the dark floor and goes to push the windows down. Still sitting on the dim bed, Catherine watches his broad-shouldered shape disappear into the hall, hears other windows close, hears his bare feet descending the stairs.

Now there is no sound but rain beating on the windows. The room's still air brightens and darkens as lightning follows thunder. Catherine sits alone in the dusk, in the steady beat of falling drops.

Wind, dense with rain, rushes through the cottonwoods. Thorn's room is alive with the sound of waterdrops on glass, a dark, sheltered place he returns to, finding Catherine in her long hair, her breath brushing against his chest as he holds her. "Tomorrow you have to go!" she cries. "And it isn't over, and how can we ever—" Her tears spill over; neither of them hears the rain any more.

They open their eyes to sun. Its brilliance strikes the mirror, the oval-backed chair, the lion's feet of the highboy: its light shines like their joy.

"But this really is all, isn't it?" Catherine asks. Happiness half shuts their eyes and binds them to the bed and each other like exhaustion. "Until I'm grown," Catherine says after a long while.

"You have to treat me like somebody younger and smaller now, but when we're the same—just imagine!" Her eyes glow. "What more could we want? Just imagine!"

14

August 25, 1939

DEAR MR. LAIRD:

I figured you want to know he has gone off to New York and is sailing to England today and then going to France. He says he has got to find his cousins there.

Any time you want to drop in is fine. Catherine has not made up her mind about going to college right away yet.

KARL TUBBIT

IV

A water tower to stand
for monumental thirst
straddles our graveyard,
bears the town's name and
brims with iron-red hard
water, a toast raised up
to common things we die
without. Across the flat land
we see that landmark first
when we turn homeward, come to lie
down under that lifted cup.

1

"You're bound to be lonely for a while," Jack Laird says, watching Tubbit pour coffee. "But in Cedar Falls you can have a little vacation, have a change, get to know people your own age."

"We're so glad you can come visit us!" Alice Knapp says, smiling. She's a plump woman, fashionably dressed in a voile suit and pearls. She looks kind. "My brother's told us so much about you that we feel like you're already part of our family."

Without Thorn this house seems overrun with strangers who all look at Catherine the same way. Their eyes slide over her as if they can read so easily what they want to see. Alice sits in the same dining room chair that Thorn once sat in, his arms around Catherine, his mouth against her bare shoulder, when he said: "She wanted you to have your eyes wide open . . . not to just feel that something was wrong, like she did."

Catherine only wanders around the house, Jack says to his sister. Alice can see how it is—Catherine stuck away out here with two men to raise her. You can see she's been crying, and she just doesn't say much, does she? Acts like she's dreaming.

The shirts in Thorn's closet keep his faint scent, and a brush in one of Thorn's highboy drawers has a few of his hairs winding through its bristles. She sleeps in her own bed without Thorn, who was the center, the core that wasn't, after all, enough.

Germans and Russians have signed a pact now; France and England are mobilizing.

"We might buy you some new clothes. That's always something that cheers a gal up. And maybe get you a new hairdo?" Alice says.

Of course she has to think. That's one of the reasons Thorn left—to let her think. She'd better do it. Stay out of Thorn's room. Listen to Alice Knapp. She can do whatever she wants to do. If she goes to Iowa, she doesn't have to stay, but she has to try living with other people now. Strange people in this house, but everything else just as it has always been—horribly just the same. She's thought it over, she tells them, and she'd like to visit in Cedar Falls with the Knapps, if they want her to come for a while.

"Of course we do!" Alice says. "We'll all be delighted! And I'll just see if I can find a good beauty shop tomorrow morning, and we'll get that out of the way, and then we can buy clothes in Waterloo on the way home."

It isn't enough, not even when the two of you come back to earth, floating like butterflies, and settle again into your own skins, still out of breath with the power of it. Books and movies and plays and fairytales end with weddings—why? You may feel like you're floating, but the world isn't different when you come down. Waking locked together, you can hear the sound of cars on the streets, or a plane going over.

The beauty shop smells like ten perfumes mixed together. Catherine sits in the hot, narrow booth and watches her hair being cut with the silvery sound hair makes against a blade. She watches them attach her, strand by strand and clamp by clamp, to a kind of chandelier on wheels.

It cooks what's left of her hair into corkscrews, and makes it smell like it's burning. There are hot places on her scalp. Then she has to lie back again to have her hair soaped and rinsed in the sink while sharp fingernails scoop the corkscrews behind her ears, and Alice chatters about her sons Dick and Stevie, and her little girl, Babs. And her daughter Margie's a high school cheerleader this year, she tells the beauty operator.

Jack and Alice and everybody think hair is very important; Catherine can see that. She sits watching them fix hers, but she isn't there at all. She's where grass is waist high, and it stirs in currents of summer morning air. You leave no track in it, and you lie naked together on that prickling floor between grass walls and a ceiling of such deep blue that you seem to turn into it on the bed of the turning world. Only grasshoppers watch, their honeycomb eyes multiplying two into enough couples to populate a world, she supposes.

Tiny mirrored ecstasies. And Alice Knapp asks how does she like it? Catherine holds up the mirror they hand her and looks at her head.

"Very nice," she says, and Alice Knapp looks pleased. She looks pleased when they've got Catherine's bags packed, and said goodbye to Tubbit, and the old Victorian house disappears behind its cottonwoods as they start the trip to Iowa. She looks pleased when she talks about the clothes they'll buy Catherine on the way home.

Catherine watches Alice's pleased face, and Jack's, but what she sees is Thorn's face at the train station, pale and stunned the way hers must have been, saying goodbye and I'll-be-back without looking at her, as if he couldn't imagine ever coming back, stunned as he was, stunned as they both were, saying goodbye to all of it.

Nothing is quite right, and Alice can't figure it out. She ought to know what high school kids are like—Margie and her friends are always running in and out, and Dick's too. The way Catherine just stands in her new clothes. Margie would be twisting and dancing around to see herself in the mirror, so fussy about every little thing that she thought made her look "too fat" or "too young" or something. Catherine just stands.

Myrtle, Alice's favorite salesgirl, sort of hangs the clothes on Catherine, saying how pretty Catherine is and how this or that is just her color. Poor Myrtle: she's trying to get Catherine interested, but all Catherine will say is that the dresses and slacks and formals and so on are very nice, and you can tell that Myrtle thinks Catherine is, well, odd. Even when Catherine tries on hats, she just lets Alice pick out a couple, finally, as if she doesn't care. It's not normal, that's all, but Catherine looks as if she thinks it is, and so you get a little mad somehow, but you don't know why. But you have to remember that Catherine hasn't had a chance to lead a normal, natural life.

2

Catherine watches Iowa fields blur, but the rippling shadow of Jack's car is steady, a black shape thrown across roadside ditches by the low-lying sun. Green walls of corn fall open to streak after streak of bare earth, dizzying as the spokes of a turning wheel— Catherine shuts her eyes, then opens them to look between Alice Knapp and Jack to the black car's radiator ornament. It advances smoothly on a highway striped with late afternoon shade.

Now and then Jack's dark eyes watch her in the rear-view mirror; she can feel them. Her throat closes, she blinks, and Jack, watching that face in the mirror, clamps his teeth, clamps his hands on the wheel, hardly sees the road.

"Margie's got extra curlers, and she'll help you put your hair up." Mrs. Knapp thrusts herself sidewise in the front seat, her plump profile to Catherine. "Even with a permanent you'll have to put it up most nights—Margie does. Do you like Catherine's hairdo?" she asks her brother's grim face above the wheel.

"Very pretty." Jack looks into the mirror and sees those dark red lips that won't say Thorn's name, and those light blue eyes, and what is she remembering, Jesus Christ. "We're a little late."

"Men don't understand!" Mrs. Knapp says with a conspiratorial smile for Catherine. "It takes time to go to beauty parlors and pick out clothes, and don't you like Myrtle? She always finds just what you want. We couldn't have shopped in Detroit—I just couldn't. All that traffic, and I don't know the stores, but Waterloo . . . " She turns to look through the windshield. "There's Cedar Falls, see? Across the river. There it is! There's home!"

Alice Knapp beams at the river between bridge rails. "There's Main Street just over the bridge—the farmers come in Saturdays to shop and go to our one movie theater."

Elms arch overhead; the streets are cool with them, and green with lawns. "There's the women's club house." A child on roller skates holds tight to a stop sign and stares at Catherine.

Alice is telling who lives in houses with wide front and side porches; strange names go by in a procession. Then a cluster of shop windows climbs a brick street. "Our local stores. The college kids call this 'Dogtown.'"

"And there's the dean's house—we have to live on campus." Brick gates are lettered "Class of 1912." Beyond the brick gates, a brick drive, a brick house. "We see lots of the students, though, living here," Alice says as the car pulls up to the steps. "Welcome home, Catherine. I hope," she climbs stiffly out of the car, "Margie and Dick aren't off somewhere."

The house is dim and still. "Here they are," whispers Dick up the stairs.

"Oh, gosh—you look!" Margie comes downstairs with Babs and Stevie. "Mom says she's got to go to the dance!"

"There's Jack the Ladykiller—let's have a swoon now." Dick scowls through the front door curtain, Stevie's head just under his chin.

"O-o-o-o!" breathes Margie, rolling her lips together to be sure her lipstick is smooth.

"There she is—getting out! She hasn't got a hat on. Brown hair . . . nice legs, anyway. Hey," Dick pulls the curtain apart a little more, "not bad. Not bad at all. Hey! In fact, good!"

"Honest?" Margie looks. "For gosh sake, they're practically at the door—they'll see us! Stevie! Babs! Let's be in the dining room and just come in!"

Jack opens the door for Alice and Catherine. The entry hall and parlors are arranged for institutional uses: smooth sofas, bare tables, thick rugs, stiff drapes, and an air of waiting. "Mar-jorie?" Alice calls to the hotel lobby silence. "Richar-r-rd?"

"Hi, Mom!" cries Margie with a little flurry of surprise, her blonde pageboy swinging as she peeks around the door and then comes in, Dick following. Babs runs for Jack, grabs him as high as she can reach, and jabs his stomach with her red head; he laughs and swings her around and asks her how his favorite red-headed niece is, now that she's almost ready for school. Stevie stands at a distance, eyeing his uncle.

"Here's Margie, and Dick . . . and Babs and Stevie. You'll have a sister in the same high school class, Catherine, and a brother who's a junior. And here's Catherine, kids!" Alice is smooth; she somehow has them moving up the wide front stairs already. "You show Catherine your room, Margie, and we'll leave you children alone until supper to get acquainted. Jack, you know where you belong." Alice and Jack go off down the hall, leaving Dick, Margie and Catherine alone in a doorway.

"Well, here's the old dive—make yourself at home," Margie says, smiling at Catherine. "Hope you can take two new sisters and two new brothers all in one day—Dick can bring up your cases." She shows Catherine the bathroom, and where her towels are.

Margie's room is ruffled and white, a nest of organdy, except for the wall behind the twin beds. Catherine has on a sharp cotton two-piece that shows her figure all right, and her lipstick exactly matches the red plaid.

"I like your hairdo," Margie says, plumping down on one of the beds.

Catherine says, "Thank you," and looks from their bobby socks and loafers to the wall above the beds, papered five feet high with brilliantly colored pictures from magazines.

"How do you like my kissing wall?" Margie says, leaning back on her elbows to look at a hundred couples in each other's arms, mouth to mouth. "Dick says it's dopey—he thinks he's been around!" She giggles at Catherine. "Say, you've been kissed lots, haven't you? How many times?" She giggles again and swings one foot. "Now that we're practically sisters."

"Yes." Catherine sits down on the other bed and looks at the couples above her ruffled pillow.

"Lots of times, I bet. Mobs of men. Well, you'll practically die in this town, that's all. There's just about two boys in our great big senior class of thirty-five that aren't zombies."

Dick swings two suitcases inside the door. "Hey—let's see all your stuff!" Margie cries, leaping up. "Want to see my formal for the dance next Saturday?" She shuts the door on Dick and drags one suitcase up on her bed.

Catherine's fingernails match her lipstick and her sharp cotton dress. Her hairdo bounces on her shoulders just like Margie's, and her legs are just the right tan. Only her eyes . . .

"Wow!" Margie says. "You got a formal for the dance!" She swoops around the room with the baby blue confection held in front of her. "I'll get Jim Becker—he's my steady—to talk to Bob Henderson—tell him you're new in town!"

"Supper, you two." Alice Knapp smiles around the edge of the door. "Don't you like Catherine's formal?"

"In the groove!" Margie says. "Come on, Catherine, aren't you starved?" Leading Catherine down the hall with one arm around her waist, Margie is watching Jack on the stairs. "Isn't he just a dreamboat?" There's the sound of feet running behind them. "For Pete's sake!" Margie says. Five-year-old Babs is trailing behind them in a long pink dress. "What do you want to wear that for?"

"It's my new dress—you got yours!"

"Well, put on your Mary Janes at least—"

"Will you look at my little princess!" Jack says from the foot of the stairs. The child gives one defiant glance to Margie, then tips her head sidewise and sidles downstairs, clinging to the bannister, all smiles. Jack snatches her up and says to Catherine, "Isn't she cute, all dressed up?"

"Honey . . . come on, you can't go to supper with your hair like that!" Alice turns the little girl back upstairs. "Where's your shoes?"

"Kids," Margie says.

"Well, well," a short, fat man in glasses says. He stands near the dining room table in the green light of a summer evening. The bay window behind him frames oaks and elms, grass, two old cannon, and students strolling hand in hand.

"Back from a late faculty meeting?" Jack says. "Catherine, here's George Knapp, Margie's dad. Catherine Buckingham, George. New member of the family."

"Glad to have you," George Knapp says in a rumbling voice from somewhere under his double-breasted suit coat. "Margie's always wanted a sister your age." He has a large, well-trained smile. "Where's Alice, and Babs?"

"Primping, I believe," Jack says.

"She wants to wear her formal," Margie says, voice descending with ennui. "You sit here by me, Catherine."

The room is too big for the big table. Through an archway Catherine can see a parlor full of stiff furniture, draperies in exact folds, and lamps too dim to read by.

"Here we are!" Alice says in a jolly voice, so that everyone looks at Babs trailing reluctantly behind. She wears a bunch of paper forget-me-nots on a hair ribbon and wrist ribbon, and shiny shoes under her "formal." Suffering herself to be led to her junior chair, she tramples net ruffles getting in, but keeps her head down even when her plump stomach is tight against the table edge.

"Oh, look . . ." Jack whispers. "Somebody's so pretty. And so shy." Glancing across at Catherine, he cannot begin to read the look in her eyes.

"Now, Babs!" Alice says. The little girl is sliding down in her chair. "Act like a little lady," her mother whispers.

"And how has the world been treating you, young man?" Jack says to Stevie.

Small for his age, the little boy is no bigger than Babs; he sits with his shoulder blades pasted to his chair back and looks his uncle in the eye. "Fine," he says gravely, holding tight to the table edge with both hands. "Did you find the erector wheels?"

"I'll tell you something," Jack says. "The stores were all out in Chicago. But do you remember when the king and queen of England were here?"

"Yes. I saw the movie," says the child gravely.

"I was in New York that day, and I found the wheels there."

The little boy's glowing eyes look as if he'd like to jump up— run in excitement. He only holds tighter to the table edge. "How nice!" Alice says to her brother. "You shouldn't have bothered."

"How's the swim team this year?" Jack asks Dick.

"Dick's top freestyler already," Alice says.

"No!" Jack says. "Well, I'll be darned! Freestyle!" He slaps grinning Dick on the back.

"Mommy?" Babs says loudly. "Can I sing my song for Uncle Jack?"

"Margie's one of the cheerleaders, too," George says, helping himself to the steak the housekeeper offers on a platter. The woman's gray hair is pulled back in a bun; she keeps her eyes down and no expression on her face. "Mrs. Hansen," George says, smiling up at her, "this is the new member of our family, Catherine Buckingham."

"Not now, dear. Later," Alice says.

"Quite an honor to be cheerleader," Jack says to Margie, his dark eyebrows rising. Margie tips her head to one side and smiles. Jack isn't watching her, but Catherine; he sees the flicker of Catherine's glance from Margie to Babs, and back again. Thorn taught her table manners, whatever else he—hate runs through Jack, hotter than the steaming coffee the housekeeper pours in his cup. Margie and Catherine sit side by side, two high school girls. He has to give Alice credit: Catherine looks just right, looks fine—beautiful.

Margie goes on and on about cheerleading; Jack hardly hears. His face wears a bland smile: he's aware Margie is tossing her head and fluttering her eyelashes. That awful long, straight hair is gone, and you can see those beautiful cheekbones she got from Janet, and that delicate little nose, and what's she remembering, for Christ's sake?

"If I don't absolutely die!" Margie pauses for breath. "If you get what I mean."

"Sounds 'super,'" Jack says. Margie drops her glance shyly and looks everywhere but Jack. George begins to talk about college enrollments.

Seeming to listen politely, Jack is aware that her eyes don't dart here and there, smiling and attentive. She gives Margie the same profound attention she gives Babs, or Alice (who now describes a recent victory George had at faculty meeting), or the housekeeper bringing in dessert.

Eating cake, drinking coffee, Jack remembers that Dorothy had been disgusted: a little girl stuck out there like that with only two men to raise her. And Shirley said it wasn't really normal; anybody could see that.

"Can I now? Can I?" Babs is out of her chair the minute dessert and the last coffee disappear. So they follow her bobbing forget-me-nots into the front parlor where the piano is.

What a cute little flirt. Jack smiles at Babs. All girl, and not even in school yet. Alice strikes a few chords on the piano and complains that she's out of practice. There had been a child kneeling to look at doll's clothes spilled out of a box, her eyes as level and thoughtful as if she were learning something. At the last flourish of chords, Babs laces her fingers together, a sweet smile on her face, tips her head to one side, and in a small, breathy soprano sings that someday her prince will come and someday they'll meet again, her long pink dress switching from side to side.

Wiggles and grins and rolling eyes. How lovely that moment will be when the prince of her dreams comes, she sings. Alice executes a long series of trills and runs, as if she, too, thinks Babs will have a prince come for her, and is embellishing the prospect.

Babs warbles that the prince will whisper "I love you," and steal a kiss or two. Jack smiles, and everybody else but Catherine is smiling, too. The kid is really cute in that formal.

The melody goes too high now: Babs has to squeak valiantly that he's far, far away but she'll find her love someday, someday when her dreams come true. She holds her dreamy smile through the last chord, then giggles and runs to Jack, squirming into his lap, her forget-me-not hair ribbon over one ear. "What a knockout!" Jack says. "You ought to be in the movies!"

Everybody claps. "Cute kid!" Jack says to Catherine, watching Babs run upstairs. He's alone with Catherine in the front parlor for a moment.

"Isn't she cute?" Jack asks.

Catherine doesn't want to answer; he can see that, and she draws away from him as if she were in some incomprehensible place. Well, this is a nice, normal, everyday family—it's not like living alone with two men—

Babs has run back down the stairs. "I got forget-me-nots all down the front, see?" she asks Jack, pulling up the net of her long skirt to show the paper flowers on the slip.

"How about that!" Jack says. What a little flirt she is. Satisfied, Babs climbs the stairs again, skirts bunched in each hand, and Jack smiles at Catherine.

Catherine doesn't smile back. Those eyes so much like Janet's . . . "It's all behind you!" Jack says suddenly, his voice as low as it is violent. "Just try to forget it all! And don't worry—you'll hear from him." He can't say Thorn's name.

"We decided not to write." Catherine's face is without any expression. "And now England's at war . . ."

"Catherine! Guess what!" Margie comes running from the phone in the back hall. "Jim got Bob, and Bob wants to take you to the big dance next Saturday! Bob's the big wheel in the senior class! Are we lucky—he had a fight with his steady!"

Catherine only stares, and here's Margie so young and cute, tossing her pageboy around and trying out her new mascara, Jack bets. "That's great!" he says. "Do you know how to dance?" he asks Catherine.

"No."

"You can't dance?" Margie looks blank.

"Aw, c'mon, there's nothing to it—I can teach her," Jack says.

"Got some records downstairs? What do you kids do around here? Jitterbug?"

"Not much. Not with long formals on anyway." Margie leads the way through the dining room and back hall and down the basement stairs. The cellar floor is painted dark red, and there are no rugs in one of the big, cool rooms. She starts turning over a pile of records by a record player. "Bob isn't wild like some of those goons. How about 'Deep Purple'? It's slow."

"Okay. Now, look, Catherine—it's simple. I just step once to the side like this, bring my feet together, and then step again and wait. One . . . two . . . three. Four," Jack says, pacing it out to the lush croon of the orchestra. "The main thing you have to do is relax and not try to go any way at all—just let the man lead."

Nothing about taking a girl in his arms is strange to Jack except taking this one, warm and light and tall and so young that she can't hide her embarrassment at being held. "Just pretend you've danced with a hundred boys—act bored," he says, without hearing the words, only thinking that Thorn must have held her as close as this thousands of times, watching her grow up, watching her become as beautiful as Janet . . .

"Hey—smooth!" Margie says, clapping and watching the brown loafers and ankle socks follow the shining black shoes. "You're getting it!" What a dancer Jack is—not like those grabby boys—and goes to swell places in Chicago with beautiful women. And those dark eyes of his, sparkling as if he's madly wicked, and his cheek against Catherine's hair, gee. He's got his eyes shut. The record wails about sleepy garden walls and the mist of a memory.

Nothing, Jack thinks. Nothing could have happened. Just a kid who's been stuck out in the country away from everything. So slim and light and warm. Janet.

He opens his eyes. "That's right!" He grins into the blue eyes inches from his. Sober as a judge. "Just relax. Hey, Margie, how about another record—I'm enjoying myself. Take you on next." Catherine's hand is wet, and she doesn't look at him any more. Doesn't she like it? Her hair shines and tumbles in curls and smells good . . .

Margie is nothing like Catherine: she chatters and smiles at him and follows his lead with little groans of "Smooth!" No feel-

ing travels from her body to his except energy, the kind Babs
gives off. Catherine is wiping her hands on her pleated skirt and
watching.

"Now a waltz!" Jack says. He demonstrates the steps to "The
Blue Danube." Catherine comes more easily into his arms this
time, and he feels dry-mouthed and breathless. Just a kid, and
he's more than twenty years older, and what will the boys in high
school . . . "Take it easy with the guys here," he says in a low
voice. "They'll be sizing you up, trying to see how far they can get
with a city girl, so you be pretty standoffish—you can afford to be!
They'll all be after you for dates, giving you a line . . . "

3

When Catherine wakes, it seems as if she hears Thorn
laugh—as if her head is on his furry chest, or the exact shape of
his mouth trembles on hers.

Then she is looking at Margie's room. Its white organdy turns
blue with dawn.

The feeling it gives her is peculiar: like trying to walk through
water, or grope in a cloud for something solid. The dressing table
is an organdy mound, and the windows are organdy-bordered
dawn sky, and all too clean to be real. Stuffed animals watch her
with empty button eyes, but above her is a wall of kissing couples,
mouth to mouth.

"Hi!" Margie says from the other bed. For a minute, half
asleep, Margie looks like a person, rather awkward and thoughtful, but then she climbs out, aluminum curlers rattling all over
her head, and begins to twist and jerk her body in the peculiar
way she has.

What's Catherine going to wear? she asks. When she comes
back from the bathroom, Margie stands at their closet door pushing clothes back and forth on the rods. If Catherine wears her
pink cotton suit, then she can wear her blue one. Or should they
both wear dresses? Slacks are hot, and it's going to be awfully hot
today.

"Do you think you'd like your hair in a pageboy?" Margie asks,
starting to help Catherine with her curlers. Margie's always trying
to be graceful, as if she wants to flutter through the day very light-

ly, but it's awkward getting the curlers out of Catherine's hair.

Catherine's head aches from lying on the curlers all night. She wishes Margie would stay like the girl in the bed, and not jerk her head on one side or the other, pursing her lips, laughing that little-girl laugh. It's as bad as her little sister rubbing up and down against Jack, and Alice Knapp does it, too—

Thirty little brown sausages hang on Catherine's shoulders. The room has nothing in it but furniture and clothes and stuffed animals. Margie is brushing and curling over and curling under, and explaining. They can both wear the pink lipstick, even if they have got red nail polish on.

"Well!" Jack says when they come into the dining room. "The beautiful twins!" Margie laughs, and Alice has that pleased look. After breakfast Jack says he's leaving, but Catherine's in good hands, and he'll be back before long for the picnic Alice is planning.

When Jack is gone, Margie says, "C'mon and I'll show you the rest of the house."

The rooms, as far as Catherine can see, have nothing but furniture and clothes and knickknacks and a few books in them, except for the kitchen.

"What do you do when you have time?" Catherine asks Margie.

"Hobbies, you mean?" Margie wears her blank look again. "Like stamps or embroidering or something like that?"

"I guess so."

"I used to collect stamps. When I was a little kid."

Catherine waits, but Margie says nothing more. "Well," Catherine says, "I'd like to take a walk around the campus and find out where everything is. You don't have to take me—I know you have things to do." Going down the stairs, she says, "I'll be back at noon. Will that be all right?"

It's okay, Margie tells her, and watches Catherine out of sight down the walk to the auditorium building. There's really nothing wrong, is there? Kids from big cities probably like to go around strange places by themselves.

Catherine comes back in plenty of time for lunch. Well, Margie and her mother say the minute they see her, where have you been?

Learning about the generators in the heating plant, Catherine says. It's hot in there with all the steam.

That explains what's happened to her hair, Margie says, and did anybody see her on the way home?

Catherine went to see the generators in the heating plant this morning, Alice tells her husband at lunch. He says that's nice.

It's just too hot to do anything, Margie complains, but if Catherine comes upstairs, she'll put up Catherine's hair again, and then it'll look nice for supper. None of the girls will be coming over today, anyway. And why don't they try the new peach nail polish to go with the lipstick?

To be able to tell Thorn how it is, lying with him in the dark buzz and sweep of an electric fan, smelling the sprinkler-soaked garden under the window. Grass blades scattered over the bed in the dawn light. To say, "It's not like movies or books—it's worse. Or is it just this family, and this place?" The remembered cottonwoods and the old house are beginning to grow huge, it seems, like a walled and turreted castle. To open the front door with its beveled window is to open a door on fields and sky. It doesn't make sense. Thorn's mouth is warm and his hair is soft and thick, and once she could almost hide in his arms, kissing . . . Catherine watches Margie winding her hair on aluminum curlers. "You had your hair real long before?" Margie asks. Catherine nods.

"And you never even put it up?" Margie asks, frowning a little.

No, Catherine says, she just washed it. Margie keeps on frowning as she turns Catherine's hair under to make a pageboy.

Honestly, Margie says to her mother just before dinner, whispering in case Catherine comes down the hall, she doesn't know anything about hair or how to put polish on, or anything, and she doesn't know how to dance—she doesn't know how to do much of anything.

"You teach her then," Alice says, wishing one more time that she didn't have to wear a corset to supper. "That's what Uncle Jack wanted us to do—help her to get used to living out in the world, not stuck away where nothing ever happens and she never learns anything."

The dean's house is quiet after supper except for Mrs. Hansen doing the dishes, and the radio in the downstairs study. Everyone is listening to Charlie McCarthy, and when Catherine whispers to Alice that she's going out for a walk and will be back about nine, Alice is laughing at the way gorgeous Hedy Lamarr is flirting with Mortimer Snerd—she doesn't really think about what Catherine is saying. When she finally realizes what it was, Catherine is gone.

"Out walking?" George Knapp says.

"She just said she was going out for a walk and she'd be back by nine," Alice says. "I was listening to the radio, and I didn't really think—"

"By herself?" Margie asks. "Boy, wouldn't I get it if I tried that!"

"It's probably all right—she won't go far," George says. "You'd better have a little talk with her, Alice."

"I'm going over to Chuck's—I'll look for her," Dick says. "If I see her, I'll walk her home."

"Good idea," George says. Dick's out through the back, slamming the screen door.

"This is just a small town, but I really don't think a young girl ought to . . ." Alice stops and looks out the curtains at College Street. A college couple strolls by the Methodist Student Center, hand in hand.

Cedar Falls is full of houses with big front porches where swings creak in the warm evening. Streetlights glow through elms. A trolley climbs the tracks in front of the dean's house just as Catherine comes out, so she gets on.

The car has flickering, dim lights, and seats whose backs reverse so that you can sit facing either way, and slotted floors. It sways and clicks through tunnels of dark leaves in farm country. Then the suburbs of Waterloo begin to show their streetlights; the car drops Catherine off on a city street corner.

There are black people sitting in the heat that still rises from sun-baked cement. The river, running through deep shafts of light, is like the river in Detroit, a little, and if she could take a bus back to Seven Mile Road and run into the back hall where the light will be on for her, and Thorn will be reading, and look up to say, "Out late?" . . .

Jack Laird isn't here, with his dark eyes always on her, hanging a heavy kind of importance around her like a blanket she has to drag everywhere. It doesn't have anything to do with who she is. He talks about her mother, but all he says is that Janet was beautiful, and men followed her around. What's the matter with him?

Catherine watches smoke streaming from stacks across the river. Maybe that's the John Deere plant—or is it the Rath Packing Company?

Catherine stays on the bridge for a while, watching the black water . . . everything is real here; it doesn't matter whether her hair is curled. Margie is always tucking her pageboy under and twisting her head from side to side, and watching Babs with a bored look, and putting up with her mother. But when she talks to her brother she has a different tone in her voice, as if he matters. She doesn't like him very well, but he matters. And she's as bad as Babs is with Jack Laird: her voice goes up high, and she wiggles and jerks. When Jack comes in the room, everyone notices, even Dick and Stevie, but the boys don't begin to squirm, and twiddle their fingers and tip their heads to one side or the other.

Lights from a drugstore stream across the pavement to the bridge. Catherine goes into the store, sniffing its scent of medicine and candy. Big fans at the ceiling are turning above bottles, boxes and packages as numberless as chips of glass in a mosaic. "What'll you have?" asks the soda jerk when she climbs on a stool at the fountain.

"A hamburger and a chocolate soda," Catherine says. Across the sink and racks of cups and saucers a girl looks back at her from the mirror, her hair curling on her shoulders, her mouth a red patch. She looks like Margie and her friends. She looks like the girl in the Coca-Cola ad under the store clock, except that her mouth isn't grinning with teeth as white and fused together as a china plate. She isn't smiling at all. She touches her hair once. Later, halfway through her soda, she looks at her legs and feet: bare brown skin, white bobby socks, moccasins.

A cold cookie, the soda jerk thinks. What's eating her? Cute, though.

"Hey, beautiful," he says, and waits for the pouty look, but all he gets is a stare. "What's eatin ya?" he tries again. "Weather's pretty hot, right?"

She looks as if she doesn't hear him at all. Then she says, "Yes. It's hot," and goes on sipping the soda.

He watches her while she pays him and gets off the stool. He likes to watch girls from the back, the way they wiggle. But she doesn't. She just walks out, and she's so pretty and all, but she sure hasn't got what it takes.

Riding the last interurban back, Catherine shuts her eyes and sees streetcars in Detroit, late: old men eating out of paper bags, and a few couples coming back from a show, and the dreary advertisements in a row above their heads, and the swinging hand straps. Coming home when she pleased to find Thorn, if she pleased, not quite asleep. From the great city, she stepped into that house and into his bed—

"Where have you been?" Alice Knapp says. The whole Knapp family is on the front porch. "Where have you been?" George asks.

She says she's been to Waterloo and had a hamburger and walked along the river and talked to people. They say: What? She's been where? They have the same look on their faces that Tubbit used to have, as if it really weren't his business.

Alice follows Catherine upstairs and tells her they think she shouldn't go off like that. She's lived in a big city—she knows how she might get hurt. She might—you know—have some man go after her.

"Be raped?" Catherine asks.

"Well!" Alice says.

Catherine says of course that's one thing that you have to be careful about. But you can't just stay home because you might get hurt, can you?

4

The Knapp family is trying to make her feel at home, Catherine knows that. But she can't help thinking that soon Alice and Margie will stop spending all their time talking on the telephone or getting dressed or combing their hair or discussing clothes, or food, or people. Mrs. Hansen is busy in the kitchen; Babs and Stevie have toys they play with sometimes, and they race up and down stairs.

"Maybe you and I can go for a walk someday," Catherine tells Babs. "I'd like to see the stores, and the library—"

"I don't know where they are!" the little girl says, her blue eyes on Catherine. "I'm not s'posed to go out walking by myself, 'cause I might get lost!" Her voice has a righteous edge to it; she climbs on her father's lap, squashing his handful of newspaper.

"That's a good girl," her father says absentmindedly, rescuing the article on state appropriations he's reading. But Babs bounces up and down in front of his eyes until he has to stop reading to admire the "little bitty doll" she has in her pocket and ask her if her baby has been good today.

No one seems to read the books much. There's a whole shelf of Hugo and Zola. Dick and George are away most of the day. There isn't much in any room but furniture and clothes.

What's Catherine going to wear? That's the first thing Margie wants to know when she wakes up in the other bed every morning and starts taking the curlers out of her hair. Maybe black and white, if Catherine wears her white outfit? Or does she want to wear blue?

Early in the morning, before Catherine opens her eyes, she can feel that Thorn is lying beside her, his fringed blue eyes always a little sad. Sometimes he lay with his eyes closed and wouldn't open them; he was too tired and too happy, he said. What mattered was not to fool yourself, but to try to understand what you were really feeling, so you wouldn't make mistakes.

Catherine watches the day come, and listens to Margie breathe in and out, until it's light enough to read *Toilers of the Sea*. Surrounded by perfume bottles and stuffed animals, Catherine reads about that insane man fighting the ocean to rebuild a ship all by himself. She looks up from such insanity to tell Margie that she'll wear blue, that's all right, or the white, that's all right, too, and Margie gets up and stands in the closet doorway, trying to decide.

And how is Catherine going to fix her hair? Margie takes the curlers out and combs it this way, and that way, being friendly and helpful. That's what they do until breakfast.

All of the morning and most of the afternoon they stay home. Sometimes they go to another girl's house. Catherine wants to talk to Dick about football, but Dick isn't home much, and when he is, he plays the radio in his room with the door shut.

Should Catherine tell Bob Henderson when he calls to order a white corsage, or a blue one? Margie's girlfriends try to decide.

"Barb Henderson's wearing pink eyelet."

"Betty's mother won't let her buy a new dress."

The girls crowd into a bedroom and pose, limp wristed and giggling, meeting Catherine's eyes with a measuring glance. Their bodies twitch and perch like Margie's; their voices go high in little shrieks. They curl each other's hair around their fingers and pass judgment on a new bracelet with crooning and hushed attention. Ann Caldwell flops on the bed near Catherine. "How do the boys kiss in Detroit?" she whispers in Catherine's ear, tipping her head on one side and giggling.

"Catherine's sure lucky—Bob's got that brand-new Chevvie!"

"You know June necks with anybody—nobody's going to ask her to the dance!"

What can be strange about this bedroom? their eyes say. The smell of hair set and fingernail polish. This is the way we are, of course. Should Catherine wear her hair up for the dance? Or down? Here—let's just try it, and what does Barb think? What does Ann think? Gee, such pretty hair.

Poor Margie. What is it that she has to explain to Catherine? After a few days she sits on her ruffled bedspread among the magazines the girls have left, and says, "You're sure shy." She picks at her fingernail polish. "You'll be all right at the dance, won't you?" she asks, her eyes down. "I mean—you've been out with boys, haven't you?"

"No," Catherine says.

Margie gets up and goes out. Catherine sits looking at one of the magazines. It has a blue sky for the cover's background. A sky like that might be over the big house and Tubbit's cottage this afternoon, hot, filmy with clouds. At the bottom it says that three million women buy the magazine each month.

Maybe she should have said yes, she'd been out with boys. If you lay watching a sky like that with Thorn, and followed the long weave of muscles down his arm with your finger, or kissed the small bouquet of hairs at his nipple, you were certainly out with a boy.

Her throat aches. A girl is standing against the sky on the magazine cover. She's a real girl in a photograph: one of her eyes is patient and a little sad, like a Patsy doll's. Her lipstick matches her rose exactly, and the ribbons on her dress and hat and belt all match, too. That's what she's doing: holding her big hat and letting everything match.

Inside the magazine nothing matches. There's a little girl

wrapped in a towel on the back of the cover, and a woman complaining about "pink toothbrush" across from her. On the next page are four women who have written stories for this issue on one side, staring into a bowl of cereal on the other.

How quiet the house is, except for Margie down on the front porch, talking to Alice.

When Catherine first saw a magazine like this, Tubbit was getting recipes out of it; he'd hang over the pictures of cakes or casseroles, mumbling in his gray mustache, cutting out bits of the pages with the end of his butcher knife. The girls sprawled on the beds this morning, giggling, looking at pictures of rubber bathing suits and rayon playsuits and Mrs. Franklin D. Roosevelt, Jr.'s wedding dress.

Catherine shuts the magazine and closes her eyes and listens to the clock tick on the landing, and suddenly the sense of space around her comes back like a deep breath of blue air with clouds in it, and she goes downstairs and out into the sunshine.

Downhill from the dean's house and the campus are farm fields, and a creek almost hidden in overhanging bushes. Someone has thrown old sidewalk blocks into it at one place, so water sheets over that mossy bridge. Even the noise of a creaking windmill in the next field is drowned in the water's rippling and bubbling.

When she runs along the highest edges of the cement blocks to the other bank and climbs through bushes, there's the windmill, pumping and creaking in hot loneliness and weeds. She stands in the shadow of the mill's weathered boards and blade, turns and looks at the teacher's college on its hill, and the roof of the Knapps' house, and the space around her. The mill keeps turning, pumping and lonely—she knows how it works with the force of the wind: a real sound. Real smells: hot black earth and weeds baking in the sun.

Milkweed grows at the base of the windmill and runs downhill, and there are Monarch larvae on it! Striped caterpillars, just the same, as if nothing has happened at all.

Catherine stays there a long time. And the next morning while Margie is fixing her hair, Catherine says she wants to do some research on Monarch butterflies to help her uncle, so she'll be out in the fields near the house every morning. It isn't that she doesn't appreciate meeting Margie's friends, or having Margie worry about her hair . . .

They certainly will have to try out the way Catherine's hair will look for the dance, Margie says, so why don't they do it this morning? Then they can wash their hair right before the luncheon bridge on Friday, and it will be just right for Saturday night. She can comb Catherine's hair the new way right now.

"Very nice!" Alice says when she sees Catherine at breakfast. George puts his paper down and says they have the two prettiest girls in Cedar Falls right there at the table. Dick whistles a little wolf whistle. Stevie and Babs are arguing, as usual, and don't like the cereal.

Alice and George keep smiling at Catherine as though they're very pleased. Catherine explains that she's found Monarch larvae in one of the fields near the house, and she's planning to spend several hours a day working on a collection.

Will she bring them back? Margie asks. Will they be alive and crawling around?

Alice Knapp doesn't know. Go out in the hot sun every day? It's still summer, after all. She's glad, she says, that Catherine has on the skirt she's going to wear to the luncheon bridge, because it's too long—doesn't Margie think so?—and she can pin it up for Catherine right now.

So Catherine climbs on a table in the kitchen, rustling newspaper underfoot. She explains that Iowa Monarch butterflies will be different from the Michigan ones in certain important ways, and she can help her uncle by going out to farm fields . . .

Maybe Dick can go with her, Mrs. Knapp says. Or Margie? She backs up to see if she's getting Catherine's skirt even.

Margie groans, and says everybody knows what the sun does to her skin, and Dick will be going to practice every minute from now on.

Dick stops in the kitchen doorway just then, and says he's meeting some guys at school to work out at the gym. He lets the back screen door slam behind him, and then there's the r-r-room-oom of somebody's "heap" turning in the driveway to pick him up.

"What do you think?" Alice says to Margie. "Too short?" They both step back to look at Catherine.

"Maybe just a little shorter," Margie says. She roams around the big kitchen. Now and then she stops to look out a window.

Mrs. Hansen comes in with the big flat pans of cake to be frosted for the luncheon bridge.

It's such a bother, Alice says, taking pins from her mouth, that the school colors are purple and gold. Of course the yellow looks good to eat, but it never seems quite like gold, and try to find purple coloring! But imagine entertaining at the state university—black and gold, for heaven's sake.

Don't they have to go shopping before the reception next week? Margie asks after a while. She and Catherine are going to wear their big straw hats, and you can't wear white gloves with straw hats.

Why not? Alice says—if they wear their white sandals it will look all right.

Standing on the table, Catherine looks down on the big kitchen. Mrs. Hansen's hair is pulled back in a braided bun. Mrs. Knapp has pins in her mouth again.

Margie leans against the mangle, picking off the rest of her peach fingernail polish.

A plane goes over. The house echoes in its empty bedrooms and parlors and halls.

Babs wanders in from the dining room where she has finally decided to finish her cereal. Now she whines that she doesn't have anything to do. Her mother tells her to find her paper dolls.

Babs doesn't want to. She crawls under the kitchen table and bangs a chair against it. The aimless clicks of metal on metal are, for a moment, the only sounds in the kitchen.

"Goodbye, ladies!" George Knapp stands in the kitchen doorway, smiling. Then his heels click briskly down the back stairs. Catherine can see him going along the walk toward the auditorium building, his shoulders straight, his briefcase swinging.

5

The next morning after breakfast Catherine says she'll go across the street to where Dick's taking a look at Gordie Bishop's car; she wants to ask him if she can borrow his Boy Scout backpack for her field work . . .

"Oh, no!" Margie says, "not dressed like that!" So Catherine has to put on her new slacks and a boy's shirt with the sleeves rolled up and the shirttails hanging out—that's what the girls are wearing. Margie combs Catherine's hair and says that she's got to put on makeup, and if she's going off somewhere, she's got to be back home in plenty of time to get dressed for the luncheon bridge.

The cars are parked at the curb. Even before Catherine crosses the street the boys see her, and whistle. She walks up and asks Dick about his backpack. She hasn't seen any of the boys before; they look her over when they think she doesn't see them doing it. Dick introduces them, and they smile and laugh, but they have a sharp look . . . the look they use for each other seems to slide back, like the eyelid of some bird, and the sharp eyes watch. She asks what they're doing with the car.

They look at each other, and Dick says it's Gordie's car. Catherine takes a look under the hood and says she's worked on a fluid drive like this one.

Well, Dick says after a pause, maybe he ought to go in with her and get the backpack because it might not be where he thinks it is. But Catherine has already borrowed a wrench from Bob Henderson, who she thinks is taking her to the dance, so she asks if Dick would mind getting the pack while she takes a look.

It's pretty quiet at the curb while Dick is gone, except when Catherine asks questions. Dick comes back fast, but she hangs around for a little while. Bob Henderson asks her about Detroit. She says she's spent a couple of days watching the Ford assembly lines, and then she describes her work with the Monarchs. If he ever wants to come out in the fields and watch, or collect, he's welcome to come along, she says. She tells them all goodbye after a while, and loads Dick's backpack, and goes off to the fields.

The walls of corn look as impenetrable as stockades, ringing in the old windmill. She finds larvae in three different instars, and eggs, too, beautiful under the microscope as something golden by Cellini, but nothing to the naked eye but a round speck. She sits under the creaking windmill and begins her data notebook precisely, carefully, and it seems as if she might suddenly look up and see Thorn. The late summer heat makes her sweat; she wipes off her sticky lipstick. The windmill turns above her in the weeds and quiet.

When she gets back to the house, she can hear Margie and her mother talking on the back stairs. What's wrong with knowing how a car runs? Alice is asking, and Margie says that there isn't anything wrong—the guys liked that all right—but, well, she just doesn't know how to act, that's all. She looks at everybody as if they were creeps or zombies or something . . .

"She's been stuck away by herself for years in Detroit," Alice says. "You know what Uncle Jack said. She's just beginning to get out in the world, and be free, and have fun with people her own age—"

"Bugs!" Margie says. "She told Bob Henderson all about her bugs, and so Gordie Bishop thinks he's such a wiseguy—he asked Bob after she left whether he had a date with 'Catherine Buggingham'! She just doesn't know! She walks right up, and she looks at boys all wrong, and talks to them and doesn't smile—she looks right at them like she knows everything, kind of, when you're supposed to . . ." Margie's voice lowers and trails off, hearing Catherine going up the front stairs. "We'd better get dressed."

By the time Margie and Catherine are ready, both big parlors and the downstairs study are full of card tables and folding chairs. No table looks the same as the next one: each has a different little bouquet to match its tablecloth and napkins.

Alice meets them at the foot of the stairs with a list in one hand and place-card tallies in the other. "I don't suppose you've ever been to a luncheon bridge," she says to Catherine.

They can practice a little, Alice says: Margie and Catherine will help Mrs. Hansen serve the luncheon plates—you serve from the left—and pour the coffee. Then they'll take the plates away from the right, and serve the cake from the left, and pour more coffee. When everyone is through, the three of them will clear the tables, but Margie and Catherine won't have to help in the kitchen; college girls are coming from the Commons for that. Margie and Catherine practice serving and clearing a table, and then the doorbell begins to ring, and Alice says the girls are beginning to come.

So many women. And this is what they often do, because they come in the front door with smiles like habit, and begin to talk as if that's a habit, too, and it's one o'clock in the afternoon, and everyone has a hat on, and they smile.

It's the kind of thing they're used to, their faces tell Catherine.

They wear pale pastel colors and flowered hats and white gloves. Everything is as it should be, their eyes say, and their high and happy voices.

Margie sees nothing unusual; she smiles and tosses her blond pageboy and introduces Catherine. Does she like Cedar Falls? the women want to know. Isn't it nice for Margie to have a friend her own age staying with her? The parlors and the study are full of their voices and their smiles and their hats, and it's one o'clock on a Friday afternoon, and Catherine fits in exactly: the eyes run over her without a break in the smiles, and doesn't she think Margie looks like her mother?

Everyone knows what to do: they sit down at the tables with their hats on, and put their gloves in their laps under the napkins. Talk flows without stopping, with little bursts of laughter, or a sudden silence at a table when Catherine puts down a plate or pours coffee and they stop talking about somebody's aunt in Chicago and say isn't this a lovely luncheon?

To be a courtier, maybe—Rigaud's courtier in the days of Louis XIV? Silk-clad legs mincing along under his skirt . . . pitched on his high heels, long curls bobbing on his shoulders. Admired. Fitting in with the others, perfectly. An old lady falls asleep in her luncheon chair, her face dropped from its cheerful expression under a plume a Watteau gentleman would have loved. What could Thorn do, his high heels making his toes ache, hours and hours on a Friday afternoon? If everyone admired his skirt and silk hose and long curls? If he looked like all the rest? "Alice has such pretty china, doesn't she?" says a blonde woman to Catherine, sipping coffee.

And all the time trucks grind as they climb College Street, and college students go by to classes.

The women would say how nice Thorn looks, and is his hair naturally curly? and talk about college boys swallowing goldfish. When the luncheon is over, each table has to have a double box of playing cards and a score pad and pencil and a dish of mints and nuts. Isn't it nice that he could come and visit? they'd say. His skirt just matches his eyes.

The trucks go by, and students and professors, and even the Good Humor man with his ice cream sticks and bell. Margie says that the lady with the big pink hat is Bob Henderson's mother. She's looking Catherine over, see?

And the blonde in the brown outfit, Margie says when the women are finally leaving, "Isn't she a knockout?"

Some faces are tired, turning away from smiles at the front door. Women watch their step, going downstairs slowly in their precarious shoes, but some stop once more to smile, and say they have a daughter about Catherine's age, or ask, doesn't she think Margie looks like her mother?

The paper boy comes with the paper. George Knapp comes home from work with his briefcase. Alice looks tired, he says, but he bets it was a nice party.

6

"I just can't eat a thing," Margie says next morning at breakfast. Not with the dance coming up that night—and she and Catherine have got to wash their hair again, because it was so hot at the luncheon . . . you can't have your hair stringy and all stuck to the back of your head.

And they've got to practice dancing some more after they wash their hair, and then call Ann, and Barb, and Betty. A network of girls' voices over Cedar Falls. "Are there girls who won't be going to the dance?" Catherine asks Margie between calls. Margie gives her that detached, measuring look that's becoming a habit and says, sure, some of the girls don't have dates—they're the ones who stand along the wall at school dances.

Margie can't eat much lunch, or supper, either. After lunch she and Catherine shave their underarms and their legs, and take baths with perfume in the water, and then rub on lotion and more perfume. It takes a long time to do their fingernails and toenails: they have to use cuticle remover and orange sticks, and then wash, and then put on two coats of nail polish and another coat of protector, and if you smear any of it, it has to be done over.

At supper they look funny in their rattling curlers, and Mr. Knapp and Dick tease them. The dance is very important to girls; Catherine tries to understand that. You have to look very different than you usually do, because you have to "wow" them, Margie says. She keeps talking about making the guys swoon, and just wait until those wolves see Catherine.

"How's that?" Margie asks her mother. They look at Catherine, who stands before Alice's full-length mirror. Catherine looks at herself and wonders if anybody can find her in all that. The fancy long dress looks like it's the important thing—somebody named Bob Henderson is going to have to lead that dress around all evening. "Just a dream!" Alice says.

You make the boys wait a little, Margie says. Her mother will answer the door and talk to Jim and Bob, and then the girls will make their "grand entrance" and "wow" them. So Catherine and Margie stand in the upstairs hall for a while, listening to the boys' deep voices. Then Margie puts on her scornful, detached look and leads the way downstairs, with Catherine teetering after her and trying to look the same way.

It's hard to tell if the boys are swooning or wowed; Catherine thinks they look embarrassed. The four walk slowly in pairs to the car, because the girls can't go very fast.

Jim and Bob are very stiff, opening car doors and waiting until Margie and Catherine get their dresses in the car and out of the way. It's a still, hot summer evening; everyone is already sweating a little, especially the boys in their suits and tight collars. Margie stays stiff and proud, as if she and Catherine are doing the boys a favor to be going at all.

It stays pretty stiff. Catherine knows a few of the girls going up the women's club house walk with their dates, and she recognizes some of the dresses, too. But there are "downtown girls" from Cedar Falls High she doesn't know, and so many strangers stare at her. The club house has a curving bannister and a ladies' room upstairs. One wall of it is all mirror, and each girl goes over to it, looks at herself as if she doesn't care for anything she sees, and then stands looking everyone else over. A few friends get together to finger each other's dresses or pin corsages on, but most of the girls look proud and stiff and scared, all at once. What are they so scared of? There are older people there, but not many. They are "chaperons," Margie says in a tense whisper when Catherine asks.

Then they go downstairs again, where the boys are standing against the walls, still looking embarrassed. Maybe the girls plan these dances, and then the boys have to come, and then they all have to act happy. The girls begin chattering and laughing when they find the boy they've come with, and they play with the little dance programs the boys are writing their names in. Bob gives Catherine hers, and she thanks him. He's just her age, and doesn't know any more than she does—he seems more scared than she is. He pulls at his collar, and shoots his wrists out of his coat sleeves.

A band from the college begins to play in the "ballroom," so everybody goes in and admires the balloon decorations and the cardboard wishing well in the center of the floor. Some older people in the balcony smile and wave. Bob gets his arm around Catherine and they start to do a fox-trot, and it isn't so hard. You have to know the steps; then you just relax and let your partner tell you which way he's going. Bob doesn't really go anywhere. Jack Laird swung her around and made little runs, but Bob just steps one way, and then the opposite way, and then back to the beginning again. After a while Catherine figures out that they aren't going to do anything else, though once they sit down for a while, and once they walk out into the big double parlor to have fruit punch and cake.

It's hot, even with the fans blowing into the ballroom. Catherine's hands sweat, and she does, too, and how does Bob feel in his wool suit? He just dances back and forth while the music goes on and on; she can't see how anyone's having much fun, but most of them are trying to laugh and talk. The girls are worrying about what they have on, or what's happening to their hair; you can tell. The boys just look hot. The music goes on and on, and the band looks hotter than anybody else. They have different kinds of dances—sometimes the girls choose the boys they came with, and sometimes the girls put one of their shoes in a heap, and the boys choose their date's shoe and dance with her. Jim comes every now and then to tap on Bob's shoulder. Then Catherine has to shift to Jim, until Bob taps on Jim's shoulder.

By eleven o'clock it's getting a little cooler, but it doesn't really matter: they're all too sticky to feel it. Catherine has asked Bob every question she can think of, and he's asked her some, too. You can't really talk when you're rubbing up and down against each other with your faces so much closer than you want them to be. You have to talk in each other's ear, or else look over each other's shoulder at all the others doing the same thing. There's a damp spot on Catherine's back from Bob's hand.

Finally the band plays "Good Night, Ladies." Everybody begins to tell each other what fun they've had, and they line up to thank the chaperons. The night is cool and breezy when the four of them climb into Bob's car. Margie giggles in the back seat with Jim. The boys get out at the dean's house, and help the girls out and take them to Margie's front door and say goodnight and thank them for such a good time. Margie and Catherine thank the boys for such a good time, and go in.

How did it go? Alice wants to know. She's waiting to find out all about it. Margie sits down and gets her shoes off. How did Catherine like it? Alice asks. Was Bob a good dancer?

Yes, he knows how to dance, Catherine says, and Margie has been lots of help, and Alice has, too. It's nice of them to help her get used to going to dances.

They're glad to help, Alice says, and Catherine will be going to school Monday; that will be nice, too. She'll be just sort of visiting, and Margie will see that Catherine gets to know the young people. It'll be such a good way for Catherine to get ready for college. She's glad the boys didn't take them out somewhere after the dance, because they'd be too tired in all this heat. Margie says she's practically dead on her feet, and she's going to bed.

7

"Have a beer." Jack hands Dick a bottle. Sitting by themselves in deep shade, they watch Margie, Catherine and Alice packing up what's left of a picnic lunch. Stevie and Babs are out on the lake with their father; their cries are bell-like over water, through trees. "How's the swim team?"

"Okay, I guess." Dick takes a swallow of beer. "But there's this Stan Beecher at school, and he thinks he's really an answer to a prayer because he's a senior. Every time I start talking to Betty Marshall, he makes a crack about am I on the dog paddle team now, and why don't I bark off? We got this new swim coach, and he's got me doing flip turns and fancy stuff—terrific."

"Sounds great." Jack opens another bottle of beer.

"Yeah. Well, this creep's got a car of his own now—big stuff— so he's got Kay George and this Betty Marshall watching each other out of the corners of their eyes—you know what I mean? Betty's pretty sick of the whole thing, I can tell, so she invites me to a beach party she's giving down by the river, and by the time the fire's down to coals, there's this jerk Stan Beecher smooching with Kay. So Betty kind of crowds up to me, and she's got this swell perfume on, so I hold her hand. Stan's got Kay in a pretty tight hold. She's a brunette with freckles and we used to call her 'Spots' on account of it, but she isn't so bad looking now, so we don't." Dick takes a long swallow of beer and coughs.

"So this makes Betty pretty sore, to say the least," he goes on. "So she gets on my lap and starts to giggle. She sure feels different than she used to—she was the most hard-muscled girl kid I ever wrestled with. I figured I'd give her something to giggle about, because I knew she was ticklish under the arm, and that creep Stan gets Kay giggling, too, and saying, 'D-o-o-n't, Stan, please!' although I bet he doesn't know the first thing about tickling women."

"Probably not," Jack says in a subdued voice.

Dick blinks at the lake and narrows his eyes. "If that log I was sitting on hadn't been as hard as a rock, I could have sat there all night, you can bet, but Betty's as heavy as lead, though it's in all the right places, of course."

"Uh-hum," Jack says.

"Darned if just about then Kay doesn't go and wreck the whole thing by knocking old Stan Beecher off his log and shouting that she isn't that kind of girl, no matter what other girls she might mention do, and she has a few points beyond which she won't go, regardless of how other people may want to show off. Old Stan really gets his, and he's apologizing all over the place."

"Quite a girl," Jack says.

"Yes. Well, the next thing I know, Betty hauls off and slugs me hard enough to be heard clear up at the Boat House, and she makes it back to the fire so fast that she even beats Kay. So when Kay finally turns up at the fire with her nose in the air, there's Betty already there with hers even higher, and they go and freeze us two guys off like, say, Siberia."

"The eternal female," Jack says.

"You've had a lot of experience, that's why I'm asking you this," Dick says. "Don't you think women are mostly emotional? I mean, they really don't make much sense."

"They certainly are," Jack says after he's taken a long pull of beer. "That's why I wanted to ask you about Catherine."

"Catherine?"

"Yes . . . do you think she fits in okay with the other girls? You have a lot of chances to watch her."

"Well." Dick finishes his bottle of beer. "She's . . . I don't know. She doesn't look the way she's supposed to, does she? Girls look at you a certain way, but she doesn't. I don't know. It makes you kind of mad sometimes. But she's pretty and all. She could be real popular if she just knew how to act."

"What should she do?" Jack asks.

"Well, gosh, I don't know. Like the other girls. You know— they kind of wait around and tease, get the guys interested without showing they're doing it . . . kind of sneaky . . . and they tell a guy he's handsome, or how they adore guys with cars, stuff like that. You know it isn't true, but that's just how girls are. And they pretend they're weak all the time, and scared of everything. You know."

"That's the way the girls in high school act."

"Sure. It makes a man feel good; that's the thing. They know how to do it, to make you feel smart. If they get good grades or something, they don't show everybody, the way Catherine gets right up in class and talks like she's Bob Henderson or somebody. And girls always talk about clothes. But Margie's got Catherine all fixed up. She looks nice."

"Beautiful," Jack says.

"She just kind of makes you mad, that's all. She goes off walking by herself—just walking around like she owns the town, kind of . . . like she wants it all explained. What's there to explain? Everything here's just like it is anyplace else, even if we do live in a town instead of a big city like Detroit."

"She doesn't know much about the world," Jack says.

"Then she ought to stay home with Margie so I don't have to go looking for her all the time—girls don't go off everywhere by themselves all the time. She says the boys at school do all the important things. I tried to tell her the girls had the cheerleading, and the pep club and all. She just kind of makes you mad, that's all. She wants it all explained all the time. What's there to explain?"

8

"But she's only been here three weeks! She only visited your school one week!" Alice says to Margie. "What will Jack think?" she asks her husband, who has just come in from a Saturday board meeting. "Catherine's out looking for caterpillars. She told me she wants to start college on Monday! Her uncle has a friend at Gilman, and she called him, and he said she can start, so she's just going—"

"She made up her mind, just like that, all by herself!" Margie cries.

"And just picked up the phone and made the call and got herself admitted," Alice says. "Of course, she asked me if she could use the telephone, and what could I say?"

"Jack could take her back with him—Gilman's on the way to Chicago. Isn't he coming this afternoon?" George says, pulling off his tie.

"Well, yes, he is, and he could, but what will he think? She acts as if she just doesn't want to stay any longer. Of course she's polite, but you know she's been . . . odd. She watches us as if she doesn't understand what we're doing."

"I've had a nice talk with her several times," George says. "Especially when I asked her not to go out by herself, and if she wanted to know about this town, and Waterloo, and farming—"

"She says Dick doesn't have to stay home, and he's only sixteen," Margie says.

"Well, gee—I told her it was different," Dick says. "I said it was just different. I could take care of myself."

"What did she say?" Alice asks.

"She said she could take care of herself, too. So what could I say? 'No, you can't'?"

"She started out so well," Alice says. "You got her that date with Bob Henderson . . . she looked just like a dream in that blue formal, didn't she?"

Margie sighs. "She's just not in the groove—I told you! The way she walks, and all. And you've got to know cute things to say to a boy, and smile, and talk about things he likes to talk about. And honestly, I think she'd wear the same outfit to school for a whole week if I didn't—"

"Were the kids at school mean to her?" Alice asks.

"Well, you don't talk about schoolwork with the girls all the time, or go up to the teacher right in front of the class and give her a clipping you think she'll be interested in!" Margie says.

"Did she tell you she thought the kids were scared all the time?" Dick asks. "She told me they were scared of looking silly, or not looking like the others, or showing that they'd learned anything."

"How can she go to college when she hasn't even got any skirts or sweaters?" Margie asks.

"And she wondered why the boys always stayed together, and didn't seem to like the girls much," Dick says.

"She just doesn't understand!" Margie cries. "You don't barge in and ask a bunch of boys questions. You've got to act kind of, I don't know, ladylike and like you don't care much . . . I don't know . . ."

"She seemed to be trying to tell me that she didn't want to stay in the house all the time," George says. "I explained how you and I make a team," he smiles at Alice, "And how you take care of the entertaining and the house . . ."

"Well, I did teach school before we married," Alice says.

"She asked if they'd have to get a new dean if something happened to you," George tells Alice.

"Now, what has that got to do—"

"She just walks up to people," Dick says. "She just walks up like she's Bob Henderson or somebody."

"We can't tell Jack about little things," Alice says. "We've got to tell him we think she should go to Gilman, I guess. I know her size, and maybe Margie and I can buy her some clothes and send them."

"It's just the way she acts," Margie says.

9

Catherine, high on the Twelfth Street hill among gravestones, watches a line of ants. Each is carrying a seamlessly swaddled larva: white dots moving on black legs punctuate the cemetery grass.

Seeing how slabs of shade fall across graves, flowers, lawn and gravel road, Catherine looks up: the town's water tower looms over this place like a giant's cup on legs, a drink flourished against the sun, enormous enough, perhaps, for any thirst.

"She says we're supposed to tell why Ophelia drowns herself." A girl's voice drifts from a clump of pines near Catherine.

"Well, okay," says a masculine voice. "So what's the reason?"

"Don't. I've got to write it down."

"Don't? Since when?"

"Now, come on, I don't mean don't—I just mean let me write it down. I've got to be home at five!"

The ants, single file, single purposed, have reasons not known; they climb over grass blades as they did in Homer's day, carrying their young like mysteries through mysteries.

"Don't." A girl emerges from evergreen shade, a clutter of papers and books in her arms. She sits on a cement bench that is ridged and knotholed to resemble a tree trunk, with "I will give you rest" in concrete letters at its base. Seeing Catherine, she ducks her head and starts scribbling.

Catherine walks out of earshot, swallowed up in a dark circle of shadow dropped by the water tower tank. In that hot dimness a row of graves still wears its Memorial Day milk bottles empty of water now, filled with dead flower heads and leaves. Tons of water hang overhead; the graves lie in that black and hovering shade.

10

Catherine watches cornfields go by, and the shadow of Jack's car streaming smoothly beside them in the deep ditches.

Now and then Jack's dark eyes turn to her; she can feel them. Lipstick is sweet and sticky, like ice cream. She licks her lips, then stops: spit only makes it worse.

She doesn't have to chatter like Margie, but why doesn't she say anything? Jack wonders. She thanked the Knapps and the housekeeper, and told them she hoped to see them again after she'd been at college for a while, but now she stares out of the car window like a statue.

And to just pick up and leave like that. Young girls don't make up their minds that way. They should think a little more. Ask somebody's advice, at least. Go off to college, just like that?

He doesn't know what to say. What in hell was the matter?

They got her hair fixed and got her nice clothes, and everything started out right, and then she just decides she can't visit any longer. She's polite enough, and says they've all been so nice to her, but she doesn't fool him.

"Thought we might stop at the Amanas to eat," he says. "Not much out of our way, and it's interesting."

"That would be nice," Catherine says, showing him Janet's profile against sun on corn. Is that all she's going to say? Rage shoots through him—what did Thorn do to her? She can't even be happy with a normal family—doesn't know how to act. Nobody said much, but he could figure that out.

And Tubbit never would say much. Stubborn. Loyal, maybe. Well, Thorn can stay away from her—stay in France where he belongs. But to think of . . . what happened? He glances at Catherine's profile. So much like Janet, and just looking at her you'd think she was only a pretty young girl, except for her eyes. And there's something wrong with the way she watches you, and how she sits, and walks, and holds her hands. She makes you kind of mad, and you don't ever know why.

A black buggy sways as it grows larger and larger in the road ahead. "Amish," Jack says, easing the car out to take a look at the highway. "That's how they still get places—horse and buggy." As the car swings wide around the swaying black box and passes the horses, Catherine sees tanned faces against green fields, and the rest is black. "We'll see more of them at the Amanas." Looking back, Catherine sees the buggy shrinking into the landscape, as if into a picture of farmland a hundred years before.

Jack glances at Catherine. The Knapps had made it clear enough: she just didn't "fit in." Maybe she'd be happier at a small liberal arts college like Gilman, where she could make friends and could send her laundry to Cedar Falls—Alice said she didn't think an old man like Tubbit would know how to fix a college girl's clothes. Catherine could come to visit Cedar Falls any time she wanted, and she'd be close enough to Chicago so that Jack could see her often; she wouldn't be so lonely.

It was nice of Alice. Coming into the Amanas, he looks sidewise at Catherine. She makes him mad and he doesn't even know why. "Good food here," Jack says, pulling up to the curb. "I'll park the car—it's so windy. You go on in before you lose that pretty hat."

The wind scoops under Catherine's dress as she gets out of the car, but it hardly stirs the heavy skirts of two Amish women standing by the curb.

For a minute, closing the car door, Catherine sees that their young faces aren't looking anywhere but at their feet. Then their bonnets box them away in black cloth. Their hands are hidden; they have no shape but folds of black.

Do they know that black-clad young Amish men are running back and forth a few feet away, laughing, carrying crates from the curb to a wagon? The young men's beards seem to belong to another world, an adventurous world of ship boarding, perhaps, or breaching a city wall. Their white teeth and red lips are wet and flashing under their broad-brimmed hats.

Catherine looks back when she gets to the restaurant door. The Amish women haven't moved; the wind scarcely stirs their skirts. They are like holes that silhouettes make in a page.

"Sorry!" A middle-aged woman collides with Catherine and the wind in the open door. The woman picks her way gingerly down the steps, high heels wobbling, hand to her hat. Jack passes her and takes the steps two at a time; he comes in to Catherine with a surge of the wind.

They are shown to a table and Jack pushes Catherine's chair in for her, and she thanks him, and Jack thinks it's all wrong; she looks around as if she owns the place or something. A woman sits down at the next table. Good looking; probably from C.R. or Des Moines, or traveling through, walking in so poised and charming with that little reserved air, and now she's leaning on the table and smiling at the man she's with. Nice legs.

The restaurant is homey, the way it's always been, and smells of fresh bread. Catherine reads the menu and tells him, when he asks, that she'll have the sauerbraten.

The woman at the next table is doing the same kind of thing Margie did, Catherine thinks. It took her quite a while to understand what Margie was doing, because it was like a dance, and complicated. First, Margie's voice changed. She had a loud, excited way of talking to her girlfriends, or else she whispered and giggled, but when she saw Jim coming up to her in the hall at school, Margie's voice softened; it wasn't loud or excited. Her eyes changed, too: the eyelids drooped a little.

In fact, Margie drooped all over. Catherine watches the woman at the next table. That was the complicated part. Margie's hands didn't hold her books and notebooks tight any more; she played around with them instead. She didn't stand on both feet or hold her head up. When she saw Jim coming, she made herself smaller—she'd slide her spine down a door frame, or if there weren't anything to lean against, she'd stand on one foot, and bend the knee that was holding her up.

Catherine, watching, had seen that Margie never looked straight at Jim, or held her head up, unless she tipped it to one side. She didn't form words with her mouth in the same way: her lips pouted instead, and hung open a little. Her eyes went up and down his face as if it were a ladder, not staying anywhere. Most of the time she looked at the floor.

Jim was different. You could see the difference from far away, just watching the two of them in the hall. He gripped whatever he had in his hands tight, and usually stood on both feet, looking down at Margie. He didn't shout, or slap her on the back as he slapped his friends. He looked uncomfortable. When he got back to the group of boys, they hit him with their big hands.

Catherine tried looking like Margie in front of a mirror once. The drooping and the eye batting were so silly, and if she imagined herself acting like that with Thorn, it made her feel like Betty Boop: all big head and eyelashes, and a little body dwindling away . . .

"You're not really my uncle," Catherine says.

Startled, Jack's dark eyes turn to her. He's been watching the woman nearby, who's leaning on her elbows now, making the table a part of her, almost, as if she's small and soft, and melts toward the man across from her . . . "No," Jack says.

"That's what I can't understand," Catherine says.

"Understand what?" Jack watches the woman run her ringed hand along her bare arm as if she loves the feel of her skin. Smiles as she talks, and gestures, her fingers loose and wide apart.

"You knew my mother and father . . . "

"The most beautiful woman I ever saw!" Jack says. "You always felt like taking care of her, protecting—"

Catherine laughs. Has he ever heard her laugh before? Janet had a soft, caressing laugh, and she tossed her short brown hair back . . . "My mother had me in a barn with nobody but my uncle to help—"

"He wasn't there," Jack says in a low voice. His eyes are so black they have no light in them at all.

"What?"

"He wasn't there," Jack repeats, anger leaking around the edges of his words.

Catherine says in a matter-of-fact voice, "You weren't told about it, I suppose, but he was." The waitress brings the soup.

Unfolding her napkin in her lap and picking up her spoon, Catherine thinks how glad she is not to be in school with Margie this morning. The students sat in rows, like the John J. Bagley School children, but now they watched each other most of the time, not the teacher. They watched each other almost all the time. They were afraid of looking silly or different—you could feel it. If they were glad when they learned something, they never showed it.

Every break between classes the girls got together in the rest room, packed into that small space, and if somebody had a new sweater or skirt or shoes, they talked about it . . . where she got it and how much it cost. They always said they liked whatever was new.

They didn't do that outside the rest room. The minute the girls were in the hall, they put their arms around each other and giggled and stayed together, but each girl was really separate, and she watched the others all the time. Everyone watched the "smooth" boys and the "popular" girls. It look Catherine a while to figure out that everyone in the halls and during classes was watching the special people.

Catherine glances up. Jack's eyes are on the woman at the next table. The most important things at school were how you looked, and getting a date. The girls worked on these things most of the time.

They were all going to get married, the girls said. As she finishes her soup, Catherine sighs, feeling a kind of freedom, even if Jack Laird is sitting across the table. She couldn't tell whether the girls loved the boys or not. They talked about catching them or "wowing" them, and they "necked" or "played the field" or "got in a clinch," but she didn't think very many of them had had intercourse, or else they hid it. If they liked boys and were going to marry them, why did they act like boys were a different kind of animal entirely, and why did the boys think the girls were just as strange? Sometimes the boys would break out of their deep-voiced groups in the hall; they'd come up shamefaced to ask a girl, Hey, Betty, how about taking in a show tonight? What's cookin', good lookin'?

The candle in the red bowl between Catherine and Jack throws patterns on the checked cloth.

"Why did you take me to the Knapps . . . and now you're taking me to college, and offering to pay for things . . ." Catherine's voice trails off as she sees Jack's eyes.

"I loved your mother," Jack says. His lips feel stiff. "It's because you're so much like her."

"Like her?" Why does she lean on the table that way, her hands jammed between her breasts and the table edge? "But I'm not—not yet!"

"You're just like her." The force of Jack's voice comes across the candle flame, almost seems to make it tremble. "Don't you know how beautiful you are?"

The spoon shakes a little in Jack's hand. Catherine stares at him across the candlelit table.

11

The Gilman College catalog showed the campus on its hill, with the small town descending on all sides into farm fields. Methodists had founded Gilman in the mid-nineteenth century, and half of its student body had always gone into business and the professions, and sent money back to give it a comfortable endowment.

The other half of the student body lives in two big dormitories, three to a room. The girls call their two bunk beds "Heaven" and "Earth," and the trundle bed that slides under them "Hell."

Each room is a packed universe: clothes jammed in two small niches called closets . . . stuffed animals . . . hot plates . . . books . . . photos of boyfriends. You squeeze through to sit in the one lounge chair, or the two straight chairs, or the lower bed (where there's no head room), or the upper bed (where your shoes dangle in other girls' faces). The window shows you miles of farm country. In cold weather you cover the window with blankets.

Ruth Stone and Peggy Schmidt are Catherine's "roomies," and they cheerfully take her in, explaining that she has to be checked in the dorm by 7:45 every weekday evening, or she'll get "minutes." Freshmen girls are supposed to stay in and study. Each dorm room has some kind of sign on it, and theirs has a picture of two brooms holding hands, with balloons above their heads saying, "We're broommates. We sweep together, dust we two." But they find room for Catherine's clothes and books and curlers, and let her store some of her dresses in their garment bags in the attic, and begin telling her all she'll have to know, since she's come late.

Boy, is Catherine lucky. She won't have to wear a freshman beanie that doesn't match her clothes, and she won't have to go through hell week—boy, is she lucky. How would she like to wear nothing but a bra and a towel and two safety pins and high heels, and crawl down four flights of dorm stairs on her hands and knees after hours, with all the upperclass girls watching? Or pass out squares of toilet paper to everybody she meets downtown? Or scrub the chapel steps with a toothbrush?

Ruth has hair as pale as blonde hair can be, and blue eyes that protrude just a little under their sweeping, dark lashes. When she puts her arm around Catherine, Ruth feels light and mostly bones, like a bird, and she thinks Catherine's blue cotton suit is swell, and can she borrow it sometime?

Peggy is from an Iowa farm, but she could pass for an Oak Park girl with cashmere sweaters, because she learns small, important things very fast. Her boyfriend at home is handsome, and they've been engaged for so long that he unfastens the back of her dresses sometimes, if her parents are asleep when she gets home from a date and she can't reach the back herself.

Was that Catherine's father? they want to know. And when Catherine says no, he's a kind of uncle—she doesn't have any father or mother—the girls think that's sad, but they say her uncle sure looks like somebody in the movies, and what a car.

You go from building to building and class to class, carrying your books. Knowledge is divided into English 101 and Speech 101 and Biology 101 and French 101 and Art 101 and Physical Education. The students watch each other, like they do in high school, but they take notes, too, and they study. You do a litte bit for each course each day to keep even, and it isn't very hard.

At meals everybody sings "Be Present At Our Table, Lord," and then there's a racket of chairs being pulled out and pushed in, and everybody starts handing big bowls of food around the table and talking, while the boys who work for board balance trays overhead. After supper there's not much time until you have to be in the dorm for the night, and then the girls pile up in Ann Denison's room, because it's a big corner room and she's senior counselor.

"Hey, Dotty's back!" Ruth says as the door opens. "Did you kiss him?"

"Not on a first date, you crumb!"

"What are you going to do when you graduate?" Catherine asks Ann.

"Get married," Ann says. "If we're not in the war by that time and Don has to fight ."

"What I want is to go on a long honeymoon out on the west coast, and go to Earl Carroll's and the Brown Derby . . ." Peggy is putting up her hair, a bottle of hair set between her knees.

"Hey, Dotty, did he feed you?"

"Quit it!" Peggy snarls through the comb in her teeth. "I'm starving—let's call the Doughnut Shop and have some stuff sent over."

"Okay. Everybody write down their orders."

Scribbling, Catherine says, "Aren't you going on to graduate study? You've got all A's . . ."

"Me?" Ann stops crocheting a mitten to stare at Catherine.

"My sister had ten showers. You ought to see the stuff she got. Last August," Ruth says.

Marie is rubbing lotion on her legs. "Joe says he's going to be a lawyer, so we'll get an apartment in New York."

"And now they're living in two rooms, so where's she going to use all that stuff? It's in our attic."

"My sister knows a girl who's going on for a master's," Ann says, "but no girl here is—I've never heard of anybody."

"Have any of you finished reading *Return of the Native* for English yet?"

"You're in biology—you could go on with work on the aphids," Catherine says.

"Well, sure." Ann laughs a little. "But there'll be maybe one girl in the entomology department, and all you can do is teach, and you don't get anywhere."

"I wish I could find some sweet guy," Marie says dreamily.

"I wish I were Ann—a senior and everything, and she's getting married."

"What's your silver pattern?" Peggy asks.

"April Rose."

"Mine's Adoration."

"And have three kids—that's what I want," Marie says. "Two boys and a girl."

"But you said your dad's head of the biology department at Illinois . . ." Catherine says.

"He thinks women get queer in the head when they do graduate work. He says he's never known a normal one."

"Hey, Dotty, did you call in the order?"

"What's chapel going to be tomorrow? I think I'll cut."

Catherine watches Ann's diamond sparkle as the crochet hook goes in and out. "Aren't there any jobs in biology? Do you have to teach? I thought maybe I'd major in it."

"Dad says the trouble is you have to go on field trips, and camp, and do experiments for weeks, and you just can't go right along with the men. But you can be a lab assistant, maybe, or a secretary, if you don't want to teach."

"Hasn't anybody read *Return of the Native?*"

12

"A dinner date?" Ruth says.

"Go ahead—tell him yes!" Peggy cries. The two girls hang over Catherine at the second-floor phone. So she tells Jack she'll be ready, and hangs up.

"He's a dream!" Ruth says. "With those looks and that car and all."

"I'll have to press my suit skirt," Catherine says.

"Suit skirt?" Ruth looks at Peggy.

"He'll be here at six."

"Today?" Peggy yells. "You never said it was today!"

She really is going to wear her wool suit. Ruth can't believe it.

Peggy ran to the telephone with wads of cotton between her toes; now she's sitting on the lower bed in nothing but a towel, seeing if her toenail polish smeared. "My God," she says, "she's really going to wear a suit."

"And her hair!" Ruth wails, watching Catherine far down the hall on her way to the ironing room. "She hardly ever puts it up! If she'd just use my big curlers and setting lotion, and turn it under the way Beth—"

"Has she even got nail polish on?"

"Of course not!"

"We can't just tell her she can't go that way! If I could get her to pluck her eyebrows and put her hair up . . . what's he going to think?"

The ironing room is little and dark; you plug your iron into the light socket plug overhead. The sink has somebody's wash soaking in it, and strings sag above, brushing you with panties and bras and slips that drip like stalactites in a cave. Waiting for the iron to heat, Catherine thinks that Jack knew Thorn, and her mother.

Tubbit didn't like to wash and iron. Pushing wet lace aside, Catherine gets the skirt on the board, inside out. Jack knew Thorn, and her mother. But she doesn't like him.

You keep your clothes hung in your mind, and they take so much time, and when you're going somewhere you think of them first, and paw them over in your imagination, looking for spots and wrinkles. And she doesn't like Jack. Every time she's with him, she's wrapped in some kind of thick, heavy importance that she has to drag along. It isn't part of her; it's something Jack hangs on her. He gives other women that feeling, too—waitresses, clerks, her roommates . . .

She thinks of his eyes: they never seem to have any expression under the heavy brows. It's the muscles around his eyes that show his senses are trained on her, like the single point where perspective lines meet. Cats are as alert as that: if you make an unexpected move, they leap to face you, too fast to see, though they've been asleep the minute before, eyes shut, tails over their jaws. Jack's lips are full, and indented at the corners like those of a Roman emperor in marble.

"Look, why don't you borrow my blue dress with the sequins?" Ruth says when Catherine comes back to put on her suit and blouse.

"Thanks for the offer, but it's cold," Catherine says. "Sometimes those places are freezing." Ruth and Peggy watch her put on a garter belt and silk stockings and pumps. She combs her hair and puts on some lipstick, finds her purse and gloves. "I'll be seeing you," she says.

"It's a crime," Peggy groans, watching Catherine go.

How does she like college? Jack wants to know. He came out in a taxi, he says—easier than driving when it's raining. He opens the dorm door and the taxi door for her, and smiles at the college kids going by. He's been on the West Coast for weeks—that's why he hasn't been in touch with her. But now she's got to see everything worth seeing around Chicago. He talks about plays and museums and night spots, while his eyes go over Catherine with their peculiar, opaque reverence.

He opens the door of the Golden Wheel for her, and checks her coat. The waiter pulls out her chair for her. Jack gives their order. She could be deaf and dumb, or walking in her sleep, or old. Or else very important. Looking up, she sees that peculiar reverence in Jack's eyes again.

Women float along so delicately on high heels. Jack smiles at Catherine. They touch their hair, and smile over the lid of a powder compact, and sit down with a little twist of the hips. And they smile. He leans back in the velvet chair and the shimmer of rose-pink lampshades and mirrors, reflected and reflecting.

"There's Jack Laird!" Ingrid Perry says, leaning close to Sally's blonde fingerwave. "Sally!"

"I don't care," Sally Quinn pouts, running a red-tipped finger around the rim of her water glass.

"Isn't he something? Didn't you go on a yacht—"

"I don't care!" Sally pouts, but she looks Catherine over between potted palms. Waiters come and go across thick carpets, and a small orchestra begins to play.

"You look so much like your mother," Jack says. Catherine doesn't answer him.

He loved Janet Buckingham for years, Jack says. Catherine looks so much like her. It seems as if Janet is still alive, and not smashed up and burned—Jack stops and looks away.

Janet was beautiful, he says after a while. Catherine has all her habits. Catherine holds her chin just like Janet did. She has those light eyes, and the high cheekbones.

The waiter lifts their soup plates away. The orchestra begins the Beguine.

"Let's walk by their table on the way out," Ingrid says, smiling at her date but talking to Sally. "I don't know who that character is he's got with him—she looks like something out of high school." She says in a low voice to Sally, "If you don't want any more of him, I'll take him on. A line as long as the Maginot, I bet, and doesn't he know his way around everything, if you know what I mean?"

"We had a fight," Sally says.

"Oh, well, then pardon me for horning in." Ingrid settles back in her chair. "Why's he so well heeled, if I may be so bold?"

"Big army deals. His company makes stuff for the army; they've retooled, or whatever."

If she liked him, Catherine thinks, maybe she could tell him how she really felt in college.

But what could she tell him? That she walked from the chapel to the dorm yesterday, when skies were streaming over her head without a tree to break their sweep, horizon to horizon, as if she were back in Detroit?

But it was almost 7:45, so she had to go into the dorm past the couples saying goodbye. College boys were wrestling on the grass, and bunches of them were on their way downtown, or to the library, or wherever the boys went after the girls had to be in.

She passed two seniors at the ironing boards, and said "Hi" to some girls in curlers and bobby pins. The back stairs rang, metal reverberating in their enclosed stories. Somebody yelled, "Hey, Barb, you got a call on third!"

Perfume mixed with soap smells, and the chemical breath of polish remover. "Corky got a box from home today," Jeanne said when she passed Catherine. "See you at ten if the hall guard doesn't make us all go back to our rooms and study."

Nobody was in the small room she shared with Ruth and Peggy. The last of the daylight fell on its jumble of familiar objects. Darkness already inhabited their clothes jammed in small closets, waiting to be ironed, and ironed again. Underwear hung on a line from the sink to the radiator. She wandered over to the dribbling faucet, running her hands through her hair. She'd better put it up.

She didn't need any light to do it, not any more. She stood there wondering which homework she was going to do first. She always worked ahead, and wrote her papers early, and was getting all A's.

Feeling in a dresser drawer for her curlers, she saw in the mirror how dark the room was, and felt as if Thorn's bed were behind her—as if, looking up, she'd see her shadowy reflection in his dresser mirror that always creaked, and behind her his long body stretched out, and his thoughtful eyes, watching . . .

She cried out then in the empty room, surrounded by bunk beds and desks and clothes in closets, clothesline and curlers and seniors at the ironing boards, ringing echoes of the stairs, a box from home, darkness like the bottom of a well. The window glass was cold when she pressed her face against it. Far away the sunset clouds descended to where the sun was going down, flowing.

"Your mother always adored dancing," Jack says. "How about having dessert later, and a dance now?"

Jammed against him on the tiny dance floor, Catherine watches the crowd who have come to sit at little tables with pink lights where they can't talk very well. Sometimes they get up and scrape their feet in a small circle of floor space, bumping against each other, looking over each other's shoulders at the pink lights and all the other faces.

There must be a kitchen, very real and smelly and busy and loud, where cooks are pushing food around on plates and wiping the edges of bowls on a rag before a waiter carries them in. Tonight when the music stops, and the cigarette smoke and the crowd disappear, people who look very different will come and take off these tablecloths, clean the carpets . . .

"You're a good dancer, if I do say so myself." Jack laughs, his eyes inches from hers.

So what's in this room now is a kind of pretending that food appears by magic, and carpets are always clean, and tablecloths grow white, like flowers, if your eyes are cool enough, if you look at it all as if that's the way it ought to be, and you deserve it.

"Get a load of that," Ingrid says, watching Jack dancing with Catherine.

"I should care," Sally says.

Jack laughs a little to himself. There's Sally. Let her look. Maybe Catherine isn't dressed right, but she's ten years younger than Sally, and the most beautiful girl in the room. If she got the right clothes . . . "Having fun?" he asks Catherine. "Want some dessert?"

Catherine sits down in the pink light from the table lamp, as fresh as if she grew there, like a flower, her eyes cool, looking at the place as if it isn't quite what it ought to be, and she deserves something better, and she does. "Tell me about Gilman," he says. "Start from the beginning and tell me about the classes, and the dates you've had—"

"I haven't had any dates," Catherine says. She tells him about her classes, and her roommate's birthday party, and the professors. Jack listens, smoking a cigarette, and then another. No dates. Doesn't look right, probably. Or is Thorn . . . has he . . .

"Look," Jack says, leaning into the pink light, "let's do something special when I come to get you next Friday. Let's go down to Henri's and let them do your hair and makeup especially for you—the works. You won't know yourself, and you can surprise your roommates and everybody. Not too sophisticated . . . a real college girl . . . see what they can do."

Catherine doesn't answer.

"Wouldn't you like that?" Jack asks. When Catherine looks very carefully at him, she sees he's genuinely surprised.

"No," Catherine says.

"You wouldn't like it?" The pink lampshade gives Jack's face a rosy edge.

"Hi," a blonde woman says, going by their table, her arm through a man's, a wide smile on her face. Another couple follows them, smiling too.

Jack stares at Catherine, tapping his cigarette on an ashtray. "Your mother was a beautiful woman—"

"Did you really know her well?" Catherine asks, looking Jack in the eye. "I don't think she had time to worry about how she looked."

"Janet loved clothes!" Jack's voice is louder than he means it to be. "I never saw her wear the same outfit twice. She went to London or New York and bought out the collections, and Rob let her—she didn't even know where the money came from, and she didn't need to. All the other women copied her—copied her hair and her makeup and the way she laughed and looked at you with those eyes of hers . . . there wasn't anybody like her!" He stops, then adds, "I knew her for years. A lot longer than . . ."

Catherine is staring across the small table at him, waiting for him to go on. He doesn't. He doesn't even look at her, but shakes a cigarette out of a pack and lights it, and blows out a stream of smoke. "I married twice. It wasn't right. Wait until you fall in love—you'll know what I mean."

His cuff links sparkle as he looks at his watch. "How about another dance before I have to get you back to the campus? Don't suppose they'd be very happy if you got in late."

Holding her, so young and light, in his arms, he looks down at that hair of hers hanging over the collar of her suit. He'll keep at her, but he shouldn't be hard on her; it's not her fault. She must be about a size 34. He's practically her uncle. If he wants to send her a dress for a present, why can't he? Those roommates of hers ought to get her to fix herself up, if she's got the dress; you know how girls are. Cute kids: Peggy Schmidt and Ruth . . . what was the blonde one's name? Ruth Stone.

It's not raining any more when they leave the Golden Wheel. Catherine lifts her face to the dark roofs and takes a long breath. "Let's walk a little, can we?" she says.

"Sure," Jack says. He stops at the cab window. "The lady wants to walk a few blocks," he tells the driver. "Follow us, will you?"

Wet wind is blowing paper down the street; Catherine dodges a newspaper in full sail, and smells autumn even here. The city hums around her with a car horn mixed in, a squeal of brakes, someone calling and then whistling, a familiar pattern of city sound that brings Detroit back . . .

Jack catches up with her and tucks her hand in his arm, smiling, his dark eyes watching her, his white silk scarf gleaming in the lights of a car going by.

Slick with rain and light, the sidewalks are nearly deserted, but the taxi follows them. When Catherine looks back, it's always there, block by block, its meter ticking.

13

There isn't any place to spend Christmas but Cedar Falls. Catherine doesn't want to go to Detroit; she doesn't know why. Tubbit writes he'll visit his relatives in South Dakota, and he knows she'll have a good time with the Knapps and young folks her own age.

The Christmas tea at the president's house is what everyone at Gilman is talking about. Each girl has to draw a boy's name from a box at chapel, and the boy has to call at her dorm for the girl, take her to the tea, and bring her back to her dorm again.

Catherine draws Bill Donnell's name, and Marie knows who he is: a real good-looking freshman, she says. The girls spend hours finding out who their dates are and what they can wear.

Catherine keeps wondering why she doesn't want to go back to Detroit.

Bill Donnell is nice looking, and he comes right on time. "Hi. You Catherine Buckingham?" he asks.

"Yes," she says. He settles his tie while she buttons her coat.

"I suppose we'd better get in the line for the two-fifteen bunch," Bill says. A line of couples snakes down the long walk in the cold wind, passing a boys' dorm.

"Do you have hours in your dorm?" Catherine asks.

"Well, the idea is—if they keep the girls in, the fellows will stay in, but I guess we don't. Not much to do in town, but one of the guys on our floor's got a car."

Catherine smiles, and Bill smiles right back and looks relieved. She should have smiled more; she always forgets. Ruth insisted on putting her hair up for her, and combing it out. Wait until you see Bill Donnell.

He can't think of anything to say, and neither can she. The president's house is close to the fine arts building, and the house door is open, swallowing up a continuous line of student couples.

There are coats heaped on beds and girls checking their hair in the mirrors. The dean of students stands at the living room door, and Catherine has been told what to say: "I'm Catherine Buckingham, and this is Bill Donnell."

The dean is a gray-haired, friendly man who says to the man next in line, "Dean Haynes, this is Catherine Buckingham and Bill Donnell," handing them over like packages.

Passing along the line, Catherine watches the men take her hand and smile, their voices rising a little. They bend toward her. Where are you from? Are you enjoying your freshman year? When they take Bill's hand, their voices deepen, their backs straighten, they raise their chins. She tries to remember to smile. What dorm do you live in? Looking forward to vacation?

The large Christmas tree ends the line with its veil of twinkling tinsel. The dining room has a table arranged with two lines of sandwiches, cakes and cups of punch. When the fifteen minutes are up, they collect their coats and are told goodbye and Merry Christmas by the president's wife at the door.

A line of couples winds back past the fine arts building to the dorms. Sunday afternoon is gray with sky and bare trees, and brown with fields of stubble and matted grass. Bill thanks Catherine for going with him, and she thanks him for such a good time. When she goes into the dorm, sack lunches for Sunday night are stacked by the desk, and the wastebaskets are already collecting apple cores and pieces of bread stuck together with white margarine.

The minute she gets up to the room, the girls want to know what Bill was like, and tell about their dates. She says Bill was nice, and he was good looking, and goes over to the sink to wash her hands. When she slips the soap under the water and puts it back, she can see Thorn's hands doing that, with their brown hairs. Narrow, long fingers . . .

"Your Uncle Jack's simply super, isn't he?" Ruth is saying. "My gosh—he's taken the three of us to that movie, and the swell stage show, and the Empire Room."

"I wish I had an uncle like yours," Peggy says to Catherine.

Ruth says, "So do I!"

They both start coaxing Catherine again. "C'mon," Peggy says. "If your uncle wants to take us—we'll never get another chance to go to Henri's, will we, Ruth?"

"And we can go home for Christmas and look like a million dollars," Ruth says. "Our crowd won't even know us, I bet! You get all kinds of grooming tips, and your makeup specially blended, and your hair styled, and Henri tells you what colors are best for you, and what ones are your next best—just everything!"

"If you tell your uncle you won't go, then we can't go!" Peggy cries.

14

They never did see "Henri"—maybe he was just a name—but the place was simply fabulous. Ruth and Peggy have to tell everybody about it. Those swell-looking beauty operators, and all the little glass booths where you go to have each thing done. Look at Ruth's hair—they rinsed it and showed her how to do it, and everything. Peggy told them she'd always wanted to have curly hair, and isn't it cute?

Catherine looks amazing, doesn't she? They gave her this super-simple hair style, and showed her how to use makeup and pencil her eyebrows and use just a little bit of rouge . . .

Jack laughs and flirts with Ruth and Peggy when he comes to take Catherine to Cedar Falls for Christmas. "Cute kids," he tells Catherine on the way home. Catherine looks gorgeous with that flat, straight, silky hair turned under just a little at the ends. Alice will notice it all right, and Margie.

And Alice does, of course. "My goodness!" she says the minute she sees Catherine, "we hardly recognized you!" She turns to Margie. "Doesn't Catherine look grown up in that hat and high heels and all?"

"Real sharp!" Margie says. Margie's room still has its drifts of organdy ruffles, and Ann Caldwell and Barb Henderson are on the other bed, surrounded by clothes and magazines.

"Hi!" Catherine says, taking off her hat and tossing her hair back. She ducks to look in Margie's mirror, and gets her comb out of her purse.

"Barb's going to Gilman next fall," Margie says. "She's got more *questions* to ask you!"

Catherine sits at the dressing table. "You're still going to go to Brymore?"

Margie makes a face. "I suppose."

"How about slacks—do you wear them to classes?" Barb asks. She's watching Catherine put fresh lipstick on. "Do you really have to study all the time?"

"Hey, tell us about going to Henri's, and about the Empire Room!" Ann says.

"What did you wear?"

"What was it like? I mean, the floor show . . ."

"How would you girls like to stay for lunch?" Alice asks, opening Margie's bedroom door. "Call your moms, and then come down when you're ready."

"Do you think I ought to take just skirts and sweaters, or cotton stuff?" Margie says, helping Catherine hang up her clothes in a hurry.

"I'd take cottons, and some blouses," Catherine says. "And jeans."

"Jeans?" Ann's eyebrows go up.

"Everybody at Gilman wears them," Catherine says. "Not girls' jeans—boys' jeans you get in men's stores, with buttons down the front, and you wear long shirttails over."

"Buttons down the front!" the girls chorus, going downstairs.

When they see Jack waiting, they burst into loud giggles.

"Mary Happel's sister has some," Barb whispers. "She goes to the U."

The other girls are so cute, Jack thinks: they sit down at the table with that flutter, their hair bouncing on their shoulders, their eyes watching him when they think he isn't looking. "But you don't wear jeans to classes," Barb says to Catherine.

"Not at Gilman," Catherine says. "And everybody wears saddle shoes and loafers . . . and lots of hats."

"For dates?" Ann asks, astonished.

"Well . . . if it's a church date, or you go to see some big show in town, and for the teas and receptions . . ."

"Let's all go shopping!" Barb says. "Get Betty, and just go looking for stuff. She's going to Iowa City and—hey—did you tell Catherine that Walt and Sue got married?"

"Listen," Barb says to Catherine, passing the rolls, "I've got to write this roommate of mine I've never seen, and we've got to get spreads for our room, and drapes . . ."

The Knapps have a "family Christmas" planned, Alice tells Catherine, and there's the Christmas play at the college, and the Christmas party at the church. Margie has twelve couples over for a New Year's dance in the basement rec room, and then a supper, and Bob Henderson is Catherine's date.

One afternoon she gets away and walks down by the creek. The snow crust is so thick she can walk on top of it most of the way in her furry carriage boots. She stands for a while under the old windmill that creaks with the wind blowing through its blades. It looks awkward and tall and lonely against clouds full of snow.

There's a new kind of gall on one of the bushes by the creek. She takes it home, hearing the sound of the windmill growing faint behind her, until it's drowned out by Dick and his friends trying out the motor on Gordie's new car at the curb.

"Hi," she says to Gordie and Dick and Bob Henderson. Bob asks her when she has to go back to college, and she tells him in two days.

"Do you have to study all the time?" Gordie asks.

"Not all the time," Catherine tells him, and goes on up the steps to the porch, breaking open the gall to see what's in it.

When she opens Margie's bedroom door and looks through the organdy curtains, she can just see the windmill over the trees.

15

Catherine's birthday in March is a thawing day, when classrooms and dorm halls are tracked with muddy water. She stays at the library until she almost gets some "minutes."

The dorm is hot and crowded; girls in slacks and shirts are studying in the parlors—you have to be dressed until the last upperclass girls come in with their dates and say goodnight and the doors are locked after them.

Girls are ironing in the laundry rooms or running back and forth from the showers. You have to watch out in the daytime: college boys clean the halls and empty wastebaskets. "Man on second!" they yell as they come; "Man on third!" Nobody cleans the rooms but the girls, if they can get roommates all together at one time to do it. Nearly everybody wears fuzzy slippers around the dorm, and they collect long ribbons of lint, like dust mops.

Catherine's hands are dirty with newsprint. In Cedar Falls she kept track of the Germans in Poland, finding where Lodz was, and the Vistula, and where the Russians crossed Poland's eastern frontier. The Knapps never talked about the war much.

"Hi," she says to girls as she passes.

And France is at war.

Radios on third floor are jumping with "Scatterbrain," but by the time she gets to her door, somebody is singing that it's time to roll out the barrel. When she walks into her room, the gang is, as the song is saying, all there.

"Happy Birthday!" they yell. There's cake and cherry floats. Peggy and Ruth have bought her a bottle of "Carefree" perfume. They give her the packages that have come: a box of cookies and some handkerchiefs from Tubbit, a table radio from Jack Laird, and a red nightshirt from the Knapps. She's eighteen.

The "phony war" drags on, but it isn't so phony any more.

Then summer begins so early—in May the weather is as warm as it was the year before in Detroit, when she was seventeen and the lunas flew in the sunshine of Thorn's room, and she said,

"We could marry." The air is full of the scent of lilacs, and the girls wear them in their hair.

They sunbathe on the dorm lawn, listening to radios set by open windows. Denmark has fallen. The Germans invade Holland. Then the Germans are in France.

Ruth sits among the blankets and books and suntan lotion with her arm around Catherine, and explains to some of the other girls that Catherine's father is over in France—not really her father, but her uncle who raised her—and it's simply awful.

Everybody thinks that America will have to get into the war now, and the boys will have to fight, unless the French win.

But the French don't win. By the time Catherine is on the train for Detroit and summer vacation, the British have evacuated Dunkirk.

The end of May is cooler. Catherine sits with a newspaper on her lap, watching her reflection travel the miles from Chicago to Detroit: in the train window she can see the turquoise of her linen suit, the black dinner plate of a hat over her eye. Peggy and Ruth helped her buy the outfit, and put her hair up, fussing over her looks, saying she ought to care.

Thank heaven it's cool for the trip. Ruth told her to wear black gloves so they wouldn't show the dirt, and warned her about the linen suit: she'd have to pull her skirt flat under her to keep it from wrinkling.

She hasn't been on a train since she took one at the station in Detroit when she was eleven, and rode it for miles, and then tried to get the engineer to explain. She'd got back home all right. Tubbit had said it was a miracle, but what she'd wanted to know was why the engineer would only talk about where she'd come from. Nobody had asked anybody else on the train where they came from, or tried to make them get on another train and go back home.

Nothing Catherine can see from her window is as wide as the Michigan fields when she was eleven—those fields streaming by on either side of the magical first train she had commanded, the way a horse is commanded, to take her somewhere.

Tubbit doesn't recognize her when she gets off the train. She hasn't seen him for almost a year, but she knows his gray mustache and stooped shoulders a long way off.

No, he tells her, no word from Mr. Wade. His eyes are on her high heels, or her hat. No word at all. He's sure glad to see her.

Thought she might come back at Christmas, but it was a long way. He liked getting her letters.

Driving home in Tubbit's new Ford, Catherine watches the familiar city streets and wonders if Irish Mac is dead, and what happened to the men who slept in abandoned cars during the Depression.

The new houses have crept a street closer now. When they drive past the "Northlawn" street sign and stop under the cottonwoods, Catherine gets out of the car and runs. Tubbit watches her go.

Months and months of days. The flowers in the beds look just the same as they did the day she left with Jack and Alice, but those flowers all died—these are new ones. The porch steps creak in the same old place.

If she's crying, it's only because the rainbows fly across the wall as she slams the door—shutting it out, shutting it all out, finally, and waiting with her eyes closed for the feeling to come. It will taste like fresh air and smell like wind in long grass, and she won't have to go out there for days and days.

Her eyes shut, she waits. The low, chuckling noise is the refrigerator in the kitchen; the clock ticks in the hall. No other place could smell like this one: old rugs, furniture polish, vegetable soup.

When she opens her eyes at last, nothing has been moved; not a thing is different. All of it is watching her, and it's just a house in the afternoon sun, with the refrigerator running and the clock ticking.

The hall floor is as bare as always under her clicking heels.

Familiar chairs spread their arms in the living room; the tall china vase on the floor sparkles in a patch of sun. But the mantel mirror's silver is wearing so thin now: she's only a blur of turquoise suit and black hat. It hardly shows her face. Her mouth is nothing but a large red spot in the mottled glass.

16

Thorn's brush is still in the drawer. His shirts in the closet are still creased with the shape of his arms. She can't sleep, night after night.

But she can't stay in all the time; she walks past new houses to lie under the elm. The sky is full of the same whipped cream clouds; the elm is heavy with leaves again. If she fills her hands with the warm, dry sand, it sifts through her fingers and blows away. She can hear a steam shovel groaning and clanking.

The NLRB is serving "cease and desist" orders on Ford, and the AFL and CIO . . . she's lost track of what's going on in Detroit. She ought to visit the Wayne County Training School again to see if they still make the children scrub and polish the wooden floors every day.

One hot morning she stops at Tubbit's fence, looking at the new backyards full of washlines and little children and toys. Then she sees that the new street named "Northlawn" stops at their lot line . . . then it goes on: at the other side of their old house and cottage and barn a new sign reads, "Northlawn."

Nights in Thorn's bed are black, and if she dozes she wakes with a wet face and aching throat, breathless, staring at what is his. Books with his name on are ranged along a shelf, the air walling them off from her as completely as if she looks through bars, as if she were Alice, only a few inches high. He had always been on the other side of that invisible wall. His eyes had that distance in them. When she shrieks at him in her dreams, that distance, sad and helpless, stares back. The room watches her as if it always knew. The carved leaves on the headboard . . . the oval-backed chair . . . the highboy with the lion's feet are only witnesses now to what has always been. A flagpole in one of the new backyards clicks in the night wind.

Her bed is narrow. Jelly glasses are still stacked on her dresser. Her books are there. The woman watches her from her frame on the wall. But if Catherine begins to fall asleep where her plants move in the breeze and the mattress has molded itself to her, year after year, she wakes with a wild cry. A sense of space shreds away from her into the summer moonlight. A dog barks somewhere in the dark streets of new houses.

17

She really looked nice, Karl Tubbit thought. Her hair cut off that way, and all the new clothes. He hardly knew her when she got off the train. But the minute she got home she put old clothes on, and washed her face, and said it was too much work to put her hair up all the time.

If she'd just stop wandering around and start working on some of those "projects" she left all over the house. She wanted to stay in the big house by herself, she said, even if it was lonely. But she'd come eat with him.

She just wandered around. Sometimes she slept in Wade's room, and sometimes she slept in her own, and sometimes he wondered if she slept at all—lights over there real late at night.

And then she started talking a lot, telling him how "crawly" she felt in Cedar Falls, when nobody else seemed to think anything was wrong.

He kept asking her what bothered her, but all she could think of was that she had to stay in the house so much of the time with the girl her own age, and they kept looking at her and worrying about her clothes and hair. Nobody ever talked like that about how the boys looked, she said, or Mr. Knapp, and they didn't have to stay in and talk about makeup and clothes and hair styles all day.

He told her he liked her hair—told her she seemed real grown up. She said the Knapps had a little girl who wasn't even in school yet, and he should see how grown up she was—just like those women Jack Laird brought with him—always smiling and twisting themselves around and showing off their clothes.

What was she supposed to do? she asked one hot afternoon when they were transplanting. He'd raised the same kind of marigolds they always had in the big flower bed, and she was handing him the seedlings. She said she couldn't just stay in this house and wait for Thorn to come back.

Well, now, that was a crazy thing to say. He told her that here she was, going to college and all, learning so many things and making friends—

And she handed him a marigold and said that they locked the dorm doors, and made the girls sign in and sign out, and didn't they know how that made you feel? The girls in Cedar Falls and at college were used to it—that was the worst part. They didn't even care any more if they couldn't get out. They weren't even curious about what kind of a town they were living in, or where things were. They just followed little paths they were sure of, and never even wondered what else there was.

That was just the trouble; he knew that—she'd always gone running all over Detroit, and now she had to learn how to be a lady and look nice and get an education. He told her she was lucky to get an education. He told her she'd get used to it all; it would just take time.

And that was when she started to cry, and he really felt bad to see her kneeling there with the marigolds, crying and saying who'd want to get used to that—would he? Would he? And nobody talked about clothes and makeup and hairdos in classes. They learned about discoveries, and philosophies, and poems and plays and novels that were more beautiful than anything on earth, and famous battles and paintings—what did clothes and hair and makeup have to do with them? And symphonies—were you going to write a symphony because you looked good?

Were you going to write a book if you wore just the right lipstick? she said, putting a marigold down and rubbing her eyes. She got mud all over her cheek. Did they really think that if you combed your hair just right you could discover a cure for some disease?

Well, of course not, he kept saying. She was supposed to study hard and learn—

Then why did everybody think the way you looked was so important? There were so many things she wanted to do, she said.

But she didn't really do much. She had a big ant project spread out in the spare room—why didn't she work on that? There was a real pretty oil painting half finished on an easel in the storeroom: she could paint. She'd always had a million things she wanted to do, and now all she did was work on the accounts. She was taking care of all their money, and she did a good job. Mr. Laird told them he'd help out any time, if they got short.

The news was real bad. The Germans were attacking along the Somme, and they said the railway stations in Paris were jammed. And then the French government ran away to Tours, and Italy declared war on France and England. By the end of June it was all over—France had been conquered by Hitler, just like that. You wouldn't think a whole country would give up so quick and surrender. Neither of them could believe it. They just sat and looked at the newspapers and listened to the radio.

He thought maybe they'd hear pretty soon from Wade. He wouldn't stick it out in France when the Germans were marching all over it like that. He must be in England. But they never did hear, not even when Catherine was about ready to go back to Gilman College in the fall.

She didn't want to go back, she said. He worried about her a lot, and sometimes they talked a long time; he liked that. Sometimes she'd read to him while he worked; she wanted to read *Alice in Wonderland* and *Through the Looking Glass* again. It was just a children's book, but he liked it, until Catherine got going in it and started being upset.

"See?" Catherine would say. "See how they treat Alice? Nothing makes any sense to her, and of course it doesn't! That's the point! She sees how crazy everything is, but when she says what she sees, everybody's mean to her!"

It really bothered her. "Not one person in either book is nice to her but the White Knight, and he's as lost as Alice is." She said she dreamed one night that she was as big as the house she was in, stuck inside it with her foot out the chimney and her arm out the window, like Alice.

She really didn't want to go back to college, and that was a shame, but she went.

He sure missed her. It was a kind of funny life, living out there all by himself and keeping two houses clean. He started going to a church not very far away. They had a bowling club and a potluck group he liked, and so he made some friends, and sometimes they'd come over to his house for a dinner, and bring their wives, and it was nice.

You had to keep the big house warm enough so nothing would freeze in the winter, and when Catherine came home for Christmas her sophomore year, they had a good time, but she was so quiet. She still missed Wade a lot—she must have—she slept in his room, and she liked to talk about him. He was helping his cousins live through the occupation, she said. That was what he'd want to do. How could they keep going with the Germans there? Roosevelt had his third term, and she was glad of that.

She worked on her ant project a little that Christmas, he thought. He never bothered it; he just dusted around all the things she called her "projects": the ants and the files and card files and paintings and notebooks and music and all. But sometimes when he came to call her to supper she was just sitting in the living room in the dark, or maybe she had a fire going.

They got a big tree like they always had, and put on all the lights, and she started talking about how people put trees in their houses and fixed them so they looked as if they gave light all by themselves. But the trees didn't have any roots. They weren't really growing. After you got tired of the same lights all the time, you took them off, and threw the dry tree out.

She said she was learning so much at college, and he said she was really lucky, but she said what good did it do? She didn't think she was really growing, or getting ready to go anywhere—where would she go? Maybe teach in some school—all these little bits of things she was learning. She stood there tightening light bulbs and asking him how many famous women he could name who had really grown up to do things, and he thought of Amelia Earhart. She held up a string of lights and they turned her all different colors—she looked real pretty—but he couldn't think of anybody else but Madame Curie. She said she didn't want to be a teacher, or a secretary, or a nurse. He'd never really thought about it.

So all her stuff just sat in that house. Of course she came home summers, and Christmastime, and there was Pearl Harbor. Thousands and thousands of Japanese got put in camps in Wyoming and places like that, and it was war again, a World War. They never heard from Wade.

Willow Run out near Ypsilanti was supposed to be turning out a thousand bombers a day in 1942, but that was a joke. People had to pay seventy cents to get to Willow Run and back on the bus from Detroit, and they were making only about nine dollars a day, so they started calling it "Willit Run." But the "Arkies" and the "Oakies" and the blacks kept coming in by buses and old tin lizzies to get the war jobs.

We were going to slap the Jap right off the map, and the Germans, too, they said. When Germany invaded Russia, everybody liked the "Reds" all of a sudden. He didn't have to plant a victory garden; he'd always had one.

Gas rationing was the first real hard thing; he only got an A sticker for four gallons a week. The trains were packed every time Catherine came home. And then there was the sugar rationing: eight ounces a week until it got to be twelve, and then coffee. You could save kitchen fats and take them to the grocer for red points, but you couldn't get anything delivered; even the milk came only every other day. You couldn't get whiskey at all, but he never drank it anyway, and he didn't miss cigarettes, either, or mind the shoe rationing.

What he got so tired of was the ration books for butter and meat and canned goods and cheese. You had to watch for the little red numbers on the shelves that told you how many points, and you had to read what points expired every day (the newspapers printed it), and then maybe there wouldn't be what you wanted anyway.

18

At first the war is like a holiday at Gilman: everyone runs and shouts and laughs and jumps up and down to think that America is finally in it.

Then the boys begin to have a different look, as if the real things are happening somewhere else now, and college isn't so important, not any more. They look at you across a kind of gap: you aren't going where they are going; you'll just be studying. The war makes the boys more important, and you can see it. People treat them differently.

Catherine often tells Jack she has to study, and can't go out with him. She sits in her room at the desk that college girls have carved and scratched hearts and daisies and initials on, staring at a piece of paper under the gooseneck lamp.

> She is as in a field a silken tent
> At midday when a sunny summer breeze
> Has dried the dew and all its ropes relent,
> So that in guys it gently sways at ease . . .

The boys begin to leave college. Catherine writes every minute she can spare from studying, and has two poems and a story of hers printed in the campus creative writing magazine.

"You're a natural writer," Professor Knowland says: Catherine thinks and writes using images; she sees feelings as things, Professor Knowland says. That's unusual.

Professor Knowland is one of the women (she tells Catherine) who thought they were a vanguard: they got PhD's and were what were called "career girls." Now she's married to a lawyer in Oak

Park, and she wears expensive clothes and perfume. And why doesn't Catherine try writing a poem made of one simile, like Robert Frost did in "The Silken Tent"? Catherine has a real gift for simile.

So Catherine writes a poem using a tent as a simile, just the way Frost did, but she never hands it in. Professor Knowland has been in the vanguard and a career girl, and she knows the girls admire her clothes. She thinks Frost's "The Silken Tent" is a lyrical sonnet tribute to his wife, perhaps, or his mother:

> And its supporting central cedar pole,
> That is its pinnacle to heavenward
> And signifies the sureness of the soul,
> Seems to owe naught to any single cord . . .

Catherine slept in a tent when she was small. Tubbit nearly had fits at first, when she stayed out all night alone in a field.

One thing she remembers about tents is that you don't touch them when it's raining, or you have to go home, stupid and soaked.

> But strictly held by none, is loosely bound
> By countless silken ties of love and thought
> To everything on earth the compass round,
> And only by one's going slightly taut
> In the capriciousness of summer air
> Is of the slightest bondage made aware.

But mostly she remembers lying in the tent in the dark, and feeling as if the tent isn't there. You can hear the smallest sound: a cricket . . . leaves rustling . . . a far-away car on Seven Mile Road. You can feel the night coolness. You can smell the grass that's soaking up dew. You might be sleeping out under the sky, except that you can't see any stars.

And you think you can get up to stand in the free night wind—but the canvas is there. You can push out into the air a little . . . then the canvas stops you, invisibly, in the dark. It sags back where it was before. There's only the one way you can get out.

On Mother's Day the dean speaks about how important women are to the war effort. He tells the rows and rows of students and faculty at chapel that our fighting men have to be sure that the home fires are kept burning. They know what they're fighting for: they'll set the world free again and then come home to the girl of their dreams and make a new, better life.

When Catherine goes to Detroit in the summer, the two houses and the barn and the cottonwoods are surrounded by all the new houses. Once in a while, looking at the cars parked at the curbs and the wagons and tricycles on the sidewalks, she thinks for a second that she imagined the sea of long grass and sumac and scrub oak in all directions as far as she could see, and the clouds in the bowl of the sky.

The next fall Dotty Smythe tells her about the new ideas on student government the campus leaders have, and she takes Catherine to some of the meetings. For a while Catherine doesn't go out much with Jack: she sits up late arguing with Dotty and Marie Carey and Don Reed and George Canaletti and Bill Donnell. She organizes the points and meets all the arguments the dean can possibly think of, and the rest of them take notes and say she's really something.

She can really think, all right, Bill Donnell says, and laughs, and brings up a point that Catherine has already discussed from every angle. He says all the same things she said; they all listen intently. He ought to go to the administration with that, the rest say. It's the heart of the argument for student government. He's right.

After the meeting Bill Donnell asks Catherine for a date. Marie and Dotty say, gee, Bill's a Big Wheel on Campus, and here she is, dating a BWOC! He's going to talk with the administration, presenting all the arguments, and here Catherine's going to have a date with him. She ought to wear her purple outfit, Peggy says. Ruth wants her to put her hair up a new way—why doesn't she try it?

Bill takes her out for hamburgers and shakes, and tells Catherine all about what he's going to do. Finally she looks at him and says that he took his main ideas from what she told the student group, didn't he? He smiles and says, sure, she's really something, does she know that? Beauty *and* brains.

Sometimes, sitting at Thorn's desk at Christmastime, she looks out at the smokestack of Bagley School over the roofs of new houses, far away, especially when she's reading the worst poems of Emily Dickinson, the ones where she's coy and cute.

But there are other poems that are as lonely as wind over snow, or a voice talking to itself for a lifetime.

> A loss of something ever felt I—
> The first that I could recollect
> Bereft I was—of what I knew not
> Too young that any should suspect
> A Mourner walked among the children . . .

She has to write a term paper on Emily Dickinson. One day she walks past the Bagley School. The same Christmas trees are pasted on the classroom windows. The same double doors clamp shut behind the children. Standing outside in the trampled snow, she thinks of a violin out of tune, scratched and battered desks, bored eyes, and a teacher after school who was followed from blackboard to blackboard by questions from a little kid in a Shirley Temple dress.

Sometimes, lying on Thorn's bed at Christmastime, she spreads out snapshots that are like windows. Is that her in the white crib? Could Thorn have brought her up these very stairs the first night they slept here? What room had her crib been in? She closes her eyes, trying to remember. The baby girl looks at her from her glossy snapshot space, her bare feet in the air, her fists waving.

The tall man and the child look out of the pictures as if she ought to know why they stand so straight, chins up, or what they are dreaming of as they kneel in a field outside Tubbit's fence, with the first houses beginning to be built a mile away.

The girl gets taller and taller, and the tall man seems sadder. They draw closer together. Tubbit was always yelling, "Move closer! I can't get you both in!" but of course he could. There they are, two people in a wilderness of uninteresting bushes or garden, tiny and close together, sunlight making caves of their eyes and showing every wrinkle in baggy pants.

How funny she looks with that long hair hanging down her back, and no lipstick, staring into the camera's eye as if she only

wants to get back to whatever she's been doing, and is only standing there because Tubbit wants to use his new Kodak.

The pictures are sharp. When she looks through a reading
glass, Thorn looks from that world with his quiet, wincing look,
as if he sees too much. And her own face swims up from the tiny
couples, bright with the sun of a world her eyes take for granted:
they are calm under that wild-looking hair. This is the way the
world is, her pale face seems to say. How else could it be?

V

Cool at last, she has no fever
to make trees waver over
her as if she were a fire; no gardens wilt
into her arms. Once she felt
sun lie hot on her skin
and a whole clover field crowd in,
fresh and common as desire.
Now every tree is as still as a church
spire.
Gardens are only flowers. Ripe clover
flushes pink and white, sways over
to nothing but the wind passing. Sun,
touching her, does not feel like anyone.

1

Bill Donnell takes Catherine to a movie in Chicago after Christmas. They watch Jeanette MacDonald carrying that soprano of hers through the most improbable situations, keeping Nelson Eddy at arm's length, cold and scornful and girlish in frilly costumes, pursued by that idiotic melting look in Nelson's eye. Imagine what's going on just out of sight: the orchestra, the cameramen, makeup crew, costume crew, professional, exacting. Jeanette manages to get a little of that melting look in her eye in the last duet, but not much.

After hot fudge sundaes and Cokes, Bill says he's had a great evening, and he doesn't know another girl he can talk to like this. But when they drive back from Chicago, he stops his car in the dark lot near the dorm and starts putting his hands all over her.

"Don't!" Catherine says, ducking her head so he can't kiss her and pushing his hands away. What's the matter with him? They're crowded close in the front seat, and it's embarrassing, and she's mad—how would he like it if she started doing that to him? "Don't!" she says, louder than before.

He's crazy—why does he think she'll let him do that? They hardly know each other, and she certainly hasn't done anything to show him she wants any lovemaking. "Stop it!" she says. They're glaring at each other like enemies when only a moment before they were friends. Can't he see she doesn't like it—not yet? He's still trying to force her to kiss him—she has to struggle out of his car and run to the dorm. Trying to be calm as she passes the desk and goes up to her room, she wonders what's the matter with him.

"Honest!" Bill says, "I didn't mean to hurt your feelings, honest I didn't!" He's at the dorm desk the next morning, waiting until she comes down for breakfast, apologizing to her the minute he sees her.

"Well, what *did* you mean to do?" Catherine asks. Backed up behind a group of chairs where their whispers won't carry as far as the desk, they eye each other. Catherine's face is flushed a little; her angry eyes sparkle.

"You're sure pretty," Bill says. He grins. "Can't blame a fellow for trying."

"Why not?"

Bill just grins, as if that's answer enough.

"Why can't I blame you for trying?"

"A girl like you? Can't a guy lose his head a little?"

Catherine gives him one angry look and turns to go, but he grabs her arm. "Listen, let me make it up to you!"

"You didn't really do anything. But I don't like to be . . . how would you like it if somebody grabbed you like that? I don't even know you very well, and you don't know me, either." Catherine shakes her arm free and starts for the dining room.

"Wait! Listen . . ." Bill catches up to Catherine at the dining room but he can't talk to her: a crowd surrounds them. She sits down at a table where there's no room for him, and he has to leave her there.

"Hey!" Peggy says, joining Catherine on the walk to chapel. Winter wind presses their coats and skirts against their long colored stockings: Peggy's are a bright red and Catherine's are kelly green.

"What do I hear about you?" Dotty Smythe asks Catherine, falling into step on Catherine's other side. "You've got Bill Donnell eating out of your hand, everybody says. What'd you do, kid?"

"Roses!" Peggy says. "A whole couple dozen of them came this morning for her!"

"Playing hard to get!" Dotty says, grinning at Catherine.

"That's the line that drives them batty! Keep up the good work!" She giggles as she sees Bill Donnell running up the walk behind them. "Come on, Peggy—four's a crowd."

"Catherine!"

Catherine turns around and waits for Bill. She thanks him for the roses, and he acts as if the roses have changed things. He wants her to date him again so he can make it up to her, he says, pleading. Finally she says she will, but she doesn't want to ride in his car.

So they have a Coke date, and then sit on the library steps. He's tall and has hair that reminds her of Thorn's, and he says he's going to go into politics. He has a government major, and works with the staff of the mayor of his town in the summers. He's going into the marines at the end of the semester. You have to have a good war record to get anywhere—doesn't she think so?

Catherine says she doesn't know—she won't get anywhere, she guesses. Bill says she has the best sense of humor, and won't she write him in the marines? He wants her to be his girl, he says. Anybody who would fight old Bill off like that: he admires it.

Why? Catherine asks him. Wouldn't he have fought back the same way if somebody had grabbed him—somebody he hardly knew? She's angry, but he laughs, that's all, and calls her a regular little spitfire, and says a man always likes a girl who plays hard to get.

She doesn't feel little, and she hasn't been playing. He's got a glint in his eyes as if he wants, for the fun of it, to be her enemy. He's peculiar. Maybe he's practicing to be a marine. Whatever's the matter, she certainly doesn't want to "fight old Bill off," which is what he seems to want. So she tells him she doesn't think they can be good friends.

Bill writes her from marine camp anyway, and says he's bushed every night, and so are his buddies. By the time they're marines they'll be dead, he says, or else solid iron.

Catherine reads his letter while girls are piled around her on the beds deciding whether to do a variety show or a one-act play for the Campus Stage Night. "Gee!" Dotty says, looking at Catherine's letter, "maybe Bill's going to send you his marine pin to wear!"

The girls stop talking and look at Catherine, interested. Lois Lester is the only one who laughs, then leans her head back against the bunk bed wall and watches Catherine. "I can't figure you out," she says. "What do you want, anyway?"

"I'd like to go fight," Catherine says. "The war is the most important thing . . . "

"How about a one-act?" Mary Ellen says. "We did a cute one in high school called 'The Wish Machine' . . ."

"If we're not good enough to fight and get shot at and get killed," Catherine goes on, but only Lois hears her. Mary Ellen bounces on the bed and flips her hair over her shoulder.

"It's called 'The Wish Machine,' and you have a big box on stage painted with wheels and dials and buttons, and people come up on one side dressed like one kind of person, and they say they want to be somebody else."

Catherine shoves her hair back of her ears and hunches up beside Lois. She sure doesn't care how she looks, Lois thinks, and she gets top grades and walks around by herself all the time.

"So then they pay their money and step into the machine and there's awful sounds, and then they come out what they want to be—except that it's really somebody else dressed up. You can't change costumes that fast," Mary Ellen says.

"When the soldiers come back, they'll have been there. They can say they've been there, and if they hadn't gone—"

"The Delts are going to do charades," Dotty says.

"They pledged Mary Langer—that brain!—all because she got an army air corps pin," Peggy says. "She was going to stay independent, but when they asked her, she said yes, just like that."

Catherine looks at the letter in her lap. "Bill found a place in the library stacks where he could sit all night." She pushes her hair behind her ears again. "It's important," she says, as if it really is. "He could stay out all night and just think."

"Hey, anybody know when senior pictures are going to be taken?" Dotty asks.

"And the professors don't look at us the same," Catherine says to Lois. "It's important. The little things are important . . . ones you hardly notice." She crawls off the lower bed under Mary Ellen's dangling slippers and looks out the window.

"I suppose we'll have to wear white blouses, and look like a bunch of babies!" Dotty says, making a face.

"So what are you going to wear to your wedding—red?" Mary Ellen asks.

"Who cares?" Dotty poses like a cheesecake photo on the edge of a desk. "Gimme a man and I'll walk down the aisle in anything!"

The hill below slopes down to a few houses, and then farm fields, white on white, tufted with stubble. At first, when Catherine was a freshman and had to be in at 7:45 instead of 10:00, she got up early in the morning before it was light, because you could get out of the dorm then; everyone was asleep.

The streets of town were blue before dawn. One of the first places to open was the Jarvis Cafe out on the highway, where the truck drivers stopped. She went out there, morning after morning, and talked with Mrs. Jarvis, and listened.

Or the nursing home on First Street behind the bank. They had their lights on before dawn, and they didn't care if you came in and talked to the old people, who sat in wheelchairs in the parlor and looked straight ahead, as if they were watching something come closer and closer.

The town streets are a map in her mind now, a grid. She had walked into the country her freshman year—out as far as the first farms. She has that map in her mind, too: the small, strange details of this or that house . . . an old barn in a field . . . pumpkins left to rot along a row of corn stalks . . .

She'll have to go out like that again. Catherine leans her forehead on the window. When she has time.

2

Spring rain drums on the dorm windows. "It's just too bad. Gee, I'm sorry," Jeanne says, and sits down beside Catherine on her bed.

"He grew up in France," Catherine says in a flat voice. "He wanted to go back and help his cousins, and then the war started, and I suppose he found a way to stay, until the Germans . . . "

"Well, sure," Jeanne says soothingly. "Sure." She gets up. "He was really like her father," she explains to Barbara and Helen in the doorway. "He raised her. And her roomies are both gone into town, wouldn't you know?"

"Gee," Barbara says. "I'm sorry."

"We're both sorry." Helen glances up and down the dormitory

hall, waiting to catch newcomers first with the news. She slides away. "Hey, Dotty," she whispers, "Catherine just heard her father got killed in France, and her roomies aren't here!"

"Oh, no!"

"Right after Paris fell that summer, remember? He had some cousins there, and finally she hears about it. He wasn't really her father, but he raised—"

"I thought her father's always driving up in that Cadillac . . . the real sharp guy who looks like Cary Grant, sort of."

"Dope! That's her boyfriend!"

"Wow!"

"He's here to take her dancing at the Empire Room tonight, and she just got the news."

"Wow!"

"Tonight! Her father's dead, and I don't know what she's going to do—he's got a tux on and he's waiting." Helen and Dotty are in Catherine's doorway now, whispering under the chatter inside.

"I've got to get ready," Catherine says in the same flat voice.

"Maybe she ought to wear something black," Dotty says.

"I've got that black jersey!" Helen's already out the door.

"She ought to wear her hair up," Jeanne says, back with Helen and the dress. "She's got to wear a girdle!"

"Here, we'll make a big wide swoop at the back of her head, see?"

"An orchid! Hey, they got an orchid just delivered to the desk for her!" A chorus of squeals.

"She's out cold, can't you tell?" Dotty helps Catherine yank the girdle up. "Put on the dress and then get your makeup on—you've got to wear mascara . . . "

"Well, hurry up—Cary Grant's down there and all the girls at the desk are swooning!"

The full, dark lips reflected in the mirror say, "He wants to marry me." The heavy-lashed blue eyes say nothing at all. Bobby pins scrape Catherine's scalp under a crown of gleaming hair. Silk stockings itch and crawl; the girdle, rigid as armor, is turning her flesh to pink, printed with round white disks.

But the image in the mirror has stepped out of the movies. When Dotty jerks its skirt up, the long, slim legs gleam under silk. Black rayon drapes the padded shoulders and gleams over the roundness of breasts and arms in the light. An orchid sprouts from one shoulder.

The girls follow her down the hall. She's got her formal coat and her handbag and white gloves. The toes of her black pumps hurt. Feeling bare and cold, Catherine goes cautiously down dormitory stairs that smell of scorched cloth from the ironing room, and the first look Jack gets is as wiped clean of any expression as Hedy Lamarr's. The beautiful thing walks up to him among college boys waiting for their dates and eyeing his tux; he thinks he'll smother, and trembles, and says in a cool voice, "Here, let me help you with your wrap—it's raining. I've got a taxi."

Nobody at the desk or in the staring dorm parlor has seen anything so much like Hollywood before. "God!" Jeanne breathes from the stair landing, "I hope she's smart enough to say yes! What more does she want?"

"Just imagine!" Dotty's eyes glow. "Just imagine . . ."

3

She has to go somewhere because of the shock, Jack says, so Catherine sits with the orchid on her shoulder, watching half-naked women tap dance in the Empire Room. And Thorn is dead.

Jack says he doesn't care if she wants to talk or cry—just go ahead, his eyes always on her as if she's a goddess and can talk about Milton if she wants to, talk about anything just to be talking: how the class sits, just sits, day after day, and the girl next to her never listens to the professor reading Milton because she has to write letters to her boyfriend, while Adam tells the archangel Raphael how he asked God for an equal: another human being like himself for company, because he was alone with the animals:

Among unequals what society . . .

but he didn't get it, Adam tells the archangel: he got Eve. But that wasn't true; Adam got Milton's Eve, simpering like the waiters at the Empire Room. Jack says she mustn't worry about a thing— he'll go to Detroit and talk to Tubbit and see what he wants to do about the two houses. And she doesn't have to think about anything like that now.

The orchid gets crushed when she dances with Jack and talks about reading Milton's *Paradise Lost* with Thorn once, and tells him that she'd raised her hand and said that Eve was the central character of *Paradise Lost,* not Satan . . . Milton couldn't help it. Eve's decision caused the Fall—she tells Jack over the orchestra playing "Go Fly a Kite"—and Eve uses Satan, and even wonders, for a minute or two, if she should share the apple and all her knowledge with Adam. She's trying not to cry, and Jack watches her and says he'll take care of her, won't he?

So Jack helps Tubbit sell the two houses and land. Catherine can't go to Detroit, and it wouldn't do any good, Jack says, so he goes. Tubbit doesn't want to live there alone; he wants to go back to South Dakota.

Tubbit cleans the houses out. He boxes Thorn's clothes, and the hairbrush with the gold-brown hairs, and the muddy oxfords Catherine used to wear in the fields, and sends them to charity. The pigeon-roosts in the barn loft, the rabbit hutches, all left behind. He packs the butterfly nets, and the glass boxes for bumblebees and hornets, and Thorn's breeding cages, and all the cases of butterflies and moths. But what happened to the beehives, brown with propolis, and the rifle target, and the waterwheel Thorn and Catherine built? Catherine never knew.

Boxes come to Cedar Falls for her; they have to be stored somewhere. She supposes they are her books, and the files and card files—thousands of entries in her handwriting, or Thorn's—records, histories, lists of books read, metamorphoses observed, sites visited, temperatures recorded . . . paper heavy with the hours they spent.

When she left Detroit that first time with her hair cut off and curled, she thought she was breaking off her projects for just a little while. She hadn't wanted to leave them very long, because they were green and growing, like her knowledge of Thorn. He was another kind of knowledge: the key on the table you hadn't been tall enough to reach until you said, "I want to begin."

She doesn't look in those boxes, not even when she goes to Cedar Falls before she graduates. She knows what the notebooks look like, full of her hasty writing: it slants across the page as if she hadn't wanted to wait to learn the next thing—had to learn it.

And between the lines a small, faint echo of another kind of knowledge: she had come from Thorn to those pages, and then turned from the pages to Thorn again.

Sometimes she goes out with Jack, because he'll talk about Thorn, and he knew her mother. Janet Buckingham was beautiful, and Thorn and Janet went riding around the dull lanes in Nottinghamshire looking for bugs. And Catherine dances with Jack on the little dance floors, her eyelashes dark with mascara, nearly fainting sometimes with the drum-drum-drum and saxophone blast and trumpets repeating the same phrase, the same phrase, the same phrase.

But sometimes she tells Jack she has to study. She sits at the desk with the hearts and daisies on it, staring at a piece of paper under the gooseneck lamp, closer to Thorn and almost more free than she can stand. She doesn't hear the dorm noise—she feels what she's going to do opening out before her like space itself. She comes home from nightclubs and movies smelling like a smoked ham, her toes aching and red lines creased into her waist and shoulders, and there are the poems and the plays and the words—the walls roll back, and she thinks she has a chance to write, write something really good, if she can stand to hang on.

She's drunk with it. Nothing, not even Thorn, comes near that feeling, because she stands alone in it, and feels strong enough. That was what she really meant when she talked about Eve on the hideous, rock-numb night when the news had come about Thorn, and she danced with the squashed orchid on her shoulder, not even crying because Thorn was dead. She was comforting herself with Eve—stupid Milton's stupid Eve—off cooking, while the archangel explained everything to Adam, and warned him. Even the girls in class didn't like it. But there Eve stood, in spite of Milton, choosing whether to let Adam share knowledge or not, and only loneliness (Catherine thought) drove her to share that stuff that made you drunker than anything a waiter could pour out of a bottle.

Night after night she watches men in uniform and their girls getting high, and she's drunker than any of them with nothing but words. *They hand in hand with wand'ring steps and slow, through Eden took their solitary way.* While Jack hums in her ear. *In the middle of the journey of our life I came to myself in a dark wood.* Jack thinks she's half crazy with losing Thorn, and she is, but she's drunk with what she's going to do, too. She's going to write about what Frost meant, and Milton. Jack whispers how beautiful she is, those solid black eyes of his twinkling with the lights by the dance floor, but what she hears is Shakespeare: *Like to the lark at break of day arising from sullen earth, sings hymns at heaven's gate.* Does she want to go someplace else to dance? Jack asks. Maybe before they go she'd like to freshen up, comb her hair?

And all the time she's pushing ahead like the handwriting in those notebooks. Losing Thorn seems to turn into a kind of force. Her professors admire her close analysis; they say they've never had a better student in the English department, not even Walter Field, who's been told already that Chicago University wants him when he graduates (he's 4-F). He can get his MA and PhD while he teaches, and then join the faculty. Catherine is their outstanding student, they say. She'll make a first-class high school teacher, and she ought to be able to get a job in one of the best suburbs—maybe Oak Park.

Catherine is president of the English Club her senior year. The freshman girls watch her, because she's one of the "campus leaders." Her friends say she's so lucky to have somebody like Jack to date when there are so few men around. Jack comes to her graduation, and so does Tubbit. Class of '43.

4

A goddamn Midas, that's what he was, with his third-floor-back, near-the-stockyards past: Jack Laird had really done it. Every contract he got turned to gold. Dorothy and Shirley were both married again: no more alimony. The business wasn't big enough to bloat and then bust if the war ended, but it wasn't small, either. Now all he had to have was Catherine. He wanted to make her happy, that was all. Thorn was gone—blown up with one of those Loire bridges after the Germans took Paris. He tried to find out more, but even the Red Cross came up with the same story: Thorn was dead.

Catherine wouldn't marry him yet, of course. She wanted to try her wings, now she had her BA. He could wait. All he wanted to do was make her happy.

She said she didn't want to teach. He called Charlie Betts at Smith and Rand Publishers in Boston—an old World War I buddy—and Catherine started in as a reader there, and found a cheap little apartment along the Charles in Cambridge. Christ, it was a hole, but she was trying to save money so that she could go to France after the war and find out what had happened, and she wouldn't take his money, not even when he told her he had more than he knew what to do with.

But he could wait.

Ten million in the armed services. He had to fight the Selective Service for men all the time. He got productivity up thirty percent and a fifty-hour work week with overtime for Sundays and holidays. A few wildcat strikes hurt him a little, but he had labor-management committees going at both plants—the newest thing—and his airplane starters were the best in the business.

Carole Emery was the only woman editor at Smith and Rand, and she took Catherine under her wing, but just the same he hated to drop in and find Catherine there, typing rejection slips and running errands. He couldn't tell her that she'd never get any farther than Carole Emery had: just the lowest-paid editor. That was the way it was. When the war was over, there'd be millions of women leaving business and the war plants and going back home.

All he wanted was to see Catherine happy. He'd loan her money to start a little publishing house of her own, he told her, but she said she didn't know enough yet, and it wouldn't be her own money, and she was going to work her way up, typing in a little cubbyhole at Smith and Rand, bringing home somebody else's writing to sweat over every night—Christ.

The North African invasion meant oil shortages; a lot of it had to go to the railroad diesels. Kaiser could build a Liberty ship every twelve days—more than 1,200 a year. In the summer Mussolini resigned and the Allies cleaned out the Aleutians, and before winter they were bombing the hell out of Germany twenty-four hours a day.

Catherine was so sweet. She didn't know anything about the world, and of course she didn't need to—let him grub around in the dirt: he'd grown up in it, running around Chicago's red light district before he was out of short pants, listening to everything, figuring everything out. You had to know how all kinds of gadgets worked: protection and kickback and pimps and smuggling, sugar in the gas tank and potatoes in the muffler and threats at City Hall. Same in a small town: he used to visit his grandmother fifty miles out in the sticks, and there were the fellows in short pants, listening in the corner of the livery stable and outside the tavern, so when they grew up they had that town down pat, you can bet, if they were smart. It all went on under the church strawberry socials and the band concerts, and those statues with big breasts and no thighs to speak of that they stuck on the roofs of county courthouses.

He took Carole Emery and Catherine to a play, and then the opera, and out to dinner plenty of times. Then he asked them both to New York for Christmas. He thought Carole would go. She was smart, and he liked her. She had to be smart, to get even as far as she had. Hard as a madam, and just as feminine; he liked her. Carole Emery had a lot of sense.

5

"Good lord, who's that?" Edna Mallory says, coming over with invoices from the mailing department. Smith and Rand editorial offices are cubbyholes beyond the chatter and ding of typewriters. Boston soot blackens windowsills, and distinguishes this week's manuscripts from last month's, gray upon grayer.

"Friend of Charlie Betts," Betty Tarr says. They watch Catherine disappear into Carole Emery's office. "Catherine Buckingham. Strictly from the sticks," Betty whispers. "No makeup, no style, and look at that hair—"

"Bet Cardiff doesn't pinch *her*."

"Listen, he's already starting to give Emery some flak about her. 'Work on her a little, Carole, why don't you?' (Whining— you know how he does it.) 'She could be a knockout. Do us all a favor.' The creep."

Edna leafs through her handful of papers. "Wesson says to copy these."

"You haven't heard the best part. This other friend of Charlie's comes in and, boy, he's Cary Grant—you can hear all the typewriter keys in the room jamming—and guess what?"

"Yeh?" Edna says, interested.

"Cary Grant's coming here to take this Catherine out! Gloria asks her, and Catherine says they're going to the Silver Slipper and then a play, and she looks like that!"

"Yeh?" Edna's mouth is open a little.

"Gloria—you know how she is—she blurts out, 'You aren't going like that?' But Mr. Handsome comes to get her at five, and sure enough, off this Catherine goes, and him opening the door for her, and all of us sitting here in a state of shock."

"Gee," Edna says, and stops. Catherine comes from Carole's office; the outer door wheezes shut behind her.

"She's got a figure all right," Edna says. "If she'd just fix herself up."

"I should care." Betty shrugs. "Maybe she's funny in the belfry, I don't know."

"Maybe she changes at his place," Edna says.

"Wait a minute—I've got some letters for Wesson to sign." Betty rummages through a file.

"Maybe she's got something on him," Edna says.

6

At first Carole Emery hardly noticed the new girl. Carole wasn't about to talk back when Charlie Betts asked her for a favor—now and then Charlie steered something besides a kiddie market book to her, and she appreciated it. So when Charlie brought this Catherine Buckingham in, Carole put her in a corner of her office and gave her some typing to do. She was a young kid just out of some little college near Chicago.

Carole was too busy, as usual—the lumberjacks were going out on strike, war or no war, and you didn't need to ask what that was going to do to the publishing business. She tried to tell the boys in the front office, but would they listen? So she got out letters to every author she had, and pushed her books through fast. She'd be sitting pretty when the rest of them started having to print on toilet paper, if they could get it.

And yet this kid sat in the corner of her office, and Carole felt how alert she was, watching. The girl ought to fix herself up— that was the first impression Carole had. Then she thought the girl was a little peculiar. And her third thought, which really

didn't fit the other two, was that the girl was smart. She'd de-
voured books for years, that was plain, and there wasn't any sub-
stitute for that kind of training. Without it, a new girl got a typewriter at Smith and Rand, and a stack of form letters, and stamps
to lick. This Catherine was a book lover, obviously, and smart—a
rare bird in this business. If she'd just fix herself up.

Catherine wore the same outfits to work, week in and week
out, and she didn't seem to care how she looked. It shouldn't
have bothered Carole, but it did—especially when Paul Cardiff
and Joe Holser came to her office one Friday late, and started to
complain about how Catherine looked, as if it were her fault.

"Work on her a little, Carole, why don't you?" Paul says, leaning on Carole's desk.

Charlie Betts comes in behind him. Charlie's got the usual
spots on his tie, and he never belts his trousers tight enough, either, so he has a baggy behind.

"Yeh," Joe Holser says, joining the crowd. "Not those old-maid
skirts every day, how about it?" Fat and bald, he shows his bad
teeth in a grin.

"She could be a knockout." Paul has a whiny voice. When his
blue jowls and strong breath lean closer, Carole manages to back
up and reach for a file folder, and she stays back. "Do us all a favor!"

Carole puts a smile on her face and gestures with her eyes and
head: Catherine is coming. Turning to watch her, they notice the
lull in the typewriter clatter and bell-ring: the secretaries have
their eyes on the man following Catherine, and no wonder. He's
a man in his forties, perhaps, with clothes from a New York tai-
lor, and looks from a Hollywood movie.

Catherine walks into Carole's office, not smiling, and goes to
get her coat and hat in Carole's closet. Charlie pounces on the
matinee idol and introduces him to Paul and Joe and Carole—
"Jack Laird, my old war buddy!" Carole hopes Charlie's war buddy is going to put money in the business: he looks like he has it.

Nobody notices Catherine; she's got her hat and coat, and she
picks up a pile of manuscripts. That's when the matinee idol stops
talking—he goes to help Catherine with her coat.

He's being polite, Carole thinks, until she sees the look on his
face. His eyes, dark under dark lashes, look down at Catherine,

and they are not merely friendly. He has not stopped talking to Charlie merely to help a lady.

Catherine stuffs her hair behind her ears in an unattractive way she has, and puts her hat on her head, and the matinee idol picks up her pile of manuscripts. Catherine doesn't smile; she merely says goodnight to Carole, then walks beside this Jack Laird down the aisle between the staring secretaries. He opens the door for her—her old hat, her everyday coat, her everyday, colorless young face.

"Well, cut off my legs and call me Shorty," Joe Holser says.

"He's a nice guy," Charlie says. "A really nice guy."

7

"He's got money to burn," Carole says to her teakettle. (She's fifty, so she figures she can talk to herself, and who's better company, anyway?) "And he looks like *that*, too."

Carole's kitchen is modern, and so is her bathroom, but around them is a Brattle Street house built before 1800. It ticks with beetles and sags with age and smells of the past, and the hand-worn, foot-trodden patina of it is Carole's delight. Through the ancient windowpanes old Brattle Street, old "Tory Row," wavers and streams like watered silk.

"So why," Carole asks the racks in her refrigerator, "does he take me along?"

There's time for a cup of coffee to keep her stomach from growling: dinner's always late at the Wayside Inn. "Hello, beautiful," she says to her new black dress and mink coat and coffee cup in the hall mirror. Maybe Jack Laird thinks the two of them look like Catherine's parents? Maybe he doesn't mind? If he doesn't, she doesn't. Her seams are straight.

Board fences. The first Yankees must have wanted their neighbors at a distance. Her high board fence, dark brown, is cut twice by a loop drive, and here's Jack's big car, headlights twinkling among November-bare shrubs. And where does he get the gas? Forget it, kiddo, she says, answering the bell. He's obviously crazy about Catherine.

So it's nice, she thinks, going down the walk with him, slipping gracefully into the back seat (he'll want Catherine in front). Otherwise she couldn't relax like this. An old friend of the family. Staring at the Craigie House railings, she's startled: that's exactly what she feels like. So it's nice. Off your guard in this guarded world, for once. You can admire his looks, and let the neighbors see who's taking Carole to dinner.

"You're fond of Catherine, I know that." Jack is aiming for Mount Auburn and Catherine's dingy little apartment, but he stops at a stop sign and turns to look at Carole. "And she admires you." His eyes seem all one darkness, pupil and iris together under the thick lashes and brows, the grooved forehead.

So that was it. "I want her to be happy," Jack says.

He turns on Mount Auburn. Carole smooths her gloves. A friend of the family. Dinners, plays, the opera, a trip to New York at Christmastime—who would say no to that? The uncles and aunts in Omaha would have to celebrate without her this year—tables loaded with little dishes, little banalities dropping among them, Christmas Eve service at the church, the smell of mothballs in her closet, cat hairs on the furniture.

Jack pulls off Mount Auburn into a paved space surrounded by garages. "She does want to succeed in the publishing business," he says, turning to Carole again as he twists the key in the ignition. "She needs . . ." He stops and shrugs. "A good friend, I guess. Somebody she admires. She won't spend any of my money, but she's got a salary now."

A compliment, in a way. And feeling in his deep voice. Watching her, Jack smiles a little, and squeezes the back of the seat with one gloved hand. "I'll go get her," he says.

Carole watches the man in the elegant topcoat pick his way through puddles, duck under a clothesline, and disappear at a store corner. A trolley clatters along Mount Auburn. Birds twitter, riding a bush in the November wind.

So she's going to have Christmas in New York, not Omaha—not the Walnut Hill house where she grew up.

Ripla, ripla, ripla rill,
We're the kids from Walnut Hill!
Are we in it? Well, we should smile!
We've been in it for a good long while!

Your father beat your brothers. Your mother and your sisters cried. Sometimes, back in that Walnut Hill house, she could hear her father's voice raging, and the sound of blows.

The defiance, the battle of wills clashed above the ribboned and braided hair at the table, and was fiercely not yours. Only Tom and Elmer and Pete whetted themselves against the edge of that bellowing voice.

If your eyes flashed with justice outraged, you got a warning glance from your mother. If you dared to speak, the bellowing voice would not be your adversary—you were simply sent to your room. You would do the dinner dishes by yourself. The eldest daughter should be an example to her sisters. The quarrel had followed her upstairs, bass voice against tenors, and had risen through the floor of the bedroom she shared with Ruth and Mabel.

But you learned by being afraid. The door to the attic stood at the head of her bed. What waited on the stairs behind that door, listening to her breathing in the dark? The thought boiled up in nightmares, sweat, choked cries until—one night when she was eleven—she waited until Mabel and Ruth were asleep, then opened it.

The black hole yawned like an open grave a foot from her sheet-covered head.

But she learned to sleep at the lip of that terror.

Sometimes, blocks away, the dark board walks of the town at midnight began to carry a rhythm over their hollows, attended by first one barking dog, then another. Aware of the black maw of the attic door, soaked in her sweat, she thought of the night out there, huge and free and mysterious, and her brother Pete, younger than she was, coming home and whistling beautifully as he strode along.

Was he afraid? He carried his tune to the very back door step and let the kitchen door shut with a click behind him. He would be whipped tomorrow, his steady footsteps said, taking the stairs two at a time, but this was his whistling they heard. He would define himself by his footsteps, by the creak of his bedroom door, by the fight that awaited him tomorrow.

Lying there beside Mabel, she listened for what was as plain as the sound of a hollow board walk, if she could only hear it. A girl was whistling in the dark, walking home from the midnight town. The midnight houses heard her. The lights of her home kitchen blinded her as her whistling stopped at the back door step. Everyone was awake. They cried her name, and the name would be talked of in every house she had passed. She would leave town.

So what was a door to an attic, after all?

Carole blinks her eyes, shaking off old thoughts, and looks up the house wall beside the car to where a light shows in a window of Catherine's apartment. It goes out.

"Come on," Jack says, switching off Catherine's lamp. It's obvious Catherine has been crying—she's just thrown her novel in the trash, she says . . . what there is of it. It's nothing but a story about two men who loved the same woman. It doesn't do anything—there won't be any afterglow, she says. You won't close the book and think: I see something and feel something I've never quite felt or seen before. Ordinary things I took for granted seem strange.

"It's just not natural," Jack says. "A beautiful young girl sitting in front of a typewriter all day, bawling her eyes out because she thinks she can't write. The whole world's out there, and you're stuck here!"

"Why isn't it natural?" Catherine says. "If it isn't natural I wouldn't want to do it."

He goes out to hunt for the novel in the trash, waving at Carole in the car, and brings it back upstairs.

"Come on," he says to Catherine, who has put on that old hat of hers now, and a coat. "Let's get away from it all and have a good time."

Watching them walk to the car, Carole thinks that Catherine isn't aware of herself—that's what it is. Most girls study themselves, and their hips and legs show it; they carry their breasts ahead of them, aware. But Catherine is all one quiet piece, as if she's alone.

She doesn't know enough to sit under a light so that it spills over her hair—she hasn't even figured out that a three-quarter view shows your breasts off and makes your hips look slimmer. She doesn't point her toe when she crosses her legs, or pose her hands attractively. Watching her wrinkle her cheek with her fist or pick a hair out of her mouth, you'd think she was retarded somehow . . . just a little odd, as if she hated herself. But she doesn't hate herself. There's nothing wrong with her, is there? Not really.

And Jack Laird helps her into his car as if she's the most beautiful woman he's ever seen. If Catherine yanks her heavy coat out from under her and sits down beside him with no more self-consciousness than a child of two, he's as blind as she is. He smiles; his dark eyes glow.

8

Carole feels responsible for Catherine now. Christmas in New York was as gala as Jack Laird could make it, and he knew how. You'd have thought there wasn't a war on.

Carole watches Catherine. Why does she sit like that? And why doesn't she buy some new clothes? Carole puts her hands to her eyes. She sounds like Paul Cardiff and Joe Holser—wanting to change Catherine, make her over. Anger washes over Carole, but part of the anger is directed at Catherine. Doesn't she care how she looks? Carole sits listening to office clatter.

Catherine's been promoted: she gets to take home manuscripts from the slush pile every night. Catherine knew what that meant: her eyes lit up when Carole told her. What dreams of glory Carole had had during another war . . . she supposed she should laugh, rather than cry, considering her mascara.

Catherine works so hard. She's so smart. Doesn't she see that none of it's going to matter?

Maybe she's too pessimistic about Catherine, Carole thinks, keeping her hands over her eyes. She thinks of the male meetings she could take another woman to, after all these years. A kind of protégé-secretary, maybe, at her elbow, learning fast.

But Catherine wasn't learning, was she? So smart, but she never showed that little bit of respect—even adulation (embarrassing as it was)—that other girls showed Carole Emery, the only woman editor in the place. Not that Carole has dreams of being a ground-breaker any more . . . the first woman to scale the wall and so on. She's looked back enough times to know that there aren't any women behind her, except maybe some crank, some oddball—Carole sighs and shuffles through papers on her desk.

What's she going to say about Catherine's novel?

She took the thing home, dreading it. Every other person at Smith and Rand was a frustrated writer—Carole was used to getting first pages of books that would never be written. But she'd had a great time in New York, and was going back with Jack and Catherine before long, and it was the least she could do.

The writing wasn't bad—it wasn't bad at all. In fact, she was impressed. Catherine knew what she was doing; you felt that same assurance a good violinist gives you when he strikes that first note out of the violin—or the expertise a master plumber shows, fitting his wrench to the pipe. It wasn't the writing that was strange.

The farther she read the stranger it got . . . whatever it was. You could see and smell and hear and taste and feel it, and the roaring twenties in Boston and England were fun. But a hundred pages farther on she didn't know what to say. The book seemed to have fallen through a crack into another world, and it lay there, almost out of reach, with a peculiar light playing on it.

Carole gets up and looks at the clotheslines and brick walls that are her office view. You can't tell a girl to her face that she makes people angry just because of the way she dresses or the way she combs her hair. You can't tell her she has to learn to smile. If she were homely it wouldn't matter so much, but she could be so beautiful, and that's the trouble—why does everyone think Carole can fix it?

The trouble Carole has to take, all the time: hours in the beauty shop, cleaning bills, watching the fashions, dressing on the narrow line where what she wears won't distract or disturb the men, but will be right, and young enough. Catherine will have to learn the hard way—doesn't she hear the whispers and see the stares? Carole has to spend hours on her looks every week, and what man here does that?

She sighs. And the men don't like Catherine. What do you do about that, when you're going to New York again with her, and Catherine thinks you're her friend?

9

There are mirrors floor to ceiling in the suite at the Plaza. Carole puts Catherine's novel on a table by the window and walks back and forth on the thick rug.

"What don't you like?" Catherine asks.

"He's so boyish and tall and awkward, and she's got all that money, and she knows how she wants to raise her daughter, and tells him . . ." Carole sums it up, then hesitates.

Catherine's wearing that same suit; Carole watches her in the mirror. And that limp hair. "Look," Carole says, "can't you give her some weaknesses so we can identify with her? Maybe she hates her husband, and loves vamping the men. Maybe her husband's playing around, so she pays him back with this kid. Maybe you ought to make them fall in love and get in bed together."

Catherine doesn't answer. She starts unbuttoning her suit coat. "Why don't you wear the rayon crepe?" Carole says. "Jack thinks we should be ready about six if we're going to get to the play afterward."

She has a great figure, Carole thinks, looking at Catherine in her slip. Catherine scowls as she hangs her suit and blouse in their closet. "The gloves have to match the hats and the hats have to match the shoes and the shoes have to match the hand-bags," she says. She sticks her head through the neck of the blue crepe and jerks it down like a sack. "Some of the girls at college even *made* their clothes. All they thought about for days were those dresses." Carole comes to button Catherine down the back. "Can't you see their minds stuck on how they looked?" Catherine pushes her hair behind her ears. "Like flies on pins."

If Carole keeps her chin up, the fifty-year-oldness isn't so noticeable, she thinks. She has good cheekbones. She looks over Catherine's shoulder to the mirror.

"And we aren't rich, are we, like Jack?" Catherine asks. "We haven't climbed to the top and we haven't got our own company. . . ."

"Turn around and let me get that belt straight," Carole says.

Catherine turns around. "So when he opens doors for us, and pushes in chairs, it's just as if we're crippled, or old." She sticks her feet in a pair of blue pumps.

The room is so quiet for a moment that Carole can hear the rain on the windows. Then Catherine comes to put her hand on Carole's shoulder. "I didn't mean you're not a success, because you are," she says. "I didn't mean that."

10

Subway cars come out of the tunnel mouth to Mount Auburn Street; they rattle between river trees and Shaler Lane past the Stillman Infirmary to Watertown. The tracks are twenty feet from Catherine's sagging cardboard Venetian blinds, but after a while she never hears the trolleys, or the constant slamming of Mrs. Reilley's shop door.

"This has got to be a big scene," Carole's note says; it lies on Catherine's mantelpiece for a long time. "He's loved her mother, and he's raised her, and now they're going to be lovers—your readers are going to be on the edge of their chairs waiting to find out how he goes about it."

Mrs. Reilley has the soft voice and hard eye of a Boston Irish woman who loves her own. Her bulldogs are her own, so her floors are a sea of newspapers; Catherine wades them to pay her rent. Mrs. Reilley's daughter is her own, slamming every door in the house, working for the telephone company. Her granddaughter is her own, and she calls her a brat. The brat's fingerprints on the woodwork began when she could toddle; now they are a black band as high as an eight-year-old can reach.

"You've got to get some passion in there. Everything that happens to the girl when she loses him and has to go to that Iowa small town would be dynamite if the reader knows she's just experienced the most emotionally turbulent affair of her life. What does she think when she goes to bed with, essentially, her father? Is there a deliciousness to the inevitable furtiveness of the affair . . ."

Mrs. Reilley's shop is her own: a room stuck on the corner of the house. Its one small lunch booth is dark and sticky. Trolleys stop before her door, dawn to late.

Catherine can listen for the trolleys, the bulldogs, the slammed doors, the customers buying a loaf of bread, and is not quite lonely. The second floor is hers; between the sagging blinds she can look down into passing cars and streetcars. Her floors are worn wood, her kitchen a closet, her bathroom festooned with laundry from the wet wash down the block. The walled-up fireplace has a mantel and hearth, but no place for a fire.

Every weekday she goes to work at Smith and Rand near Boston Common, until one late March afternoon, when she looks up to see Carole watching her.

"I don't want to hurt your feelings, because we're friends," Carole says. She props her elbows on the desk and makes a hammock for her chin with her white fingers. "For a while I thought you didn't care, or maybe you hated yourself. Really. I thought so. You know I used to write?"

"You told me," Catherine says.

"And I don't want to hurt your feelings." Carole raises her eyebrows above her sharp, straight nose. "People are kind of cold to you, aren't they?"

Catherine hesitates, then says, "I ask questions. Nothing looks quite the same to me as it does—"

The telephone rings. Carole tells somebody that no, they'll lose the book if they can't get the paper, and hangs up. "That's why you've got to write," she says to Catherine. "You see things." She shuffles the papers around on her desk. "But you're not going to get anywhere in this business—not any business. That's just what I've got to tell you."

Catherine says nothing. Carole looks out at March snow, brick walls, lines of washing, blank windows. Her hair is glossy brown; her clothes are expensively simple. "At first I thought you were numb, or didn't care, or hated yourself. I was way off the track. Now I don't even know where the track is. But I know you're not going to make it in business."

"I've watched you," Catherine says. "When you took me to the lunches."

"And it didn't work, did it?" Carol ticks each off on her fingers. "We didn't sew up Waring. Jones said no. *The Man Who Wanted a Million* went to Random House. I thought for a while that my luck had gone out the window, but it was just you. And it wasn't your fault."

The phone rings again. Carole listens, then says to someone, "I told him we thought Kransky had another *One World,* but we can't print that many. Promise him a second printing." She hangs up. A fire engine wails by on the street. She looks at Catherine, then away. "Men don't like you, and women don't like you either, do they? They always want to make you over, I'll bet. Change everything."

"You don't," Catherine says.

Carole clasps her white hands as if wringing them. "I'm a crazy failed writer!" She sits thinking for a while. "I don't even know what we're talking about—do you want to write?"

"Yes. If I can."

"Then write!" Carole leans toward Catherine. "That's the way you can go straight up on your own—women have done that one thing for centuries. Have you got money?"

"Not very much. I can live on it."

"The artist in the attic? Oh, come on! You've got Jack Laird!"

Catherine says nothing. Why doesn't she do something with that hair? Catching herself, Carole puts her white hands to her eyes and begins to laugh. "Marry him, for God's sake. You can write all day. I'd jump at a chance like that!"

Catherine can see that she would. "Why?" Catherine asks, astonished. "It wouldn't ever be your money—it would be Jack's."

"That's not it." Carole's eyes are glowing. "It's a game, and you win. He's crazy about you." She laughs again. "You can write. All you'll have to do is look nice for his friends now and then, and entertain a little, maybe. The rest of the time you can write."

"But you have to get energy from inside. When my uncle . . ." Catherine stops. "If I just married Jack, I couldn't get enough . . . I wouldn't be doing anything, or being anything . . ."

"Jack'll let you have whatever you want—he's crazy about you."

Catherine frowns. "He thinks I'm like my mother, that's why, and he didn't really know her at all. She wasn't always thinking about clothes and parties, and flirting—"

"You get a man like that—really get him—he's working for you!" Carole cries. "Everybody knows it. Handsome and rich and all yours. It's like a game. Women are going to envy you, and if you're not like them it won't matter—they'll start copying you because you got him. They'll want to be your friend, and you get time to write, and you can even have a family, too. What more could you ever—"

The telephone rings. "He did?" Carole says to the twittering voice. "No. I didn't know about it." She slams down the phone. "You want to get ahead in business? Well, just go right into the john with the boss and all the men!" She laughs, a hard sound. "Go right in there and listen while they decide everything. I swear, they pee together in there and settle half the business, and then come out with the word, and maybe they tell me. And how

about the locker room at the athletic club? Stag parties? Hell!"
She glares at Catherine. "High-class hookers in this town know
more than I do about Smith and Rand—you want to bet?"

Catherine doesn't answer. "Write about that!" Carole says.
"I'm good, but if I go on trips, what will their wives say? And what
if one of them asks me to bed? If I sleep with him, I'm his little
helper from then on. If I say no, I'm a hard bitch. Either way I
lose, and the men know it, so when the really important things
come along, do they tell me? Oh, sure, they ask me to a meeting,
or to meet somebody important, because they know I can't go, or
I know I won't be welcome. So they can ask." She shoves papers
back on her desk. "They do all the important things. They're
trained to do them, and helped to do them. That's all."

Carole looks out at the snow. It's as if Catherine's not there. "I
can't keep a job here much longer, because I have to meet the
public—I have to sell young ideas. Look at me. Men don't like
older women. Women don't, either. Neither do kids. I go out to
walk on the Common before work, and do you know what young
punks say when they pass me, just loud enough for me to hear?
They say, 'How about paying me, Grandma?' They say, 'Guess
who's got cobwebs you know where.'"

Catherine says nothing for a while. Then her low voice explores
the silence, tentatively. "I used to visit the Negroes on Brush
Street in Detroit. The women told me I was pretty, and ought to
dress up, but they treated me as if I didn't know anything, and
never would." She glanced once at Carole, then away. "The
mothers brought in all the money, because the men wouldn't
clean toilets, I guess, or wash clothes. So the women worked all
day and then came home and cooked and cleaned and fought the
men and got the kids off to school and went to work again. And
they were sweet to their sons . . . they coddled them and
dressed them up and let them lie around. But not their daughters."

Snow strikes the window behind Carole; the light is beginning
to fade toward dusk.

Catherine looks down at her hands. "I want to write about the
little things. Nobody sees them because they're so little. When
you think about them, you say to yourself, 'But they're only little
things.'"

"My God," Carole says. "You sit there watching all the time."

"I'm watching how you do it. I can learn."

There's no sound in the office for a while. Then Carole says, "You'd better try the writing." A subway car rumbles past, and when the sound of it dies, they can hear the typewriters and the hiss of snow on the window.

"It's like dogs, isn't it?" Carole says in a low voice. "Wagging behinds and whimpering with pleasure and squealing—"

"You don't. You just smile, and make yourself small, all curled up. You look sleepy, and talk like a little girl who just happened to think of the right thing accidentally." Catherine's direct eyes are on Carole. "I can do that. I've already found out that I can say just what I think if I smile. If I tip my head to one side and look sleepy, like you do. I can watch you. I don't want to act like the girls in college, but I can act like you."

Carole says nothing at all. She watches Catherine go out to get her coat.

"Goodnight," Catherine says, looking in at Carole's door. "I'm sorry I wasn't any good at the job. And thanks."

The Boston Common is so open and so wide—to walk to the subway through the sharp, snowy air is enough to give you a feeling of freedom even if you feel like crying. Catherine joins the crowd going down, shoes clanging on dirty subway steps stuck with gum, and runs for her train.

There are uniforms here and there in the subway car: khaki and navy. The faces people wear in the subway are usually blank, but the servicemen have a severe, even proud expression, as if the uniform is important and heavy.

Tile walls fly past. When Catherine gets out at Harvard Square, two Harvard professors are discussing a new English study of Chaucer, and Catherine lingers for a moment near their subway bench to listen.

Climbing the steep stairs, Catherine sees the clock without hands on Massachusetts Hall, up to its shoulders in ivy and neither wrong nor right. Newsboys hawk a Vichy crisis at the subway entrance in small clouds of their own breath, but Harvard Yard, walled in brick, scatters the news of one more war in echoes between Widener Library and the chapel.

Frank Sinatra croons from a newsstand radio, and shop windows follow the curve of the stores around to Brattle Street, ruling the sidewalk into hot yellow spaces. Snow and pedestrians kindle before each glowing shop window, wink out, then break into color and light again.

Spinning like sparks, snowflakes cloud car lights going down Brattle away from the Square. Stores thin out here, and famous old houses keep company down Tory Row with rooming houses painted the same warm yellow. Pedestrians thin out, too; only one old man is fighting the wind by Pratt House.

A woman beats her evening newspaper empty of snow on a railing as Catherine passes. No tourist buses are pulled up at the ball-topped gates of Craigie House now; the cream yellow facade gleams in the last light, and Catherine stops as she always does, because Longfellow lived there, and George Washington.

She never could explain it well enough to anyone else—her sense of the past she found in Boston. She could have explained it to Thorn. Snow thickens on her wet lashes. Cars move on velvet along Brattle, snow swarming in their headlights.

The sense of the past is like a pull. Catherine watches a dim light behind one of the Craigie House curtains. Washington wrote by candlelight there once. He saw snow fall on this place, just as she sees it now. And Longfellow had to put one word down and then another; there wasn't any other way. So there's a chance you can do something, too, and that's the pull that comes from the past. How long had Henry watched this snow before "It was the schooner Hesperus, that sailed the wintry sea" had found its second line, and its plot: "And the skipper had taken his little daughter, to bear him company"?

The old man ahead of Catherine shuffles through snowdrifts and tufted air. The wind fills her eyes with tears. The scent of thousands of wood fires had soaked into the walls of Craigie House or Paul Revere's house—even in summer you could smell it, and so the past reaches out and pulls you. But Thorn's dead.

> Blue were her eyes as the fairy-flax,
> Her cheeks like the dawn of day,
> And her bosom white as the hawthorn
> buds,
> That ope in the month of May.

If Thorn were here she could tell him.

The boxed-in winter doorway of Craigie House wears its

Christmas wreath. She could ask Thorn why her mother had chosen him.

But the Thorn that Carole imagines walks that upstairs hall in the dark. The hall smells of beaverboard, and the bathroom smells like soap, and they're real. But the man Carole imagines is fascinated by a girl—he's going to teach her delicious things, Carole says.

The raindrops on the bedroom windows are great, Carole says, and of course the kid doesn't know what she's doing when she gets in bed with him. She can imagine the girl pulling off her nightgown and then falling asleep—that's great, it's really funny. That's a good start.

The old man ahead of Catherine noses through the dark, turning his head slowly in the ring of his muffler as if he knows someone is coming up behind him. Then he stops under a streetlight at a corner and turns, his eyes lifted to Catherine's through lenses as thick as ice.

"Miss?" he says. "Miss? Could you direct me to Mason Street?"

His face is blind, like a mole's. "You've come too far along Brattle Street," Catherine says. "I'll show you." She offers her hand but the old man takes her arm and presses close to her as they cross.

My wallet's in my other pocket, Catherine thinks. He weighs on her arm, pressed close as they walk in snow that is darkening to gray. His voice is shuddery. "It's hard for me to see just at dusk," he says. As they cross a streetlight's round, snow-dimmed arena, he lifts his face, but she can't see his eyes through his thick lenses. "You're the Edison girl, aren't you?" he asks. "And your mother's dead." He says the last word with a peculiar intonation: it's almost an accusation.

"No, that's not my name," Catherine says. "Here's Mason Street." They move into another streetlight's funnel of bright snowflakes. "Would you like me to find your house?"

"No. This is fine. I can turn here and find my way home. So now you're going to live with your father," the old man says, and shakes his head. "Thanks," he tells her, and shuffles off down the lonely sidewalk.

Catherine watches him disappear in the dimness between thick, wet flakes. He has her mixed up with someone else. Running back to Brattle, she feels released from the old man's half-steps, the weight, the glass-incrusted face. To not be blind—to see the world, even if it makes no more sense than talking cards or painted roses. She can write about it. He won't see her running. Picket fences leap past; she slides on packed snow. Night air makes her lungs ache; it tastes of space and clouds.

Brattle Street again, and Craigie House. Through the receding perspective of falling flakes the great facade lifts its nine shutter-flanked windows. One of them glows.

George Washington was there on a snowy night like this, and there was a war going on, just as there is now. The young men, severe and proud in their Revolutionary uniforms, knowing they were important enough to die for their country.

But the air stands up in windless distances. Snowflakes, each a constellation, slide down to her like beads slipping an invisible string. Is the snow moving—or the earth? Tory Row seems to rise with the night, lifting through flakes that stand still, and for a minute Catherine is lifted, too, because she sees the strangeness. She cries out, and feels the pull, and starts to run again.

"Say!" A woman comes along a side street to join Catherine at the corner. "I just thought I'd better tell you. That old man walks along here and picks out young girls to walk with—that's what he wants. I thought I'd better tell you." She crosses Brattle Street.

For a minute the only sound is Catherine's breath as she watches the woman disappear. No cars pass. The wind is gone.

A house door opens down Brattle Street: a small eye of light. Then it closes. The silence is so deep that she can hear the click of the lock.

11

When she stops working at Smith and Rand, Catherine begins the book again at the beginning: the sky, stretched over wild grass and sand, horizon to horizon. If feelings are things, what feeling is that sky? And the planes going over?

But who'd read about some little kid crawling around in high grass, or concocting messes out of sumac leaves to see if they'd make a dye? The joys of childhood in one more novel. Women flew all the planes.

Or farther back? Rob Buckingham had gone to Harvard. That

little floppy piece of muscle and skin. She couldn't believe that mothers and fathers felt that way, until she went to Cedar Falls. Until she saw Stevie sitting so straight in his chair, or heard Dick leaving the house, the screen door slamming.

"Read Colette's books about Claudine," Carole says. "It's the same thing—Renaud is her father and lover, too, and she's tired of being alone, being her own boss. It's only natural."

The war grinds on, as if all the bodies thrown under it slow it down. Allied armies creep up the Italian boot. Russia fights, city by city. Gold stars multiply in windows. Lists of wounded and dead lengthen. Rationing. The rat-a-tat of broadcasts from the fronts. And she's trying to write about what happens when you say, "I want to begin."

"It could be really delicious," Carole says. "She doesn't know the score, and she wants to . . . can't they be in that barn, and accidentally brush against each other, you know . . ."

Jack's office is at the top of a Chicago skyscraper with a view of the lake. Typists sit outside his door, desk after desk. Jack lounges on a corner of a big table in his beautifully cut business suit, his hair a little gray here and there, his dark eyes on Catherine. He's only a small cog in the war effort, he says; the big boys are making the money.

"I got started down there on the Chicago streets without a cent—got in the machine shop with old Israel when I was twelve. I was lucky, that's all. Built the business up on nothing but luck." Jack smiles.

"I knew how radios worked when I was ten," Catherine says. "I could take every kind apart and put it together. I could do that with cars, too."

"You bet you could." Jack's smile broadens to a grin. "Never saw a girl who could ask the questions you did at the plant—made me proud."

What about the young men with no arms . . . without legs . . . blind . . . who are coming home now? She could be a Wave, or a Wac, and at least type or file or switch calls for Uncle Sam, who isn't asking her to die.

Every morning she walks for an hour in a different direction—it doesn't really matter which way, as the Cheshire Cat said, because the suburban houses stretch for miles, and she asked the questions about them years ago. Downtown Boston is thick with men in a hurry: miles of office buildings and industries and colleges and universities and stores. She can sit in Longfellow Park and watch mothers and children and baby carriages. When she goes out with Jack, she can ask him about her mother.

"Her eyes were a light gray," Jack says. "She had a way of holding her head so that her hair fell on her cheek, and you knew she was teasing, and that she wasn't happy. She didn't fit into that Boston blue-blood crowd, but she put on a good show, the way women do." He seems to believe the impossible things he says. "Janet could have given my whole life meaning—what good is working if you can't make anybody happy?"

"You've got that old house," Carole says. "Maybe she could get a little drunk and start doing the chasing—that would be hilarious. Here's this man who's been around, and this girl who doesn't know anything, and he's backing up as fast as he can . . ."

Catherine wanders around the five and dime, and talks to Mabel Burns at the lunch counter. Mabel leans on the pie case while Catherine has lunch, and keeps up the conversation as she watches sandwiches toast on the grill.

Catherine tries not to watch Mabel's legs, because they look as if they're slowly melting into her runover shoes. Mabel says, "Kid, I been working here since I was fifteen, and I never had to lay on no back room stock table to keep my job, neither, and I ain't going into no war work. The women'll be out on their cans the day after the war's over—you watch."

Mabel likes Catherine. Mabel says Catherine looks so sad, and what's a cute kid like her doing looking sad? "Get yourself a 4-F boyfriend," Mabel says. "Read the magazines. The girls in the stories all quit their jobs the minute Mr. Right comes along, you notice?"

Catherine keeps buying little plants in the five and dime, until the windowsills in her apartment are full. Forel and Wheeler and *Alice in Wonderland* watch from her bookcase as she types, and so does the watercolor portrait from one of the boxes Tubbit sent to Cedar Falls. Now the middle-aged woman watches Catherine, and the sagging Venetian blinds, and a slatted view of Mount Auburn Street.

Catherine can go anywhere now. One night there's a street fair in the Italian section: Italians dance and shout and laugh and hang out windows; children are asleep everywhere. Statues of the

Virgin watch Catherine the length of the street: a procession of impassive life-size women in blue, wearing wreaths and ruffs and bracelets and belts of dollar bills. The public beaches on hot summer days are acres of bare flesh from the pop stands to the water. Nights along the river chatter with radio after radio on the blanket-paved park grass. Citronella flavors the war news.

She tries to begin her novel again, in Boston, the way it must have been when Thorn came there the first time. Janet was exploring Boston and learning, and she kept a journal, and was curious, and intelligent, and knew exactly how she wanted her children to be raised.

"Janet's father had cotton mills. That's all I know about where her money came from," Jack says. "I don't think Janet ever saw a cotton mill. Rob had good lawyers, and he was smart—Janet never had to worry about money." He smiles at Catherine between acts of a new play. "Thorn and I were the poorest of all the men she had following her around." He scowls. "And then she went with Rob in that car.

"Drive?" Jack says. "I never saw her drive. She didn't know a thing about motors or cars or how things worked—why should she? She was almost as beautiful as her daughter, do you know that?"

Jack tells his friends that Catherine is writing a novel. "It's going to be a best seller," he says.

Janet Buckingham is like paint flaking off a wall. Thorn has been gone four years, and already her eyes and her mouth are dissolving.

12

Carole told Catherine how lucky she was, and how many times did she think Jack was going to ask her to marry him? He wasn't in any hurry; she could think it over. But didn't he have his pride, a man like that? He didn't look more than forty, whatever his age was, and if he didn't know what a woman liked . . .

But then Carole stopped talking about Jack, because she could see Catherine was feeling very low. She tried to talk about Catherine's novel instead. Carole said it was getting so much better, now that Catherine had put in those love scenes she'd suggested—the reader was going to die wondering which older man the girl picked, especially when the two men hated each other like that. "Like *Daddy Long-legs,*" Carole says, laughing. "Pygmalion? Gods and their virgin daughters?"

Catherine was so quiet, and she looked sad. And Jack is beginning something new—she knows it—shifting his grip slightly, as if she isn't experienced in such things, as if Thorn had never been hers, like a city, to explore. When Catherine watches the ballet, a hand is on hers. The male dancer, a pivot, centers the rosette his partner makes in the air around him. Their mouths are both open in a wide and panting smile.

"I've got to go back and see Detroit," she tells Jack at intermission. "I can't hold on anymore. I had it once. I was moving with it, until they cut my hair, or the man on the steam shovel wouldn't explain . . ." Seeing his face, she pushes her hair behind her ears and tries to smile. "It's all so silly. All the little strands are so silly, breaking one by one, and then you're not hanging on any more." She thinks of the premiere danseuse gliding in on sweat and muscle, fresh from the tower, the hedge of thorns, the trackless wood, the glass mountain, to float all white in the prince's grip, as if that were possible.

"The servicemen on the subway have ribbons now, and decorations—they shine like the things Alice sees on the shelves of the sheep's store." she says. "They move away when you reach for them, even if you have the money to pay, and you know what you want."

Jack looks blank. "Well, sure! We can go to Detroit, but don't you think it'll make you feel—"

"I could have taught English in Oak Park," Catherine says, her eyes as bright and hard as the blue mirrors of the box. She stares at the noisy opera crowd. What if Thorn had stayed, so that she could touch him only when she had to, less and less, until she stood free . . .

"I'll go to France the minute the war's over," Catherine says. "If he isn't dead, I'll find him." How sad her face is. "It's all so silly," she says again. "I can be a secretary, or a teacher. Courtiers have always learned how to do it, but Carole thinks I'm too old."

The theater lights are dimming. Jack doesn't have to answer.

So he gets the gas coupons and they drive to Detroit one week-end after the Allies have liberated Paris, when it seems to Catherine that the war will never end—she can't even remember what it was like before the slogans and war songs and posters and ration notices and communiqués and sugarless recipes and quotas began to cover ordinary life: bits of red, white and blue sifting down to become drab, like old snow. Like watching the trolleys on Mount Auburn. Like a novel you work over and over, trying to catch feelings you're not even sure of, now.

And you're handed like a fragile package from the car to the Statler Hotel—she hasn't been there since she was eleven and went in to have dinner by herself. Dirty paper blows back and forth on the hot Detroit streets, but the Statler towels are thick, and the chrome bath and sink faucets look as if no one has ever used them.

Catherine pushes the drapes of her room open and leans out the open window. The hum of Detroit goes on without her, goes by, not needing to be understood, after all. The novel's a year old and it doesn't mean anything to anybody else, not unless you write it the way Carole wants it. Women driving trucks on Seven Mile!

Down there, there on the corner, she'd learned about a planetary transmission in a rainstorm, water pooling with oil on a garage floor and a man letting her see how it worked. Thorn stood in a doorway across the street where she could see him past the rolled-up door and the rain.

Supper at the Statler gleams discreetly, like faucets no one seems ever to have touched. When Jack dances with her, Detroit is a gloss on him, like the shimmer of his lapels, because he has put her in the Statler, because when he was twelve there was nothing he could do but earn his living.

She had to come back to Detroit, she tells Jack while they eat. She'd had a city map, and all the streetcar lines were hers. Jack keeps watching her. "The man always yelled, 'City maps a die-yum!'" Catherine says, and Jack smiles.

"You can learn Boston the same way, or New York, even if people crowd against you and pinch you," Catherine says. "And whistle at you, as if you weren't in your body at all."

When they've eaten supper and get up to dance again, Catherine says, "If I tell about Bill Donnell sitting in the library stacks at night to do that extra thinking, that small extra time that puts him ahead . . ." She shakes her hair back. "What does that mean except that I'm sorry for myself? I could have stayed out every night and got expelled from Gilman. I didn't have to iron clothes or put up my hair, or smile, or watch the freshman boys walking downtown at 7:45. I didn't have to stay at home with Margie."

Jack holds her tight as they dance and says against her hair, "You'd better turn in early and get a good night's rest."

Detroit is cool in the morning, just as Catherine remembers. A woman marine grins from a poster on the Campus Martius: "I have freed a Marine to fight. You can do it, too!"

When she'd graduated from Gilman in June of 1943, thousands of white people had roamed Woodward Avenue looking for blacks to beat up and kill, until the 701st MP battalion had finally moved in. Jack weaves through the morning traffic, driving out toward the mile roads.

There's the old Roxy Theater. Its marquee says, I TAKE THIS WOMAN SPENCER TRACY BUY WAR BONDS AND STAMPS AT THIS THEATER. Catherine keeps trying to remember what Thorn said—that Tubbit drove the Model T, and she slept in a baby buggy wedged between the front and back seats, and the gravel road led through sand and wild grass for miles, until they saw the sumac thickets and the cottonwoods, and the old houses and barn.

The Cadillac passes mile after mile of Detroit's bungalows. Jack grins at the car ahead, not at Catherine beside him. "Remember when I came out here to see you the first time? Thorn answered the phone when I called, and he sounded like he thought I was a ghost—never supposed he'd hear from me again."

Catherine watches Jack's handsome profile against the streets that are beginning to be familiar now. Five Mile Road. The door of Joe's Meat Market slaps shut where the Cadillac's reflection slides across store windows.

"Remember when this was a whole subdivision laid out, and it stayed that way all through the depression?" Jack says. "A regular wilderness." Catherine turns in her seat and remembers how Thorn's car left paired tire marks, two lonely lines, block after

block, when trees and bushes stood in house lots full of snow
here, and there was nothing more to see but a few tumbleweeds
blowing across untracked miles.

Six Mile Road. There had been piles of red-gold sand here, and
steam shovels under the long-ago blue summer sky. Now block
after block of brick houses line the streets, and small trees are
casting shade in the parkings.

"Seven Mile," Jack says.

"Seven Mile!" Catherine cries. The houses have cut off her
view—she's missed the last row of them, and then the beginnings
of the gravel road. "Go back!" she says.

"Back?" Watching her, Jack frowns and turns on Seven Mile,
turns again. Block by block the new trees line the street. Small
children play on the sidewalks. A dog lopes across their path.
"You know . . ." Jack begins.

"Turn again!" Catherine cries.

Jack turns back on Northlawn. "You know the old house is
gone, of course," he says, feeling sick to think of what he did this
for—so that she would see that Thorn was gone? That it was no
use dreaming, after all this time, that he was alive?

All the streets are the same: an unbroken grid. Catherine un-
derstands that at last. If they drive for hours, turning and turning, they won't ever come to the gravel road. The rows of houses
cast their cool blue shadows on their lawns.

"Stop!" Catherine says at last. She's crying, and Jack wishes he
could put his arms around her, kiss her, tell her he's sorry, that
he'll make it all up to her, that all he ever wanted was to make her
happy. But she doesn't want to be touched or comforted—all she
wants is to find a certain street sign, and at last they do.

A green and white street sign that says, "Northlawn." Catherine blinks and rubs her eyes and looks at it. The nearest sign of all
those signs that had marked off empty house lots as far as they
could see. They'd passed it for years, going in and out by the
gravel road. How could any of them have guessed that it would
be the only thing left when the fields of grass went, and the sky,
and the roads stretching away . . . and Thorn?

"All those years," Catherine says as if Jack weren't there. "And
all it ever said was 'Northlawn.'"

13

The fall of '44 was profits and more profits at Smith and Rand; Carole spent Thanksgiving with Catherine and Jack, then hardly saw them until Christmas in New York. Catherine was very quiet and thin and tired, Carole thought, and she said she was spending most of her time on her novel.

The new year's paper quotas and taxes hardly put a brake on the publishing boom. Books were selling, really selling, and if people were buying *Forever Amber*, they were still buying *One World*, and *Cass Timberlane* and *The Thurber Carnival*, too. The houses put their paper and money into half as many titles as usual, and picked up more profits from the paperback Armed Service Editions. Smith and Rand lost men to the war; Carole worked extra hours every week. She didn't have much time to think about Catherine and her book.

Carole was out of town in January. When she came back, there was a message from Jack waiting: Catherine was sick; she'd been taken to the hospital by ambulance. Carole started the secretaries on correspondence, then caught a cab.

Slush and rain and mud in Boston . . . a January thaw.

"She nearly died." Jack's almost too angry to be polite when he meets Carole in the hospital waiting room. "That's what the doctor says. Didn't you catch on? You knew how she just sat in that little hole on Mount Auburn. Especially after we went to Detroit last summer. All winter long in that hole, except when I could get here. And all the time I've been away—"

"She didn't come to the office," Carole begins.

"Why didn't you check on her?"

"I just thought she was busy writing, and God knows—"

"And you took that job away from her—left her high and dry, and all she had left was sitting in that place trying to write—a whole year of it now!"

"Her landlady said she had flu," Carole says. People are listening.

Jack takes Carole's arm and they start toward Catherine's room. "She just lies there," Jack says, his voice trembling. "I told you how it upset her to go back to Detroit, and I couldn't get here as much as I wanted to this winter. Then I had to go west. I shouldn't have gone. And she just lies there and doesn't know me, and says that no girl is going on for a master's degree, or a doctor's degree—things like that. She said somebody named Walter Field wasn't as smart as she was, but she couldn't go on field trips."

Two fashionably dressed people, Carole and Jack skirt hospital carts, nurses, orderlies. "Who's this Walter Field anyway?" Jack asks. "She keeps saying that he's going to get his PhD and teach at Chicago U."

"She never talked about him to me," Carole says. A nurse looks Jack over as he passes.

"Catherine hasn't had a chance—that's all." Jack scowls down the long hospital corridor. "And you know all I want is for her to be happy. She doesn't have to work! She can write all day if she wants to. But she lies there and worries about having to look nice, and says she can't get anywhere in business, ever. She goes on about this Walter Field. Some college boy she knew." Jack stops before the door of a room and opens it for Carole.

To see a familiar face on a hospital pillow is always strange, but Carole hardly recognizes this one. Catherine's eyes are wide open, yet she doesn't know where she is or who they are; Carole is sure of that. Catherine gives them a sad, confused look and tells them that it isn't enough.

"What isn't enough?" Jack leans over her but she doesn't answer. "She's so hot!" he says to Carole. "They're getting the fever down as fast as they can."

"And the wiggling . . . grinning . . . rubbing against things!" Catherine's voice is as thin as she is. "Awful," she whispers. "Putting cloth together and dragging it around."

A nurse comes to take Catherine's temperature; Catherine lies quietly with the thermometer in her mouth. Jack retreats to the door with Carole. "Can you figure out what Catherine's talking about?" he asks in a whisper.

"I'll have to give her another sponge bath," the nurse says, shaking the thermometer down. "You can wait in the waiting room."

"She's obviously worried to death about something," Jack says, walking away from Catherine's door with Carole. "She told me this morning that she had 'wanted to begin.' I said that anything she wanted to begin was all right with me, if she'd tell me what she wanted. But all she'd say was that there was nowhere to go. Where does she want to go? I'll take her anywhere!"

"Pardon me." A doctor stops Jack. "Are you the Buckingham girl's father?"

"No, but I'm responsible for her," Jack says. "Anything she needs—"

"She'll be all right now, I think. Flu. Her temperature is coming down." The doctor has a fierce black mustache and black eyes. "Starving themselves to look like some movie star," he says indignantly. "These girls ought to be spanked. She's lucky to be here. Try to get some sense into her head." He walks off, his stiff white coat crackling with starch and exasperation.

Jack looks after the doctor, the creases deepening between his heavy eyebrows.

"Maybe she got lost in her writing and forgot to eat," Carole says, going into the waiting room with Jack. "I knew a novelist . . ."

"There wasn't a single page of her book in her apartment," Jack says. They find two chairs near a window. "I went to look after I came here, because she was talking about writing, and whether she could write a novel if her hairdo wasn't right." He offers Carole a cigarette and takes one himself. "She talks about her uncle in France, and some invisible wall or other, and this Walter Field." He glances at Carole. "Why don't you go in when they'll let you, and see if you can figure out what's bothering her. She's so fond of you."

When Carole goes back, Catherine's room is dim and still, and Catherine seems to be asleep. Jack's flowers already surround the narrow bed, and cards are propped beside them saying, "Get Well Quick" and "Sorry You're Ill." Carole looks at the thin young face and smells the hospital's chemical breath.

Catherine's brittle voice startles Carole. "You can't go on field trips or do anything and that's why you get queer, because they don't want you, do they? They have to like you." Catherine's voice is a monotone. "All the time." Then she cries: "Like being crippled! Or old!" Tears are running down her cheeks in the dim light. "I want to go to France!"

"It's all right," Carole croons, bending to kiss Catherine and push damp hair away from Catherine's face.

Tears keep sliding down Catherine's cheeks. She murmurs something about hanging on, and clouds, and a dark wood. Then the room is still for long time.

Jack opens the door softly. "How is she?" he whispers.

"Asleep, I think," Carole whispers back, and joins him in the hall.

"Did she say anything about this Walter Field?"

"Not a word," Carole tells him. "She wants to go to France."

"I'm going to take her!" Jack cries. "As soon as she's well, I'm going to take her over. I've got a place in Paris, if I can get it fixed up, and I've got a lot of friends still there—I lived there for years, you know. We'll go over and look for her uncle, though God knows he can't be alive. But I know a lot of people. It'll give her a real break from all this—what do you think?"

"She certainly wants to go to France," Carole says as Jack opens the hospital door for her.

It's a warm day for January. It stays warm for a week while Catherine gains her strength back. Her room is full of roses Jack sends every day. She's so thin; Carole wonders if that's why she seems so different, but after a while she thinks the difference is in Catherine's eyes. Catherine's hands shake when she begins to feed herself again. She takes slow steps on the nurse's arm.

Jack has a big radio delivered. The negligees and perfumes—where does he get such things in wartime? The nurses take turns coming in to see.

Catherine sits by the window and watches Carole and Jack. Jack has wrinkles in his forehead and grooves beside his mouth, and his hair is gray at the temples. If he notices how women's eyes follow him, he never shows it. He calls Catherine his darling little girl, and says she should never go back to that hole on Mount Auburn Street.

"How about one of those new apartment houses on Memorial Drive? The ones they built just before the war started." Jack passes a box of his chocolates to Carole. "How about letting me line one up for you, and find some furniture—then when they let you out of this place next week, you can settle right in there?"

Catherine's eyes exactly match her blue negligee, and they watch Jack for a moment, then drop to the hands that she is twisting in her lap. "All right," she says.

Jack is so delighted that he carries everything before him—

Carole goes shopping with him because she can't resist the joy he spreads around him as lavishly as he spends his money. Catherine is going to let him take care of her. "That's all I want," he tells Carole in the showrooms and warehouses and back offices where they feather Catherine's new nest. "That's all I want." But of course it isn't. Carole knows that.

And she's angry. Anger runs through Carole's days like a snagged thread through silk. It doesn't help to ask why the anger should be there, or what she's angry about, when everything is turning out all right. Catherine is well (she's only a little weak), and she's certainly not going to be stuck away in that place on the trolley line any more. Jack treats her like a princess, and the man looks handsomer than ever, and if Catherine isn't the luckiest girl around, who is?

And what resources Jack has. Boston isn't his town, but he knows how to make it his with a name here, money there, and the odd kind of barter and switch of wartime shortages. Nothing but the best will do for Catherine.

On the day she's discharged from the hospital, Jack insists that Catherine ride in a wheelchair to the car. It's raining, so he brings umbrellas for Carole and Catherine, and ushers them into Catherine's apartment house with a big grin on his face. "Housewarming!" he says.

The place is gorgeous. Polished floors shimmer with the colors of new furniture, and beyond it all flows the Charles, carrying its bridges and lights beyond windows, balconies and rain.

Jack gets them settled on a big divan and goes to the buffet table's glass and porcelain. "Champagne!" he says, waving the bottle. Where does he get champagne?

Carole watches Catherine take a glass of it from Jack. "She's so thin," Jack says to Carole. "Won't she have to have a whole new wardrobe?"

Carole waits, feeling that small current of anger flaw the surface of what ought to be satisfaction. When Catherine simply smiles at Carole, Carole stares at them both. "I guess so," she says almost reluctantly, and hears her peculiar tone herself, and tries to force heartiness into her voice to suit the occasion. "We can certainly fix that!"

Jack's voice is hearty, too. "If we're going to France. Get her some nice things to travel in."

Carole nods. She listens to them talk, and keeps an indulgent smile on her face. But when she says she really must get back to Smith and Rand, and smiles some more, and Jack goes to get her a taxi, she feels an absence in the very brilliance of the lamps and the colors of the furniture. Even though the view is lovely, and they are all looking so cheerful.

"Maybe when we've traveled around France and looked for her uncle, Catherine will be more settled in her mind," Jack tells Carole as he opens the cab door for her. "If Catherine says the word, we can be married in Paris—but what will we do without you?" He grins. "We'll have a coming-home party! If it all works out. A big one in New York, just for you."

Jack is still grinning as the taxi pulls away from the curb. It's a warm day for January. A newsboy on Boylston Street yells that the Russians have taken Warsaw.

14

Catherine and Jack were in Paris when Roosevelt died. Carole got a letter from Catherine saying that they were traveling through France looking for her uncle. Then Jack sent a note to say that a relative had seen Catherine's uncle killed when Paris fell to the Germans. It was hard on Catherine to give up hope, he said. He was taking her back to Paris.

Then Berlin fell. The Germans surrendered at last. Catherine wrote that she and Jack had been married in Paris. They planned to fly back to New York soon, she said, because she wanted some time to get new clothes and fix up the place on Central Park before their coming-home party in August. Carole must come —she'd be the guest of honor.

Smith and Rand were expanding now; Carole could go to New York only at the last minute. A new kind of bomb had been exploded over Hiroshima. Russia attacked Japan. People stopped talking about how many American boys would be killed in the Japanese invasion. Another bomb was dropped, this time on Nagasaki.

So the war was over on the day she finally got away to New York. The train was full of excited people; Carole watched a group of students wave newspapers and bounce on the battered train seats. Everyone smiled at everyone else. The war was finally over.

There were young men on the streets now, some of them crippled, all of them with the short, short hair that Carole thought looked ugly. They grabbed girls and kissed them and shouted that the war was over; New York was bedlam. Carole got to her hotel at last, and changed for the party. Jack called and said he'd come to get her; she'd never make it otherwise.

"It's a mess out there—Times Square's got more than a million people in it. They're watching the *Times* sign and cheering and dancing and wading in paper." Jack holds the taxi door for Carole, waiting until she gets her long skirts arranged. "You look gorgeous!"

"It's been months," Carole says, smiling. "How's the bride?"

"Beautiful!" Jack's eyes gleam. "I think she's really happy. The New York place has given her a lot to do, and she was so thin . . . she had to have all new clothes and hairdo and all, and it took time. I steered her to some of the nice shops and salons, and then I had to get to Chicago. This peace means a lot of changes." Shredded paper falls around the taxi; crowds block each intersection.

"Next corner," Jack tells the driver.

Jack's new place on the park is as fancy as Carole expects it to be, and there are expensively dressed people in the lobby and elevator; Jack slaps the men on the back and introduces Carole to everybody. It looks as if Catherine's first party in New York will be a big one, and it is. The huge apartment is as crowded with faces and glitter as Times Square.

"Come in, come in," Jack says, giving Carole's wrap to a maid while the butler opens the door to more guests. Jack wears a tux as if it's ordinary, like a watch or a pair of glasses. "I've got a couple of friends here tonight who might put some money into Smith and Rand—I'll introduce you," he tells Carole.

She watches the women turn their faces to Jack, sunflowers to the sun, as he welcomes them to rooms full of dancers and food and music. All day she has thought of Catherine in a hospital bed saying that it isn't enough. *Wiggling . . . grinning . . . rubbing against things!* Jack is Carole's friend and not an ordinary friend, either—yet Jack, his apartment, his fashionable crowd set her teeth on edge tonight. Even though the war is over, and it lasted forever, and luxury like this party is a craving that shows in everyone's eyes, even hers. *They have to like you. All the time.*

But if Carole's teeth are on edge, she sets them, and goes into the brilliant rooms angry, and angry with herself, but smiling a little, oh yes.

Women are dragging cloth around here tonight. Their eyes run over Carole's dress. Let them; she looks as classy as any of them: she has to in her business. She follows Jack through the crowd and takes the drink he hands her. They wait for a minute or two outside a group of men, a palisade of tuxedos.

Then several of the men, seeing Jack, break ranks; the black fence opens and Catherine is at the center of it, saying, "Carole!"

Carole kisses the air beside a smooth cheek, a glistening wave of brown hair, and steps out of Catherine's arms. The face is recognizable. If the eyes aren't the same, the perfect oval of the face is, and those cheekbones. Every woman in the room craves a figure like that: the plain white gown clings, like the classic shape of her hair. "Let's talk when we can!" Catherine says to Carole before she takes Jack's arm and smiles, and the crowd closes her away.

There's a wall nearby; Carole takes her drink there, and watches the people around Jack and Catherine. The women draw a little away from her as Jack introduces her, but the men step closer, their eyes fastened on her, jockeying for a chance to talk. Catherine laughs. When she tips her head, the curve of her hair swings wide. She drops her eyes to her cocktail glass often, as if she's shy.

Carole sets her drink down and walks away. Hours and hours of fittings, and mornings and afternoons in beauty salons. So what's the matter with that? So . . .

"What a bash," snarls a voice at Carole's elbow. "Where does Laird dig this booze up? He liberate Paris or something?"

Moe Moeller. So he's one of the financiers Jack's going to introduce her to tonight? Well, Carole knows Moe already, and Moe has money all right, but not for Smith and Rand. Definitely not for Smith and Rand. He thinks they're a textbook house.

"Something like that," Carole says, smiling, and asks herself what on earth is the matter. She gives herself the onceover in a mirror framed in palms while Moe chatters about the end of the war. If her father could see his daughter Carole now: a businesswoman and looking good at fifty. Him with his shoulders rounded and his arms long as a gorilla's with lugging a salesman's cases. *How am I doing?* Carole likes to ask that father, who poses in her past with his mustache and gold watch chain.

Now Catherine is dancing with a dancing bear in a tuxedo, a hairy hand against her bare back, a smile on her beautiful face.

Jack has a group of men to one side. None of them are smiling.

Carole says yes, she'll dance with Moe. Moe isn't smiling, either, but Carole is. What the hell does it matter, she thinks as she steps this way and that with Moe. You get old and they give you the gold watch, but you've got stocks and bonds and an apartment house in Omaha. Yes indeed.

Carole takes a glass of wine from a butler's silver tray. Everybody's beginning to loosen up; they're having a good time. So the party will be a success. "Hello," Catherine says. Jack has told her Moe is here, and Catherine recalls what he thinks of Smith and Rand—it's visible in her eyes when she smiles at them both. But Moe won't remember where he's seen Catherine before. "Mr. Moeller?" she says. Moe holds Catherine's hand much longer than it takes to shake it. "Carole? Come and have something at the buffet."

Carole follows them. "Not really," Catherine is telling Moeller when Carole helps herself to the caviar. (Caviar! Where does Jack get it?) Catherine says, "Not really" in her soft voice, smiling, and Moeller, who isn't at all fond of being contradicted and will slug wildly in all directions when drunk (as he already is), simply fills his mouth with olives and then caviar, and listens while Catherine tells him about Smith and Rand's *bogus* reputation as a textbook house. Catherine laughs at the very thought, then stretches a warm, bare, slim arm inches from his shirtfront, spearing a slice of ham prettily. Moeller blinks, and follows that figure of hers as it slides between chairs, undulating.

"Carole, I'd like you to meet an old friend of mine," Jack says behind her. "Carole Emery—George Armour. George is interested in Smith and Rand. I told him what you were doing with paperback books for the servicemen . . ." Jack puts a hand on George's shoulder, smiles at Carole, and leaves.

Ask him about his business. Let him talk about himself. It's second nature; Carole begins. But Armour takes her arm and draws her to one side. "Say, who's Jack's new wife?" he asks,

244 AN ACCOMPLISHED WOMAN

breathing gin into Carole's ear. "Can't he pick 'em, though? Don't have to be smart, but they sure do have to be stacked, and the ones he marries are even pretty." He winks. "Jack says you know her."

"Yes," Carole says. "I used to. She's a writer . . . from Boston. Worked in the publishing business."

"Writer?" Armour's sparse eyebrows draw high. "Well, well." He pokes Carole with an elbow. "Good on the bed scenes, I bet. Can't beat experience! 'Write about what you know,' that's what my teacher always said, and that's why I live it up—helps the Muse."

Moe Moeller comes to spoil Carole's chance with Armour: he drapes an arm over George's shoulder and says, in a slurred voice, that George is his old buddy, and doesn't Carole keep herself looking great, though? The two men give her the grins they reserve for women who keep themselves looking great. Carole says, "Thanks, Moe," and turns away, a smile on her face. What does it matter? They'll find some young things to look at very differently; there are always such things at parties.

"We missed you, Carole!" It's Catherine, her hands outstretched, fingers glittering with rings.

"How was the wedding?" Carole asks. Catherine gives details of time and dress and ceremony with the smoothness of a college senior or a seasoned officer, in step without thought, able to think of other things. She stops to give a butler directions, then says that the wedding was a small affair because they knew her uncle was dead by then.

"Honey, the war is over!" a well-dressed man says, hugging Catherine as he passes.

"You found out what happened to him," Carole says.

Catherine examines her long red nails and a diamond on her finger. "We found out he'd been killed after the Aisne front collapsed in June of '40—remember? The Paris government took barges, trucks, cars, anything, and got away to Tours, and French soldiers were roaming Paris, and farmers were driving their livestock through . . ."

"It must have been terrifying."

"My uncle's cousin Marthe saw it. Streets full of abandoned belongings and garbage, and anything that had wheels going out from Les Halles. Can you imagine three million people on the roads?" Catherine seems lost in her thoughts.

Carole shakes her head.

"Smoke and fire everywhere—they were burning gas and oil depots around Paris. Cows left behind on the quays, lowing all night. And the Germans coming . . . going right through Paris to Angoulême."

"Listen," says a man beside Carole, including Carole and Catherine in his conversation, "there's a hundred and forty billion in savings and war bonds out there—what're they going to spend it on, huh?"

Catherine looks at the crowd around her as if she doesn't see it. "Millions of people and soldiers all the way to the Loire and waiting to get across. They must have looked like ants when the Germans machine-gunned the roads. To keep them open. And blew up the bridges while the people were crossing."

"Nylons!" a woman says.

"New cars!" says a man.

"That's where your uncle was killed?"

"He wasn't really my uncle." Catherine smiles at their neighbors, then turns her back to them. "He wasn't related to me, except that his mother married my grandfather, that's all. He raised me."

"Outside Chicago," Carole says half to herself, her eyes on her glass of wine, not Catherine.

"Detroit," Catherine says. Carole stares at her glass, afraid to say that it was a Victorian house with a barn and a cottage behind it. An old man in an apron, new houses rising, a child with a doll—they all seem to be shifting in her head like heavy furniture, moving to positions so correct that she will be able to walk among them, if she can get alone to think.

"Thousands . . . millions on the roads, and the Germans machine-gunned, and that was when Marthe saw Thorn killed. She couldn't even go back for the body. She and her children went on with a man nobody trusted, though she didn't know that then." Catherine's makeup is perfect, Carole thinks. No one would guess those were false eyelashes. "Somebody from her village paid to have Thorn buried near the bridge, and gave her his belongings. We found the grave."

"I'm so sorry," Carole says, looking up to see a face she remembers: Catherine is staring at the room around them as if she can't
understand the most ordinary things . . . why people should
crowd together, the women in the newest coiffures and gowns,
the men in never-changing black and white . . . "Nobody over
here knows yet what really happened, what people did to other
people." Fear, for a second, runs through Catherine's eyes.
"They killed Thorn."

"I'm so sorry," Carole repeats gently. What else is there to say?
A lawn sprinkler whirls in her menory like the illumination fire-
works give, white on black. Scratched desks at a school.

"When we found Marthe, she was starving, I think. She was in
a place Thorn remembered—a miner's house in a little town, so
small and clean and empty. And there she sat with what was left
of her family." Catherine's eyes suddenly fill with tears. "Jack got
some food fast, and a doctor. We set her up in business with a little shop there; that was what she wanted. She's all right now."

Carole puts her hand over Catherine's young, diamond-bright
one on a chair back, not knowing the size or shape of what she
mourns with Catherine. "Best wishes to the beautiful bride!" a
man says, kissing Catherine. "Jack's a great guy! You got to come
see us at my place in Miami!"

"Marthe gave me a package of Thorn's things: sketches, papers. Then Jack and I went to Paris and got married." Catherine
takes a long breath, and her face, always changeable as clouds or
water, becomes still under the shining fall of her hair.

"I want to know all about you, dear," a large woman in a red
dress says to Catherine. "Jack Laird has been a friend of mine for
just ages, and now the war's over I hope he's going to take it
easy . . . you've got to see that he does!" She beams at Catherine and leads her away, nodding at Carole.

Watching Catherine go, watching the men watching Catherine, Carole has a sense of absence again: something missing in
the very brilliance of dresses, flowers, laughter, music. Even
though the place is so handsome, and the war is over, and everyone is looking so cheerful. Far away on a midnight board walk in
Omaha a young girl walks home, whistling . . . Carole shrugs.
Hasn't everything turned out right?

George Armour stands at a window nearby, looking at the

street far below. "Conga lines," he says to Carole. "They're dancing in conga lines all over town, chanting, "*Hey, the war is oh
ver!*"

"So you're a writer?" Carole asks, just the right blend of surprise and admiration in her voice.

Armour's eyes light up. He's off on the story of his life. Carole
can stroll beside him, glass in hand, looking as if she's listening
closely while she waits to tie something he says in with Smith and
Rand, with the possibility that a man who *writes* . . .

"I've always thought I had a book in me," Armour says.

Jack and Catherine stand together as Carole passes. "How do
you like my wife?" she hears Jack ask a tall man with a beard.
"Isn't she a beauty?"

"You've had so many interesting experiences," Carole murmurs. If Catherine leans against Jack and runs a finger down the
shining curve of her hair, why should it matter? Jack is whispering in her ear; if Catherine raises one shoulder so that her dress
clings to the shape of her breasts, who cares?

"Would you like to take a look at the manuscript I've got so
far?" Armour asks eagerly.

"I certainly would," Carole tells him. Jack's place is as big and
beautiful as she expected it to be; New York shrinks to a hum and
a spangled expanse beyond the curtains and lamp glow. Looking
back, she sees Jack and Catherine alone for a moment. Jack's arm
goes around Catherine, who stands quietly, her face turned away
from him, her eyes on the glitter of New York.

"Say, I'd like to hear more about the paperback business at
Smith and Rand," George says.

Carole looks in a mirror as she passes it. Her hair is as smart as
any woman's there; her figure is still good. She's never really
lonely, she tells the woman in the mirror. She's used to it. She
likes it. Anger makes her eyes sparkle.

Armour wants to know if she thinks paperback books are just a
wartime phenomenon, or should somebody put money into the
idea, now that it's peacetime?

Carole finishes her drink and gives her sales pitch at the same
time. She can do more than two things at once. And she's looking
good. Furious, not knowing why, Carole smiles all the more
sweetly and tells Armour that paperback books are the books of

the future. But what she's thinking of is her father. He'd better be watching from wherever he is, the bastard. Does he know she's got all those stocks and bonds? And the biggest apartment house in Omaha?

15

"Exquisite," Miss Wainwright is saying when the telephone rings. Jack has brought her from New York to "do" the Oak Park house for Catherine; sample books and swatches are strewn about the back parlor. These wide lawns and clumps of trees make the house "like a jewel," Miss Wainwright tells Catherine. "It's secluded enough for royalty," she says.

Neither of them hears the phone ring; the maid answers it and says that Mr. Laird isn't at home. Miss Wainright eyes Catherine and says Catherine ought to have blues around her, with those eyes and that hair. Catherine has a madonna-like quality, she says. Shy and elusive. Very feminine, of course. Not red or orange . . . definitely blue. The maid says that Mrs. Laird is at home, and comes to the back parlor.

"Excuse me a moment," Catherine says, smiling, and leaves the interior decorator considering the view. Jack's huge house, muffled in the splendid furnishings he wants to "modernize," spreads room after room before her; she takes the call in Jack's den.

Not a thing in Jack's den is familiar to Catherine. The walls are lined with expensive sets of books some past decorator chose for their jewel-like colors, no doubt, red against green against blue. Crossing the room to Jack's big, cluttered desk, Catherine thinks she hasn't had time, in three months, to open a single volume. The wall beside the phone must be a poetry collection, she thinks, picking up the telephone receiver. Has Jack ever read Browning, she wonders, or Tennyson, or Eliot? Shakespeare? Dante? "Hello," she says.

"I'm sorry to disturb you, Mrs. Laird," says the voice on the other end of the line.

Catherine doesn't hear the words, not yet. Later that night they begin to come back to her, the words that he must have said, but now all she feels is the world pouring through the phone receiver into her head with the timbre and cadence of that one voice in the world. She floats in blackness with a mouth on hers, voices calling her to supper, hammer strokes, the scent of an old barn, Tubbit's eyes, grass blades, a bed at dawn, wind, clouds, space . . . "but I'm an old friend of Jack's, and I'm trying to locate Catherine Buckingham. Do you happen to know where I can reach her?"

"Thorn." Her voice is too low for him to hear it; six years are thundering through her head like an express train traveling so fast that what it leaves behind is a cold vacuum filled with leather-backed volumes of Tennyson, Browning, Keats, Dante, and the maid's white cap as she glances into the den, then closes the door.

The voice is waiting patiently on the other end of a line that can't exist, a connection with a grave near the Loire, a phantom house in phantom cottonwoods. "Mrs. Laird? This is Thorn Wade," it says. "I've been in France . . . perhaps Jack has mentioned me to you? I'm calling from New York. I've tried to reach a house of mine in Detroit . . ."

She can't answer.

"Has Catherine been with you lately, or taken a job somewhere? I'm her uncle . . . can you tell me where I can reach her?" Fields of long grass. Dark night full of the rustle of leaves. She tries to say his name.

"Who is this?" His voice is closer, older, and sharp. He might as well have her in his arms. "Mrs. Laird?"

"Yes," she says, her eyes shut in the cold vacuum of six years passed.

He says nothing for a moment. Then he says, "Catherine?"

"Yes."

The leather books before her eyes are acting strangely: they're blinking on and off like Christmas tree lights. Just in time she grabs a chair and doubles up with her head between her knees, the receiver cradled at her ear. "Thorn," she says.

"Are you all right?" He asked that always after the bruises and cuts, temper tantrums and disappointments, and after the first time . . . "Catherine?"

"I'm all right," she says.

"I didn't want to shock you," Thorn says. "I intended to reach Jack first, and then see you myself after you knew." Thorn's bedroom is dim in Catherine's memory; the shadows of leaves move over the white sheets and the oval-backed chair. "You're visiting him?"

"No," Catherine says. If she keeps her eyes shut she's there; Tubbit is calling the cats from the barn and a robin sings beyond an open window.

"I was hurt, but I got into the mountains with the Maquis," Thorn says. "Then I got hurt again, badly, and they didn't know who I was for a long time. They couldn't let you know I was alive. A couple of weeks ago I finally came back to consciousness, and got well enough to travel, and got some money . . . ."

"You're all right?" She can feel his thick hair under her fingers, and traces the line at the corner of his mouth while his blue eyes watch through their dark lashes.

"A little weak yet. How are you?"

Her throat closes. She can't answer that most ordinary question, so ordinary that it opens at her feet like a black hole. "Fine," she croaks at last.

"Catherine?" he says. When she doesn't answer, Thorn says, "The maid told me that Jack's wife was there—is he married again?" He's making conversation to give her time, to make this conversation seem normal . . .

Jack has come from somewhere; he bends over Catherine, shaking her, trying to see her face. "What's wrong?" he asks. He lifts her up to sit in the chair and takes the receiver from Catherine. "Who is this?" he says belligerently.

Sick as she is, Catherine watches Jack's face change, sees him take a breath to answer Thorn, to tell him that—

"No!" she cries, snatching the receiver from Jack, speaking to the voice and the old house, the fields, the sound of rain outside a dark room. "I married Jack. I married him last May." If there is an answer, she never hears it; she runs away down a hall to a bathroom, coolness, dimness, silence.

The various blue sateens, cottons and velvets are now spread in rows in the back parlor. "There you are!" Miss Wainwright says briskly when Catherine comes back with her husband.

The man is good looking and rich, too; Miss Wainwright looks them over. With a wife young enough to be his daughter, and he's crazy about her; that's obvious. Miss Wainwright pats her hair and smiles, and holds up a sketch of the dining room. "Don't you think blue is your wife's color?" she asks.

You talk to the husband (Miss Wainwright always tells her assistants), but you keep your eye on the wife. "Of course you want the whole house to express her personality . . . her special quality!" she says to Jack.

Decorating really bores men—it's understandable. Their interests are all elsewhere. It's the wives, Miss Wainwright tells her assistants, who haven't anything else to do but spend the money.

16

Everything had turned out pretty well—Jack often told himself that. Even when they found out that Thorn hadn't been killed after all.

When the news came, Catherine was in the middle of fixing up the Oak Park house; they'd been married for months by that time. He'd told her the money was hers to spend, and the interior decorator was there, talking about Catherine's coloring and personality and what Catherine ought to have in her house to complement them, when Thorn's first call came through. He wanted to talk to Catherine, and of course it was a shock to know he wasn't dead.

The Oak Park house was a real challenge to Catherine; it kept her busy running around with swatches of cloth and books about antiques. It was about time she had some nice things. That room of hers in Detroit with a blanket for a bedspread, and all those bottles of ants . . . of course she'd been lonesome in that Detroit place, roaming around with nothing but fields of grass to watch, and old Tubbit mumbling. Such a pretty young kid, looking in the mirrors at herself, he bet—wondering if she'd ever have a boyfriend.

But now she had a big house of her own, and enough money to decorate it; it hadn't been done since his divorce, and Shirley never had had good taste. Working so hard on it cheered Catherine up after that trip they took trying to find Thorn . . . bombed-out families and Jews from the death camps and prisoners of war roaming around Europe trying to find each other—they'd depress anybody. They talked with you and traveled with you and were almost there, but not quite. "Displaced persons" were what they were called, and what they were, too, because in the middle of the most ordinary conversation you suddenly got the feeling that they couldn't understand you, couldn't understand how your mind worked. So you felt as if you were making unintelligible noises, not talking, and they looked at you the way Catherine sometimes did.

So of course the trip to France upset Catherine, and just when she was beginning to perk up, that call came, and she told Thorn they were married.

Thorn had sense enough to stay away—you had to say that for him. And it wasn't his fault that he'd been dragged off half dead from that bridge over the Loire; one of his boyhood friends had taken care of him. Nobody ever told his cousin Marthe: she was traveling with a man they didn't trust. So they told her Thorn was dead and buried. Saved his life that way.

Catherine got over it. For a while she wanted to talk about Thorn fighting with the Maquis until he'd been so badly wounded he couldn't ever get word to her that he was alive, and nobody knew who he really was, or whether he had any family. No wonder—the mess Europe was in for a year or two.

But they had a nice honeymoon in Paris anyway, and he was the happiest man in France, and Catherine was having such fun doing the house when Thorn's call came. Thorn had sense enough to stay away. He was turning out to be quite an authority on some kind of insect or other, and he got professorships at different universities, traveled around. He called them now and then.

The whole airplane business changed after the war. Centrifugal compressors in the turbojets were being superseded. The Junkers 004 and the GE TG-180 had axial engines, but the low pressure ratio was the problem. So he got men working on components—had some first-rate minds at his Chicago plants—and for a while all he talked about was efficient high pressure-ratio axial compressors, and that was pretty boring for a woman. But Catherine got him to explain the idea to her, and she understood it, too. She really had a head for mechanical things.

Everything had turned out pretty well. It was up to him to make her happy; he knew that. And you couldn't say he hadn't practiced long enough. He wasn't young, but he knew a few tricks that old Don Juan or Casanova couldn't sneer at.

So they were pretty happy, though she always seemed like the girl with the long hair who'd said, "I'm interested in engines"—an island nobody had ever really discovered—that was the way she seemed. It was Thorn's fault. He'd stuck her away out there on the edge of Detroit until she saw everything in a funny light. Butterfly nets—Janet had laughed at him. Damn. But now Catherine had all the money and freedom to make her happy, and she looked like a million dollars, and after Truman's Fair Deal fell through and the railroad brotherhood strikes and old John L.'s strikes were over, they lived in Paris for a while.

Catherine loved the Paris house, and they did a lot of entertaining when his business friends flew over. The fellows would praise Catherine's marvelous food (she found a cook who was a miracle), and wail about Truman and the twelve billion the U.S. was spending on the Marshall Plan—Truman didn't win in '48 with *their* votes. But when the Korean War started, Catherine came back to New York with him, and then Chicago; he was expanding his plants again, thanks to the war orders.

He liked things nice, and so did Catherine; they got along well that way. "There's a kind of perfection," Catherine said when they bought a place near New York and she was doing it up. "It's made of details. If your luggage is scratched, for instance, it can't really be made perfect again—the leather will always look scarred. And if your clothes are washed or cleaned, they look just the least bit lifeless. You can work at perfection the way you work at anything—with a very critical eye." He figured she was right about that.

McCarthy scared a lot of people; you realized you weren't saying what you thought out loud any more—it was spooky. And old MacArthur got dumped by Truman, and went all over making speeches. Truman muscled in on the steel industry—that was something, too. But Catherine wanted to go back to France, and he figured they could. He was pushing sixty, and he started delegating a lot more authority in the business. He could afford it.

Catherine thought she'd try to write, and she got to know Marie Sido, an old French writer. Catherine had a certain something, Sido told him. Catherine was exquisite, of course, but she was so unexpected: you never knew what she would say; she never saw life quite the way everyone else did. She put on a sleepy look, and her wit made her seem like a little girl unexpectedly wise—that was what this Marie Sido said. She was a very successful writer. She had a sea house on the Côte d'Azur.

He liked work. When he was just sitting around he got bored. Catherine had their different places to keep up, and all that, and she kept busy, he thought, but he liked to work all day, and then come home at night and put his feet up and watch television—he had a set put in every room at the Oak Park house. Television was really something.

So he lived in Chicago most of the time, and Catherine did as she pleased—visited Tubbit, or Carole Emery at Carole's big Omaha house, or sometimes went abroad. When she was gone he led a quiet life—had a chauffeur drive him home after work . . . had his supper and an evening of television. When Catherine was there, she kept busy shopping, going to shows, that kind of thing. Sometimes they entertained.

It was a good life. He thought they got along as well as anybody did after being married eight years.

17

Every Thursday afternoon Catherine had her hair done downtown, and met Jack for dinner afterward at the Empire Room. One Thursday in 1953 they never got to the Empire Room: Jack had a heart attack in the lobby of the Palmer House.

An ambulance took him to the hospital, and the first night he seemed to rally. The next morning he could talk to Catherine; the results of tests would be coming back soon. He could have a fairly normal life, the doctors told Catherine, if his heart weren't further damaged.

Catherine watched that day pass, hour by hour; she went in for her allotted five minutes each hour, and talked to Alice Knapp on the phone. Jack was nearly always asleep when she looked in; he groaned in his sleep. Before night Jack's doctor told Catherine that Jack might not live.

Alice sobbed into the telephone and said she would come at once. Catherine went back to hold Jack's hand. He opened his eyes and groaned, and said, "Janet."

Catherine squeezed his hand. "I'm here," she whispered. He said something about "happy" and "beautiful" and "damn fast cars," and then the nurses asked her to step into the hall for a moment, and it was all over.

VI

The day lily keeps honey in her well.
Bees let themselves down, heavy and eager.
They sway with her on her stalk.

When they climb out, they are pollen-yellow.
Before dark, each in her narrow cell
rubs down her bright black fur.

Down in the lily, white is gold now.
Folding, the great wet bell
wrings herself closed in the last light.

1

Thorn's plane will come in tonight over Antibes and Nice where the last foothills of the Alps block the north wind. The lowland drops to the Mediterranean just here, and if Thorn knows where to look, he can barely see the green speck of this terraced slope Catherine owns, and the stone mill where she sits now in a nest of sheets and velvet and wool, his voice still in her ears.

Thorn hadn't been dead, of course, but he might as well have been.

Still holding the telephone in her lap, Catherine remembers the old house: it enclosed her like the voice she has just heard. The round window in the front door. The darkening mirror in the parlor. The narrow upstairs hall with light cutting across from her room, and Thorn's room.

How many times in the last fifteen years has she heard his voice on the phone, saying that he has come from one place and is going to another, that he's fine, that he has a visiting professorship or grant, and how is she?

And now to be coming. After fifteen years.

Her hair. And what about the bed? After all these years when he never came, not even when Jack died. To be flying into Nice. To be driving up tonight. After fifteen years.

She's shaking, and feeling a little sick now, as if she's traveling in a train, backward, too fast. Thorn's low, hesitant voice without the slightest edge to it. So quiet. As if they still had the big house, and she was seventeen and standing at Tubbit's gate to see the grass blowing in the wind.

She can use the white sheets, the ones with the hairpin lace from her mother-in-law's attic that she cleaned out, and would recognize Jack's mother as girl and wife and woman now, recognize her at any point in her life: the high school graduate with the diploma at her feet, or the old woman who kept every favorite dress and a wicker baby carriage and hairpin lace. And get rid of the mattress cover that crackles, and put on a new bed pad. And her hair—can Yvette fit her in for a shampoo and set?

But all the time the feeling of long hair comes back, when it was only something down your back, behind your face, to be washed and dried and pushed out of the way. Sometimes Thorn braided it in the air of fans . . . his brown hands twisting it out of her way, or his . . . hot afternoons when they lay naked and listened to Tubbit's grass shears clipping, a sound as dry as the zing-zing-zing of cicadas in the heat before Thorn went to France, and never wrote, and Jack took her to visit his sister's friendly family in Cedar Falls, Iowa.

And why cry, for God's sake—red eyes and splotches around your mouth, and you've got to go and get your hair done.

Her hands are wet, dialing Yvette's number. French crackles along the wire from town. No, it is too bad, Madame Laird, but it's impossible today. Not today. Not even a minute, it's too bad. The polite voice—does it imply that she's the stranger, after all, the widow, the American who bought the old olive mill?

She'll have to wash her own hair because it's full of sweat from gardening. And all the time she remembers hair falling behind her, nothing but hair, and the day's going to be hot.

She strips off her nightgown. Nothing seems real. The sun has topped the hill across the river, and is a ray of yellow in her room, slanting through windows set in walls two feet thick.

Nothing seems real. Her triple mirror yawns like a triptych. When she looks in, she sees only what the sun spotlights: a slim torso yellow with sun, like old marble dug up in Greece without a head or arms or legs, and yet the breasts command. The very turn of the hip is goddess enough. But when she steps back, she is only the blue, naked shadow of a woman beyond the golden

shower of sun, and she sees Thorn's quiet face as he reads to her.
She's small, and sits in his lap, and remembers the taste of milk
toast with butter floating on it.

He's younger than Jack was when he died. In his early fifties.
What can she do with her hair? It ought to wave around her
face—Jack always liked it short. When he brought her something
nice, he always said that she was the only woman more beautiful
than Janet Buckingham. Poor Jack.

But all the time the wideness of Detroit fields is there . . . the
quietness that the steam shovels trundled into, gorging and dis-
gorging, shrieking, rattling. They were as ugly and useful as elephants. The drivers wouldn't answer her questions. Red-gold
sand rose in hills. "Make a mud pie for us, blue eyes! Put lots of
raisins in!" And the earth-floored cellars smelled of urine. You
could learn how a house was built if you watched what they did
every day. Standing beyond the sunlight with her hands on her
wet eyes, Catherine can't remember why she climbed up and
down and drew pictures of the houses as they went up, labeling . . .

She rinses her face at the bathroom sink and pulls on a shirt
and jeans and sneakers. What can they have for supper? An omelet. A light supper, she'll say, because they always overfeed you
on planes. A tossed salad. A chocolate mousse. She made a
mousse for Jack once . . . in London after the war, when you
could see the sky through the windows of beautiful old houses,
and she knew Thorn wasn't dead after all.

Her big bedroom seems so close and small. Even when she
runs into the living room, its huge space isn't enough. There's no
fire laid under the white hood of the hearth—she'll have to do it.
The mill's great beams, four centuries old, and the beautiful
French wooden pieces, and the paintings—he'll see them. See
how she's come along . . .

But that face of his! She had dreamed of it smashed, split open,
flies crawling in the cracks of her horror . . .

The morning air beyond kitchen and dining room makes her
sigh, and breathe deep, and try to stop crying. There's her garden
above the mill wall, sun-warm already and simmering with bees.
The abandoned road beyond is a deep green tunnel of shade. At
her back are the mill's stone walls that will be cool at noon, because the hill climbs against them. The sky is what she has come

for—the Mediterranean blue, free space streaming beyond the
red tiled roof and the patio and the hill and the railroad bridge
that leaps like a squirrel above the river.

All the same, the tears keep running down her face, and she
still feels small and trapped, even under that sky, like Alice, in
Wonderland or through the looking glass, with the key high
above her on the table. Rubbing her wet eyes, she hears Thorn's
voice opening the way back to so much free space that she's dizzy, standing among the roses in the garden, as if she saw smoking
ruins, or had missed a last, horribly dwindling train.

Silly. Make yourself some breakfast. Without Jack, she can
have the food she likes—odd things: quiche Lorraine, or nothing
but fruit for breakfast, or the fish paste they make in Vence,
spread cold over hot potatoes.

Thinking of it, she begins to laugh. When she's out in the
morning sun again, squinting from her patio at the railroad
bridge, she laughs and cries, and claps her hands, and feels hungry enough to hold her orange juice to the sun, a gold toast to
gold. Bread and ham and melted cheese taste good.

Sit down and eat. Look what you've got. Say to yourself: what a
day this is going to be. No matter how it ends. It's only a few
hours to get through. Even supposing he says: *Shall I stay tonight?* Hours never stop, and neither do your heart or your
lungs—they work by themselves like a conveyor belt, carrying
you through anything, and why should she care what he thinks
after all these years? After she'd thought he was dead.

So stand here. Take a deep breath. Say (to remember if he
leaves . . . if you're here alone tomorrow morning eating your
breakfast by yourself and watching the railroad bridge leaping like
a squirrel)—say, What a Day. What an Evening.

2

After she goes shopping she'll wash her hair. The last time
Thorn saw her it was hanging down her back, and nothing could
have been worse—what had she looked like? A Mary Magdalen,
probably. Or an Indian squaw?

Young women wore "hairdos" then, shoulder length or less,
with little dabs of waves or curls here and there—the same way

they stuck bows or sequins or cloth flowers on dresses. No wonder Jack's sister got her to a beauty shop before she took her to Cedar Falls. But what had she cared what they did to her hair?

A cheese omelet, or one with sour cream, and chives from the garden? All day the cuckoos seesaw back and forth with a call here, an answer there. What if the nightingales come tonight to sing? The kitchen is new and clever, but there aren't enough eggs, and no lettuce.

She closes the refrigerator door and smells the bayberry candles and geraniums and old stone of the dining room beyond. Once the dining room was the mill's loading space, open to cartloads of olives or grain, so it has just three walls and a ceiling, like a stage. The fourth wall is nothing but the light and air of the garden . . . the patio terrace along the mill wall's edge . . . the abandoned road.

Eat supper here. Zeus returning to Minerva . . . *Athena*, it was, goddess of wisdom, who cast her stone for Orestes—

> For I did not have a mother who bore me.
> No, all my heart praises the male.

Don't mix Greeks and Romans. Moths will come through the missing wall tonight, with the sound of the river plunging below. If they have to cry, or get away from each other, there'll be the dark garden, full of night noises, or else the big mill room and the fire. Either way they can escape.

What if he never reaches out, never says in the candlelight . . .

But he'll remember the omelets made in that old Victorian kitchen in the dark so that Tubbit wouldn't guess how hungry they were in the middle of those nights. So they could sit at breakfast eating Tubbit's oatmeal and muffins and tell him, with no looking at each other, that they were going into the fields for Monarchs again, and would take a lunch if he'd pack it.

She'll have to shop, but first—what about the bedroom? There must be flowers—she'll pick broom, yellow broom from the side of the hill, massed on the windowsill with damp night river air blowing through. Thorn would wait, always waited, those deep blue, long-lashed eyes of his as vulnerable as they were quiet. Until, shutting her own and being swallowed up in him, she'd never looked to see if his eyes closed. In Cedar Falls she'd stayed awake night after night trying to remember if she'd ever seen his eyes closed then, torturing herself under a wall of paper couples kissing . . .

Early morning yet, but the sun is already baking fragrance out of the roses; a breeze blows it in the dining room's open wall. There are new candles in the table drawer; it takes only a minute to set the table with dull green glassware on white linen. She picks roses for the centerpiece. Then she goes to get a bouquet of broom.

The abandoned mill road, arched over with leaves, is cool. There's no sign of the wild cat or her kittens.

Long ago the slope at road's end had been ringed with terraces—girdled and stayed with rock walls that some peasant must have spent children and grandchildren building. Now the vineyard has gone back to weeds, spilling like a Rubens nude to the river, yellow with broom.

She steps off the road that's going back to meadow, into terraces that are going back to hill. The sun is hot but the afternoon and night are coming: she can smell and feel them, as if they're the wild mother cat, or Bacchus waiting to dance in the ghost of grapevines. Damp soaks into the canvas of her sneakers. Bushes catch at her jeans. She remembers a windmill creaking in the wind, and sits down on a flat rock, feeling its grainy warmth under her hand.

He will want to understand. He'll come to the mill and sit down and wait. He won't ever say, *Shall I stay tonight?* She should have remembered that she'd have to do it all. She'll have to begin . . .

Where? Sun and olive leaves make a pattern over her, a formless, dancing shade that makes, nevertheless, a shape on the ground. They cut her hair. She watched Margie and her friends, their twitches and giggles as bizarre as the actions of a spastic, and the women played bridge at two o'clock in the afternoon. Can Thorn sit there and imagine the faculty women at the reception on the lawn, each one with her house to talk about, and her children, and Catherine and Margie in their big straw hats, listening, fitting in?

Does he know that college boys hung around their dorm rooms in the clothes they'd worn all day, and then they went out in the dark and talked until two in the morning with a traveling sales-man, maybe, or a truck driver? Or they could think, quiet and alone on the top floor of the library stacks where there was a table and a light bulb?

The cuckoos are monotonous as a creaking door—Catherine climbs down into the broom. Broom's hardly a flower; it's as tall as she is and like an architecture: spikes rounding to flowers as fleshy as lips. To pick a huge head of it above the bruise blue shadows is a kind of violence, and when she carries back an arm-ful of heads and sticks them in crocks and bottles on her window-sill, they stand above her bed, a solar constellation.

Now her three mirrors show a bedroom yellowed with the flow-ers in the sun—a charming, leaning, off-plumb rectangle of a room (trapezoid?) that's four centuries old and all primrose yel-low now.

Yourself the primrose path of dalliance tread. The primrose of that path had to be pink, she'd always thought, but when she looked it up once, after "primitive" and "primordial" and "primp," the dictionary said it was a reddish yellow "of medium saturation and high brilliance," which was one of the most breathtakingly right and wrong definitions . . .

He'll sit there, and she'll say: what was it like hiding from the Germans with Marthe, who could play number games so well, and whose white apron was what he always remembered, a white flutter in a doorway when he rode off, free, with the Jaubert boys? What was it like to find Claire, who could pantomime anyone in the village, really dead, and not pretending? He had worked in the Resistance, and in the Maquis, knowing parts of France as a boy learns it, mile by mile.

How had it felt to be fighting?

Catherine hears a plane from the Nice airport circle once as it aims for Rome, or London . . . startled, she finds herself before her three mirrors again, looking at her figure that's all right yet. Standing on one foot, the other knee bent, she tips her head to one side. She's only five years younger than Thorn was when he looked at her under the elms that morning, and Jack was asleep in the house—just a man visiting, with a new car and a girl, that was all. Except that she and Thorn had talked about Jack, and then Thorn turned away, and there had been that first flaw in the clearness between them.

She'd been part of the "war effort." Every Monday night the college girls went downtown to a room over the police station and wrapped bandages for the Red Cross. You washed your hands, and then you measured the gauze with a ruler, and put the cotton inside. "Don't you know there's a war on?" everyone said, and everybody helped, and sang about "the boys over there," and bought war bonds and war stamps, and carried their ration books to the stores. A kind of warm fellow feeling came from it; you were all in it together. And what you were doing was so important, they said. The boys had to have bandages, and they had to have V-mail letters.

Not enough eggs, and no lettuce. To have to put on her make-up, and then take it off and put on more later. Go into town once without? She laughs and begins adding one by one the infinitesimal blurrings and shadings of base and cream that look like nothing and take skill, and then the darker brows and lashes and pinker lips that are what people think they see, when what they're fooled by is the background, the natural skin that's nothing of the kind, and kept her home sometimes—just the idea of having to put it on. Lazy.

And put on clothes that look so simple and have to be so right, because it isn't a matter of what the color does to your spirits, or whether you feel good in it—it's strategy, especially from behind—being an elephant will do you in, all wrinkled from the rear, or bulging under a shirt not quite long enough, or tapering in the least from smaller above to larger below . . . looking in the mirror, she feels good. She doesn't look young, but she doesn't look old, and she's got to hurry.

What does she look like? (The mill path is dry—they need rain.) An American, whatever that is to these people. (The old lady, her nearest neighbor, is out scratching around the new pigeon house in her garden.)

A woman with money, to fit into a world of rich, strolling couples along the road into town where bits of blue Mediterranean show through trees. Along the road a chink in a hedge or wall lets you see great jugs planted with roses, or a pride of cars being hosed down by somebody's gardener. The chapel at the corner has fresh flowers stuck in its ancient wooden grating.

Christ, full size and full color, hangs on his cross where the larger road into town runs by. In spite of a glass olive jar full of roses at his feet (a young peasant girl grinning from the jar label), he only looks like somebody hung up there, painfully and for no reason, and then painted over with poster paint.

The never ceasing fountain, a cut artery, wells up to run downhill. As usual, cars are nosed in under the crucifixion, and people are filling jugs and bottles with the water. Crucifixions were something—weren't they?—that you ought to see in one horrendous flash, tearing veils, and then nothing but the cross left? What did it do to people to see cadavers every day, oozing red paint beside their plastic water jugs? And who stuck flowers in bottles of water wired to the old chapel's grating? Women, most likely, wanting something, or thankful for something to somebody who, presumably, liked flowers.

She pulls in her stomach, watched by well-dressed people who exhibit taste by preferring this water to that. Is taste a continuum, so that to be a connoisseur of life you can't appreciate, say, the shadows in a Vermeer without knowing the subtleties of water? Or is one single true, close perception enough? Are you then equipped to distinguish, and thus be distinguished?

But what would a visitor from space think of crucified men stuck up on crosses all over a beautiful planet? And where do the starving fit into this late afternoon, crouched over their misery under this sun somewhere, uncomplaining, allowing her to think about whether she should put polish on her fingernails—allowing that distinguished-looking Frenchman to drive away from the fountain in his expensive car?

The market will probably be out of lettuce already. The granite statue of a woman with wide stone haunches folds on itself above the geraniums at the intersection. Between one plane tree and another down the shaded road, she reminds herself not to feel or be ordinary on such a day, but like a procession, thinking of Thorn waiting for her in the grass, or cottonwood shade, or wherever she pleased, and Jack, so intent and so skillful, poor man.

Beautiful young things cross the street ahead, hair flying above brown arms and legs, never noticing her, of course, but she can watch them. They have to strip crowds to those who are young and handsome (to be reckoned with), those who are only young (to be carefully ignored), and all the rest of the human family less than ignored . . . blurred, a backdrop waiting for the occasional man who might be interesting, might turn, look, speak. But she can watch not only the brown knees twinkling along tandem, but others: the woman with the pocket-sized dog in her shopping bag. Or another creature whose skeletal body rattles along under a small fortune's worth of chic clothes.

Traffic now, and the Mediterranean at a distance, a blue glare. Hurry. To walk past shop windows, thinking you know how you look, only to see yourself, a woman of thirty some, sliding across displays of vacuum cleaners or travel posters, a reflection. The old church wall has Roman tombstones built into it: Christianity absorbed everything, even olive bottles. The church door breathes out the black inside: a belligerent darkness only dappled by candles that lean obscenely together, dripping to death in a crypt.

And the woman with the shopping bag dog. At first Catherine thought there was nothing alive in that bag, but one day a passing hound barked at it—stopped, and stiffened, growling. Then she saw a little dog's head, all of three inches long, stuck out of the corner of the shopping bag, yipping back.

Look there: the woman with the shopping bag puts it down. Out pops the little dog and pees—one, two—against the church wall, then jumps back in and is carried along again beside the woman's buttock shift and churn under her short skirt. Wonderful, to think of that, the coordination, the brisk business of it, beside a fat baby trotting along, hung by one arm to his mother's hand. Children must be iron-armed, like baby monkeys. There's lettuce yet in baskets under the trees in the square. And eggs. She buys them and starts home.

But the knuckles of trees over the square stop her. Every summer those trees put out green branches to roof the square, only to be hacked back to knobs to do it again another year. The well-dressed natives and tourists come and go by the shadowy, narrow streets and gateways, the medieval fountain is playing, and the hotel wall that is too old to be either salmon pink, gray or green is all three. A boy sprays one of the high windows and rubs it behind reflections of mottled stucco and sprouting trees.

Because it's this day, she sits down under the trees and orders lemon beer, knowing the French for it and other things, but learning no more than enough French because—why else?—she doesn't have to. "Don't bother your head, Beauty," Jack always said. He called her Beauty because he was the Beast, he said, whom she changed to a prince (at least he felt like one). And she supposed she hadn't bothered to learn much French because Thorn came here, came down and back to France, sick and angry, she imagined, for years after, and seldom wrote or telephoned. Old pavement, worn slick by centuries, is set with plastic-covered tables. Marie comes now with lemon beer.

What does it feel like to be Marie? To have been Matisse's model, to wear a small white apron and a businesslike air, making change, and to have been, as Marie has been, kept for posterity in every line of her solid body and peasant head, aging now? To have been kept for a turn of throat, a something that Matisse brought from his past, investing it there in ocher or sienna (because she was so brown), watching the woman's body that rippled its skin and smiled, posing, being so there and yet so not, and so forever on museum walls without ever having been there, less than a table Matisse had kept, so that, seeing it in a glass case, you said, "Ah! That table in his pictures! There it is!"

Deep shade slips over a bus that comes into the square, missing windowsills by inches as it wheels to a stop. She gets up and keeps her stomach flat and her back straight until she's as far as the flowering hedges and can let herself go. She has some French ground of her own now . . . yes. She has a fury as complex in its colors as shadows on a peeling wall, or the patterns leaves make, fingering from the knuckles of trees.

3

Leaves above the mill road move in afternoon breeze, heavy, a weighted swinging above her, and the dining room is a dark hole in stone. Just as she puts down her shopping bag the telephone rings in the bedroom, and Brian's voice begins the minute she picks up the receiver—he knows she's the only one there, silly, all alone in that mill when everything worthwhile is going on offshore. Come on out of your hole—drive down to Nice and board, and we'll cruise. Nobody but me and the captain and crew and a cook I've just got—fabulous—come on.

There's an old friend coming, she says, but I'll see you at Adrienne's tomorrow, I think. Unless my friend stays. No, a really old friend, friend of the family, yes, that kind, she says, feeling the push-resist of conversations with a man. They made the game, the dance of it, so complex and a challenge. You got a feeling of power out of it, as if you controlled what a man wanted most, which was a lie, of course, although he hid it. That's what made it fascinating: thinking of another person as intricate as yourself being dependent on you, yearning . . .

Brian's voice is gone, pressed down and away in the phone cradle, and she is trembling again, and weeping over a wine bottle in the kitchen. It didn't matter. She'd be washing off all her makeup and starting over.

Get the wine cool. Make the mousse. She doesn't think about what she's doing or even see the kitchen around her: she thinks he won't stay. They can't be seventeen and thirty-seven again. If they went back, the new brick houses would be all they'd see, covering the cottonwoods and the elms. A cement gridiron is stamped on Tubbit's garden. Houses are built around the very air that had once been walled in by a vanished Victorian house, swans and fountains in a bathroom, a round, beveled window, Tubbit's doilies, and the barn where she had said, "I want to begin. I'm not afraid"—and kissed Thorn, and added too much together all at once. The only thing she could do was run—run into the house and up to her room, thinking maybe she would choke to death, breathing and breathing where there didn't seem to be any air.

He had kept back, leaving the space and silence around her. He canceled even the waiting out of his eyes and voice, so then the absence of it told her it was there, and she knew, perhaps for the first time, exactly how much he could do with so very little, and how much he had done.

Or did she only see that later, when she was twenty-two and was being stalked, day after day, by a man playing another game? If she hadn't had Thorn, she would have thought Jack was more exciting than any man in the world—he knew every trick, even the trick of not seeming to have any. Yet you knew it was a trick to hide tricks, with Jack.

Thorn wasn't hiding anything except his waiting. And who had ever been, as she had been, neither the stalker nor the stalked, but only the younger, given the towering excitement of reasoning and feeling your way toward a silent man?

You never thought about clothes, or perfume, or how you

looked to him. He wasn't somebody you fascinated, or enticed. Had she even owned any perfume then?

Putting the mousse in the refrigerator, she can't stop laughing at herself, at such a question, except that she's crying, too, in a town not far from Grasse, for God's sake, as if she hasn't learned to love trailing scent behind her pretending it was her smell—not dead plants and animals, glands and roots and petals and secretions, crops for sale, dirty barrels rolled off freighters.

She didn't need to smell delicious then . . . what she had to ask herself was: should she touch Thorn? Kiss him again? Why did she want to, and what did he want?

It was hard to remember now: that tremendous pull to Thorn. He wasn't really "handsome." He wasn't going to make her feel triumphant if she "got" him. He was just the Thorn she had always known, except that now, like the moon, he had another side.

Thorn made no move. Not one.

Chopping walnuts for the salad, Catherine laughs, remembering how she crept around thinking about how she'd begin, or if she should, or if she could. The condoms he'd have to wear. The act that wouldn't be—couldn't be—dignified. If no one had ever told you how it was done, wouldn't you be appalled? Wouldn't you say, Oh no, that can't be it!

Sometimes at night she had curled in a tense ball in her bed. But as she listened to the quietness of the house, the spring wind, the rain blown on the wind, she felt the space. It was her choice, and the excitement wouldn't last; she had the freedom not to do anything at all.

Gathering up walnuts from the block, she knows she never had that again—that freedom to do nothing. There had always been the man's steady pressure, the urging he thought was natural: do this . . . do that . . . kiss me . . . take off your clothes . . . never once, except once, had she been free not to move unless she pleased. To think and plan forever, if she liked, while he was as busy with his own work as she was with hers. Unless she wanted to talk about it. Unless she put her arms around him without a word while he held her. While he waited.

At seventeen, standing that way, suspended, she had to think of everything. He was twenty years older. How would they get along when they stopped being yanked toward each other like this, and were separate again, and looked around them at the world?

There had been so much she was going to do. Her hair was only something that hung down her back, and she washed her face, that was all. She wanted to write; she was pretty sure of that. She'd travel by herself after she'd been to college for a while. Whatever she did she'd do alone, so that it would be hers. Thorn would be gone for a year, perhaps. They wouldn't even write letters.

"You should be all by yourself now," he had said once when there was a storm, and the old house was as dark at noon as if it were twilight. "I can't help you much any more—never could." Thunder cracked overhead and she had felt, for a second, as if the whole world lay before her and she had wings. Years later she had seen the *Winged Victory* at the Louvre.

Thorn had been watching the new brick houses blotted out by rain, until only the nearest street sign stood against that blown, smoke-colored curtain. Then the cottonwoods had streamed in the wind, and the window flooded with rain until the world outside had been nothing but streaks of yellow and brown. If she could have stayed there always?

Then the wind and the rain had begun to weaken, and she had seen Thorn's long profile against the clearing glass. The sound of raindrops had slackened and grown soft and scattered.

"She married," he said. "It was so easy."

4

What should she wear? It all depends on whether she can get her hair to look right—that smooth curve. If she can't, she'll have to wear a scarf. If her hair comes out right, she can wear the long, sheer caftan. She tries it on, posing for a long time in the mirrors. She had tried everything with Thorn, whispering in the dark, not afraid or shy, experimenting until they both laughed and shuddered with joy.

Or she can wear the green linen with the chain of jade and gold links, and the matching sandals.

There's the blue Dior. Pretty with her eyes, and the scarf would do with it. Very bare sandals, with only a twist of leather here and there. He won't make the first move. She'd forgotten. He'll never say, in the candlelight: Shall I stay?

Ever since she heard his voice, she's worried about what to wear. Maybe the yellow print? It would be bright in candlelight, like a candle itself. The dresses are piling up on her bed, a rainbow thrown over the white linen and hairpin lace; they look helpless, limp and still.

Pants, maybe? The plain white pants and top. Cool. She walks back and forth for a while, fingering her hair. Can she possibly leave it the way it is? Of course not. He'll smell it if he gets close, and he will. But he won't . . . he'll be quiet, listening. He'll wait—for what?

Well, make your mind up after you see how your hair turns out. After you shave your legs and take a bath. Stripping off her jeans and shirt, she's crying again, thinking how she must have looked at seventeen, coming into Thorn's room to sleep with him, just sleep with him, night after night. Getting used to him.

He understood, even the first night. He moved over without a word, and she lay hearing the spring wind flowing through the window, rustling maps on his desk. At Gilman she'd dreamed herself back in Thorn's room, her face against his broad back and her arms around him, and wakened in a dormitory room, knowing he was dead.

He hadn't been dead. Catherine watches tears run down her breasts and waits for the tub to fill. But he'd been torn out of her anyway—with that orchid on her shoulder, hardly seeing the dancers in the Empire Room, Jack watching her as if she were a queen, a goddess, who could talk about Milton, for God's sake, on a dance floor, talk about Adam telling God what kind of a mate he wanted:

> Among unequals what society
> Can sort, what harmony or true delight?

The bathroom mirrors reflect a naked woman waiting for a tub to fill, her cheeks wet, her breasts wet. But the only woman Milton could give Adam was Milton's Eve, and she wasn't what Adam asked for . . . except that Milton was a poet great enough to slip into truth unaware. So he made Eve the central character after all—it was Eve's decision that caused the Fall (she'd told

Jack over the orchestra), and Eve uses Satan, and even wonders, for a minute or two, whether she should share the apple and all her knowledge with Adam. She'd been trying not to cry, and Jack watched her and said he'd take care of her, wouldn't he?

She dumps perfume into the bath water and sinks into it; the warmth surrounds her as Jack's voice did, and his arms, and his plans. Ruth and Peggy couldn't believe she didn't want to go out with him.

Catherine listens to birds chirping in the garden, and cuckoos calling from one riverbank to the other. The cuckoos will stop soon, and leave the air to the nightingales, as courtly about time and space as Thorn, who had never so much as visited Mr. and Mrs. Jack Laird for reasons of such time and space . . . who had let more than a year go by since Jack had cried out once in a hotel lobby, and fallen at the feet of a little girl who kept asking, "Mommy, is the man dead, Mommy, is he dead, Mommy?" while Catherine stood horrified at the time and space flash of death cutting so close. Time and space came again in papers from lawyers. She could, literally, do as she pleased, and choose.

She had thought she could choose at Gilman. She went out with Jack in Chicago, her eyelashes dark with mascara and her breasts pulled up and out by the new kind of bra until Jack could, no doubt, feel them through his tuxedo, holding her close on those little dance floors while she nearly fainted with the drum-drum-drum, and blast of saxophones and trumpets repeating the same phrase, the same phrase, the same phrase—poor Jack.

Catherine steps from the perfumed water and watches it sink and disappear. All the bathroom fixtures are new, and the chrome, porcelain and glass shine on the old mill walls like a soap bubble. Drying herself, she stops and holds the towel to her face for a long time. She shouldn't have seen where the houses in Detroit had been—she couldn't bear it.

Years later in Jack's London house, she'd opened the notebooks full of her hasty writing that hurried to get to the next thing she wanted to learn. The writing raced across yellowing, round-cornered paper, and Thorn was between those lines like the slightest scent. She had known he wasn't dead by that time. She had been talking to the interior decorator in the Oak Park house when Thorn's first call came, and she had to tell him that she'd married Jack.

Birds call in the garden, and cuckoos echo each other across the rushing river. The heat of the day is beginning to go. Her bath perfume and the perfume she sprays on are the same, but the lotion she uses on her shaved legs smells different: she tries to wipe most of it off. She scours the tub and sink, and puts out towels for Thorn.

Her hair. She runs naked to wash it in the kitchen sink, because it has a spray. No one can see her. The cooling air carries the smell of the river. Looking out as she towels her hair, she sees old Devereux hobbling across the back of the bridge's magnificent set of arches, high against the blue sky: the very portrait of an obsession. His bridge. His view from up there, exclusive as God's. Lonely.

She wraps the towel around her and climbs the winding stairs to the big rooms at the top of the mill. Great sunken windows are like deep-set eyes under roof tiles; they look up and down the river to both bends, and catch a sliver of the Mediterranean between trees. She stands in one of those eyes, imagining Thorn here, working here.

He can work in one of these big rooms. Her books and notebooks and files and typewriter are in the other one. Maybe she'll try writing some short stories first, to get used to fiction. She's free to write now. No more of Jack's clients or friends or fellow businessmen to entertain, and no houses to travel between with the season. Open this apartment, close that country place—eight years of it.

Thorn will see how spring changes the looks of this river and the vineyard slopes, and how the fall here is so different from anything in London or Italy or the midwest. If he stays.

5

Soon every blade of grass in the mill garden will be doubled by a red edge, thickened by sunset, bloody and lush. The trees above the abandoned road move in a breeze, heavy, a weighted swing that plays on her. Bathed, wearing perfume blended for her, her hair all right and her slim body sheathed in a white crepe top and pants, she vibrates; the summer air breathing across her makes her quiver.

The road loops below the mill, turning back on itself, then buries itself in trees below the bridge. For the last half hour Catherine has heard every car. Now the bridge, high above, is black on sunset: a Roman aquaduct, night's architecture with niches of red air.

Lighting the candles, she freezes, hearing a car stop. A car door slams. She's a statue in the gap between match and wick, between three stone walls and one of air. Then she walks out, her white slack top blowing.

What she sees, waiting in the roses, are the leaves between her and the path she described to him on the phone. She's ready, she thinks, for anything: a bald head, eyes that are a cold, fringed blue, or a stoop—whatever fifteen years have done to him. Jack had been his age, almost, when he played a lover like all those in films and books who courted, pursued—

And now she thinks she sees Thorn, splashed with sunset red as he climbs, half of his tallness doubled and thickened by scarlet, the other half as shadowy as the path and stones crackling underfoot. She imagines, mercifully, only the look of one of those fringed eyes, blue-green threads in their blue; the other is in shadow under the touseled hair. The mouth's width and creases are grooved in place now, a sad triangle over the jutting chin.

Nothing as easily understood as romance, lush as leaves he will step from in his wrinkled suit, briefcase dangling from one hand. Nothing so simple as love, father to daughter and back again. Nothing like a mouth remembered, or any intimate touch forgotten. "Catherine," he will say, and she will say nothing. She'll walk into his arms so she won't see his eyes, and he will smell the same—tobacco, and the scent each body carries, distinctive as a Japanese prince's. They'll kiss, because what else is there to do?

Shivering, he'll admire the mill and the railroad bridge's arched leap. Deaf and blind, she'll smile and tell him the bridge isn't used—not any more. The war smashed up too many bridges linked to this one; they couldn't be rebuilt. Now only one old man travels the bridge to his house across the river: a sour old peasant with a ladder he hides. No one can reach the bridge without it. No one can take that high way but him. It must seem as high as a high wire up there, without a net. The red will fade from the hillside.

Waiting for Thorn to wash up, Catherine will be dizzy: he's

come and the candles are still burning, the salad is still crisp in its bowl, the omelet has cooked perfectly. When his lash-shadowed eyes are watching her across the table, she remembers he has a mole at the base of his neck, and another on his hip, and pours their wine. "Tell me about Brazil," she'll say, leaning on the table until she seems to be a part of it, and smiling, the wineglass barely touching her lips.

"None of the color plates for my new book can begin to get the butterflies' colors. How have you been?"

"Lonely, of course," she'll say, and he won't look at her. The downward slash of his mouth's corners . . . the full lower lip . . . and under his suit his old thinness . . ."since Jack died. But he left me enough to do pretty much as I please."

He won't look at her. He tells her about visiting in South Dakota. Tubbit's getting old, and lives alone. Thorn will watch the candles, or look out at the garden. When he pours wine, his hand, unsteady, might be her own: every knuckle and crease of it are familiar. She'll eat the omelet, but it won't taste like eggs: it will taste like vegetable soup and the smell of an old kitchen's dark air. He keeps his eyes down.

She's talking about the time she plans to spend in London now. She feels once for the smooth curve of hair on her cheek. Once she meets his eyes, and they might be Jack's eyes at the Amanas: bemused, with pity in them, sliding instantly away.

She says Jack's heart attack was so quick. Such a shock. If they'd had children. But it's been more than a year now. She takes the plates into the kitchen, and brings the mousse and another wine. When she sits down across from him again, her lashes drop, and she smiles a little over her wine, tilting her head. The sad face in candlelight, her partner, turns away.

As if she were a cripple.

No, he'll say, he never has got around to marrying.

"Well, you must see the mill," she'll say after a while, when the mousse and coffee are gone. The kitchen is bright; the big room beyond is dim under its immense beams, and rich with a fire under the hearth's swelling hood. Her short brown hair feathers on her cheek; she shakes it back. "You're here for a while?"

"No," he says. "Not for long."

Doesn't he think such old buildings are fascinating—these high, narrow stairs up and down? Sockets in the floor for the mill wheels—they're just big enough for a table in the middle, and she had benches built around the edge. This is where she plans to write—beautiful views from up here in the daytime. And there's another room, just as big . . .

Beside the fire with him, she'll light a cigarette and lean back in a quilted chintz chair, the shifting light playing over her round, bare arms, the river's roar below the open windows.

"I'm glad you're so well settled," he says. She leans through her cloud of cigarette smoke, narrowing her eyes. His socks show his bare legs; his suit is wrinkled. He doesn't go on, but sits looking at the seventeenth-century tables and the paintings, each glowing beneath its small light.

The grass will be dark to the mill wall. (The wall had sagged in a half moon and fallen the summer before, burying a garden and lawn chairs and a stack of books, biting off a section of the mill road.) The rose scent is heavy in the dark, mixed with the forest floor odors of the abandoned roadway.

Another moth attacks the candles left burning on the table, then veers into the dark again where a nightingale has begun to sing, against all feathered rules, to the dark and not the sun. Catherine draws deeply on her cigarette, then uncloses her lips to soft smoke, and thinks Thorn shivers.

A shadow detaches itself from mimosa shadow. Two patches of shadow follow. The wild mother cat, alert to the moon rising, brings her kittens to the dish Catherine filled. Silhouettes flicker across patches of moonlight; six eyes blaze like beacons at the shed wall.

When the nightingale stops the cats have melted into the dark. The moon inhabits the mill garden. Catherine and Thorn will step from candlelight, and the river fills the valley with the sound of falling. They stop together at the top of the downhill path where a cat's eyes blink for a moment, and are gone.

Thorn looks up at the bridge, then starts down. She hears his car start, and take the road that loops below the mill, turning back on itself, running through trees.

When the sound of the car is gone, she can hear the spring by the road. It flows above the rush of the river, coating ivy with lime: great white-frosted sprays cling to the rock, and are not so much leaves as frost patterns in the hot night, wet down there.

The rose scent will be left, and the cat, somewhere along the road with her kittens. A faint breeze comes through the road's tunnel, fragrance of broom on its breath. The mill stands as solid as the bridge against the stars, and the nightingale begins somewhere else farther down the valley.

The candles are nearly guttering; she'll blow them out and lock the kitchen door behind her. There's the greasy omelet pan and what's left of the salad, wilting in its oil. Jeannette will clean it up tomorrow.

The river moves away with every window she closes, until the living room is all that's left of the evening: firelight behind a screen, flickering on each chair and table she has chosen, each wood surface and flare of oils calculated in effect, without seeming to have been brought from somewhere, or to have been bought, but to have grown where no such things grow. In the cellar are the worn mill wheels still in their sockets, the rancid odor of olives, the damp of a millrace that ran under this roof once, under a bridge that thundered once as trains crossed a chasm in a few seconds against the sky.

The fire is small flames now, tame behind its screen, but cold moonlight is in her bedroom. When she opens the door, that icy light turns even the yellow broom colorless, and every blue-white fold of the bed has its inked shadow. There is nothing there but a light like frost, and the rush of the river.

She can shut the door on that moonlight: the big mill room will be warm. She'll lie on a couch with a shawl over her to keep her from shivering, and now and then the fire will put out a tongue, a pointed foot, a finger, warm and yellow.

She'll smell the salad vinegar; Jeannette will clean it up. There will be breakfast on the patio, and another morning. She'll lie half asleep, listening to the rhythm of her breathing, and her steady heartbeat.

6

No, Catherine says.

Waiting for Thorn, lighting the second candle, she hears the car that isn't Thorn's pull away from the curb, take the loop in the road below the mill, and fade away. Thorn hasn't come—not yet. Dizzy with his imagined presence, she runs past kitchen and fire and her bed to her desk to find paper and pen.

She had thought first of what? Her hair, and then the bed. The candlelight balances in its pools of brilliance with green glass, butter curls, the wineglasses: a beacon above the path Thorn will take when he comes, beyond the leaves, stones crackling underfoot. Now Catherine's note stands between candlestick and flowers. When her footsteps fade away up the mill path toward town, the candles grow steady: pillars of light.

The pigeon house in her neighbor's garden catches sunset along its roof; a frog croaks from somebody's fish pond. At three points along the winding road are three evergreens anchoring a hedge: they are tall, and trimmed into curves like a woman's. They watch her as she approaches them, as she passes. Her sandals scatter pebbles, a dog barks, she hears laughter and the chink of glasses from a gap in a stone wall. Her hair, and the bed. A shampoo and set. And what to have for supper. The scent of flowers, heavy and sweet after the hot sun and bees, comes and goes across her path.

And he'll see how she's come along: see the paintings and the sculpture and the money it took. The yielding, shapeless sound of the fountain grows along the road, and she draws back into the deep door of the chapel among bottles of flowers wired there. A car turns the corner, coming from town, and—for a second—sunset on the chapel's white wall sets Thorn's profile against dark trees, the cross, the fountain.

Then Thorn is gone with the sound of a car traveling away, the reflection of red sun on its windshield carried before it as a man carries a lantern in daylight; it flashes upon another wall, a gate, and then, one by one, the three tall, undulating evergreens. They bear the scrutiny of that light in turn; rejected, they stand green, darkening toward night.

Someone knocks jugs together, filling them at the fountain. The granite statue is losing all the colors of its flowers but the reds: geraniums will give off a blackened scarlet in the dark that's coming. Between one plane tree and another down the road she thinks of the church. No one will be there now.

Lovers kiss on a bench in the shadow of plane trees. Streetlights flicker on above the traffic. Vacuum cleaners and travel posters wait in shop windows for morning. Couples, groups, solitary strollers step around a temporary fence into the street, skirting construction in a vacant lot.

Clothes piled on her bed, and perfumed bath water.

The surface of the Roman tombstone built into the church wall is worn to nothing but an uneven swelling, but now a streetlight indents what might have been a waist, a neck, a hand raising a cup. To the dead, she supposes.

There's no one in the church except the candles leaning together, dripping. Sitting down in a corner, she hears a violin tuning up somewhere, whining up and down from the clear, true note.

7

The mill leans as defiantly away from the downslope of its hill as a Boston Back Bay house. Seeing it, Thorn parks his car and looks for the path.

It's growing dark. Gravel announces him, crackling under his shoes. His hand sweats around the briefcase handle.

Her eyes will be light, with their dark pupils like a gun pointed at you when you aren't trusted, just at first, by the Maquis. "Catherine," he calls, and the mill answers: his voice echoes away in corners of stone and massed trees in the dark. Then the river water runs on, as tranquil a sound as the wind in pines, or the low hum of insects.

There's an open-sided room; he sees that now. Candlelight defines it against the dark fragrance of roses. A cat leaps from a mill wall that's half fallen into the garden below as he picks up an envelope from the table to read Milton's few lines.

Silence among dull green plates and glasses, and roses on a white cloth. The glasses are half full of wine, and above the candles a medieval icon of the Virgin watches him from a wall, a headdress like a helmet on her head.

His face looks white to him in the mirror on the kitchen wall: a cowboy face with eyes that wince, grooved cheeks, a mouth set and grim. Tall, skinny, he stares into a bowl of salad and rubs his damp hand on his pant leg. The kitchen's stainless steel and expensive glitter surrounds him; tropical fish swim in a tank on the wall. He looks back at the table and garden. No one is wading through the dusk as it swallows up the roses.

The mill's huge living room floor is black, old, worn and polished; it shimmers with a dance of flames and the repose of paintings under their small lights, pieces of sculpture, and the sound of the river beyond windows, terraces and silence. Sitting for a minute alone, Thorn wedges himself in an antique chair, his hair mussed, his socks showing a sliver of leg below his trousers. He ruffles his hair, his fringed eyes moving over a sculptured male nude . . . modern pigments clashing in their frames . . . a Giacometti woman as lonely and narrow as a young boy.

Standing at the fire now, he puts his briefcase down near a vase and stares at its painted Chinaman as if he were a shape in a coffin, familiar and lost. Beside it a fire snaps under a mirror that is losing its silver . . . a row of souvenir plates . . . but when he looks, the great hood of a centuries-old French hearth bulges like the forehead of a skull, and has no mantelpiece at all, nor does it look back.

He climbs winding stairs, whitewashed and unevenly curved as clay under a potter's palm; they lead to rooms she has left half lit. The first room stops him: where has she found these things? Packed up by Tubbit? Lugged all over Europe? Stored for years somewhere in Iowa?

Framed expensively, his sketches of Nottinghamshire flowers and grasses and insects wait for him on these walls, and Janet rides high in a rented Ford down cowpaths and winter fields, her lips pink with rouge, her eyelids shiny with grease, bringing this lichen back to Marleyshall in a lichen-gray glove.

This bumblebee is a *Bombus lucorum*, where Janet's face was white across dim and dusty air, lightning lit. This one is a *Bombus pratorum*, and Janet's eyes filmed and filled until she rubbed them, and sobbed, and pulled her dress up and off, and kicked it away. The drawing of the bumblebee is smeared in the corner. It had rained when they were in the barn.

He never had a picture of Janet; he had burned them all in Detroit one afternoon, watching the faces under the fancy hats crackle and blacken across their smiles. Thorn picks up the photo on the new desk. As dated in her Castle stance as a nickelodeon or a ukulele, Janet puckers her mouth in the rosebud look of the day. Her face is tilted, looking sidewise under a hat close fitting as a helmet. Her skirt dangles between her pointed shoes; her sleeves are too long with their flopping cuffs. An immense collar dwarfs the small, remembered head.

Beyond the picture of Janet, Thorn sees the next room, as big as this one, with its new typewriter, the desk as blank as a sleeping face, fresh paper in a rack, and sharpened pencils: a rosette of lead.

8

Catherine can't stay in the church. The air is old enough to have come from a burial mound. The only things alive are Catherine and the candles, and the candles writhe and twine, burning against each other. A statue of the Virgin holds its hands out, the fingers broken off short, like trees.

Is Thorn at the mill now, walking from room to room, seeing the lovely things Mr. and Mrs. Jack Laird bought in Greece and Italy and France and England? When Catherine walks away from the blue glance of the Virgin, the statue holds out its stubby hands to the place where Catherine was.

By the time Jack took her to Greece, the mountains could look on Marathon and so could she, cold as they were, because the world was split down the middle. What could Thorn have done about that? She didn't know when it split. It must have begun as a hairline crack, the way splits began at York Cathedral; she'd seen them. They started sometimes when stone was actually bending under too much strain: Purbeck stone bowing slowly in a vast, monumental curve at Salisbury (if you could imagine it), or a crack running up the face of York, setting it just a little off from top to bottom: two halves not quite fitting.

When you think of it, how do you know she's the madonna if she doesn't have a baby? But who else could she be? The candles are busy, like tongues, because there's a draft.

When nothing quite fit, then whatever came from the past stopped. It broke right there, at the crack. Nothing came down to you any more. You could see even the Parthenon and know it had nothing to do with you. Athena had cast her stone for Orestes by that time: he'd only killed his mother.

The Virgin has a bottle full of day lilies at her feet. Tubbit grew day lilies: Catherine remembers how they opened their throats for one day to the bees, like a temple to the vestals: small black ladies who went back to their hive at night and unloaded pollen and honey, while the great day lily bell shut like a dying parasol, and drove her strength down to her root. But these lilies don't have any roots. They're closing already, and they'll stink by morning.

What does Thorn think of the mill? All those beautiful things that cost so much—and her, exiled in his country? With Jack's money she could live anywhere in the world, but what did it matter, as the Cheshire Cat would say? The lord of this French town where she stood right now (all in white and smelling delicious, her hair shining and no place to go) had had four daughters.

It was the thirteenth century then, but what did that matter? The four princesses were all beautiful, and they must have known—being princesses—that they had all been married at birth to a foreign country, so to speak. Princesses, if successful, are always exiles. So from this garden four fleurs-de-lis were plucked: the first was bride to Saint Louis, the second Henry III's Queen of England, the third Empress of Austria, and the fourth Queen of the Two Sicilies. All from one small town. Did they ever come back, dragging their trains behind them?

Catherine laughs. The church echoes. She ought to commemorate the day. She hangs a day lily from one of the madonna's partial fingers. The flower is slimy already, and drips like the candles.

The air is better outside, and there's music: the usual dance in the little space in front of the Hôtel de Ville. Catherine turns away from the sound.

Streets climb up and down, crowding her, black with cobblestones, stinking with garbage, their walls worn by hands; they echo fiddle scrape from their dark throats like sibyls parroting the birds. An old Roman town. A bishop's town. Picasso and Matisse loved it. Her white slack suit gleams lily white as she grows nowhere, like princesses, in any town of buildings no one like her has built.

This town has small brass hands for knockers on so many of its old doors. Catherine touches one. Open Me.

You go to the Vatican and there are breasts everywhere, decorating lives of the saints and deaths of the martyrs. The breasts

Nancy Price   283

have eyes like two fried eggs on a plate, and then another blank face above, and waves of beautiful hair, and usually wings to intimate what's missing, like asterisks, like the spaces between the faces in Raphael's *School of Athens*, left blank for people like her, broken meats from all the tables:

> The knife is in the meat and the drink is in the horn,
> And there is revelry in Arthur's Hall,
> And none may enter but the son of a privileged country,
> Or a craftsman with his craft.

But when you get to the crack or the last hedge, and there's a crown on your head, it really makes no difference at all, because you're still about twelve years old like Alice: everybody can see that. Or if you have poems in your head, like Alice, they come out nonsense. How doth the little crocodile. Or they might as well. It really doesn't matter.

The Hôtel de Ville shows through an archway; Catherine watches dancers bob up and down to music that's across the crack from her, too. Then she climbs dark cobbles to the main square. Under the mutilated trees are the round tables, Marie in her little apron, and fashionably dressed people lounging in the cool night air.

Catherine hears a deep voice behind her say, "Hello, neighbor" in American.

She turns to see a man a little older than she is. He smiles down at her. "Sorry there's no one to introduce us—Bob Barclay's the name. I've bought the place down the road from your mill—the place with the three trees." He makes an undulating outline with his hands and laughs. "I call them Faith, Hope and Charity."

The three trees flicker in Catherine's memory, then blacken.

"Catherine Laird," she says.

"Won't you be my guest?" Barclay asks. He pulls a chair out for Catherine. The chopped-back trees block the streetlights here; the tables are in the half light of their moving shade. Two women in marvelously chic summer dresses are watching Catherine with interest; a man gives her the usual look. She leans back and smiles at Bob Barclay, her eyes on the square's expanse of lights, flowers and strolling people.

"What would you like?" Barclay asks, signaling to Marie.

"Lemon beer, please," Catherine says. Violins at the Hôtel de Ville are playing something vaguely familiar. Beyond Marie's small apron and businesslike scribbling, Catherine sees Thorn far across the square.

"You're spending most of the year at your mill?" Barclay asks when Marie has gone.

Catherine's eyes are on Thorn; he has seen her. "I have a place in New York, and one in Paris." Thorn's suit is wrinkled and his pockets are crammed full. He shifts an old briefcase from one hand to the other as he waits to cross the street.

Barclay lights Catherine's cigarette, his smile white in his tanned face. "And you've lost your heart to Vence?" The smoke from their cigarettes rises between them and Thorn who is approaching now, stuffing one hand in a pocket, his eyes on Catherine.

"I love this place," Catherine murmurs. The night is warm, her hair is smooth, her perfume surrounds her, and Thorn has stopped at their table. She looks up at him, then at Barclay. "Here's an old friend of mine," she says. "Thorn Wade . . . Bob Barclay."

Thorn shifts his briefcase so he can shake hands. Marie comes with their order; he's in the way. Won't he bring up a chair and join them, Barclay suggests, and won't he have something to drink?

Thorn looks around for a chair. "No, thanks, I won't have anything." He carries a chair to their table and sits down, his briefcase in his lap.

"Thorn is a sort of uncle of mine," Catherine tells Barclay, smiling. "He brought me up when my parents were killed. And he's an entomologist. He travels looking for rare specimens."

"Interesting work," Barclay says, holding out his cigarette case to Thorn. Thorn says no, thank you. "Found any new varieties around here?"

Catherine is watching Thorn's long, narrow fingers that grip his briefcase. Her white shirt is faintly green with light through leaves. The sound of the fountain in the square rushes under voices speaking French, English, German. "No," Thorn says, "I haven't."

"I've been telling Mrs. Laird that I've bought the place down the road from the mill—can't get enough of this part of the country." Barclay taps the ash from his cigarette and smiles. "Where have you lived in the States?" he asks Catherine.

"Chicago," Catherine says. Leaf shadows spangle her smooth hair with flecks of yellow from the streetlights. "New York." She keeps the conversation moving in its smooth, sociable groove. Her husband was a manufacturer, she says. She's furnishing the mill with period things, and some art pieces she likes.

There are insects in the trees and flower beds of the square; they keep up a faint, insistent chorus. Barclay sips his drink and leans back in his chair, smiling. "You'll have to come see my place, give me some pointers. I'm interested in period furniture, too."

Marie hovers discreetly. "Another beer?" Barclay says to Catherine. "Won't you have something?" he asks Thorn cordially.

Leaves move over their table: light from the square falls on Thorn's face. His eyes are so close that Catherine can see the blue-green threads in their blue, and a shimmer of white she knows is herself, reflected for a second in their depths. Then he looks down at his briefcase and his wrinkled pants and hitches a pant leg up, and says he'd better be going.

A night breeze ruffles Thorn's thick hair. "Won't you come up to the mill?" Catherine asks him. Cigarette smoke wreaths her face. "I'll be going back soon."

"Or come to my place!" Barclay exclaims. "Visit and give me some suggestions . . . make an evening of it!"

Thorn unfolds his long legs and stands up. He says he's sorry but he must be going. His deep blue, wincing gaze moves over the people, the square and the fountain's spray: a rustle of water in the shadows.

Catherine says nothing. Barclay holds out his hand and grins. "Maybe you'll come over some other time," he says in his friendly voice. "Glad to meet you." He watches Thorn pick his way between tables and wait to cross the street. "Nice fellow," he says. He sits beside Catherine again and takes up his drink. "About those art pieces of yours—what do you like? I'm a kind of collector myself."

Catherine is watching Thorn cross the street under the bright lights. He seems so out of place in that wrinkled tweed suit, making his way through strolling couples who are dressed for the south of France, a summer evening . . . as if he's lonely, or embarrassed, hurrying with his long-legged stride. But when he turns his profile to her a last time, his deep blue eyes and the straight, grim line of his mouth are not embarrassed. He looks up at the trees.

"I have a Giacometti I like," Catherine says. Night wind from the square moves leaves above her; light floods the short, shining helmet of her hair, her still eyes, the drink in her hand. Then leaves move back, and she speaks from the spangled dark. "And a Renoir."

9

Karl Tubbit stays where he can keep warm—no sense heating a whole house when the kitchen's the best place to spend your time. The rest of the house is full of furniture his mother would have given five years of her life to own, and he keeps it warm enough so the stuff won't crack or loosen up these South Dakota winters. He's no fool.

Karl Tubbit's no fool. Move to some "home"? This is home. He even talks to it sometimes. "It wasn't my business," he says to the stacks of old newspapers, or his suspenders on the chair. He'd been born in South Dakota, and he could die there.

He can talk to the cat. Damn talkingest cat he's ever seen, but that cat won't eat scraps of meat off wax paper—has to drag them on the linoleum and grease it up. But he'll answer you back for ten minutes, just like a conversation. "I can see her just as plain," he tells Waldo, the cat. He could, too: three years old even, maybe, with dirty overalls on and that look in her eye she'd had from the very beginning.

And my God, the questions. Give her a house like this, he tells the cat, and she'd want to know every dad-blamed thing about the pipes and the bell-bottomed jackscrew holding up the floor by the fireplace—she'd be after your brains like a worm after an apple. Why was the fire blue? What made a spoon look crooked when you stuck it in water? If you didn't answer straight, Thorn Wade jumped on you like you'd killed Christmas, and took her off and explained it all. What did she have to know that stuff for?

Long as he lived he'd remember that look coming out of a little

girl's face—she honest-to-god thought she could do anything.
"Smart kid," friends of Thorn's used to say, but they didn't really
mean it as a compliment . . . don't know how they meant it, except usually people got kind of mad when she looked at them and
asked questions. She'd come right up and want to know—made
you uncomfortable. Kids usually stand back and act shy, you
know, duck their heads and just watch and listen, unless they're
so little they don't know any better.

Oatmeal for breakfast this morning, cat. That's why he's lived
so long—oatmeal. You can cook it once a week, and then warm it
up. Use the stove and you can shut off the heat register for a
while, cut the bills down.

Sit there and talk when she wasn't four yet, right in there with
his men friends and women friends, and them not liking it, especially when she knew something they didn't know. Milk froze every winter in that milk chute because she'd asked the milkman
what kind of cows his milk came from, and he didn't know.
Wouldn't close the chute door after that. (She found out and told
the milkman it was Guernsey.)

"Look at that chair you're sitting on," she'd say to him. "It's got
a little platform with four feet and a back, because we've got a
bend in us. If we bent the other way, what kind of chairs would
we have? We couldn't sit in this kind—we'd be sitting with our
fronts backward."

Could have built her anything—a playhouse, with a stove and
sink and tables and chairs and icebox and beds for dollies—he
could have. And let her go to school and be with the other cute
little kids with their pretty dresses, playing hopscotch after
school. She said she didn't like school—well, who ever does? You
got to go and learn anyway, and the girls didn't have to know how
steam shovels worked. Women truck drivers. My God.

Never was the cuddly kind, not like Shirley Temple, all cute
and dimply—see them on the streetcars with their mamas, all
dressed up. She hadn't had a mother; that was some of the trouble. Here comes the milkman, and it's just about light out now.
Another day.

Yes, the houses are starting to show across the street, coming
out of the dark. She was helping to make jelly once, and she said,
"Don't you ever wonder how we all go to sleep at night and then

come back to the same place to wake up in the morning? Nobody ever gets lost in the Middle Ages, or way off in Africa. You come back to just one little dot of a place on one little dot of time." There's Mrs. Ackerman across the street, coming out for the milk; she's got an organdy apron on. So neighborly, always bringing something over, and so dainty. She was just baking and she thought he'd like a piece of cake—patting her hair and apologizing for looking such a mess. Good cake, too. Well, she did get away. She married Jack Laird, and now she's a widow and living in France, and maybe she'll come visit again before long. And she's really all right—she got married and had a normal life. So it was really all right.

And it was none of his business, after all, he tells the cat. He goes out to bring in the milk before it freezes. Women flying all the planes. My God. But she was all right now. Everything had turned out all right.

HB3J